Little Bird: Book One

Jennifer Reynolds-Cook

To Mammina
To my favourite footy players who inspired Brendon and Troy
To the beautiful game

Content Warning

L ittle Bird is a tragic love story set in the Taunton, England, which includes elements about abuse, mental health, addiction, alcohol abuse, emotional and physical abuse, graphic language, and sexual activities. Readers who may be sensitive to these topics, please read with care, and prepare for Little Bird.

Also by

Prologue

B rendon Cook was angry. His body filled with sparks. He imagined them dropping like spiky raindrops, slashing through the cottony clouds, and disintegrating before they reached the earth. His father sat beside him. His brow furrowed in concentration. Brendon hoped the silence meant David Cook was focused on listing the names of the senior judges recommended for the Supreme Court of the United Kingdom and was having a hard time choosing who to advocate for. Brendon would title the flight home from Germany, die Kacke ist am dampfen, the shit is hitting the fan.

1 Dum Spiro Spero

Brendon

Golden sunlight illuminated meticulously groomed grass. Once nothing more than a weed-infested field, a set of dilapidated bleachers and standard goal nets, a hefty donation transformed Taunton Park into the envy of any visiting Southern League team. Steel stands rose from the ground, housing black and blue molded stadium seating. A royal blue awning boasted Taunton First in block letters. Five First players chased after the ball, hollering 'get after it' and 'push up.' Brendon braced himself; dewy grass squelched beneath his cleats. He grinned confidently, snatched the ball, and rolled it onto the pitch.

"I've let three in so far. Is anyone going to get one past Mr. Football?" William McGregor said.

"Nothing gets past my mate. He's the top keeper in the Southern League," Troy Spence said, smiling. "I can see another championship in our future now that you're home."

Brendon wasn't happy to be back. He thought he was finally rid of Taunton College, Taunton Park's 'okay' pitch, and William McGregor. The sparks had gotten him into trouble again and sent him home.

Brendon tugged at the hem of his Borussia Dortmund jersey and swiped it over his brow. A girl with waves of red hair made the shape of a heart with her fingers and held them up. Heat crawled over his cheeks.

"Don't they have better things to do than watch us practice?" He jerked his jersey down and scowled. "I didn't have to deal with squealing girls in Dortmund."

"You should have kept your mouth shut, Cook," William said.

Troy batted William's arm and frowned. "Leave him alone. He's only been home for an hour." He nudged the ball under his foot, tipped it into the air with his toe and bopped it from knee to knee. "Just ignore the tarts of Taunton. Tilly and Rachel do this for attention. They think we like the giggling and cheering."

Brendon rubbed the nape of his neck and pulled his gaze from the gawking girl. "I wish they wouldn't. I come here to practice."

William placed his hand against his heart and swooned. "What I would give to spend one night snogging Matilda Morimoto."

Matilda gave the illusion she was aloof and mysterious. A glossy onyx fringe hid her ebony eyes. The constant gum chewing and giggling put an end to the bougee façade.

"Did you forget about your girlfriend, Will? Her name is Gemma," Troy said. He dribbled the ball to midfield and kicked it towards the net. Brendon stepped to the right and caught the shot, rolling it onto the field. Rachel Jones cheered and shouted, "Du bist erstaunlich."

"There is no harm in looking," William said, throwing a confident wink in Tilly's direction. "Who would you choose, Spence?"

"Neither of them. I'm taken," Troy said, rolling the ball under his cleat.

"What about you, Mr. Football? Who would you snog if given the chance?"

Brendon grabbed a pylon and stacked it on top of another, tossing the tower towards the locker room door. Sparks lit.

"Can we finish the drills? I've had a terrible morning."

"Your girlfriend isn't around, Cook. Pick," William said, flashing an overconfident smile at Tilly.

He snatched a water bottle stuffed into the net and chugged it in four gulps. "Rachel Jones."

William snickered. "I've shagged her."

"Who hasn't," Troy said.

Brendon crumpled the bottle in his hand and glared. "I didn't say I fancied her. I like her hair."

"Temper, temper."

"Shut it, Will. I just got my mate back, don't be causing any sparks, not yet. We're here to practice, not talk about girls."

Brendon hurled the empty bottle into a recycling bin and tried to ignore the tiny flutter dancing in his belly. Talk of Rachel Jones had flooded the locker room for years. She was as bold as the untamed locks that cascaded over her shoulders.

"I think we're done."

"Who made you coach?" William snarled.

"My mate's in charge when Liam isn't here. He earned the role of team leader."

"Taunton's bleeding hero," William said, batting the ball between his feet. "Your bollocks at corner kicks."

Brendon snagged a ball from the pitch and flung it into the air. "Says the second-choice keeper."

William flipped up his middle finger and sauntered over to the girls.

Brendon grabbed a net bag and stuffed the ball inside. "I survived a two-hour flight with my dad. I'm not in the mood for Will's shit."

"He's pissed off your back. He only wears the jersey to pull a girl."

"William needs all the help he can get." Brendon tied the bag closed and slung it over his shoulder. "I forgot to ask, how did the Man U trial go?"

"I was bleeding nervous, mate, got into my head, couldn't concentrate."

"There will be scouts out all season. I could ask Walt to have Lukas fly in."

Troy chuckled. "And play for the Bundesliga? The Premier League is the only place for me. Manchester United all the way."

"Germany *is* football. Brilliant coaches, younger players get a chance, consistency. Should I go on?"

"Your daft. Premier players are ace; Old Trafford, Emirates Stadium. The English invented football."

"The Bundesliga has the highest average attendance."

"Only because the ticket prices are so low." Troy took the bag of balls from Brendon and smiled his sunshine smile. "Race you, mate."

"I'll beat you. I trained with the U19 squad."

"Bollocks. You haven't beaten me yet." He dropped the bag and readied himself. "On three. One, two, three."

The race was on. Troy clomped to a stop, beaming. "Nice try, mate. Still got you beat."

They walked into a locker room that could rival any professional team. Each player had their own gleaming wood cubby, their jerseys hung game ready. Offside the dressing room was a training area equipped with a variety of high-tech machines and gadgets. Winning began in the locker room, and this one had winning all over it.

"Disappointed to be back?"

Brendon grabbed his body wash and towel from his backpack. "A promise is a promise."

"At least you have a contract. I'll be stuck on the farm forever if someone doesn't notice me."

"You're the quintessential centre back, tall, strong, and fast. No one shuts down the opposition like you. Someone will notice."

"I'll keep trying and wishing," Troy said. He dug his school tie out of his bag and draped it over his blazer. "You coming to school today?"

Brendon masked his disappointment with a thin smile. "Tomorrow. Dad needs to go over the rules with me, and then we're meeting with the headmaster."

"You got manure on your boots, Spence," William interjected. He barged into the dressing room, held up his cell phone and flashed Tilly's number. "No professional squad wants a player stinking of cow shit."

"Do you have to be a wanker?"

"Not everyone can pay one of the Bundesliga's top scouts to watch them play." He tore off his practice jersey and stuffed it into his knapsack. "Look at all the dough your mom dumped into this place. You're a shoo-in for any pro team."

Tiny sparks flickered. Brendon inhaled, counted to four, and exhaled. "I'm a good keeper."

"You've got money, that pretty face," William said, shrugging into his white button-down.

"My face has nothing to do with it."

Brendon stuffed his practice jersey into his backpack, his body tense. "A quick punch will wipe the bloody smirk off your face."

"Keep breathing, mate. Wait until the second half of the season to punch him."

"Always bloody Switzerland."

Troy wound a towel around his neck and grabbed his shaving kit. "Someone must be."

"You should have stayed in Dortmund," William said, ripping his backpack from the hook.

"And let you fuck up the season."

William stomped from the locker room. Brendon grinned and plunked onto the bench. Just like he had— fucked things up.

"Don't get all mopey," Troy said. He pointed to the tattoo on Brendon's wrist and tried his sunshine smile again. "At least you have that as a souvenir."

"Dum spiro spero, while I breathe, I hope. I'll keep breathing and hope I get through the school year."

"You'll be alright. Just do as you're told and keep the sparks to a minimum. You'll be back in Dortmund in no time." Troy walked to the shower stalls with Brendon in tow. "Will has blabbed around school your Uncle Walt's getting married."

"That's the rumour."

"Who is she?"

"He met her in a park in Paris. That's all I know."

Troy's cobalt blue eyes twinkled mischievously. "Is she anything like the Russian girl he was dating?"

"Anastasia Morozova. She has over 100,000 Instagram followers."

"How come Walt didn't propose to her?" Troy drew back the privacy curtain and twisted on the taps. "They dated for a year."

"She wanted to move to LA to model. A billionaire was sending her DMs and enticed her to fly to California. She never came back."

"Blimey! Was Walt upset?"

Brendon stepped into the shower. The hot water felt good on his aching muscles. "Walt doesn't get upset over women. There's always another one waiting in the queue."

"There won't be now if he gets married. I looked forward to meeting Walter's newest girlfriend."

"She hasn't said yes."

Walter

Walter Pratt stepped out of the taxi, grabbed the picnic basket, and smiled. The sky was endless blue. The air perfumed with the scent of dahlias. Parc Floral de Paris was luminescent under the sun's glow. Just as she promised, Angelene Hummel basked on the park bench. The slip of yellow cotton barely covered her thighs and looked as if picked off the rack at a charity shop. Charcoal pencils and papers surrounded her bare feet. The concentration on her face as she sketched was endearing.

"You didn't run today."

"You've been harassing me since April, Mr. Fancy Suit."

Walter set the basket on the ground and dropped beside her. "I would call it dating. Few wives run from their husband."

"We aren't married yet."

"You'll marry me," Walter said, tucking a strand of hair behind her ear. "Your drawing is interesting."

Angelene shuffled her illustrations into a pile and stuffed them into a book. "It's Lucifer's side of the story. Do you find it interesting now?"

Walter chuckled at her prickly tone. "I guess everyone's story must be told."

He opened the picnic basket and reached for a bottle of wine. The game had been fun, chasing and wooing. He liked a challenge. Angelene Hummel had been his biggest yet.

"Your words are black, Monsieur Pratt. Not pretty night sky black, but overwhelming, powerful black."

Walter handed her a glass. "Call me Walter or darling, something other than Monsieur Pratt."

"Why did you choose me? Out of all the women in Paris, you picked a girl in cheap clothes."

"I see something in you," he said, his eyes crinkling as he smiled.

Under the tangled ponytail and flimsy sundress was a beauty. He wanted to be the talk of Taunton. Not because his wife was almost half his age, but because she was beautiful. He would do a better job than Henry Higgins. Angelene Hummel would outshine all the other ladies in Taunton. He would see to it.

"You don't know what you are getting yourself into." She gulped a mouthful of wine and ran her finger over a dribble on her lip. "Maybe my drawing is my story."

"Maybe, and maybe it's poor Lucifer," Walter said. "Take it easy, that's a Chateau Mouton Rothchild. It's for sipping."

"Wine is wine, non?"

"No, it isn't." He opened the basket and set a baguette, brie, and grapes between them. "What made you stop running?"

"Strong hands," Angelene said, popping a grape into her mouth. "Broad shoulders. You have a strong exterior and a stronger interior. You're the epitome of normal. A home in the countryside, goodbye kisses, dinner on the table. Normal has never fit. It will now."

There wasn't anything normal about the waif sitting beside him.

A concrete beast rose into the clouds. Food wrappers floated in a river of rainwater collected in the gutter. Limp laundry clung to the rusting steel slats. An occasional pot of flowers added a pop of orange or red to the dismal beige complex. Walter gazed from the graffiti-tagged walls to a man lumbering back and forth in the foyer, push broom in hand. Something sent him into protection mode.

"I'll walk you to the door."

Angelene bristled and flapped her hand. "See you next Saturday."

"I'm a gentleman. A gentleman walks a lady to the door."

"I am no lady, Monsieur Pratt."

They weaved around scraps of sun-bleached newspapers floating in puddles.

"You haven't invited me to your apartment yet."

"I promised God I would not bring you to my flat."

Walter chuckled, took her elbow, and guided her around a puddle. "I won't be staying long. I'm having dinner with a friend. He's a scout for the Bundesliga."

A beefy hand slammed against the door and pushed it open, leaving a sweaty imprint on the smudged glass. The gold chandelier and porcelain tiles gave the impression that the building was classy and impressive. The ceiling had buckled from years of neglect. An out-of-order sign dangled from the elevator door. The man grunted and wheezed across the fleur-de-lis tiles. Little whirlwinds of dust flew around the broom.

"Where have you been, little bird?"

"None of your business."

Walter curled his fingers protectively around her shoulder.

"You promised to wash my sheets," the man huffed.

"Tomorrow," Angelene hissed.

He grumbled, slapped the broom on the floor, and puffed away.

"Who was that man?"

"My landlord Emile Douchette."

"Why did he call you little bird?"

Angelene opened the door to the stairwell. Dank, mouldy air assaulted Walter's nose.

"I'm not his little bird."

"It's fitting. You're so tiny and delicate, like a baby bird finding her wings."

"I'm Angelene. Although I don't like to be called that most days."

Walter followed her up the stairs. Each floor held a distinct scent. Cumin, boiled potatoes, floor four smelled sweet and earthy. He cleared his throat, wiggled Angelene's elbow, nodding towards the door to five.

Angelene jerked her elbow free from his fingers and knelt in front of a girl. "Yasmine, what are you doing? It isn't safe."

"I forgot my key," she said, collecting her crayons. "Are you the man Maman told Mademoiselle Hummel to stay away from?"

Walter grinned, reached into his pocket, and handed her a handful of Walker's toffee.

"Maman says you're too fancy."

Angelene hid her smile behind her fingers. "Come wait in my apartment. You've been practicing drawing."

"I added lots of detail, like you said."

"I like the knot in the tree and the owl hiding inside it."

Walter collected a glittered backpack and followed them down a peppery scented hall. Years of abuse dulled the beige walls and tiles.

"You can leave now," Angelene said.

The slap of a broom and heavy, asthmatic breaths reverberated off the walls. Angelene's shoulders stiffened. Walter took the key from her and unlocked the door.

"I'll stay until the girl's mother arrives."

The sun set the scratched parquet floor on fire. A sticky breeze lifted a cornflower-print tea towel, moving the scent of sandalwood and stale cigarette smoke through the stagnant air.

"May I sit on the window ledge? I love the view from your apartment. All Maman and I can see are the garbage bins."

"It's my favourite spot to sit. Go ahead."

Yasmine smiled, bounced onto the bed, and scrambled upon the sill. "Why is your bed in the living room?"

"That's a good question," Walter said.

"The view of the stars is nicer out here."

Walter's stomach quivered. There was something unnerving about the flat, like it housed terrible memories and sadness. There wasn't much in the apartment. A shabby green velvet chair, a spindle-legged table cluttered with cans of paintbrushes, and a bed that had seen better days, took up most of the space. Her breakfast of a boiled egg and cheese sat next to an overfilled ashtray on the counter. Stacks of well-loved books piled ten high leaned precariously against the faded peony wallpaper.

"Where's your telly?" Walter said.

"Why do I need a television? I have my books."

"Where do you sit? That chair looks like it could collapse."

"On the window ledge, Monsieur," Yasmine said, twirling the end of her pigtail. "What is your name?"

"Walter."

"You aren't French."

"Monsieur Pratt is from England."

A knock rattled the tiny apartment. Angelene's cheeks paled. She drew Yasmine to her side.

"You forgot your key again, silly girl," Lisette Gagnon announced.

"I should introduce myself. I'm..." Walter thrusted out his hand.

Lisette waved his hand away, dismissing him. "I know who you are, Secretary of Defence for the United Kingdom. Come, Yasmine, you have troubled Angelene enough."

Angelene jumped from the ledge and stood next to Walter. "I couldn't leave her alone. Douchette is wheezing through the halls. He would have pestered her."

Walter wound his arm around Angelene's shoulders. She recoiled and rushed to the kitchen table.

"Take these. You'll be a proper artist now."

"Look, Maman," Yasmine said, holding up a fistful of charcoal pencils.

"Neither you nor I have the money for art supplies," Lisette said.

"Angelene will have the world," Walter said.

"We'll see, Monsieur." Lisette plucked Yasmine's backpack off the floor and gave Angelene a look. Walter was sure it was a mixture of disapproval and condemnation.

"Tough woman."

"She's protective of me." Angelene rambled to the window ledge, nestled into the corner, and dug around a stack of books for her cigarettes. "She's as unhappy as God. I promised no more men."

Walter grinned and rested beside her. "Next Saturday, Parc Floral with Father Charbonneau and the peacocks."

"I haven't said yes."

He unbuttoned his suit jacket and pulled a velvet box from a silk-lined pocket. "I have something for you." He snapped open it and studied her face, waiting for a smile, a gasp. She stared blankly at the diamond pendant, fumbling in a packet of Gauloises cigarettes.

"I won't accept it."

Walter laced it around her neck. He leaned towards her and puckered his lips. She ducked, slipped past him, and sank into the chair.

"Is Taunton peaceful?"

"I live in the countryside. In a pretty home. Next door to my friend."

Angelene twirled a piece of thread dangling from the cushion around her finger. "Is this the friend you share a flat with throughout the week?"

"David Cook. Rosewood Manor has been in his family for decades."

She tied the thread tighter and tighter, strangling her fingertip. "His wife?"

"Sofia is wonderful." Walter watched her fingertip turn purple. "She can be a little feisty. She balances David's dull side."

"Do they have children?"

Walter snapped the thread from the cushion and unwound it from her finger. "One. Brendon's a good kid. Tries his best, which should count for something." He lifted his cuff. "I have to meet my friend Lukas. He was ecstatic when Brendon signed."

Angelene rubbed at the purply indents and glanced up. "Is there something special about the boy?"

"He's an extraordinary footy player."

Walter laid his hand on Angelene's cheek and studied her grey-green eyes. "I'm glad you finally stopped running."

"I promised God: no more talking to men. You kept pestering me."

"I'm not any man. I'm Walter Pratt."

"I asked God if I made a mistake."

Walter grinned and smoothed her hair. "What has God said?"

"He hasn't answered yet."

"I suppose I shouldn't ask for a kiss goodbye."

"Go away, Mr. Fancy Suit."

Walter blew her a kiss. He didn't need to wait for God. He knew he had done the right thing.

Angelene

Angelene slid onto a polished chair and clasped her rosary. The sun radiated through the stain glass windows, washing her face in a glow of red, yellow, and blue. Praying from her apartment window was getting her nowhere. She needed to try God's house.

Saint-Étienne-du-Mont was her favourite of all the churches in Paris. The asymmetrical wonder had taken one hundred years to build. The white spiral staircases that flanked each side of the pulpit and the cherubs brought her peace. God had to give her a sign. She appreciated His forgiveness and love. God's love was the best kind of love.

'Please, God, I've been waiting for you. I sat with Victor Hugo and told him I would miss him. I visited the Dean of Fine Arts at the Sorbonne and asked her to wish Professor Piedmont well. Her office smelled of mouldy potpourri and her books, squished together. The covers were torn. I wanted to save them all.'

Angelene pressed her shoulders back and stared at the arched ceiling.

'Walter is handsome. He's powerful. We ran into Mademoiselle Cadieux from apartment 415 in Parc Floral and she blushed. He's tall, athletic looking, jogs, plays football with his friends. He takes up a lot of space when he's in the room- grand gestures, expensive suits, gold watches. Is he the one? Tell me. If you flutter my hair, I'll know you're happy with me. If you poke my belly, I'll run.'

The air was still and heavily scented with frankincense. Angelene clutched her rosary, sweat dribbled down her back. The memory was vivid.

Monsieur Krieger, you're back.

What makes you so sad, little bird? Who made you feel so tiny that you believe you must face all of life's storms alone?

2 Schwellenangst

Brendon

The steady tick of the clock drummed in Brendon's ears. The only phrase he understood was 'Sapre aude, dare to know.' It had been Taunton College's motto since the school opened in 1880. The only thing he dared to know was the Bundesliga team stats.

A trickle of sunlight danced over his desk and bounced onto the paper. He didn't know why his father thought Latin was an important subject. It made no sense, and after surviving all his classes, he couldn't care less about carpe diem. All he wanted to seize was a football before it went into the net. Outside the classroom, the end of the day was sweeping down the hall; feet shuffled, students chatted. From across the classroom, Rachel Jones stared at him from behind her textbook. His cheeks warmed. He squeezed out of the too-small desk and loosened his tie.

"Destitutus ventis, remos adhibe." Theodore Campbell stood by the door in a brown blazer, fingering his bowtie, expressionless. "If the wind fails, use the oars."

Brendon rolled his eyes, dropped his unfinished quiz on the desk, and followed the flow of students. The hallway was a sea of navy and grey. Buffeted from side to side, knocked by sharp elbows and backpacks, Brendon moved with the crowd. He wondered why they seemed so cheerful cooped up in Taunton College. A museum curator could have decorated the hallway. It was as stuffy and antiquated as the classrooms.

Did they like coming to school? How did they cope with quizzes, book reports, and the dizzying drone of teachers? He had been happy to replace the uniform with Dortmund's black and yellow kit. He thought he had finally said goodbye.

"You were brilliant on the pitch." Rachel stepped in front of him and blocked his way. She reached for his tie, moving her hand up and down the plaid silk. "Are we still on for German lessons? I wouldn't want you wandering around Dortmund not knowing how to ask for the loo."

Brendon tugged his tie from her fingers and tore his gaze from her ample chest. "That's the plan."

"Did you know your name means prince?" She bit into her bottom lip and smiled.

Girls had always made Brendon uncomfortable. He would become tongue-tied and flustered at his blazing cheeks. Embarrassment layered on embarrassment. This girl, with her rolled kilt and snug blouse, had him beyond flustered. Brendon Cook didn't associate with the tarts of Taunton. He was a good boy who dated nice girls.

"Get your jubblies off my mate."

Troy's voice pulled Brendon's gaze away from the freckles on Rachel's exposed chest.

"I heard you chatting him up." He stepped between them and folded Rachel's lapels over her chest. "Did you know your name means tart?"

Rachel flicked Troy's chin. "Rachel means beautiful in form." She wiggled her hips and beamed. "It's in the Bible."

"Since when do you read the Bible?" Troy said.

Rachel adjusted her lapels, pushed out her breasts, and smirked. "The prince of the pitch. It suits you. Auf wiedersehen."

A group of girls giggled, turned, and called out, 'Hiya Brendon' in unison. His flush deepened to crimson.

"Never a problem with the girls." Troy inspected his hair in a class-room door and grinned.

"Rachel gave my tie a wank in front of Mr. Campbell. It's embarrassing."

"Girls have been chatting you up since reception. The first day of school Ellie Harker shared her biscuit and kissed your cheek."

Students parted, making way for two of Taunton First's finest. Brendon Cook and Troy Spence were the footy club. It gave them status. Girls swooned and boys envied them. Teachers couldn't care less. They should be proud to walk the halls of the reputable Taunton College. Neither Brendon nor Troy cared about A-levels. For Brendon, it was a promise. Troy needed something to fall back on.

"I don't pay attention. I have a girlfriend." Brendon nudged Troy and nodded towards the end of the sun-drenched corridor. "Like you."

"Troy Spence, you were supposed to meet me."

Charlotte Donovan swung her hobo bag back and forth like a cricket bat. She tucked a wisp of chestnut brown hair into her fishtail ponytail and pouted. Charlotte was a spoiled fashionista. A slender, shapely, cooing dove with a blue-eyed, 'please little crumpet' stare. Her make-up—perfection, nails manicured to match the Manchester United kit. Brendon laughed inwardly; the practiced pout was working on Troy.

"Where have you been, babes?"

"Can't I meet up with my mate? I'm excited he's home from Dortmund, even if he isn't."

"Not when you're supposed to meet me. Give me your keys and I'll wait at your car." She gripped his square jaw and nibbled his chin. "I love my little crumpet."

Charlotte bumped the door open with her hip and skipped across the lawn in her navy Doc Marten boots. Brendon had always admired Charlotte's carefree attitude. Her biggest concern of the day, how to doctor her school kit so it resembled the outfits she adored in Vogue and Glamour.

Brendon pushed open the door, glad to be free of the musty air and rules that came with attending the illustrious Taunton College. They were as suffocating as his father's 'thou shalt not' and the Gentleman's Code.

"You got time to go to the pitch? I've been practicing my volley kicks," Troy said.

They trudged towards the car park. Waiting patiently by his car was Margaret Thornton. Kilt knee-length, white cotton blouse buttoned to her neck, fresh-faced with blue blossom eyes. The kind of girl who found solace in the library. The kind of girl Brendon Cook brought home to Mammina.

"Can't. I promised Dad I would catch up on the schoolwork I missed. It's part of my punishment."

Troy's face erupted into a smile. "When you get bored with studying, you can sneak off to the Beemer for a snog."

"There will be no time for snogging. Not when the library and history are involved."

"Hurry, my delicious little crumpet."

Brendon glanced from Maggie to Charlotte's fluttering kilt. His eyebrows raised. Her panties were lace.

"I'm down here," Maggie said.

"Are you wearing lacy knickers?"

"Don't be daft. Mom would give me an earful if I wore anything like that."

Brendon kissed the top of her head and lifted the hem of her kilt.

"Nice one, mate," Troy yelled. He dove into the car and revved the engine. "Have fun studying." He barrelled out of parking lot in a spray of sand and gravel.

"I want to see what style of knickers you're wearing."

Maggie gave him a playful swat. "Mrs. McGregor was at the salon and told my Mom Walter got married."

"Mom's been bloody cranky. I thought it was me. She's been grumbling over lists and whispering to Dad about being disappointed."

"Who is she?" Maggie said, chomping on her thumbnail. "Should I be worried? Walter's ex, the Russian slag, fancied you."

"Mom said and I quote, 'Walt should bring her to Taunton in a pram.' Dad wasn't impressed."

Maggie wound her arm through his and snuggled into his side. "I'm glad you're home. These last four weeks have been awful."

The sun illuminated the collection of Victorian buildings. Immaculate green lawns surrounded Taunton College, with fields and trees on all sides. They walked past the chapel and ivy-covered administration office. Brendon kept his eyes on the ground. The headmaster, Julian Dawson, popped up in the window and bellowed for all to hear. "Three strikes, Mr. Cook."

Maggie stifled a laugh and yanked open the library door. "Mr. Dawson not happy you're back?"

"The only thing he was happy to see was Mom. I swear he was hiding his biggie during the entire meeting yesterday. Dad must have been too bloody pissed off to notice."

Brendon hooked his foot around the chair leg and fell onto it. He scrubbed his cheeks and sighed. An irritated 'shh' blew from within the rows of books.

"Look what I did for you." Maggie smoothed out a chart, pushed her tortoiseshell glasses on, and smiled. "I did it in Dortmund's team colours."

Brendon stared at the mapped-out assignments. She had written each subject in bold black and highlighted them yellow: English, French, history, and Latin.

"You went to a lot of trouble. Thanks." He kissed her cheek and slid his fingers between her thighs.

"Stop before someone sees." Maggie pried his hand from between her legs and put it on the table.

"I missed you. Let's snog."

"I promised your father I would get you organized. You've missed two weeks of school."

"Those were the happiest days of my life."

Maggie rolled her eyes and tapped her finger against his notebook. "You're starting with The Sorrows of Young Werther in English, Henry VIII in history."

"Can we talk about something else?" Brendon touched the diamond solitaire on her finger. "Like how bloody brilliant I played for Dortmund's U19 squad." He nuzzled her neck and raised his middle finger at the tsk-tsking coming from the aisles of books.

"I was gutted when you were away."

"I called you every night at 10:00." Brendon lowered his voice to a whisper. "I dreamt about you."

Her eyes fluttered shut. The kiss was gentle and sweet.

"Not in the library, Mr. Cook. Three strikes," the librarian said sternly.

"Does the whole bloody school know?"

Maggie clicked her pen and listed the due date of a French assignment. "Kids have been placing bets for weeks. Someone bet five quid you'd only last a day in Dortmund."

"People need to piss off." Brendon undid his tie and tilted the chair back. "I talked to Rachel. I thought you should know; in case the bets start."

Maggie scrunched her nose and flipped through her notebook. "What did Taunton's tart want?"

"She's going to teach me German. Madame Lafavre recommended her."

"I promised after the Franca incident I wouldn't get jealous."

It was a promise Maggie had difficulty keeping. Brendon couldn't help girls flirted with him. He didn't ask his cousin's friend to skinny-dip in the pool. The girl batted her eyelashes and flaunted herself the entire two weeks she stayed at the manor. Brendon hung out at the pitch and Spence farm to avoid her flirting.

"I need help learning German. I couldn't understand the goal coach. I promise I'll follow my dad's daft Gentleman's Code."

Maggie rested her cheek against his arm. "I'm glad you're back. I missed you horribly."

He kissed her and glanced at the accumulating list of assignments and quizzes. "All that in one year?"

"These are your A-levels. What did you expect? Worksheets and colouring pages?"

The walls of books shrank around him. The smell of dust and aging paper tickled his nose. He wanted to tell Maggie about the mistake he made, the regrets he had. There was something about the way her glasses sat precariously on her nose, how her eyes reminded him of the bluebells in springtime, made him change his mind. He had seen enough disappointed people since arriving home.

"You want to get out of here?"

"Your dad will be mad if you don't start an assignment."

"I'll take you for pizza."

Maggie shoved her notebook into her bag and folded her glasses. "Can we go for a walk in Vivary Park after?"

Brendon grabbed her overstuffed book bags. "We'll find a bench and start the history homework. I should have brought you to Dortmund with me. I might have done better."

"Next time," Maggie said.

Maggie

A fit of giggles stuck in Maggie's throat. She lounged on a fuzzy pink pouf in front of a white veneer vanity. The sweet scent of cotton candy and vanilla clung to the pink and lilac throw pillows, filmy white curtains, and her blankets. Her room smelled like a candy shop.

Maggie pulled her fleecy unicorn and rainbow housecoat tighter around her chest. She gazed at the assortment of photographs propped up between perfume bottles and lotions: Brendon in his football kit, on the steps of Evans Hall, in his car. She grabbed a pair of scissors from her drawer and clipped out an article from the Taunton Times. 'Borussia Dortmund's future. Welcome home, Brendon Cook.' Maggie's heart swooned. Everything about him, the throaty timbre of his voice, his dark eyes, how he moved effortlessly on the pitch, was perfection and all hers.

"I have the perfect hairstyle picked out," Rosie Thornton announced.

She was middle class; born into middle class and wore the label proudly. It stood for hard work and pride that all she and Kevin Thornton had; they earned. If she had food on the table, clothing, and they paid the mortgage, she was a blessed and happy woman.

Beneath her caramel-blonde bob, Rosie hid her disapproval behind a façade of a smile. She set down a plastic caddy filled with brushes, hairspray, various clips, and nudged the photos towards the mirror. Rosie wasn't happy Brendon Cook was home. She hadn't been happy the day Charlotte Donovan planned the double date. Brendon was everything Rosie despised: money, prima donna footy player, and a politician's son. Not just any politician, England's Lord Chancellor. If anyone asked Rosie her opinion of Taunton's footy hero, his snooty mother coddled and spoiled him. He was no good for her darling Margaret.

"Do you need to have so many pictures? It's bleeding creepy having him stare at me."

"Photos were all I had when he was in Dortmund. Besides, I love looking at him. He's the most attractive boy I've ever met."

"You've only been to Paris. There is an entire world of handsome boys." Rosie's mouth dropped into a frown. She lifted a chunk of Maggie's hair and teased the roots. "What about the boy from drama?"

"Michael? I don't like him like that. I only want Brendon."

"Would you think he was so special if he didn't drive that BMW or live in some posh manor?" Rosie said, yanking Maggie's hair into a sixties-inspired ponytail.

When Charlotte introduced her to Brendon, it wasn't about the car he drove or where he lived. It amazed her that he was even interested. There was something about Brendon, not his goalkeeping skills or being the Southern League's dishiest player. He was sweet, thoughtful, and admired her intelligence. He bragged to his dad how smart she was and the perfect girl to help with A-levels. He was the first boy to notice her, and that meant the world to a girl who loved the library.

"I don't know what it is with girls and footy players," Rosie said. She placed her hands on Maggie's shoulders and forced her to look in the mirror. "Isn't it brilliant your mom is a stylist?"

Maggie titlted her head from side to side and handed Rosie a pink rhinestone clip. "I always have a great cut and highlights and don't have to spend three-hundred pounds like Charlie."

"I earn my paycheque. What does Mrs. Cook do all day in that fancy house?"

Maggie covered her face as a mist of hairspray fell around her. She coughed and blinked, tired of the conversation. Two years of justifying how Sofia Cook filled her time, and that Brendon was a gentleman. He had a code to follow.

"She does lots of things."

"I suppose planning posh parties and shopping fills her days. She could be on that show, *The Ladies of London*," Rosie said. She smoothed Maggie's bangs and shot a blast of hairspray. "They could rename it the Ladies of Taunton and have Victoria McGregor on it. Nosy cow."

"Mrs. Cook is brilliant with me. That's all that should matter."

"If buying you expensive gifts makes her nice, then what else do you need," Rosie said. She angled her head beside Maggie's and grinned at her work. "There. You're as pretty as Julie Christie in Doctor Zhivago."

Rosie's gaze shifted from Maggie's perfectly coiffed ponytail to a beaded mini dress with puffed sleeves.

"How much did that cost?"

"It reminded me of the dresses I saw in *The Great Gatsby*."

"You're supposed to be saving for uni." Rosie set the brush and hairspray in the caddy and slumped onto the bed. "Your father and I barely scrape by every month, and you're spending money on some daft dress."

Maggie hung her head and shoved her thumbnail into her mouth. "I used my birthday money."

Rosie huffed out her irritation. "It looks a little short."

Maggie dropped her housecoat to the floor, shielded her lace bralette, and shimmied the dress over her slender hips. "See, not too short. It covers my bum."

Rosie rubbed her knitted brow. She reached for Maggie's wrists and pulled her down beside her. A well-loved teddy bear tumbled into Maggie's thigh. She cuddled it against her chest.

"What's with the lacy knickers?"

"Charlie told me to buy them. She said a girl should always wear posh knickers under a fancy dress."

"I'm sure Charlotte Donovan knows a thing or two about knickers, not to mention other things. Running around Taunton, groping Troy Spence. Not a way for a young lady to act."

Maggie laid her hand over Rosie's and ran her finger over the cracks in her palm. "I wanted to feel pretty all over."

"Don't get yourself into trouble."

"If you saw what some girls at school wear under their uniform, this is plain in comparison."

The frustration that furrowed Rosie's brow dropped. Maggie knew the look on her mother's face: worry, love.

"I love you and Jack. You know I only want the best for both of you."

Maggie could see the 'don't-make-the-same-mistake-as-me' look in her mother's blue eyes. She squeezed Rosie's hand. Her beauty had faded. She looked beyond her thirty-nine years.

"I know, Mom. I love Brendon and gosh, Charlotte, even Gemma, who is as boring as me is... well, you know."

"I was fifteen when I had you. Don't rush into sex."

"Brendon is a nice boy. He respects me."

Rosie laughed and patted Maggie's thigh. "No boy is nice when it comes to that. They say they'll wait, but trust me, they won't."

"Brendon will. We've talked about it."

"Taunton's hero wait." Rosie stood; a sigh blew from her lips. "I want you home by eleven tomorrow."

The sound of footsteps pounding up the stairs shook the thin walls. Maggie rolled her eyes and opened the top drawer of her vanity. It was filled with sweets. Jack, her little monster, the brother who was nine years younger than her, bounded into her room and snatched a handful of candy.

"Why'd smelly Brendon have to come home? I was happy he wasn't coming around here on Sundays. I got to see Charlie instead."

"Don't eat all those sweets," Rosie said. She grabbed the caddy off the vanity and ruffled Jack's hair. "One, then climb into bed. Maggie can read you a story."

Jack stuck out his tongue, punched over a picture of Brendon, and dashed from the room.

"Do I have to read him a story? We've read that Batman book about a hundred times."

"Yes. You'll be off to uni next year. Jack will miss you."

Maggie doubted it.

"Mom."

Rosie turned and leaned into the door frame. "I'm over the dress. You look pretty. I just hope Brendon Cook sees how beautiful you are."

"I was going to ask who Julie Christie is."

A grin broke through Rosie's pursed lips. "Ask your father."

Maggie shook out her hands and gnawed on her lower lip. She had to prepare for another performance. It had been her tactic at all Sofia Cook's parties. Act, pretend she was on stage, lines rehearsed, ready to dazzle the audience.

"Every damn do, you get yourself all worked up. This party is no different from the last one."

"It's incredibly special, Mom. Mr. Pratt got married."

Rosie choked on her laughter. "I told Simone Batra hell must have frozen over. Take the dress off and go read to Jack. I can hear him bouncing all over his room."

Maggie took another look in the mirror. She didn't care what her mother said. It was love. Brendon Cook wasn't a spoiled dolt. He was a 'hold the door open for her, call before he fell asleep,' kind of boy. Out of all the girls who loitered around the pitch, vying for his attention, he had chosen her. Bookworm, sweet as springtime, Margaret Thornton.

Angelene

Angelene stared at the building across the street. She laid her hand against the glass. His spirit hovered in the window. A shadowy touch, the smell of rose and pomegranate, haunted her. She followed the setting sun's glow to the faded peony wallpaper. Roman Krieger brought the hand-painted paper back from London. It was one of the few moments she saw her mother smile.

Angelene sniffed and wiped her nose on her sleeve. She had cried among the tired walls, screamed, hid, and cuddled with Roman in the faded green chair. Memories swarmed her head, snapshots of moments flicked through her mind in a series of black and white pictures. She was drowning in her memories, oblivious to the door opening.

"Will you look at this place? I can't see an inch of the floor."

Yasmine jumped onto the chair and wrapped a shawl around herself. "You could open a boutique."

Jars of wilted flowers disguised the kitchenette and spilled from the bedrooms. Price tags hung from clothes slathered over the kitchen table. Angelene touched the emerald-cut diamond that spanned the length of her slender finger and forced a smile.

"Monsieur Pratt has been very generous."

"Your husband," Lisette said. She picked up a bottle of perfume and sniffed. "Pretty."

"Keep it," Angelene said, sliding off the window ledge. "He doesn't like patchouli oil. Roman used to bring it home from India for mother. I loved how it smelled on her skin. It was the only thing I liked about her."

Lisette turned the box over. Her eyebrows lifted. "190 euros, I couldn't."

"I don't want to smell flowery."

"This feels soft, like a bunny," Yasmine cooed, rubbing a shawl against her cheek.

"It's angora, sweet pea," Lisette said, removing the wrap from her fingers, "and expensive. What do you know about this man?"

Angelene twisted her fingers through her hair. "We've discussed this."

"Did God give you a sign?"

She tugged her hair and smoothed it. "There were too many. Walter's a politician, you know this."

"Him, not how he makes his money."

Yasmine whirled a pashmina wrap around herself. "He wears fancy suits, Maman."

"Is it the money?"

Angelene lit a cigarette, took a hearty drag, and slung her arm out the window. "This is my chance to get out of Clichy-sous-Bois."

"Do you love Walter?"

Angelene tossed the cigarette and paced. "I'm not sure." Angelene tossed the cigarette and paced. "I like his tattoo."

"Is that it? An anchor tattoo."

"Walter's been very kind to me."

"Clothes and jewellery are just things," Lisette said, fingering the price tag of a Christian Dior blazer. "Your soul mate could be out there. He could be in Taunton. What will you do? You're married to a man you don't love."

Angelene paced back and forth, dodging vases of flowers and shopping bags. "Love will come."

"You make terrible decisions." Lisette held up a black silk dress. "This is not you. Where is the colour? The patterns?"

Angelene kneaded her knuckles and moved methodically across the floor. A few beats passed before she spoke. "I still have my them. My whole life has been nothing but patterns."

"Your perfume, your clothes, shouldn't he love you for you?"

"Oh, mon Dieu, Angelene, you are making me dizzy," Yasmine said.

She ignored Yasmine's plea and marched on. "I suppose Walter should. I've never had a normal relationship."

"You've made poor choices," Lisette scolded.

"It's too late for a lecture. He'll be here soon."

"Douchette," Yasmine whispered, pressing her fingers into the faded velvet. "Where will I go when I forget my key?"

Angelene stopped pacing, kicked a Louboutin shoebox across the room, and dropped to her knees. "Where's your key?"

Yasmine dug in her sundress pocket and dangled it between her fingers. Angelene unclasped the diamond necklace and laced the chain through the hole.

"Now you'll never forget."

"Monsieur Pratt gave that to you."

"He can afford another."

"Give her a piece of ribbon, some string," Lisette said.

"Promise never to remove it. You must protect your light."

Lisette slammed her hands on her hips. Her tone was both teary and harsh. "I insist you take it back."

"It will keep her safe."

Lisette yanked Angelene from the floor and shook her. "You frustrate me."

"I have something else for you." She broke free of Lisette's grip and scrambled to the kitchen, rummaging underneath the clothes for a book and a collection of pencil crayons.

"You love Schellen-Ursli. Monsieur Krieger gave you the book," Yasmine said.

"I have my memories. It is your turn to help Ursli chase winter away."

Angelene turned from Yasmine, gathered an armful of clothes, and tossed them into a bag. The perfume was next; the angora shawl and navy blazer. She shoved it at Lisette.

"Take them."

"Walter bought these for you."

"Wear them, sell them, I don't care. Please keep Yasmine's light safe."

The frustrated look fell from Lisette's face. "In my pocket, in case you get hungry on the plane."

Angelene thrust her hand into Lisette's cardigan and pulled out a rectangular box. "Lemon macaron."

"Only the French can make a macaron. Be safe."

Angelene blew a flurry of kisses and slumped onto the armrest. Patterns, poor decisions. She had been exceptionally good at both.

The elevator doors hissed and bumped open. Angelene pressed her bottom against the door and dragged a duffel bag inside, followed by two suitcases. The doors thumped shut, and she struggled to breathe as it lurched and clunked between floors. Years of counting each level, cursing Douchette when it was broken. She would have new stairs to count, a proper kitchen to mess. The doors hissed open; Angelene lugged the bag and suitcases through the lobby. Slivers of fading sunlight shone between the buildings. The concrete scenery was her home.

"Little bird."

"What do you want, Emile?"

"You forgot something. I was going to throw it down the garbage chute."

Angelene ripped a jewellery box from his hand, unzipped the duffel bag, and shoved it among the clothes. Douchette slid behind her. She could feel his round belly against her back. He placed his nose on her neck; his plump fingers snaked through her hair.

"Walter will be here soon. If he sees you touching me."

"Your lover will not want to muss his fancy suit."

"He's not my lover. He is my hus... husband."

"You still have trouble saying that."

Douchette's breath rattled in her ear. An empty Orangina can clattered across the pavement. In the distance, a horn beeped. Angelene wiggled free as the black Rolls Royce she had spent the summer travelling in pulled alongside the curb.

"Always the big shot. Sac de merde."

"Be quiet, Emile."

She tugged at her blouse and teetered in her new shoes. She had scoffed at the red-soled shoes. So much money wasted on a pair of heels she could barely stand in. What she needed was a glass of wine, a cigarette to settle the tremors shredding through her stomach.

"It's a glorious evening," Walter said.

"If you say so."

Angelene gave the building another look. She had hated the concrete monstrosity; today she was in love.

"Hand me your bag. We have a flight to catch."

Angelene tore her gaze from the building. Her face blanched. "I've never been on a plane. I'm frightened."

"We have our own suite. We'll celebrate with champagne. It will take your mind off the nerves," Walter said, loading her bags into the trunk.

Douchette huffed. "Don't listen to him. You sit in a seat and pray it doesn't fall from the sky."

Angelene gripped Walter's suit jacket, her eyes frantic. "I'm not getting on that plane."

"He's an idiot. We'll be in the air for an hour. You'll be fine."

Angelene shook out her hands and wiggled her fingers. The voices in her head quarreled: *stay, run.*

"You shouldn't be leaving. You're French," Douchette said.

"She'll still be French, just in Taunton."

Douchette shook his head, his chins jiggled. "This is her home. She's my little bird."

"Stop," Angelene said, holding her hands over her ears. "I can't listen to the two of you bickering. My own thoughts are enough."

"You think there is a heaven in her, Pratt. She's all devil."

"I'll take my chances."

"Mademoiselle Hummel," Yasmine called.

Angelene stumbled and stared at Walter. "Why did you buy me these ridiculous shoes?"

"They're Louboutins. You'll be the envy of every woman in Taunton."

She scowled at Walter, bent down, and clasped Yasmine's shoulders. "You drew me a picture. Is that my home in England?"

"It will be spring every day."

Angelene drew Yasmine into her arms, pressing her nose into her apple-scented hair. "Your light is so bright. I'll miss you." She glanced up at Douchette, her eyes damp. "Run to your mother. Go."

Angelene licked her lips and rubbed at an ache in her chest. The building warped; Lisette's 'see you soon' swept down from their balcony. Memories flooded over her in scents and colours.

"I'm homesick and we haven't left. How will Lisette protect Yasmine?"

Walter kissed the crown of her head and nudged her towards the car. "Don't worry about the Gagnons. I have a plan for them, too."

The farmhouse was modest, with black-framed dormer windows, its walls and walkway covered in wisteria. The trees surrounding the drive sheltered it, casting shadows across the lawn. Grass crept up around the door in scraggily patches; weeds choked out the marigolds. Angelene shivered and pressed her thumb on her pulse. Thirteen listless beats. It was like the sun never reached it or warmed its rooms.

"It looks haunted."

Walter parked under the limbs of a willow tree. "If you want ghosts, head up to the manor. There's one in every room."

"The forest. Is that part of the property?"

"All the way to the manor and beyond. There's a path that leads from here to Rosewood. The fun David and I had in the woods."

Angelene stepped out of the car and swallowed mouthfuls of air. This was her home now. A farmhouse in the middle of a moor, in the middle of nowhere with no one. She dug her fingernails into her wrist, '*what have I done*' stuck in her throat.

Walter handed her the keys and grinned his crinkly smile. "Go on, little bird. I'll pop the boot and get your things."

She walked in slow, precise steps, afraid she'd stumble in the heels he had been so eager to buy her, afraid of what she might find beyond the door.

"Go on," Walter called. "I had no idea I purchased so much stuff in Paris."

The key shook in her hand.

'*Schwellenangst. I'm scared to enter this house and start a new chapter.*'

Sweat trickled down her spine. Something didn't feel right, like the house was pushing her away, like it knew of her arrival and wanted her out.

'*It's just you, Angelene Hummel, now Mrs... it sounds strange. Here goes, I hope you are with me, God.*'

Shadows waltzed across the foyer and over the dull white walls. The sharp sting of citrusy bleach bit her nose.

"Amelia was here. I must send her flowers."

Angelene jumped at the sound of his voice. "Who's Amelia?"

"The Cook's housekeeper," Walter said, plunking her duffel bag on the scratched parquet. "She's more family than an employee."

"Do you have a housekeeper?"

"I prefer to do my own cleaning. I'm very particular."

Angelene cocked her head and glanced into the front room. Nothing but an aging leather recliner and more dismal white walls. She rubbed the goosebumps erupting over her skin.

"Wh... where's the kitchen?"

"Right this way. I keep thinking I should remodel it. I have fond memories here. The island is new."

The space was well-loved and charming, with whitewashed cupboards and a sea-foam green, white, and beige backsplash. A window seat, covered in a dingy sage cushion, overlooked the moors. Angelene licked her lips and ran her hand over the weathered wood island. "I can't cook."

"You'll learn. That's the sitting room."

She spun on her heels and gazed at a worn leather sofa and gargantuan television sitting atop an antique bread hutch.

"It's not what I expected."

"What more does a man need? Were you expecting something posher?"

"You're so particular about your clothes, your fancy watches."

"Between London and travelling for work, I'm not here much."

Angelene shrank against the island, overwhelmed and feeling out of place.

"Let me show you the upstairs."

She followed, surrounded by more white walls and empty rooms.

"You said I would have a room where I can paint."

"There's one at the end of the hall." He stood in a doorway and waved his hand. "This is our room. I'll grab the luggage."

A mammoth bed dominated the space. It was an unsightly focal point, making the knotted pine dresser and nightstand insignificant. Angelene pulled off her shoes and padded across the room like she was stepping on glass. She dropped onto the bed and clutched the duvet.

The closet is bigger than my flat. A bathroom, right here in my bedroom.

A thud jolted the thoughts from her head. She gathered her hair around her face and twisted the sun-bleached strands between her fingers.

"I can't breathe."

"What's the matter?" Walter dropped a valise nestled under his arm to the floor and joined her on the bed. "You were so excited on the plane, talked the entire flight."

"I was worried it would fall from the sky." Angelene blew out a ragged breath. How could she be a wife? How could she act normal, do normal things when it never existed in her?

"This room is ugly."

Walter smiled his crinkly smile and brushed his lips over her hair. "I suppose the whole house needs a makeover."

"I want to go home."

"This is your home now."

Angelene sniffed and turned toward the window. At the top of the hill, wrapped in rose gardens, stood the manor. Her room faced a sash window on the second floor. A shadow shifted behind its curtain and a shiver ran through her. Something strange, static, prickling, pulled her toward that room. It stole her breath and made her insides tremble.

"Do you have to work in London?"

"I thought you enjoyed being alone."

She tore her gaze from the window and picked at the raspberry-red nail polish. "I'm overwhelmed. I must go to this party and remember all the rules. No gulping the champagne, no fidgeting."

"Please stop picking. I spent forty euros on your manicure."

She shook out her hands, lifted her bottom, and shoved her fingers underneath.

"Where will I go? What will I do? Back home, I could go to Parc Floral or sit with Hugo."

"We have parks here. You'll have Sofia."

Angelene stood and tugged on the pull of the duffle bag. The jewellery box rose on a wave of clothes and tipped open. Scraps of paper and postcards spilled onto the floor. Edelweiss tinkled in the air.

"What's that?"

"Just an old box."

She stuffed the papers and postcards inside, closed the lid and cradled it against her chest.

"There will be no secrets in my home."

"It's a few old memories, nothing more."

Walter unzipped a Chanel garment bag, expecting to see a black cocktail dress. It housed a saffron dress with beaded straps.

"Where is the dress I bought you?"

The words trembled from her mouth. "I gave it to Lisette."

"You want to wear this?" He held up the slip and shook it. "My friends will be there, my colleagues. How will you hide..." He stopped mid-sentence. Tears sat in the corners of her eyes.

"I love that dress. It's my favourite colour. It will make me yellow, less frightened."

"Do you know how much the Chanel cost?" Walter touched her trembling lips and grinned. "Of course, you don't. This will have to do."

"I'm sorry."

"No need for apologies. I'll make you a cuppa. Did you see the window bench in the kitchen? It has a wonderful view of the moors."

Angelene scraped up and down her arm. She had lived her life blending into the background, trying to fit in, trying to do normal and be normal. She had doubts she could be a wife and do the things wives do. It was as strange and scary as landing in a foreign country: new language, new customs.

"My stomach hurts. A friend suggested it was my nerves. Mother said it was God's punishment. Is God trying to tell me something?"

"You hardly ate today. Just pecked at your breakfast, pecked at your dinner. Just like a little bird pecking away."

"I feel dizzy."

"I'll make you tea. You can sit in the window," Walter said, reaching into the depths of the duffel bag. "You have your book, *The Hunchback*. Everything will be fine."

"Please don't leave me alone tomorrow."

"I promise."

3 Hiraeth

Brendon

Brendon drove along Taunton Road, following a charm of goldfinches. They dipped above the treeline, over the farmhouse, settling into the arch of ancient trees framing the laneway. Brendon zoomed through the tunnel of contorted trees, the branches unravelled and presented Rosewood Manor.

The stately Georgian home draped elegantly across the grounds. Ivy clung to the ivory stucco walls and framed the sash windows that overlooked the gardens. At night, the house loomed over the moors, haunted in darkness, mournfully weeping, surrounded by a forest of bent and gnarled trees. It was his mother's pride and joy, his father's disdain, and one day—his.

The manor had always been a silent sentinel overlooking the moors. Today it was bustling. Caterers carried in crates of produce and bulging paper sacks. Decorators came and went, arms full of twinkle lights and urns. Brendon parked beside his mother's Maserati, grabbed his backpack, and stepped over containers of pressed linens. He opened the servant's door, his eyes widening at the buzz of activity. A team of people had hijacked the spacious kitchen. Silver tiered trays crowded the black walnut island. Opened boxes of petit fours and pastries sat between piles of vegetables and fruit. He leaned against the counter and smiled. Amelia Potter flew from the pantry and slammed jars of spices into a heap of flour. A cloud of white exploded into the air. She coughed and sputtered, scooting between the chefs like a determined mouse dodging a trap.

"Ame, you're not humming."

Amelia crumpled onto a stool and tucked a strand of grey hair into her bun. "I'll be humming the death march soon. Look at my kitchen."

The chefs had ransacked the cupboards; bottles of olive oil and vinegars covered the countertops. Crumbs and vegetable peels dusted the travertine tiles. The usually immaculate and obsessively organized room was in disarray.

"I'll have to alphabetize my spices again."

Amelia jumped from the stool and lifted a dome, exposing artfully arranged slices of Battenberg cake, Victoria sponge, and cannoli. "Help yourself," she said, glaring at the head chef. "He charged into my kitchen, ordering me about. Go on, mess up his fancy display."

Brendon hitched his backpack over his shoulder and snatched a piece of cake.

"Where's Mom?"

"I don't know. I told Sofia a simple meal with a few close friends would be fine."

Brendon chuckled. "Mom doesn't do simple."

"Miss Amelia, I need basil, fresh, not dried," the chef demanded.

Amelia huffed and dragged a bundle of basil from within a pile of herbs. "I'd get out of here before he puts you to work."

"It's almost over."

Brendon dodged two men carrying urns of red roses and stopped in the middle of the foyer. The house was as magnificent inside as it was outside. Other than the extension built to house the indoor pool, Sofia had not altered the original design. The drawing room, ballroom, library, study had preserved woodwork, crown moulding, fireplaces with ornate mantels. Sofia's colour palette, navy, midnight blue, black, gold, and cream, rescued the home from David's father, Richard's reputation.

Collywobbles Manor no longer existed. Rosewood Manor stood for elegance and grace.

"Be careful up there," Brendon said.

Peter, their groundskeeper, leaned into the ladder, polishing the crystals dangling from the chandelier. Brendon ducked past a parade of caterers carting displays of fruit and buckets of champagne and bounded up the split staircase. The hallway stretched on either side. Sash windows brightened the cream walls and elaborate wood trim. Sunlight bounced off the polished parquet floors. Chandeliers hung from the coffered ceiling and created a sparkly pathway leading to the nine bedrooms. Sofia had decorated each room with a different theme. Springtime in Ireland, the Art déco masterpiece, Mediterranean dreams, whatever had inspired her. One bedroom remained locked. It was off-limits. It had been for as long as Brendon could remember.

Brendon flicked on the light, grabbed his Latin textbook, and dropped his backpack by the walk-in closet. There were signs a teenager lived amongst the built-in bookcases and antique furniture. Clothes draped over a Victorian button-back chair, stacks of football magazines, a collection of scrunched Red Bull cans cluttered the dresser. Nestled among his favourite childhood stories sat Paddington. The bear was well-loved and had played in every imaginary football match in the garden.

Brendon flung the textbook onto the bed, tugged his tie from beneath his collar and tossed it on the heap of clothes. A weird energy hummed in the air, and he didn't know why. The atmosphere was electric, like a storm approaching. He stripped off his school blazer and caught sight of the light coming from Walter's bedroom window. His heart fluttered as shadows moved across the walls. His parents hadn't said much about the mysterious woman who stole Walter's bachelorhood. Over the years, Walter had introduced him to a collection of brunettes and raven-haired models with plumped lips and overly accentuated body parts. Anastasia had been the last of Walt's beauties. The flirty brunette would comment on his dimpled grin and dark eyes. He would blush. Sofia would curse. His looks had earned him the title of the Southern League's dishiest player. He purposely forgot to shave and didn't bother styling his messy fade, hoping to deter the girls and social media polls. It hadn't kept Anastasia away, his cousin's friend Franca, and only irritated his mother.

Brendon flopped onto his bed, opened his Latin text, and stuck a pen in his mouth. From deep within the house, an ear-splitting crash and stream of Italian reverberated off the walls. He cringed, then laughed. He pitied the poor soul who had to deal with a furious Sofia Cook.

"Why didn't you say hello?"

His mother's entrance was grand, like a commander going to war. She marched to the bookshelf, straightened the trophies and Paddington, and walked to the bed, her silver bangles jangling. Sofia Cook was strength, elegance, passion, silk, and red lips. She had a face that turned men's heads, a body his friends ogled, and a love that was fierce.

"I just got home."

She brushed her lips over his cheek and planted herself on the bed. She moved a pillow, angled another, adjusted, and readjusted.

"What are you working on?"

"Latin. I don't understand."

Sofia dragged her fingers over her bracelets. Her red nails swept back and forth *jingle, jingle.* "Ask your father for help. He loves Latin."

"He'll get frustrated and tell me I'm not applying myself. I'll ask Rachel tomorrow."

Sofia stopped playing with her bangles and moved on to twisting her wedding band. "Who's Rachel?"

"A girl."

Brendon jotted down an answer, rewrote the sentence, and scribbled it out.

"Are you still upset we wouldn't let you stay in Dortmund? We haven't spoken much since you got back."

"I don't want to talk about it." He flipped to the glossary in the text, ran his pen down the definitions, and attempted an answer. "Dad's disappointment is bloody heavy."

"If Walter hadn't brought Lukas around, the Bundeswhatever wouldn't know who Brendon Cook is. You'd be here in Taunton with me."

"I don't want to be in bloody Taunton. I tried. It was a lot, studying and football."

"Education is important to your father. He wants you to have something to fall back on when you're too old to play and your body is broken."

"Lukas had his eye on me when I was seven. Dortmund wanted me at sixteen. You two said no."

Sofia tapped her finger against his textbook. "None of them care about you. You're a commodity."

Brendon had heard this for years. He'd be in his twilight years at thirty with a broken body and no safety net. David Cook's son would be well-rounded, respectful, and smart.

"I'm trying. Doesn't that count for something?"

Voices swept up from the foyer: 'Good afternoon, sir,' 'Nice to see you home,' 'How was Parliament.' Brendon pictured people on bended knee and curtsying as his father moved across the hallway and up the stairs.

"I see I'm not the only one looking for a hiding spot. It's a circus down there."

If there were a picture beside the word respect in the dictionary, Brendon would place his dad beside it. David Cook, in his tailored suit, silk braces, and stylish tapered hair, symbolized respect.

"You two talk," Sofia said, adjusting David's suspenders. "I want you both with me when Walter arrives. Twenty-five years old. Cretino." She left with a flap of her hands and a long sigh.

"Everything good in Parliament, Lord Chancellor?"

"The usual. Argue and debate, debate and argue."

"Is she really twenty-five?"

"I told Walter to think about marrying someone so young. He went ahead and did it. I have my fingers crossed."

Brendon tried another answer, hoping to appease the lingering disappointment on his father's face. Rumours had been spreading around town about the mysterious woman Walter Pratt married. Some were good, and some washed in filth.

"William told us she modelled nude."

He could feel his cheeks burn. He wasn't the type to listen to gossip, especially the stuff that spilled from William's mouth. Brendon wouldn't put it past Walter to marry someone with a story.

"Word travels fast around Taunton, doesn't it?"

"Everyone knew about my mishap in Dortmund before the plane arrived at Heathrow."

David flipped Brendon's notebook around and stared at the three sentences scribbled on the paper.

"She posed for art students, not in those magazines you and your friends look at."

Heat crept down Brendon's cheeks and over his neck. There was Mr. Respectable again. He slid his notebook into his backpack and dragged his fingers through his hair.

"Done your homework?"

"I'll do it later."

David took off his suit jacket then pulled his suspenders over his shoulders. "You promised you'd try harder."

"Dortmund wanted me to stay."

"You didn't learn your lesson last spring. You've gone and messed things up again."

"Aren't we supposed to be getting along? Mom expects a perfect family."

"My apologies. You're trying, *again*." David pinched the bridge of his nose and forced a grin. "Has mammina laid out our suits?"

Brendon pointed to a garment bag hanging from the closet door. "Did you expect them not to be? I'll have my homework done before school."

Brendon wiped his sweaty palms on his thighs. The entire time he was swapping his blazer and tie for another, questions bombarded his head. Who was this girl? Was she sultry and aloof? Outgoing and vibrant? Was she really a nude model or a sometimes-nude model? Did nude mean bare breasts or everything on display? Questions continued to elbow one another for his attention. What did he care? This was Uncle Walter's wife.

"When are they going to get here? The canapes and hor d'oeuvres will spoil." Sofia paced and fiddled with her bracelets. "Perfect. Everything has to be perfect."

"Will you sit? You're making me dizzy," David said.

"Maybe it's the scotch."

Brendon grinned at his mother's remark. "You'd think Prince William and Kate were coming over."

"I wish you two would stop." Sofia marched across the den and plucked a piece of lint from Brendon's blazer. "Five months and married."

"I knew the day I saw you eating sorbet with your mother on that piazza in Milan, I'd marry you," David said.

"Troy fell in love with Charlie the first time he saw her."

Sofia smoothed Brendon's lapels, worry furrowing her brow. "We were together for two years."

Headlights brightened the den. Brendon slid off the corner of the desk. The moment had arrived. Blonde, brunette, youthful, sophisticated?

"Get over here. I want to hold your hands," Sofia said, reaching for David and Brendon.

"Bloody hell, Mom, you'd think some stranger just showed up. It's Uncle Walt."

"Ten quid, she's Swedish and moved to Paris to pursue her dreams of becoming an artist," David said.

Sofia smirked. "She's Spanish, a runway model."

"She's an exotic dancer with legs a mile long and flaming red hair."

Sofia arched a meticulously manicured eyebrow and squeezed Brendon's hand. "Walter would not date an exotic dancer."

"There was that girl from Liverpool."

Sofia frowned and snapped David's suspender. "We don't talk about that girl."

Brendon smothered his laugh. The doorbell rang, and they looked at one another. The answer was on the other side of the door.

"Bloody hell. Is no one going to answer it?"

He let go of his mother's hand and yanked open the door. His smile dropped. The world slowed and blurred. She was neither Swedish nor Spanish. She didn't have mile-long legs, red hair or over-plumped anything. She was the most beautiful woman Brendon had ever seen.

"Angelene, meet my friends." Walter nudged her, jerking her strap over her shoulder.

The yellow dress skimmed over her body, highlighting her delicate curves and breasts. Brendon swallowed; she wasn't wearing a bra.

"Bonjour."

"It's nice to meet you," David said. "Let's head to the ballroom. I opened the Lagavulin for you."

Walter tugged his sleeve from Angelene's fingers then clapped a hand on David's shoulder.

"Your home is lovely." Angelene's eyes darted around the foyer as fast as her chest rose and fell. She wove her fingers round and round. Her wrists, full of bangles and beads, jingled.

"David wants to sell it. He's sick of the ghosts," Sofia said. She eyed the fallen strap. Brendon knew she was resisting the urge to fix it. Perfection, always needing perfection. As if sensing Sofia's uneasiness, Angelene hooked her finger beneath the gilded strap and tugged it over her shoulder.

"I've never seen so many lovely things... only in books..." The sentence struggled to leave her mouth and what words she managed wilted from her lips.

"Mom spends a lot of time at auctions."

"Some of the furniture belonged to David's family, some from mine," Sofia said.

Angelene had no response. She stood, eyes wide, hands trembling. The jeweled strap fell down her shoulder.

A server strolled past. Brendon grabbed two flutes of champagne and handed one to Sofia, the other to Angelene. She whispered, 'merci' and gripped the glass so tight, her bracelets tinkled against the stem.

"You could play football in here," Angelene murmured.

Brendon grinned. The ballroom made an excellent pitch on a rainy day. He had fond memories pretending he was in Dortmund at Signal Iduna Park with 80,000 screaming fans, him in net, Paddington out front in defence.

"I have."

"We let Brendon and Troy kick the ball around in here when they were younger." Sofia's gaze swept over the food stations and décor. "We don't use this room very often."

It amazed Brendon that his mother had managed to put something so extravagant together in such a short time. Candles flickered from ornate candelabras illuminating the food. The air was heavy with the scent of flowers and a melange of hors d'oeuvres. A jungle of red roses covered every inch of the room. The baby grand was in danger of collapsing under the weight of roses arranged on its lid. It was everything Angelene wasn't: elegant, posh, comfortable.

"Where in Paris did you live? David and I stayed in Saint-Germain-des-Prés a few years ago. It was exquisite."

Brendon looked at Angelene, waiting for her answer. He wanted to ask her himself, but like her, he was speechless.

She stared at her feet as she spoke. "Clichy-sous-Bois."

"Those riots happened there." Sofia looked at the seafood station, studying it, pulling the drawing she had made from her mind. What went where. The chilled items, hot items. "Two boys died."

"Dad said they didn't have police records. They were just two kids playing footy."

"They hid from the police in a substation and got electrocuted, knocking the power out," Angelene said. She took a hearty gulp of champagne. The glass dangled from her fingers. "It was chaos. I didn't leave my apartment for weeks. The neighbourhood has never been the same."

"Is your family still there?" Sofia said.

Brendon couldn't take his eyes off Angelene. He was oblivious to what was happening around him. All he could see was the trembling girl in the yellow dress.

"I don't know where my mother is." Angelene frowned as she spoke, then faced Sofia like someone had told her the rules of conversation. "She's excellent at running from things. I have a serious lacuna in my family tree, quite a desolate gap. It says a lot about me and my values, or lack of."

Brendon touched Sofia's fingers as they clicked across her diamond and ruby bracelets.

"The seafood station is all wrong. The lobster toasts are supposed to be on the tiered platter, not shoved at the back. Excuse me," Sofia said.

Angelene picked at her manicure. Tiny flecks of raspberry polish fell to the gleaming parquet. She scowled at the fallen strap.

"Merde!"

Brendon moved the strap over her shoulder and tightened the clasp. Her skin was warm and soft. She shrank away from him. Little beads of sweat dotted her clavicles and upper lip.

"What are you doing?"

"It shouldn't fall down now."

Servers strolled past carrying trays of mini beef Wellington and Scottish salmon. Couples Brendon didn't recognize wandered into the ballroom, blurted out greetings and exchanged curious glances at the girl in the yellow dress.

"You're sweating."

Brendon handed her a handkerchief; she blotted her collarbone and clutched it. Tiny sparks burned inside him. Walter was welcoming guests. His mother was arguing with the chef. Women hid their looks of disapproval behind flutes of champagne. There were no hellos. Everyone was pretending not to stare.

"Ang, come meet my friends."

Walter's voice carried over the music. All eyes were on her. Instinctively, she shrunk into Brendon's arm.

"I'm going to trip in these ridiculous shoes."

"Do you want to hold my arm?"

Angelene pressed the handkerchief into his hand. She placed the champagne flute on a table beside a sign— 'Congratulations Walter and Angelene' and held out her arms to steady herself. Brendon held the handkerchief to his nose. The scent was intriguing: smoky, earthy, sultry.

"You're brooding, sweetheart."

Brendon jumped. He stuffed the handkerchief into his pocket and placed his hand on his thundering heart. Had Mammina seen him staring at Angelene? Had she caught the exchange of words?

"I can't make sense of her," Sofia said.

Angelene hid beneath Walter's arm. No smile, cheeks pale.

"It must be overwhelming."

"The others were so vocal. They never had enough to say."

This girl was not like the others. What was it about Angelene that tugged at his heart and made his belly flop? She was awkward, unconventionally pretty.

Brendon cleared his throat and reached for a glass of champagne. "She can barely stand in those shoes. Why isn't Walt holding her hand?" He guzzled the champagne and set the glass between platters of antipasti. "Mrs. Batra is staring down her new nose at her."

Sofia touched his tousled locks and grinned. "Simone Batra is gawking at you, sweetheart. I had to remind her she has a daughter your age."

"None of your friends have spoken to Mrs. Pratt."

"She hasn't mingled."

Brendon stabbed a bocconcini with a toothpick and nibbled it. "Why would she when everyone is giving her the evils."

"Speaking of my friends. I'm going to rescue your father from Victoria McGregor. He doesn't do well with gossip."

Sofia presented her cheek; Brendon kissed her and glanced at the ceiling as a whisper of *'he's such a good boy'* reached his ears. He stepped away from the table. Walter was centre stage, the crowd mesmerized. Just like the fans who cheered Cook when he made a save, Walter had his own audience. The person who needed his attention stood offside, hidden among the urns of roses.

"This is like a proper do."

He gazed at Angelene. A little voice in his head reminded him of the Gentleman's Code—rule number eleven: don't covet another man's girl.

"Excuse me, earth to Brendon."

He felt a tug on his sleeve and looked down at Maggie, smiling a shaky grin. "Oh, hey, Mags."

"I texted you to say I was here. A bloke wearing white gloves escorted me."

"I had to leave my phone in my room. Dad didn't want me watching football highlights."

"How do I look?"

There was something about Angelene that made him feel like he couldn't breathe. Her skin glistened in the firelight. Grey-green eyes yearning to be somewhere else. Skin and bones and blue veins.

"I asked you how I looked?"

"Brilliant."

"You haven't looked at me. Charlie said my dress is posh. No one would know I got it off the sales rack at Debenhams."

Brendon tried to think of something dazzling to say. Thoughts of Angelene held the words hostage.

"Are you going to introduce me to Mrs. Pratt?"

Collywobbles attacked his stomach. It wasn't the house prickling his skin or the ghost of his grandfather Richard haunting the ballroom. It was the odd attraction to Walter's wife.

"Is she dead gorgey? The kids in drama were placing bets," Maggie said, snatching a blini topped with caviar. "Farrah Swindon heard she was on the cover of French Vogue."

"She's just a girl."

Brendon blotted his forehead with his tie. The code bounced around his head: take Maggie's hand, don't curse, be polite. He laced his fingers through Maggie's and led her through the crowd.

"Here's Taunton's hero," Walter boasted. He vigorously shook Brendon's hand before he leaned in for a half-hug. Four hearty pats. Good old Uncle Walt—grand gestures, flashy, powerful. The gold wedding band flickered in Brendon's eyes.

"I wish you wouldn't say that. I'm just a keeper."

"Don't be so modest. Number one in the Southern League."

Brendon let go of Maggie's hand and rubbed his sweating palms on his trousers. "Maggie, this is... Mrs. Pratt."

Walter withdrew his arm, pressed his fingers into the small of Angelene's back; she wobbled forward.

"Angelene. Bonjour."

"It's nice to meet you. Gosh, that's some ring."

"I want people to know she's Walter Pratt's wife."

Brendon glanced at the glimmering diamond. It screamed she belonged to Walter Pratt.

"Sorry Davy boy didn't let you stay in Dortmund."

"Dad wants a kid with an education. Now he'll get it."

Walter snorted and clapped Brendon's shoulder. "I told you he was a good kid. Always does as he's told."

"I don't want to fight anymore. What's eleven months?"

"An entire season," Walter said, scanning the crowd. "I'll be damned. Patrick Carrington is here. You must meet Paddy. We were in the Royal Navy together. Chin up, Brendon, we'll get you back to Dortmund."

Angelene's eyes pierced his. He could have sworn he saw 'help me' flickering in them.

"Ahem," Maggie said. She looked from her simple pink lacy frock to the tiny yellow slip and jabbed her elbow into Brendon's side. "You can stop staring at Mrs. Pratt.

"Bloody hell, I wasn't staring at her."

"You were gawking at someone. I doubt it was Mrs. McGregor."

Brendon's thoughts were a mess of why? Who is she? How come I fancy her? She isn't pretty. She's beautiful. He grabbed Maggie's hand and scanned the ballroom. Angelene had disappeared.

"Are you going to admit you fancy her?"

"No."

"I'm not a dolt. You had that same daft look on your face when that French exchange student called you her petit chou."

Sparks twitched and sizzled. "I thought you were working on your jealousy."

"Did you see her dress? She isn't wearing a bra."

"I hadn't noticed."

The lie slipped out. He had noticed her golden hair, her wobbly ankles, and twitchy fingers. He had followed the curve of her spine and her perky breasts.

"Every man here has."

Maggie gazed at him in a way that said, 'I adore you.' Guilt took hold of him and shoved the Gentlemen's Code in his face. Rule number four: treat a girl the way you want your mother treated.

"Do you want a drink?"

"Something fizzy, not champagne. It gives me the hiccups."

Brendon shook the sparks away and left the ballroom. He walked down the hall wrestling with the Gentlemen's Code, a few smouldering sparks and guilt.

Stepping into the kitchen, he opened the fridge and grabbed two cans of soda. An orange orb caught his eye. The glowing dot disappeared, then reappeared. Brendon glanced at the doorway, then back to the glow. Rule number seven: help a woman in distress. He set the cans down and walked to the door.

"What are you doing out here?"

"Hiraeth." Angelene dragged on the cigarette. Smoke curled around the words. "I'm homesick and I can't go back. I can't breathe in there."

Goosebumps erupted on her arms. She wobbled in the stilettos. "You can scrub shit off anything, but the stink remains. I'll never be what he wants."

Brendon peeled off his suit jacket and held it towards her. "Put this on."

"I shouldn't."

"I'll feel bad if you catch a cold. Besides, it's the gentlemanly thing to do, rule number six."

Angelene wrapped the jacket around her shoulders. It was as long as her dress. "That's my problem."

"Do you catch colds easily? I usually get the lurgy around this time of year."

Angelene tilted her head and hid her smile behind her fingers. "I don't think. I dive right in."

Her accent was thick and syrupy. She dropped the cigarette and slammed her heel into it. "I'm not good enough, or pretty enough, or sophisticated. Your mother is so elegant, so fucking confident."

"You're the most beautiful woman I've ever seen." Mortified, Brendon looked away and cursed.

"Your words are brown. You're brown." She shrugged off his jacket and handed it to him. "Call me Angelene. I'm having trouble with Mrs. Pratt."

Brendon fanned his tie over his heated cheeks. He said she was beautiful and her response, he was brown. He didn't know what that meant. His hair was brown, his eyes the same deep shade. It was an odd thing to say; she was an odd girl.

'It was just a dream.'

He grabbed the cans of soda and repeated the mantra.

'It was just a dream.'

The conversation, the compliment, handing her his jacket, all a dream. With every step to the ballroom, he repeated, *'it was just a dream,'* guilt hurt less.

"What took you so long?" Maggie said.

Brendon shoved the can into her hand and brushed his lips over her honey-blonde hair. Rule number five: honesty.

"I was talking to Mrs. Pratt."

"You've been chatting up Mrs. Pratt."

A groan rumbled deep in Brendon's throat. He chugged the soda and crumpled the can.

"You think I was pulling Walt's wife?" Sparks smouldered. Guilt pecked away at him.

"I bet she's a tart."

The words were harsh. He was sure every woman at the party thought the same thing.

"You don't know her. Nobody does."

"Is that what the two of you were talking about? Poor Mrs. Pratt, nobody likes me," Maggie said. "If she wore a dress that didn't show off her bits, people wouldn't stare."

"Stop whingeing over Mrs. Pratt. Did you bloody hear that? *Mrs.* Pratt."

Sparks whirred, setting his limbs on fire. He inhaled slowly and imagined them as ash.

"Are you going to accuse me of pulling Rachel? I'll tell her to forget about German lessons, if that's the case."

"Nice boys don't date girls like Rachel Jones."

'Breathe Brendon, you know Maggie is the jealous type.'

"I'm curious about Mrs. Pratt, just like everyone else."

Maggie grinned. "I forgive you, only because I need to try the dumplings. I have ten stations to sample before I go home."

Brendon kissed her cheek and scanned the crowd. Simone Batra smiled and winked. Victoria McGregor stood next to the dessert station; her plate piled high. His parents sat by the fireplace. He spotted Walter by the bar, no Angelene. Groups of people gathered around the food stations. The sofas and wingback chairs Sofia had rented for were empty, except one. A tiny tug yanked at his heart. Angelene was sitting alone. He wasn't doing anything wrong; no one was talking to her.

"Would you like anything? Champagne? Something to eat?"

Angelene fiddled with her bracelets and slowly shook her head. "I can't have anymore champagne. It's for sipping. I gulp it when I'm nervous."

"Did Walter say you couldn't?"

"He's so happy his friends came to celebrate. I don't want to make a terrible impression." She hid her smile behind her fingers and laughed softly. "I've already made the wrong impression."

"It's not like there's a couple of people here. I'm overwhelmed."

Angelene flicked at her engagement ring. Her voice was tiny and quivering. "Were you given instructions? Were you told how to act, what to say?"

"Give a firm handshake, say hello, be polite, use a napkin, don't ramble on about football."

"Je veux aller à la maison."

"I'm bollocks at French."

Angelene weaved her fingers in and out, pushed and pulled on her knuckles. "I want to go home."

"I'll get Walter and tell him you feel iffy."

"My home. My flat in Paris with the faded peony wallpaper and the stars outside my window."

"We have lots of stars in Taunton."

Angelene shook out her hands and shoved them between her thighs. "I don't know how to be a wife."

"You just have to be you."

"Your light is powerful," Angelene said. She met his gaze and looked away.

"Liam, my coach, talks about firing up the dragons before a match. Is that the same thing?"

"It's within you, sometimes dull, sometimes intense and blinding. Mine is barely a flicker."

"It's not so bad here. Mom grew up in Milan. She didn't like Taunton at first."

The saccharine-sweet scent of vanilla filled the air. Maggie jerked on his suit jacket and glared as she chomped on a dumpling.

"I was just talking to Mrs... she was alone."

"Taunton is cleaner than Paris. No offence," Maggie said.

"I hear that a lot. Paris is dirty. To me, it's beautiful."

"Mrs. Pratt was telling me about the light people have."

"Everyone has it. It's what drives you. Have a dumpling," Maggie said. She smirked and forced it into his mouth.

Brendon's lips flattened as he chewed. He caught another smile hidden behind Angelene's fingers.

"Walter is finally alone. Thanks for keeping me company." She teetered to her feet, held out her hands to steady herself, and walked away.

"Do you think she's Einstein? Everyone knows about a person's light." Maggie gobbled the last dumpling and patted her mouth. "I've eaten about a hundred of those."

"Why would you say Paris is dirty?"

"When Charlie and I visited, I nearly stepped in dog poo every day. There was rubbish in the streets."

Brendon spotted Angelene. She hid beside Walter, her head bowed. Prior to the party, he hadn't given much thought to who she was or what she might look like. His mind emptied of football highlights and save percentages and was stuck on the yellow dress. He couldn't get her out of his head.

Sofia

"Why her? You spend all week with Walter. What's so special about her?"

Sofia glanced at her reflection in the mirror, touching the fine lines around her eyes.

David pressed his lips against her gardenia-scented shoulder and ran his hand under her hair. "She makes him smile."

"He said that about Anastasia and Branagh, Ellie. Kate."

"She shared quotes from her favourite books. She paints," David said, resting his chin on her shoulder. "You're upset about Brendon. That's where this is coming from."

Sofia dipped her finger into a pot of moisturizer and dabbed it under her eyes. "She could hardly stand in those shoes. She picked at her nail polish. It was all over the floor."

"Walter likes a challenge."

Sofia dissolved into David's chest. "There's something about Angelene, something I can't put my finger on."

"Have you been talking to your mother?" David smoothed her hair and kissed the crown of her head. "She'd make anyone suspicious."

"As soon as I saw her, the hair on the back of my neck stood up." Sofia kissed his neck, breathed in the scent of his skin—Italian citrus and vetiver. "There was a shadow surrounding her, dripping black and sorrowful. It was there when Brendon opened the door. She didn't want to be here. She didn't know what she was supposed to do, how to act. She barely spoke."

"It could be the ghost of my father. You know he haunts the house. He's still angry at you for getting rid of his Chippendale desk."

Sofia arched her eyebrow and touched the grey weaving through the hair at his temples. "Her eyes are so sad."

"They're also green. Mine are hazel, yours are brown." David kissed her and slipped his fingers under the strap of her silk nightgown. "Give her a chance to settle in."

"Did you not see the fidgeting? All night long."

"She was nervous." He placed his lips on her neck and kissed a trail to her ear. "Can we talk about something else?"

"How about your son? You've said maybe two words to him since he got home."

David sighed softly and dropped his forehead onto her shoulder. "It's the same conversation with him, over and over. We let him sign with Dortmund and he finishes his A-levels. Dortmund calls him up to play; we agree if he continues his studies. He's horrible at keeping promises. I won't fight with him anymore. He can buckle down and finish school. You need to stand by me."

"I said I would." Sofia took his hand and led him to the four-poster bed. "You didn't get a weird vibe from her? Nothing prickled your skin?" She turned back the blankets and slid underneath. "I have a bad feeling."

"This week has been difficult. Brendon's home. We had to meet with Julian Dawson, who couldn't keep his beady little eyes off you."

Sofia laughed. "It could be Ralph Fiennes staring at me and all I would see is you."

"La tua bellezza mi toglie il fiato."

"My beauty still takes your breath away. I felt old standing beside Angelene."

David covered her mouth with his and spoke around kisses. "Walter can have his young bride. You're an incredible woman and all mine." He pressed himself against her and lifted her nightgown.

"Are you seducing me, Lord Chancellor?"

"Yes."

People always stated if there were a couple meant to find each other, it was David and Sofia. Sofia couldn't say the same about Walter and Angelene Pratt.

Angelene

Angelene perched on the nightstand; smoke trickled from her mouth. The party had flown by in an array of colours and sounds. The only colour that stood out was brown. She inhaled sharply and tossed the cigarette out the window.

"I hung up your dress," Walter said.

"You can throw it out."

She jumped off the nightstand, slid onto the bed, and hugged her knees. Her mind was full; dizzying little bullets pummelled her brain. She would never belong in Walter's world. She had spent most of her life trying to fit in and realized she doesn't. She folded her jagged edges and hid her scars in hopes no one would see the things that made her different. Disguises never worked. Her sharp edges poked through her skin, and her scars glowed, neon and bright.

"People pretended not to stare. They laughed at me."

Walter popped his head out of the bathroom, toothbrush dangling from his mouth. "You shouldn't have given the Chanel to Lisette."

"I was the talk of that ridiculous party."

The water ran from the tap. His toothbrush clattered in the glass. "People want to get to know you."

"You left me alone." She yanked at the blankets and crawled underneath, wrestling them to her chin, making a cocoon, squeezing her eyes shut.

"You should have introduced yourself to Victoria or Simone. They just got back from Provence."

"Sofia doesn't like me."

Walter tugged at the sheets and curled his body around her. "If you continue to hide away, she never will." He nuzzled her neck and ran his hand over her stomach.

"Let me sleep."

"I'll ask Sofia and Brendon to stop by. You liked his company."

Angelene stuck her arm out from under the tomb of blankets and groped for her cigarettes. "He was the only person who spoke to me."

"No more." Walter reached across her and batted the pack to the floor. "They're stinking up the house."

"It calms me."

"I know another way," he said, tracing around her nipple.

Angelene pushed his hand away and shrank under the blankets.

"I've given you a new life. No brute of a landlord. No more scraping by."

"Become a servant of God. You have proof of heroic virtue. I'll be a miracle, the new and improved Angelene. The Vatican will canonize you, Saint Walter."

"You say the most amusing things." He slipped his hand under the covers and cupped her breast. "You were the envy of every woman tonight."

"You're full of yourself."

Walter chuckled, kissed her neck, and swept his fingers along her stomach. "Guess who I bumped into before we left Paris?"

Angelene clamped her thighs together, imprisoning his hand. "Brigitte Bardot."

"Your friend Pierre Piedmont."

"How do you know Pierre?"

"I donated to the Sorbonne. You love the Hugo statue," Walter said, prying her legs open. "He was coming out of the Dean's office. I heard her mention they had let you go."

"Why did you speak to him?"

"I was curious how he knew you."

"You should have left him alone."

Walter pressed his mouth against her ear. "I told him I married you. Do you know what he said?"

His fingers slid into her panties. She squirmed, a cold tremor slithered down her back.

"If you want to fuck me, just do it and stop talking."

"He said, good luck."

4 Wabi-Sabi

Brendon

Brendon stared at the English assignment like it was an intricate math problem or a foreign language: list the character traits of Lotte. He had thought of two: flawless and angelic. The list had transformed into what he liked about Angelene: the earthy, spicy scent of her skin, the yellow dress.

"Brendon Cook. You're behind two weeks. I suggest you get your head out of the clouds," Harriot Hudson said. She had been part of the faculty for over twenty-five years, bled Taunton plaid, and could recite random quotes from Dickens, Bronte, and Shelley. She was squat, stodgy, and bland. Brendon had never seen her in anything but beige. Even her squared-off bob was drab brown.

Troy laid a pencil stub on the edge of the desk, closed his eye, and aimed. "Psst, mate." He fired it into the air. Brendon shot out his hand and snagged it.

"You heard Ms. Hudson. I need to concentrate."

"You haven't mentioned Walt's wife? All Maggie told Charlie was the dumplings were brilliant."

Brendon leaned across the desk and shielded his mouth with the novel. "Promise you'll keep your gob shut. That means no telling Charlie."

Troy rolled the novel into a tube and nodded.

"Walt pulled a tidy one. She had on this yellow dress. You could see everything."

"Was she better than that Polish girl or Anastasia?"

"I hope you are discussing Werther and not football," Ms. Hudson said.

Brendon lowered the book and flashed his dimpled smile. "I was telling Troy, Werther's love interest is named Charlotte."

"Perhaps he'll read the novel then." She plunked her ample bottom onto the chair and pointed a pen at them. "There's two minutes left. Use the time wisely."

"She wasn't wearing a bra. I'm not sure she had knickers on."

"What were her jubblies like?"

Brendon peeked over the novel. Ms. Hudson flipped through an essay, happily slashing red pen across it. Warmth crept over his cheeks.

"Small, a little more than a handful. They were perky."

"I've got to meet her."

"I shouldn't be talking about her that way. She's Walt's wife."

"No harm in looking, mate."

"The assignment is due tomorrow. I want quotes, one that resonates with you," Ms. Hudson announced.

Brendon shoved his notebook into his backpack. Troy's philosophy, a peek doesn't hurt, was simple—make it quick. Brendon had peeked and stared. She had haunted him since the party.

"Good luck in French."

"I'm meeting Maggie first," Brendon said. "She's doing a fantastic job pretending not to be nervous about German lessons."

They strolled out of the classroom, swept down the hall by the rush of students.

"Keep away from Rachel. That list is infamous."

Brendon pushed open the door and blinked. It took a minute for his eyes to adjust. "What list?"

Troy shrugged, smiled and sprinted across the lawn. Streams of yellow light filtered through the treetops; sparkles of amber twinkled along the branches and bark. Angelene was all around him. The girl he should be thinking about was walking towards him.

Brendon grabbed Maggie by the arm, dragged her behind a grove of cedars, and pressed his lips against hers. She tasted like a cupcake.

"Someone might see."

"We have five minutes. Kiss me."

Her breath danced over his lips. "We shouldn't."

I'm not good enough or pretty enough... you're the most beautiful girl I've ever seen.

The words soared through his mind. He kissed Maggie, breathed in her sweetness, ran his fingers up her spine. He needed to get Angelene out of his head. It wasn't right. She belonged to someone else. She was Uncle Walt's.

"No more. Mr. Dawson patrols the school grounds between classes."

"Just a little longer."

Maggie squirmed out of his arms and straightened her blazer. "I can't be late for class."

"Can we meet in the car park after German lessons? I parked under the willow tree."

Maggie adjusted her kilt and hiked her overstuffed book bags over her shoulder. "Everyone knows what happens beneath the willow tree. Behave yourself with the ginger tart."

"I'll follow every daft rule in the Gentlemen's Code."

"You better. No thinking about any other girls. That goes for..." she stopped herself and stood on her tiptoes.

"What were you going to say?"

"One more kiss."

He pecked her lips and fluttered her kilt. "Lace knickers today?"

"You've been awful randy since coming home from Dortmund. See you."

'No thinking about Mrs. Pratt, bloody dolt. Walt brought Lukas to Taunton. He gave you the BMW when he bought the Aston Martin. Walter is more dad than dad.'

The words bumped around Brendon's head. He told himself Mrs. Pratt was off-limits. Maggie was his girl. He had French class to worry about.

French.

France.

Angelene.

Brendon swatted her name from his mind and dashed to class.

The German flag drooped over the chalkboard; framed posters of Karl Marx, Bach, and Goethe hung in various corners of the classroom. A dish of roasted almonds, an Oktoberfest must, sat beside a bruised apple. Brendon's leg bounced under the desk. Not thinking about Angelene while reciting 'bonjour,' and 'd'accord' had been harder than he thought. Now he had German and the spirited Rachel Jones to contend with.

Brendon fanned his tie over his flushed cheeks. The room felt hot and stuffy. The Gentlemen's Code flicked through his brain like pages of a book.

"Guten Tag, mein gutaussehender Prinz."

Rachel strolled into the classroom and tossed her hair over her shoulder. She dragged a chair across the floor and straddled it. His eyes darted from her freckled inner thighs to her enormous breasts squeezed into her blouse. The Gentlemen's Code flew out the window.

"I'm surprised Thornton is allowing this."

"I need to learn German." Brendon shoved the desk forward and moved his chair closer to the wall. There was no escaping her. He had seen flirty. Rachel Jones was what his mother would call 'coquettish.' The good boy in him shunned her fluttering eyelashes and temptingly full lips. The bad boy found her freckles and cantaloupe-sized breasts alluring.

"I was a little lost in Dortmund."

"I'm here to help." Rachel scooted closer to him. She twisted a strand of her hair around her finger and grinned. "Won't Dawson let you take it again?"

Brendon pressed open his notebook and dug in his pocket for a pen. "I called Mr. Lochmann a poofter, told him he could shove his roasted almonds up his arse. He won't have me in his class."

"Now you're stuck in French."

Brendon wiggled closer to the wall. The temperature in the classroom climbed another ten degrees. Rachel's presence filled the room and all the ignored parts of his body. "My dad thinks everyone should be fluent in two languages."

"Why didn't you take Spanish? I liked it better."

"Mr. Klaussen didn't want me either."

Rachel moved to the edge of the chair and squished herself next to him. She had him pinned against the wall. Brendon's nose filled with the scent of cigarette smoke and tuberose perfume.

"Wurst du man Freund sein," she said, brushing her pinky over his. "Will you?"

He didn't know where to look: the chart of German expressions, the sky, her breasts.

"I don't know what you said."

"I asked, will you be my friend?"

"Why do I need to know that? What if I have to ask for a bloody taxi or directions?"

Rachel ran her fingers up and down his pen. A flirty smile on her lips. "You want to be my friend, don't you?"

Brendon ran his tie over his forehead and swallowed nervously. Her smile was intense. Amber coloured eyes. Red hair, breasts, pale freckled thighs. He was speechless, flustered.

"You're fit as fuck." Rachel didn't blush or look away. "You have the perfect footballer's physique. How tall are you? Six-two?"

Compliments were nothing new to Brendon, never so bluntly and never without it, followed by giggles.

"Am I making you nervous?"

"Bloody hell, yes. Can we get to German?"

"You're even dishier when you blush."

"I'm going to leave if you don't stop."

Rachel flashed him an 'you're-no-fun' pout and plucked the pen from his hand. "Ich brauche ein Taxi." She wrote down the phrase and smiled. "Repeat it, handsome."

Brendon rolled his eyes, repeated the phrase, and relaxed against the wall.

"You can ask for a taxi now. Try this one. Ich wurde gerne der Gründe für deine schlaflose Nacht sein."

"Bloody hell, you're going to have to say that slower." Heat bloomed over his neck and cheeks. "What did you bloody say?"

"I would like to be the reason for your sleepless night. I'll write it in your book."

Brendon chuckled and flicked her hand away. "Don't do that. Maggie will know what it says, and there go German lessons."

"You're no fun."

"What if I get lost and need to find Signal Iduna Park?"

"Wo ist Signal Iduna Park?"

"What if I need to use the loo?"

"Wo ist die Toilette? I'll write them down for you."

He twirled a strand of her red hair around his finger. It hit him. He fancied the girl no boy fancied. Brendon pushed the feeling deep inside. Mammina would not approve of Rachel. A gentleman chose a lady.

"Why did you ask me for help? I could ruin your reputation."

"I need someone who can speak German brilliantly."

"You think I'm a slag."

Brendon had heard the rumours, listened to Maggie and Charlotte go on about the tarts of Taunton. He never gave it any thought. She was just a girl with fantastic red hair.

"I asked Madame Lafavre who was the best student in Mr. Lochmann's class; she said you."

Rachel unglued herself from his side, clicked his pen, and shoved it in his pocket. "Twice a week at lunch break?"

"Are we done? It's only been thirty minutes." He dropped his notebook in his backpack and zipped it shut.

"I've got to eat and have a ciggie before classes start." Rachel pulled a hair tie from her purse and piled her locks into a bun. "Up or down?"

"Down. I like it down."

Rachel brushed her fingers over his flushed cheek. "See you in Latin. Ich bin bis uber beide Ohren verliebt."

"You didn't ask for a kiss, did you?"

"I'm head over heels in love," Rachel said. She shaped her fingers into a heart and winked. "Glad you're back, Mr. Football."

Brendon had spent most of Latin ignoring Rachel's advances. It had been hard to concentrate when she wiggled her tie at him or fluttered her heavily mascaraed lashes. He was glad the school day was over and even happier to be home.

Brendon opened the door. Sofia stood in front of a rosewood bijouterie table, positioning a Royal Worcester vase between a 1920s hat stretcher and a bronze letter rack, re-angled it, moved a framed photo, and rearranged it again. She wore a black pencil skirt and a blouse the colour of red wine. The afternoon sun shone through the transom window, casting a spotlight on her raven hair and curves.

"Beautiful," Troy muttered.

"That's my bloody mom," Brendon said, punching him in the ribs.

Sofia turned, her ruby-red lips quirked, and she exhaled. "Your home."

She swooped in; her arms outstretched like silk wings. Brendon shot up his middle finger at Troy and shrunk away from her embrace.

"Every day around this time."

"Don't be cheeky." She smoothed his hoodie, looked at him, and took his backpack. "How was your day?"

"I pissed Mr. Campbell off. That's the fourth time this week."

"What did you do?"

Troy chuckled behind his hand. "He was staring at Rachel's jubblies."

"It was a quick peek, then she was sent to the back of the classroom."

"Did her boobies distract Mr. Campbell, too? She really does need to wear a larger shirt," Troy said.

Brendon gazed at his trainers. Heat prickled his ears. "She asked if there was a scroll in my trousers or if I was happy to see her."

Sofia's mouth gaped into an O. "What a thing to say. You've missed two weeks. Can't you pay attention?"

"It's Latin."

Troy laughed. "English, French, history."

"You're not helping, bloody prat."

Sofia touched her silver bangles. The tiny charms jingled with each flick. Brendon heard the worry in her voice.

"Your father rang this morning. Walter would like your help."

Brendon made it through the rest of the day without thinking about Angelene. Rachel's flirting and Mr. Campbell's frustration were a welcome distraction. The mention of Walter's name shot her back into his mind. Her trembling fingers, the way her mouth moved when she spoke, the yellow dress.

"He's planned his own party and wanted to know if you could mow and hack down at those overgrown shrubs. I told him; you're not a gardener."

Brendon kept his voice light and easy. "Add it to my list of punishments."

"That's what he said." She clicked through her bracelets and tried to mask her concern. "He wants us to check in on her. If she's so lonely, buy her a cat. Don't those artistic types like cats?"

Brendon avoided her eyes and turned to Troy. "I've got nothing better to do. You in?"

"I said I'd like a look at..." Troy hung his head and rubbed the back of his neck. "I have more experience mowing."

"The idea of you pruning and trimming that mess."

"Walt's done lots of stuff to help me out."

"You're dressed for it," Sofia said, tugging on his hoodie. "Ever since those girls blasted that silly poll over social media, you've completely given up on your looks. So what if people find you attractive?"

"I've told you a million times, I'm a keeper, not a face."

Amelia scurried across the foyer, pointing her duster. "That's how footy players make extra money. Look at Beckham toting those posh underpants."

"Don't be too long. I'm making spezzatino di manza."

"Bloody hell, if you don't stop, we'll be there until midnight."

Brendon gripped Troy's shoulders and twisted him out the door.

"Your mom cooks?"

"Don't be a dolt."

"Every time I'm at yours, Amelia is slaving away. You have a perfectly good mom to make you dinner."

"She's busy."

"Doing what? Looking fit. My mom has fed the cattle, prepared supper, got things ready for work, all before seven."

They rambled down the drive. The sun dappled through the leaves, golden and bright. Branches swayed and clicked. Swallows darted from limb to limb. Shadows grew and shrank. The air, sweet and warm. The farmhouse, a few steps away.

"How come Walter doesn't have a gardener?" Troy said.

"He likes to do this stuff. He says it keeps him grounded."

Troy laughed and kicked a stone down the road. "Your dad and Walt are like us."

"What are you going on about?"

"You're a nancy and I have to muck stalls, feed the chickens."

"Stop talking bollocks."

"What was that? I couldn't hear you. Your silver spoon is in the way."

Brendon froze at the edge of the farmhouse drive. He grabbed the hem of his hoodie and twisted it between his sweating hands. He was steps away from the girl who had changed his world and shouldn't have.

"This is ace. I can't wait to meet her." Troy straightened his Manchester United t-shirt and smiled boyishly. "I'm all set."

"Don't act like a dolt. She's shy."

"Hurry, mate, before my hair gets mussed," Troy said, giving him a little nudge.

Brendon unwound his hoodie from his hands and took a few quick breaths. Wisteria dripped from the trellis on either side of the cobblestone path. A trail of purple petals led them to the front door. He lifted the door knocker and lightly tapped it. Every nerve zapped with electricity. The door opened. He felt like he was standing under a heat lamp. She wore holey jeans, a flimsy shirt; her hair was as golden as the day, her eyes dull green. Troy fixed his gaze on her, blinked, glanced at Brendon, then back. He scratched his hair, smoothed his bangs, and blinked again.

"Got something in your eye?"

"No. I'm... blimey... I don't get it."

They stumbled into a clutter of paint cans and rollers. The scent of turpentine and fresh paint hung in the air. The front room was empty. All that remained were three shades of blue swiped across the wall and a tarp covered in wood trim and nails. Brendon glanced from Troy's puzzled face back to her. She was imperfect, hesitant to smile, and as she dug in a bowl for a skeleton key, he imagined the graceful movements of her fingers on his skin.

"Thanks for helping Walter."

Her syrupy voice snapped Brendon out of his reverie. He floated behind her, mesmerized by her heart-shaped bottom.

"You've got drool on your chin."

Brendon shushed him and knocked his elbow into Troy's side. "I'm not drooling."

He didn't think he was. He had never seen a bottom that shape before. A flush stung his cheeks. He wasn't doing anything wrong. A quick peek was harmless. He cursed under his breath. It wasn't a peek; he was staring.

They stepped into the mudroom, over broken trim and cardboard boxes filled with yellowed curtains. When Brendon was younger, the green door led to an imaginary pitch and thousands of screaming fans. Walter would take him to magical places where mermaids enticed, and pirates were ready to pillage and plunder. The little room took on a whole new meaning.

"Qui est votre ami?"

"Troy Spence."

"Il est mignon."

Troy's eyebrows raised, and he swatted Brendon's arm. "Did you hear what she said?"

"I'm bollocks in French."

"She said I was cute."

Angelene placed her hand over her mouth and clutched her smile like it didn't belong.

"Will you visit me sometime? This house frightens me. It makes all sorts of noises."

Brendon could hear his own heartbeat. He looked around the tiny room. All he could see was her. "Sure, I mean, I guess until you get used to the house."

"Come on, Casanova," Troy said, tugging on Brendon's hoodie. "I still have chores to do."

Angelene opened the door and stopped. She had a look on her face like she had just heard the most incredible thing. "You live on a farm?"

"Unfortunately. Right next door. Spence Farm."

This was the happiest Brendon had seen her. Her cheeks were pink. Her eyes were more green than grey and wide, like his had been the first time he saw Signal Iduna Park.

"Do you have animals?"

"Cows and chickens."

"You don't like the farm?"

"Getting up at dawn, manure wafting through my bedroom window." Troy lifted his shirt and sniffed. "The constant noise."

"What's the matter?"

"Sometimes you can't get the smell out."

Angelene stepped closer and placed her nose on his neck. His cheeks flushed. "You smell nice, like a forest after it rains. What is it?"

Brendon laughed. "Eau du chicken feed."

"Thanks, mate."

Brendon shielded his chest from Troy's fist. He glanced at Angelene, amazed at how tiny she was. The heels she had struggled to walk in gave the illusion she was Walter's type: leggy. She barely came up to his shoulder.

"Do you play football?"

The sound of her voice knocked Brendon back to the mudroom. He was staring again.

"I'm part of the defence team, a centre back," Troy said. "I protect his pretty arse."

"I'll have to get Walter to take me to a match."

Flutters ripped through Brendon's belly. He envisioned her in the bleachers, cheering and shouting 'Cook.' The flutters disappeared. Walter invaded the dream.

"Everything you need is in there." Angelene pointed to a shed walled in woolly willow and butcher's broom. "I'll let you get to work. You'll be okay, oui?"

"Sure, Mrs. Pratt."

"Please, Brendon, call me Angelene. I'm struggling with being a Mrs."

She held his gaze and walked away.

"I didn't see it at first, mate."

They trudged through the overgrown grass. The sun was beginning its descent, lighting the moors on fire.

"I was expecting Miss. Poland, I got Miss. Awkward instead. Has Walter lost the plot?"

"I think she's beautiful."

"I wouldn't say beautiful," Troy said, glancing at the farmhouse. "Something about her sticks."

Brendon understood. She had been in and out of his thoughts, confusing him, enticing him, and giving him a severe case of the guilts.

"You sure Walt didn't meet her in a creche?"

"What the bloody hell is that?"

Brendon shoved the key into the padlock. The door screeched open, releasing a musty odour into the air.

"Daycare."

"Age doesn't matter. You love who you love." He searched through the garden tools and held up the shears. "Prune or mow?"

Troy grabbed the shears, pointing them toward a hawthorn bush. "I'll prune and start right over there."

Angelene had burrowed in the corner of the window bench, book in hand. A cigarette dangled from her mouth.

"I thought she wasn't pretty."

"It's weird. I didn't think she was. It's like she crawled inside me, and I need a second look."

Brendon sparked the mower to life. It rumbled and vibrated in his hands. "It's a quiet beauty. It creeps up on you."

He pushed the mower past the window. She glanced over the book. A knot tightened in his belly; something haunted her eyes. Who was Angelene Pratt? Shy, awkward, a mystery. Brendon mowed the length of the garden, met her gaze again. She was sunshine hidden behind a wall of clouds, wintry and pale. She was the most beautiful woman he had ever seen.

Maggie

The town library was one of Maggie's favourite places. Books made brilliant company when Brendon had practice. It wasn't cool hanging out at the library. Maggie had never been cool, not until she started dating Brendon. The kids at school still questioned how she scored Taunton's hero. Her friends thought the pairing of athlete and scholar was weird. Weird or not, Maggie thought she was the luckiest girl alive. A studious thespian, the girl rated six out of ten, had the most popular boy in school.

"I love history. I could study it all day."

"You're daft," Charlotte said, dropping her purse onto the table. "I cut my shopping trip short. This better be good."

'Shh,' hissed from behind a towering bookshelf.

"Maybe if you spent more time in the library, you'd get better grades."

"I'm only finishing my A-levels for daddy." Charlotte thumbed through a book and crinkled her nose. "I have one plan and one plan only."

"You should go to school for fashion. You have a brilliant sense of style."

"I'm going to be Mrs. Troy Spence, live in a posh house and run all over Manchester with the other footballer's wives."

"Those are some lofty dreams," Maggie said, jotting down a few sentences about Henry VIII in her notes.

Charlotte rooted inside her hobo bag; tubes of makeup and mini bottles of potions tumbled onto the table. "How was the do?" She spotted a pot of lip gloss and swiped the arsenal of beauty products back into her bag. "You haven't talked about anything but those dumplings."

"Brendon and I got into a spat."

"Was Mrs. Batra chatting Brendon up again?" Charlotte smeared lip gloss over her lips, smacked and applied another layer. "That gobby cow told babes he had a nice bum."

Maggie glanced around the library and jammed her thumbnail into her mouth. "We fought about Mrs. Pratt."

Charlotte's blue eyes brightened. "Rumours are she looked poorly, pale-faced, skinny."

"She's different." Maggie plucked a piece of thumbnail from her tongue, flicked it onto her notebook, and started on her pointer finger.

"Does she have an arse face?"

"You remember Mr. Pratt's last girlfriend?"

"There's been so many."

"The Russian. He brought her to a football match. The entire team was gawking at her."

"Miss photoshopped face, I gave babes the biggest pinch for staring at her."

Maggie tore at her fingernail and sucked at the blood bubbling around her cuticle. "Mrs. Pratt is tiny, barely came up to Mr. Pratt's chest, and plain. She's quiet."

"That's rubbish. Mr. Pratt wouldn't marry someone like that," Charlotte said. "Was she wearing a banging outfit? Something from Chanel or St. Laurent?"

"Her dress looked like it came from a charity shop, what there was of it. Her arms were more covered up, bracelets to her elbows." Maggie rubbed her finger under her nose. The colour receded from her face. "Brendon couldn't take his eyes off her."

"Shouldn't you be worried about the ginger tart?"

"It was the way Brendon looked at her, like he fancied her but didn't fancy her, or was confused about fancying her."

Charlotte tossed her lip gloss into her bag and pulled Maggie's finger from her mouth. "Have you thought about humping him?"

Maggie rolled her eyes and bit into her fingernail. "It always comes back to... *that*."

"Don't you get a flutter in your fanny when you're snogging Brendon?"

Maggie tore at the tip of her fingernail, picking the glittery bit off her tongue. "Do you? With Troy."

"As soon as babes' lips touch mine." Charlotte yanked Maggie's finger from her mouth and frowned at the mauled manicure. "His spunk won't kill you."

"Mom says the stuff is as bad as the plague," Maggie said, tapping her highlighter against her notebook. "I don't want people to think I'm like Tilly and Rachel."

"No one will think you're a slag," Charlotte huffed. "You can't expect Brendon to bang one out every time you feel scared."

"That's disgusting. You don't think he does that, do you?"

"Every boy wanks."

A smile replaced the disgust on Maggie's face. "Do you think he does it in the shower?"

Charlotte clutched her stomach and laughed. "They'll touch their knobs any chance they get. Mr. Dawson caught Philip Morris in the custodian's cupboard last term."

Maggie stopped giggling and bit her lip. "I bet Brendon did that after the do, thinking about Mrs. Pratt."

Charlotte wrapped her arm around Maggie and squeezed. "He might have, or he might have fallen asleep. Worry about Rachel and her list, not homely Mrs. Pratt."

"I can't get her out of my head. I try to think about an assignment or Brendon and Mrs. Pratt is there."

"You've had a rough go. Brendon left. He came back moodier than ever. Rachel has her tart hands all over him."

Maggie flipped over the page in her notebook. A heart with M.T loves B.C filled the page. A feeling like something dark was going to happen prickled her skin.

Troy

Troy reached beside his bed, grabbed a T-shirt off the floor and brought it to his nose. "There you are, Charlie. Right here with me." He laid it on the bed and cradled a pillow under his arm. "Now you'll get out of my head, Mrs. Pratt."

Troy had never thought about anyone but Charlotte. In his friends' opinion, he was crazy. Being a footy player on a semi-pro team meant he could pull a girl just because he wore the First kit. After getting his heart broken by Eleanor Duncan, he swore off girls. His mother, who was the smartest girl he knew, other than Margaret Thornton, told him he'd meet a girl who was so unlike anything he had ever known. She would say the right things, make him laugh, drive him wild, and he'd do the same back. Charlotte Donovan knew who played for Manchester United, and not just the gorgey players that the girls giggled over. She constantly made him laugh, and it felt good to be with her. He did the same for her. He shopped with her and commentated as she walked down an imaginary runway. His friends thought he was stupid to settle at sixteen. After two years, Troy couldn't see himself with anybody but Charlotte. Mrs. Pratt had changed that, and he didn't know how. There wasn't anything special about her. She paled compared to Charlotte. Still, she had somehow snuck into his thoughts and stirred his heart. The only person who should give him the feels was Charlotte.

Troy swatted a stack of magazines to the floor and grabbed his cell phone. He dialled Charlotte's number. The whole time his heart thrashed about, and a weird, nauseating flutter stormed his belly.

"Hey, babes. I just got home. Maggie made me go to the library. It was just awful. It smelled old and musty, like my great-nan's house."

"I love you."

"Ah, babes, do you miss me?"

"I just need you to know that."

"Have those tarts been hanging around the pitch again? Bleeding Matilda Morimoto bet five quid she could pinch your bum. Cheeky cow, no one pinches my babes but me."

"Rachel and Tilly were there, but she didn't touch me, I swear. I wanted to tell you I love you, that's all."

"You're the sweetest little crumpet. Look, babes, I must run. I left my shopping bags by the front door, and my mom is having a conniption. I'll call you before I go to bed. Love you."

Troy brought Charlotte's T-shirt to his nose and inhaled her scent: vanilla and flowers.

'Out of my head, Mrs. Pratt. Only Charlie belongs there.'

Angelene

Smoke curled around Angelene's head. Ash dripped to the floor. Images of Brendon haunted her: broad shoulders, slender waist, lean muscles. He had an incredible glow. His light was bright; she'd call him her boy in brown.

"Forgive me, God, for thinking such things. It's my pattern."

She squashed out the cigarette, dropped it on an ash-filled plate and tugged at her hair. The memory was vibrant and ran like a movie through her mind.

I got here as fast as I could. I had to wait for father to fall asleep.

The quiet is killing me. My scars are on fire, ready to burst.

I'll fill them with gold. Kintsugi, you'll be even lovelier.

You're ridiculous. My scars are ugly.

Wabi-sabi, embrace your imperfections. There is beauty in your scars.

Tell me a story, fill the silence.

Once upon a time there was a boy who built the grandest castle Paris had ever seen. The boy lived alone and wished to share his home with someone. One day, a winter storm blew furiously. Within the flurry of glittering snowflakes was the prettiest girl he had ever laid eyes on.

Angelene fell onto the bed and cradled the pillow. She heard Lisette's voice, sharp and piercing, blaze like fire through her head. '*You don't go looking for trouble; it falls at your feet.*'

The words strangled her. It had been her pattern, greeting trouble and asking God for forgiveness.

5 Limerence

Brendon

Brendon bounced down the steps of the modern languages building. The sky had clouded over; vast stretches of grey engulfed the Victorian buildings. Maggie was waiting by the dining hall, prettily composed. The crimson glow on her cheeks told him differently. There was a storm brewing inside her. He'd use Troy's tactic, compliment, then a kiss. If that didn't work, beg for forgiveness.

"You look nice."

She crossed her arms and scowled. "I look the same every day."

He bent to kiss her; she swatted his arm.

"Bloody hell, did you not get the part of what's her name?"

A glimmer of frustration shot through him. His scoop saves had been outstanding. He hadn't stumbled over the agility ladder like William. All the exhilaration he felt at training puddled at his feet. He smothered the sparks and shoved his hands in his pockets.

"Her name is Ophelia. Michael is going to be my Hamlet."

Brendon chuckled. "You and that swot again."

"Michael is a brilliant actor," Maggie said. She shifted her overflowing bags, wobbled from the weight, and kicked her shoe into his. "I told you I got the part of Ophelia at the party."

"What the bloody hell is the matter, then? I've had a brilliant morning."

"My mother forgot to wash my favourite tights; these are horribly itchy. Jack sucked on his finger and stuck it in my toast."

"How is your brother spitting in your brekky my fault?"

A gang of students lingered near the dining hall doors, loitered around the privet hedges, and placed their bets. Two-pounds Maggie Thornton was ready to have a tantrum. 50p Brendon Cook would scream the king of curse words.

"For two years, at exactly ten, the theme from Zeffirelli's *Romeo and Juliet* plays."

"Is something wrong with your ringtone?"

"No, wanker. I waited over an hour for you to give me a ring, half an hour the other night."

Brendon raked his fingers through his hair and glared at the crowd of onlookers. He shot up his middle finger and turned back to Maggie.

"I've been busy."

"You never forget. Even when you were in Germany, you gave me a bell."

"I was at Walter's. The Bayern and Dortmund highlights were on. Bloody homework."

Something flashed across Maggie's face: frustration, jealousy, anger. Brendon didn't know which.

"You saw Mrs. Pratt?"

"You're seriously asking if I was with Ange... Mrs. Pratt?"

Maggie's mouth tipped into a pout. Wagers whispered in the wind. Two pounds, Maggie was about to cry. One pound Brendon would explode.

"Walt asked me to mow the fucking grass. Was I not supposed to talk to her? She bloody lives there."

Maggie's chin trembled; she sniffed and ran the sleeve of her blazer over her nose. Hot sparks filled his hands and fingers. He curled and uncurled his fists.

"Will you lot fuck off."

The crowd scattered. Peals of laughter followed Brendon into the dining hall. The smell hit him first: lasagna, garlic bread, an array of perfumes, the savoury tang of Caesar salad. Conversations about who was pulling who, and the Christmas formal created a joyful hum.

Brendon's stomach turned.

"I got you the veg lasagna, mate. It's a far cry from your Nonna's."

Brendon mumbled, 'Thanks' and dropped into a chair.

"You're dark and broody, Mr. Football. Did you not make a save this morning?" Charlotte smothered Troy's cheek with kisses and traced her finger over his ear. "I wish I were an octopus. I could touch all the parts I love."

Maggie flopped onto the chair and dumped her bags at her feet. She leaned into his arm. Her cloyingly sweet perfume assaulted his nose.

"Ask your friend why I'm pissed off."

"Don't blame Magpie," Charlotte said. She plucked a crouton from her salad and tossed it at him. "Do you want to go to the pub tonight? We'll celebrate me getting the part of Queen Gertrude. I'm not sure why Miss. Baxter gave it to me. She didn't like the dress I chose for the tryouts."

Maggie giggled. "They didn't wear mini dresses in the eleventh century."

Brendon flipped over a layer of lasagna and ran his fork through the roasted vegetables. A debate started in his head: *go to Angelene, leave her alone.*

"I have to help my mom after football."

"Can't Amelia or Peter help?" Troy said, poking at his lasagna. His gaze shifted around the dining hall, grin forced, cheeks flushed.

'Troy's hiding something. Is he thinking about Angelene, too? Charlotte could be giving him a wank under the table. Angelene. I should check in on her. I want to. Dad said it was okay.'

Thoughts cluttered Brendon's mind. He took a small bite of lasagna. An excuse. He needed an excuse.

"It's part of my punishment."

"We haven't been to the pub in a while," Charlotte said.

Chatter clogged Brendon's ears and, in his head, Angelene.

"We went to the pub before I went to Dortmund. I got bladdered and barfed at training. Liam fined me twenty quid."

"Cut the apron strings, mate."

'I shouldn't go to Angelene. The code, I need to follow the bloody code. I want to see her. Why do I want to see her so bloody bad?'

The thoughts were dizzying. They banged around his head and choked his breath.

"Come over Saturday after the match."

"I can show you my new bikini, babes."

"That isn't a bikini. It's a bunch of strings," Maggie said.

Her breath tickled his ear. Brendon yanked his arm free and loosened his tie. The dining hall was as hot as a desert. He tugged at his collar, needing to escape, from Maggie, from the thoughts spinning around his head. Brendon yanked at his cuff and dabbed his forehead.

"I need some air."

Maggie looped her arms through the plethora of straps and handles and pushed back the chair. "I'll come."

"Talk girlie stuff with Charlie. I'll be five minutes."

Brendon dodged around the tables. Conversations halted; students stopped eating and stared. A few bets followed him through the double doors: two pounds Dawson would have him in the office, one pound Maggie would rush after him.

Brendon scanned the hallway for the exit, barreled down the hall and tore off his blazer.

"Blimey, mate, what's up?"

"Maggie was hanging all over me. My mind is racing about the... the match. I couldn't breathe."

"She can be clingy."

Brendon was confused. How could a thought about Angelene leave him feeling suffocated?

"Don't tell Liam about this. If he thinks I'm not in top form, he'll put Will in."

"I just got you back in net. It's our secret."

I'm not good enough or pretty enough.

Angelene's voice whispered through his ears. She slithered inside his mind and through his thoughts. A little shiver trickled down his spine. He loosened his tie and unbuttoned the top buttons.

"If Dawson sees, you'll get a uniform infraction."

"I'll fix it before class."

"Tidy yourself up, mate. Your mom will have you benched if you fool around."

"She only said that to make dad happy."

The dining hall doors burst open. Students milled about the lawn, their eyes on Brendon. He had a reputation for angry outbursts; they had never seen him shaken. Within the crowd—red hair, kilt too short, blouse too tight. Rachel wiggled her fingers at him, and a strange sense of calm washed over him.

"Walk me to class, babes."

"You going to be okay, mate?"

Brendon nodded and stuffed his hands in his pockets.

"You look better, not so pasty," Maggie said, pulling his hand from his pocket. The ring he had given her on a whim poked into his palm. "Why is the tart coming over?"

Brendon stared at his feet. A flush crept over his cheeks. Rachel was as bold as her red hair.

"Guten Tag, Mr. Football."

Brendon wrapped his arm around Maggie and jerked her into his side. He grinned awkwardly as the flush moved down his neck. "Hey, Rachel, um... guten Tag."

Maggie's fingers clenched around his in a 'he's-my-man-stay-away' grasp.

"You looked brilliant at training. That tip over the crossbar, ace," Rachel said.

Brendon cleared his throat and ran his finger around the collar of his shirt. "Maggie and I are on our way to history."

He inventoried Rachel: nice hair, amazing breasts, freckles on her collarbone. His skin tingled; she was an eight out of ten. It was as if Maggie had read his mind. Her grip tightened, cutting off the circulation to his fingers.

"Can you go away?" Maggie said.

Rachel ran her tongue over her glossy lips and smiled in a way that said, 'Make me.'

"Shall we watch the highlights again?"

Maggie swung her bags into his hip. Guilt slapped him hard in the face. He had daydreamed about Angelene, sized up Rachel like a piece of meat.

"That was a one-off. I had to see if Gladbach moved up the standings."

"What's the tart going on about?"

"We better get to history. I'll see you in Latin."

Rachel lifted his cuff and looked at his watch. "You don't want to be late; three strikes, Mr. Football." She glanced into his eyes, then back at his wrist. "You have a tattoo. You're even dishier now."

"Get your hand off my boyfriend."

"I'll save you a seat, knuddelbär." Rachel winked. He could have sworn she put an extra wiggle in her hips.

Students moved around them, sneaking glances, fingers pointing, muffling their laughter. Brendon tugged his hand loose and shook out the pins and needles from his fingers.

"She just asked you to cuddle or called you cuddle bear. Cheeky cow."

"She wants to piss you off."

"Are you going to tell me what was the matter? And don't say the veg lasagna, it was delish."

"This place."

Drizzle cooled Brendon's face. *'Visit, don't visit. Respect Uncle Walt. I'll decide after classes.'*

"Why did you watch football with her?"

Brendon slung Maggie's stuffed-to-the-brim book bags over his arm. He rested his hand on the small of her back, ignoring the snickers and side glances. Bets had been placed and lost. Maggie Thornton held onto her tears, and Brendon Cook squashed the sparks.

"We always watch the highlights together. It drives me bonkers but it's our thing."

"What highlights did I show you on the drive to school this morning?"

"One team had blue shirts, the other red."

Brendon held the door open. "See, you don't watch, and I didn't ask her. She moved her chair next to mine."

"Ignore her next time."

"She's harmless."

Maggie's mouth dropped open. "Everyone knows you're at the top of her list."

"What list?"

There had been rumours before he left for Dortmund that Matilda Morimoto and Rachel Jones had listed the boys they planned on pulling before the school year was finished. He was too excited Dortmund called him up that the rumoured list was nothing but rubbish, more shit spewed from William's mouth. He was beginning to believe the infamous list existed.

"Don't play innocent. You know what kind of list the tart keeps."

Brendon placed her bags on the floor, wrapped his hands around Maggie's waist and lifted her into his arms.

"Hold my kilt down. I don't want people staring at my bum."

"I'd have to touch it then."

Maggie giggled and placed her forehead against his. "Put me down."

He dropped her to her feet and snuck a kiss. A hoarse 'ahem' bellowed down the hall.

"Into class," Mr. Clark said.

Brendon glanced at the man who believed his ancestors belonged to the House of Tudor. He was short, stout, and spherical. His blonde beard was trim, hairline receding, and if he wore a fur-trimmed crown, Brendon might be convinced.

"You may enter my classroom once you have straightened your tie. Three strikes, Mr. Cook."

Brendon wiggled the knot in place and prepared himself for an over-enthusiastic lecture on Mr. Clark's family tree.

Brendon cast a brief glance at the farmhouse. Rain dribbled from the sills and dripped from the wisteria. Sorrow and grey clouds swathed the house.

'*Go home. This is daft.*'

He put the car in reverse and hit the brakes. She had asked him to visit. A ten-minute check-in wouldn't hurt. Brendon jiggled his keys and stepped into the rain. He jumped over puddles and thumped the door knocker. Rain melted his hoodie to his chest. He pressed his ear to the door. It opened, and he stumbled over the threshold.

"Look at you."

Brendon ran his hand through his wet hair and grinned. She wore patched jeans and a stretched-out shirt. Her hair fell from a messy top-knot. Tiny splotches of black paint covered her shirt. She didn't seem to care that she looked dishevelled.

"I was just driving by. I thought... I'm not sure what I was thinking."

"Do you like it?"

White paint replaced the dismal ivory walls. She had stained the cove moulding deep amber and hung Linolscnitt prints of rabbits and birds. Teal, orange, and white added a touch of whimsy to the puny foyer. Sandalwood incense snaked into the entry in long, twisting swirls.

"Go sit by the fire. I'll get you a towel. I haven't put the laundry away yet. Walter would be so upset."

Brendon rubbed the back of his neck. This was Uncle Walt's house, his wife. If he stayed, all the strange, confusing emotions that had made him irritable and dizzy might return. Brendon sighed and stepped into the front room. It took a second for the changes to sink in. A hulking olive-green sofa leaned against the indigo blue wall. Turquoise, vermil-lion, and floral print pillows smothered the couch. She had piled massive plum and teal pillows by the fireplace. Brendon ran his fingers over a peacock feather. A cluster of black ink illustrations: faceless creatures and dancing fairies lined the mantel.

"Do you like it? The wall colour is the same shade as a friend's eyes."

"It isn't Walt's taste."

Angelene handed him a towel. "Walter has no taste. Will you stay for tea?"

Brendon clenched the towel. He should be grumbling over his home-work or at the pub. He stumbled through a quick mental list of why he should stay: she was sad, lonely.

He collapsed onto the worn brick ledge, yanked off his soggy hoodie and laid it on the warmed bricks. "One cup."

"Your mother came to visit today."

Angelene poured tea and passed it to him. He shivered as her fingers skimmed over his.

"How was Mammina?"

"Votre mère est intimidant, » she said, holding up a tiny pitcher of milk and a sugar bowl.

"Just milk."

"She told me in the politest manner, if I hurt her family, she would send me back to Paris." Her fingers wove in and out, press and push.

"I'm sorry."

"Don't be sorry. She adores you." Angelene pointed to his chest. "You're wearing a cross."

"I'm Catholic."

"Me too. Do you go to church?"

"When I was younger. Mom had a question for God; he didn't answer. She lost her faith."

Silence stretched through the room. Brendon sipped his tea, his gaze fixed on Angelene. The flames flickered in her eyes. He didn't know how to feel. Her voice, raspy and syrupy, sliced through the quiet.

"I'm glad you stopped by."

"The first time I went to football camp in Dortmund. I was bloody scared. You must be feeling the same way."

Angelene sipped her tea and set it on a chipped saucer. "I'm feeling many things: fear, elation, loneliness. I'm also grateful, hopeful." She laid a plum pillow at his feet and nestled onto it.

'I fancy you; I don't. I think you're beautiful; I don't. I want to be with you; I shouldn't. You're in my head and out of my head. I'm losing my bloody mind.'

"Bloody hell, it's hot in here."

Brendon plucked at his t-shirt. She had done it again, slithered into his head and lit a fire in places she shouldn't.

"What do you do all day, other than redecorating?"

"I read and paint. Would you like to see my artwork?"

Curiosity stirred inside him, another layer to the mysterious girl.

Brendon set down his cup and followed her up the stairs. Paint cans, rollers, and splattered tarps cluttered the hallway. She had smeared a stripe of chocolate brown, sienna, and burnt umber on the wall. An assortment of throw pillows, swatches of fabric, and a can of paint sat in the centre of each room he passed.

"This is where I spend most of my day."

The room smelled of turpentine, walnut oil, and sandalwood. Brendon didn't recognize Walter's boyhood room. The walls were white. She had clipped yellow saris to the brass curtain rods and angled a saffron lounge between the two windows. He approached a table. Illustrations of gnarled trees, distorted figures, dancing horned creatures lay between a palette and tubes of acrylic paint. The collection of drawings was haunting and morose, another layer to peel away.

Angelene laid her hand on his arm. A flutter rippled through his belly. Her touch was light and hesitant.

"Yellow is my favourite colour. I thought if I decorated this room yellow, I would be yellow. What's your favourite colour?"

"Think about it and tell me later. Here's a hint. It's not brown."

He picked up a painting of a woman with the head of a goat reaching for her horns; her body stretched like elastic.

"You drew all these?"

"Do they frighten you?"

"They make me sad."

She burrowed into his side, taking up a place beside him as if she belonged there.

"Tell me why."

"The woman in the painting doesn't like what she's become. She's trying to break free." Brendon thumbed through the drawings. "Something has happened to all these women. They're running, hiding, or trying to beat a creature off. There's no one protecting them."

Angelene lifted her cuff and scraped along a faint scar. He pushed up her sleeve and inspected her forearm, pale crisscrossed lines, tiny crosses.

"Please don't do that." He traced over a faded cross. Beautiful, bruised. '*Uncle Walt's.*' "Do something else, scream, punch a wall like I do. Well, used to do. I'm working on my temper."

"My screams are as lost as I am."

Brendon slid his thumb between the strands of beads. She tugged her arm free and hid her smile as he yawned.

"You're sleepy."

"I get up early to train, rush home, rush to school."

"Is that how you spend your day? Rushing around Taunton?"

"Mom and Dad are making me finish A-levels. Liam, my coach, keeps us on an intense schedule. I'm busy."

He followed her out of the bedroom; the stairs creaked under his feet. They stood silently in the foyer. A strange sense of comfort wrapped around him. The silence was as loud as the rain pelting against the door. After a few minutes, Angelene spoke; her voice was far away.

"I love football."

"What's your favourite team?"

Could this be true? Did she love football as much as he did? Most of the girls he knew either despised it or watched for the players, not 'the beautiful game.' Maggie humoured him. Charlotte adored her little crumpet.

"Paris Saint-Germain."

"I thought you'd be the art gallery type."

Angelene's eyes were bright and glittering. "I am. I love a good match. Walter said you play professionally."

"Semi-pro in Taunton. I'm on loan with Dortmund's U19 squad."

Her voice was soft. "Your words are bruised, black, disappointed blue."

"Education is important to Dad." Sparks flickered and faded. "I didn't do well last year. I've had a few mishaps with my tutors."

"Football is your passion, non?"

Brendon dug his car keys out of his pocket and jingled them in his hand. "It's a long story."

"Will you share it with me sometime?"

"It's a tale of a boy whose dreams got shattered by expectations and ghosts."

"I would like to hear it and watch you play."

Brendon opened the door. The wind swirled wisteria petals into a dizzying waltz, depositing them at her bare feet.

"You're in luck. We have a game Saturday."

Her hand covered her smile. Brendon's fingers tingled with the urge to pull it away.

"I'll beg Walter. Cry."

Rain pelted against his back and pooled under his feet. Brendon looked into her eyes. He was curious about her story. He titled the night, 'Silent screams, scars and the tugging thread that ties us.'

"I'm happy you came."

Angelene stood on tiptoes. Her lips grazed his chin. His heart leapt and crashed. He touched the spot. It radiated warmth like the happiness, confusion, and guilt raging inside him.

"Will you be okay? Bloody hell, there's a mess on the floor." The words spilled from his mouth. The spot her lips touched was warm.

"Don't worry about me. Go home."

"The highlights will be on. You'll have to sit through the Premier League first. They'll eventually get to Ligue 1."

"The puddle will soon be an ocean."

"Goodnight, Mrs... Angelene."

"See you soon."

Brendon flew to his car; branches swayed; chilly rain pierced his skin. There would be a next time, and another after that. There was nothing wrong with checking in and chatting. They could talk about football, and he could convince her the Bundesliga was better than Ligue 1.

Brendon pulled into the carport, the thread that tied him to her tightened. He touched his chin; the spot tingled. If he found himself lost, the thread, the odd, wrong, and unbelievable connection would lead him to her. Water splashed around his feet as he dashed to the door.

"Mammina."

He wiped his T-shirt over his face and walked to the dining room. The scent of candle wax and cedar lingered in the air. The rain and midnight blue walls made the room darker, sinister. The decorative header above the window added charm to the outside. Shadows cast across the table looked like prison bars. The theme for this room, 'erase any trace of Richard Cook.' Brendon swore his grandfather joined them at meals, pissed off Sofia had replaced the heirloom Chippendale table for a mid-century Gangso Mobler masterpiece.

"You didn't answer my text. I thought something happened to you."

Brendon jumped and clutched the back of the chair. "Bloody hell, don't do that."

Sofia was trying her best not to jingle her bracelets. Her white-knuckle grip on the plate she was holding was a dead giveaway she was worried.

"You could have been dead in the ditch. Two texts unanswered."

Brendon sank into a chair and stared at the rain snaking through the ivy. The thin ribbons crisscrossed through the leaves reminded him of

Angelene's scars. Brendon rubbed the chill from his arms. He had carried her scars home.

Sofia set his dinner in front of him and slowly arched an eyebrow. She was trying to be observant, like his Nonna Nicola. She hadn't mastered the skill yet.

"Where have you been?"

Brendon rpushed his fork through the sweet potatoes. He could lie, say he was at the pitch. Lying went against the code.

"I was at Walter's."

"Doing what?"

She had given up trying to read him and gave her 'mom' stare.

He crumbled under her gaze and poked at the rosemary-scented chicken breast. "Making sure Ang... Mrs. Pratt was okay."

"I want you to stay away."

It was time to try another tactic. A compliment would get him nowhere. She was in her pyjamas. Interior decorating was a passion of hers. Other than attending auctions, Sofia loved to decorate and redecorate according to her mood. Before he left for Dortmund, she had named bedroom number five 'an ode to Sweden.' When he came home, she had papered a wall in a black and gold floral print and renamed it 'subtle sophistication.' There was nothing subtle about it.

"Did you see Walt's front room? I thought you were obsessed with pillows. Stacks of them and in the nicest colours. It doesn't look like Walt's place at all."

"The style is bohemian, sweetheart."

Angry mom averted.

"Did you look at her drawings?"

"I thought the crayon drawing was wonderful."

"Not that one, bloody hell, it had the name Yasmine in the corner. The ink sketches."

"They're awful, like nightmares."

"Where do you think the ideas come from?" Brendon scooped up a forkful of potato and chicken and shoveled it into his mouth.

"Manners, sweetheart." She dug into her housecoat pocket and tossed a napkin at him. "Her imagination."

"Do you think the paintings could be about her life?"

"I hope not." Sofia's gaze swept over the mahogany chiffonier side-board, the Art déco vase filled with roses, and over each of the twelve chairs positioned around the table. "I need you to stay away from her. Those paintings frightened me."

"I saw worse in my art history class. There was one called *Severed Heads*. Mrs. Pratt is harmless."

A frown creased Sofia's forehead. Brendon laid his fork across his plate and reached for her hand.

"I won't visit Mrs. Pratt anymore."

"You didn't get a strange feeling when you were with her, that, *be aware*, feeling?"

"I see a girl with bloody, twitchy fingers." His cell phone buzzed in his pocket. "That's Mags, she'll get whingey if I don't answer. Thanks for dinner, Mammina."

Brendon rambled into the kitchen, placed the phone on the counter and hit speaker. "It's not ten yet."

"Where were you?"

He could tell by her sour tone she was sulking. He yanked open the fridge, grabbed the milk, and spun off the cap, glanced towards the doorway and gulped.

"First Mom, now you."

He chugged another mouthful, whirled the cap on, and shoved it back into the fridge. If he wanted to end his night peacefully, he needed to choose his words carefully. If he gave her a compliment, it would be insincere. He knew she would be in either unicorn or mermaid print pyjamas. Before he left for Dortmund, he snuck her in to sleep over. He hoped for a frilly baby doll but got mermaid jimjams, an old bear jammed between them, and a horrible case of the guilts.

"You looked nice today."

A groan bellowed through the speaker. Stupid, he had used that one already.

"Don't try to charm me. I want to know where you were. I called Troy, Charlie answered the phone, giggling. I don't know what Troy was doing. She could barely speak."

"He was probably visiting Australia, down under, you know."

"I *do* know, and that's disgusting."

"It sounds bloody smashing."

"I'm waiting."

"I was at Walter's." He closed his eyes and waited for the backlash. All he got was a breathy, annoyed sigh. "She's redecorating and needed help to move furniture."

"You must be tired. You helped your mom. Mrs. Pratt."

Brendon leaned his head in his hand. He had forgotten about the lie he told at school.

"Can you drop it? I'm bloody knackered."

"Limerence."

"Bloody hell, you're as bad as my dad, always dropping words I don't know."

"Charlie learned about it in psych. It's infatuation, deep longing, like how I felt about you after our first date. You better not be obsessed with Mrs. Pratt."

"Good night, Mags. I love you. I'll see you in the morning. Sweet dreams."

The whiny sigh turned into a giggle. Danger of a miserable Maggie averted. He was on a roll.

"You're a wanker, but you're my wanker and I love you."

Brendon stared at the tattoo on his wrist, 'Dum Spiro Spero.' The Latin phrase, 'While I breathe, I hope,' had ruled his life. He had hoped to be in net for Dortmund; it had come true. He clung to the hope he could finish sixth form with no trips to the headmaster's office. He hoped, despite his mother's warning, to see Angelene again.

Troy

There were four reasons Troy enjoyed spending time at Charlotte's house: it was quiet, it smelled nice, no hay or dust to contend with, and no brothers. Charlotte lived in Stonegallows, in the southwestern outskirts of Taunton, in a five-bedroom executive home. The house was bright, modern, and airy with a large garden the sun shone on daily. What Troy liked best about Charlotte's house— her.

"What do you think, babes?"

Troy rolled the pouf back and forth under his feet. It was the fifth ensemble showcased in the Charlotte Donovan fashion show. This number, skinny jeans with strategically placed holes, an oversized off the shoulder sweater, and booties, perfect for a day at the pitch.

"It's brilliant. Those jeans make your bum look fantastic."

"You said that about the last outfit," Charlotte said. She yanked off the sweater and tossed it onto the dresser. "What's with you today? You've hardly said two words to me, well, maybe more, but you haven't been yourself. Did you do something?"

Troy flicked at the pull on his hoodie. "Yes. The Aussie kiss."

"Troy Alexander, you better not be hiding anything from me."

Visions of Angelene tumbled into his head. He still didn't understand what it was about Angelene that made her so attractive. He liked brunettes, always had. He preferred someone extroverted to balance out his introverted side. He liked Charlotte.

"Where were you yesterday after school?"

"Brendon and I went to the pitch. I told you that," Troy said. An incessant throb took hold of his heart. He didn't know why he felt he had to hide meeting Angelene. He was doing Walter and his best mate a favour. Maybe it was shame eating him up inside. He had been a bad boyfriend ogling Mrs. Pratt. He didn't deserve an amazing girlfriend like Charlotte, but it was just a peek, and a peek was okay. Who was he fooling? It wasn't a peek. She lingered like her perfume had on his T-shirt. He wasn't supposed to think about anyone but Charlotte.

"You sounded funny on the phone. Were those slags from King's College at the pitch again? I told you to tell me if they showed up. Cheeky mare, asking you to watch Netflix and chill."

The throbbing captured his lungs, and a heaviness settled into his chest. He looked at the girl stripped down to her lacy knickers and tattooed the image in his mind.

"Walter needs some help in the garden. He asked Callum, but the little bugger said no."

Troy waited for her reaction. Depending on her answer, he might spill the truth and suffer a pinch. It would be better than the suffocating guilt he was feeling.

Charlotte pulled a denim shirt dress from a shopping bag and slipped it over her shoulders. "Tell Mr. Pratt to do his own yard work." She clasped a belt around her waist and studied herself in the full-length mirror. "What do you think, babes? Cute, isn't it?"

"It's brilliant. You always look brilliant."

"You aren't thinking about mowing Mr. Pratt's lawn, are you?"

Troy zipped and unzipped his hoodie. "It wouldn't hurt to help. Walter has done lots of stuff for Brendon and me. He took us to that Chelsea match. He was the first one on the pitch the day I got my concussion."

Charlotte walked over to him and wedged herself between his thighs. "I don't want you around Mrs. Pratt."

"You haven't met her yet."

She lifted his chin and stared into his cobalt blue eyes. "Maggie told me she pouted the entire night of the do. Mrs. Cook puts on *fabulous* parties. They're legendary in Taunton."

Troy wrapped his arms around her waist and placed his cheek against her belly. "I won't help."

"Promise me, babes. I don't want you near her until I meet her. Maggie has a feeling."

Troy tossed her on the bed and undid the latch on her belt. She laughed and kissed his nose.

"Again, babes. You're terribly randy tonight."

"I can't help myself. You look so beautiful."

'And every day, every night, every hour. Just this time, I'll keep a secret.'

Angelene

Angelene filled a glass with wine, picked up her book and shuffled to the front room. Wind rattled the windows and blasted rain against the panes of glass. Had she not been afraid of her new surroundings, she would have gone for a walk, let the wind lash through her hair and the rain soak the Ecole Nationale Supérieure d'Architecture T-shirt. It was safer to be inside. God was angry, and she hadn't figured out why.

Angelene lounged on the sofa. Something black caught her eye. She crawled across the couch and peeked over the armrest. Her heart slowed and her breath returned. Angelene held Brendon's hoodie to her nose and breathed in the scent of warmed citrus. The smell was invigorating. If she were to put a colour to it, it would be dazzling amber. She tugged it over her shoulders and lounged into the cushions.

"God, please do not see this as bad. He smells so clean, pure white. I promise to return it."

Her gaze drifted to Yasmine's drawing. She held her cuff covered hand to her mouth and smiled; it was not springtime in Taunton. It was the season of unknowing and unwanted transformation.

"I painted the wall the colour of your eyes. Now I have you with me. My boy with inky blue eyes."

Angelene tucked her nose into the collar. His scent was all around her. *'The devil lives within him. His devil wants to break free.'*

6 Metamorphosis

Walter

Walter sat on his bed. His phone rested by his thigh.

"I got the bill from Maisons du Monde. Fifty euros for a pillow, little bird."

"It's the colour of a plum."

Walter sighed and grabbed his watch from the nightstand. "Can I have a treat when I come home? It's been a while."

"It's been a week. I won't make any promises."

Walter swallowed the grumble simmering in his throat. "Have fun at lunch today. As much as you can with Victoria and Simone. The black wrap dress is pretty."

"I'm feeling like someone has put a plastic bag over my head and secured it around my neck. I'm breathless and hot."

"Do this for me. People are talking."

"Let them. Goodbye, husband."

Walter held onto the silence, released the stifled groan, and strolled to the kitchen. Grey light lit the polished concrete floors and stark white walls. Outside, people rushed about; traffic snaked along Chapter Street. He placed a mug on the counter and filled it with coffee.

"Busy day for you?" David said.

"Budget meetings."

"I'll be tied up in judicial policy all day. Eat. You look miserable this morning." David shook muesli into a bowl and pushed the box at Walter.

"Little bird needs to fly back to Paris," Walter said, pouring milk over the cereal. He rammed a spoon into the bowl and growled.

"Give her time to settle in," David said between chews.

"Rumors are circulating."

"What did you expect? You and Kate were in Paris a month before you met Angelene."

Walter slurped back a mouthful of coffee and pushed cereal around the bowl. "Kate and I went as friends."

"Friends don't stay at the Ritz."

"Things didn't work out."

David tipped the remaining milk into his mouth and dropped the spoon into the bowl. "Things didn't work out, or you didn't want it to work out?"

Walter scraped the cereal into the bin, rinsed his bowl, and slid it into the dishwasher. "Save the lecture for Parliament."

"You've been miserable. I'm concerned." David placed his bowl behind Walter's on the rack and closed the dishwasher door. "You're a newlywed. You should be happy."

"Have you met Angelene? There isn't anything happy about her."

David topped up his coffee and leaned against the kitchen island. "At the party, she hid her arms with bracelets."

"Nothing to be concerned about, Davy boy."

"What do you know about her?"

Walter puffed out his cheeks and groaned. "She was born in Marseille. She loves art and Victor Hugo." He finished his coffee and set his mug in the sink. "We have to catch the tube."

"If she wasn't hiding by your side, she was scratching her skin," David said. He drank his coffee and passed the empty mug to Walter. "She may be too much for you."

"There isn't anything I can't manage, especially a woman."

"Do you love her?"

"Maybe. Not yet. Soon. All the above."

David grabbed his briefcase and shook his head. "You married someone you may or may not love?"

"Not everyone can find an heiress to a $32 million textile fortune. Some of us must create one."

"She isn't a project. Something tells me Angelene might not want to change."

"I like a challenge."

"Angelene may be your biggest yet."

Walter smiled and clapped David's shoulder. "I'll make a sophisticated woman of her yet. I'm Walter Pratt. I don't fail."

Sofia

Sofia blotted her nose and appraised the sky. It had been a fickle morning. The sun would shine, then clouds would flood the sky, threatening rain. The weather matched her mood. She had spent most of the morning swinging between calling off the lunch date and hoping someone else would. David had reassured her a quiet meal with proper introductions would be good for Angelene. When Sofia had watched Angelene teeter down the walkway, she wasn't so sure. As they sat in the car park, staring at the restaurant. She still wrestled with the idea.

"I phoned Walter and said I had a stomach ache. He said I need to meet people." She tossed her cigarette out the window and burrowed into the seat.

Sofia grinned at the confession. "You'll love my friend Kate. She has a bit more couth than the other two."

"I don't do well in social settings."

"Brendon told me he stopped by." Sofia glanced at Angelene and argued with herself. What was she looking for? Blushing, a twinkle in the eye? It was bold of her to even bring up the subject. It had haunted her all night and woke with her, joined her for coffee.

Angelene's voice was brittle and faint. "He's a nice boy."

"All those years David drilled the Gentlemen's code into Brendon's head, he did the respectable thing."

"Gentlemen's Code?"

"David and Walter wrote it when they were fourteen. They vowed to live their lives by it." Sofia pulled the keys from the ignition and dropped them into her purse. "David stuck to it. Walter faltered a few times. You ready?"

Angelene fluttered the bow on her blouse. "I've been practicing what to say. I'm afraid I'll forget something or disappoint Walter."

"Just be yourself."

"It's hard to be me."

"Then act. Everyone at the table will put on their best performance."

They stepped out of the car. Angelene wobbled. Sofia took her elbow, masking her impatience with a smile.

"How do I look? Walter said to wear a dress. Trousers were more comfortable. I hoped my yellow blouse would make me calm."

"Is it working?"

Sofia had chosen a black A-line dress. Understated was what she was going for. Anything to keep Angelene's jitters at bay.

"I'm afraid not. You look beautiful," Angelene said, smoothing the ends of her hair.

"I've had years of practice. Now, do as I do. Shoulders back, chin up. People will think you own the place."

Angelene's shoulders sagged, her lips trembled around the words. "I can't."

Sofia clicked her fingernails against her purse. Her tone was sharp. "Yes, you can. Take a breath."

"When have you ever felt like this?"

"I've had moments. What's something that calms you, besides the colour yellow?"

Angelene buried her fingers between Sofia's bangles and clutched her wrist. "His eyes. They're as dark as the Makonde figurines I saw on display at the Louvre."

The hairs prickled under the sophisticated knot tied at the nape of Sofia's neck. It was like looking into a shattered mirror.

'*I'm not scared of you. You have no control over me or my son.*'

"You'll be fine, Angelene. I'm right here."

Sofia opened the door; the aromas of focaccia and roasted garlic wafted from the dining room. She gave Angelene a little nudge and caught her elbow as she stumbled.

"Merde, merde. These ridiculous shoes."

"I've tripped over my gown before. Those two have stumbled."

Victoria McGregor and Simone Batra whispered at each other from behind their wineglasses. Victoria was an all about impressions woman, from her frosty blonde hair to the Botox smoothing her face. She was overprocessed, brassy, and stuffed into her blazer and skirt. Simone Batra's enthusiastic, nasally voice was enough to get her noticed. Her philosophy—stay young forever, at whatever price.

"Have a seat before you fall over," Sofia said, pulling out a chair. "Walter should have bought you pumps instead of stilettos." She slid into a chair, hooking her purse strap over the back. "You remember Victoria and Simone."

Angelene nodded and clasped her hands in her lap.

"This is my friend Kate."

"It's nice to meet you," Kate said.

"And you," Angelene warbled.

Friends for twenty-three years, Sofia could always rely on Kate to calm her when things got crazy. Kate was not a worrier. She focused on the present, looked for reasons why, reeling Sofia in before things spun out of control. Kate Miller was the type of woman who could knock back a few cocktails in a designer dress and look good while doing it. She took care of herself and stood up for others, while keeping her hands clean. Sofia thought Kate was a catch. She had yet to be caught.

"We missed you at the do, Kate. Was it too difficult?" Victoria said.

"I was in London, wedding dress shopping with my niece. I heard it was a lovely evening."

"Nothing but the best for Walter," Sofia said. The server set down two glasses of wine. She thanked him and passed one to Angelene.

Simone tore apart a bread roll and pointed it at Kate. "Weren't you and Walter in Paris? Still harbouring feelings for him?"

"I loathe Walter. He's chauvinistic, overconfident," Kate said. She ran her finger around the rim of her wineglass, her tone softened. "And the most charismatic man I've ever met. However, I respect him and his decision."

Victoria leaned into Simone's shoulder and smirked stiffly. "Does that bother you, Angelene, knowing Walter and Kate dated?"

Sofia arched an eyebrow at Victoria, then lowered her gaze to Angelene's weaving fingers. Angelene ignored the question and spoke to Kate instead.

"Walter mentioned you're a barrister?"

"I am. What did you do in Paris?"

Sofia's ears perked up. She had heard bits and pieces from David, the gossip that vomited from Victoria's mouth. There had to be more to Angelene Hummel than horrifying paintings and twitchy fingers.

"I worked at the Sorbonne." Angelene's flushed cheeks deepened to crimson, the twitching stopped, she froze.

"Interesting," Simone said. "Tell us more."

Sofia held up her wineglass and shook it at the server. "It's okay, Angelene, no one here will judge you."

"How's Brendon? I haven't stopped thinking about him since the party. I told Eshana he's the one to go after," Simone said.

Sofia's jaw tensed. "Can't you stay on topic?" She forced a grin and laid her hand over Angelene's fidgeting fingers. "My son is fine. Breathe, Angelene, it will help."

"Every time my heart beats this fast, a friend, Roman Krieger, would say, breathe, little bird." She exhaled a long, ragged breath. The words, 'I did some modelling,' hung off the end of it.

"You're a little short," Victoria said. She slathered butter over a slice of bread and had a hearty bite. Her magenta lipstick left a smear on the crust. "My niece walks the runway. She's five-foot ten. What are you? Five feet?"

"You don't need height to be an art model," Sofia said.

"Don't art models pose nude?" Simone said. She turned to Victoria and struggled to raise an eyebrow.

"Not necessarily. David mentioned you did some other work for the university."

Sofia took a sip of wine and patted Angelene's hand. A friendly gesture to say, 'I've got you.' Brendon would be proud of her. She was being a friend, steering the conversation away from Victoria and Simone's nosy questions.

"I set up the art rooms." Angelene's voice was raspy, her accent thick. She spoke into her lap. "Collected textbooks and sometimes, Professor Piedmont would ask my opinion about a student's work."

Sofia glanced at the menu. A nice bowl of pasta would settle Angelene's nerves. It always worked for her. "Angelene paints and draws. She has a wonderful imagination."

Angelene weaved her fingers. Her gaze darted from one exit to the other. Sofia doubted pasta would work any magic on Angelene.

"I love Kandinsky. He heard sounds as colours. The notes of a song became a colour and an image. I found that interesting," Kate said.

Sofia grinned. Kate was playing the game of 'keep Mrs. Pratt comfortable,' too.

Angelene stopped weaving her fingers and exhaled a short, quick puff. "Kandinsky had a theory that geometrical elements make up every painting. There was the point, line, and basic plane." Weave in and out, push and pull. "A friend drew a castle using Kandinsky's Point theory."

Victoria nudged her elbows on the table and clasped her hands. "Were you born in Paris?"

"Did you surround yourself with artistic men? Voulez-vous coucher avec moi ce soir. Right, girls?" Simone said. She flipped her golden-brown hair over her shoulder and licked her plumped lips. "Well?"

"That's a silly phrase," Angelene said. She moved from her fingers to the napkin, strangling it instead. "No one in France says that."

"Just ignore Simone. She's worse than a teenager."

Sofia crooked her finger at the server, smiled graciously, and pointed to the antipasto platter.

"I'll have the orecchiette with broccoli rabe."

They placed orders. Angelene guzzled her water and appeared to be studying the entress. Sofia sighed softly, took the menu, and handed it to the server. "She'll have the same."

After a brief silence, Angelene spoke.

"I was born in Marseille." She spat out 'Marseille' like it was poison and needed to rid her body of it. "Mother moved us to Paris when I was two."

Victoria clapped her ring-clad hands together, her face cracked into a smile. "We took a trip to Marseille. Sofia begged us to drive to Italy."

"I suggested it," Sofia said, laying a napkin across her lap. "Simone pushed. You wanted to discover the men of Turin."

The server set a platter of antipasto in the middle of the table. Sofia picked up her fork, rolled two olives on her plate, and lifted her eyebrows at Kate.

"Where in Paris did you live?" Kate said, biting into a polenta square.

"Who cares about that. I want the juicy details," Victoria said. She stuffed salami in her mouth and spoke while she chewed. "How did you meet Walter? I can't imagine a man who was in the Special Forces taking an art class."

Simone's boisterous laugh dominated the breezy sound of Vivaldi's *Stabat Mater*. Diners turned their heads and stared.

Angelene gripped her wineglass, sipped, then gulped. "We met in Parc Floral."

"One of Walter's favourite places," Kate said.

Sofia patted her heated cheeks. Angelene's tiny slurps and hearty guzzles grated on her nerves.

"Didn't you think it was odd, a man of Walter's age interested in you?" Victoria said.

"I've been with someone older." Angelene's tone was quiet yet piercing.

Victoria leaned into Simone's ear. "Probably married."

The attempt at a whisper did not go unheard. Diners peered over menus and raised eyebrows at the accusation. Sofia looked at Kate with wide, 'you've-got-to-be-kidding' eyes. Angelene hobbled to her feet. The dishes clattered. Wine spilled.

Sofia steadied the table and hid her frustration under a grin as the server passed out their entrees. "What's the matter with you?"

"It must be true. Look at her, trying so hard to fit in," Victoria said. Her smile was as fake as her hair colour.

Sofia glared at Victoria. "You would know. She's gone and hid in the powder room."

"We've all done things we aren't proud of," Kate said, spooning parmesan over her ravioli. "You invited that man, or should I say boy, back to your room in Ibiza."

Simone dabbed her mouth and stared down her new nose at Kate. "He played for Real Madrid."

"We all have baggage; that's all I'm saying," Kate said.

Victoria stabbed at a rigatoni and pointed her fork. Sauce flicked across the table. "Angelene has steamer trunks."

Sofia shifted her gaze to the hallway. The escape to the loo had done nothing to ease Angelene's trembling. She wobbled towards them, her hands clenched and unclenched.

Sofia touched Angelene's shoulder as she collapsed onto the chair. "You'll love the orecchiette. It's comfort in a bowl."

Angelene murmured, 'Thank you' and dragged her napkin over her lap. Sofia had seen Brendon anxious before a match. She had never seen anyone dissolve the way Angelene had.

"Is it Burnham-on-Sea or Milan?" Kate said.

The sour expressions on Victoria's and Simone's faces screamed they had no desire to hear about vacation plans. Sofia didn't care. She had lunch to rescue.

"I'm hoping for Milan. You know how much David loves Burnham."

"There wouldn't be a choice. If I said we were going to Milan, that would be the end," Victoria said.

"I'm with you. All those Italian men," Simone said between bites.

"I'm the single one, yet you keep going on about men," Kate said.

Angelene kept her eyes on the bowl, poking at the pasta. "You have a home in Italy?"

Sofia finished chewing and patted her mouth with the napkin. "It was my uncles. He left it to me and my brother Gianni."

"You're lucky to have seen so many places," Angelene said.

"Have you not travelled?" Kate said.

Angelene set down her fork and fiddled with the ropes of sea pearls around her wrist. Sofia gazed curiously. The night of the party, strands and strands of bracelets; today the same. The day she visited the farm-house, she wore a collection of copper and silver bangles.

"My friend Roman Krieger travelled for business. He would tell me about the places he visited. I vacationed through him."

Sofia hesitated before speaking. Angelene was finally opening up. "Those bracelets are lovely. Did Walter buy them?"

"Walter thinks my jewellery looks cheap."

Sofia exchanged a look with Kate. "He means well."

"My friend Lisette said he was trying to change me."

Sofia tapped her fork against her lip, searching for the words. "Walter sees the beauty in you. He's trying to bring it out."

"I guess."

"You guess?" Kate said, slicing into a ravioli. "You have magnificent bone structure. Women would die for a complexion like yours. We'll plan a spa day, the works."

"That will be wonderful," Victoria said. She burped into her napkin and shrugged off her indiscretion.

"No one is inviting you," Sofia said. The feeling that gripped her at the wedding reception flitted around her belly.

"You're still good for tonight?" Kate said.

"What are we doing?" Simone said, laying her napkin over her empty bowl

"We're." Sofia paused and pointed at Victoria and Simone. "Doing nothing."

"Cheeky mare," Victoria said. "What made you decide to marry Walter? Was it his looks? I never go for the rugged type."

Simone chortled at Victoria's serious expression. "We know your type. Sofia's David."

"Did you enjoy your meal, Angelene?"

"Stop twisting the conversation, Sofia. I want to know what drew her to Walter," Victoria said.

"Walter was a fool marrying me."

Sofia glanced at Kate, who glanced at Simone, who struggled to raise an eyebrow at Victoria. Sofia was curious now. She didn't know where to take the conversation or if she wanted to continue it. The annoying feeling swarmed her stomach.

"I'm a mess. I have been for a while."

Silence hung over the table and thundered louder than Sofia's beating heart. What did mess mean? Her appearance? Her story?

Brendon

Dusk painted the sky purply grey. Brendon could hear his mother telling him to stay away. Another voice told him it was okay. A tug of war battered his brain, *visit, go home*. He raised the door knocker; it was heavy in his hand. Stay, *go, follow the rules*. Stay won.

"Mrs... Angelene. You should keep the door locked."

She strolled from the front room, in Walter's pyjama bottoms. Graphite smudged on her fingertips. Her hair piled into a tangled mess. She was beautiful chaos, melancholic and dishevelled.

"You're wearing my hoodie."

Angelene tugged at the waistband and lifted it over her chest.

"Keep it."

He knew he should take it back. She wore a look that said she needed comfort. Brendon told guilt to '*fuck off*' and flopped onto the sofa.

"I tried. I was drowning," Angelene said, in a raspy slur.

"Would you like a cuppa?"

Angelene raised a glass of amber liquid. "I have this."

"Scotch?"

"C'est dégoûtant."

The coffee table was a muddle of illustrations, stained tissues, and pencils. Brendon picked up a sketch—two women cackled into their wineglasses. Their faces stretched taut across their skulls.

"I hope that isn't mom."

"It's Victoria and Simone."

She gulped the scotch, cringed, and dropped the glass to the floor. "Your mother and Kate were kind. I call that drawing tweedle dee and tweedle dum."

Angelene yawned, crept across the couch, and curled against him. Guilt, or someone with excellent marksmanship, shot an arrow and pierced his heart. She held him like he used to cuddle Paddington when the ghosts visited. Her breathing was drawn-out and steeped in scotch.

"I'm a monster."

"Don't be daft. You're just a little rumpled."

Angelene flapped her hand over her mussed appearance. "Someone so lovely and pure. Here you sit, with this."

"I wanted to make sure you survived lunch."

Angelene squeezed him and squished into the cushions. She swiped her cigarettes from the table, flicked a lighter, and took a long drag. "Tell me about your day. What's your school like?"

Brendon coughed and fanned the smoke from his face. "Bloody pretentious. You are somebody if you go to Taunton College."

Angelene hauled on the cigarette. "What are you studying?"

"You really want to hear about this?"

She nodded. The cigarette smouldered between her fingers. Ash dripped onto her lap.

"I have English. We're reading a book called *The Sorrows of Young Werther*. The ending is going to be sad. I know it."

"Good books have tragic endings."

"Then I have French, history. I had a match today, so I had permission to bunk off Latin."

Angelene tossed the cigarette onto an ashy plate and wiped her fingers. "Did you win?"

"I stood around most of the match." He glanced at his watch and hesitated. "I need to go."

"Do you have to?"

His mother's warning assaulted his brain. He didn't want to leave her with her friends scotch and ciggie. It was best he went home. He was still walking a fine line after the Dortmund fiasco.

"I have a ton of homework to complete. If I don't start applying myself, Dad will never forgive me."

Brendon screwed the cap on the scotch and hid it behind a mountain of pillows. He shoved his hands in his hoodie pouch. The room fell quiet. He had never been a 'fall head over heels' type of guy. This mess of a girl had changed his mind. He had fallen into the 'can't breathe, can't concentrate, can't think about anything but her' trap. He had fallen for Uncle Walt's wife.

"I'll stop by again." Brendon tripped over his feet and his words. "Sometime... after practice or when Walt's home."

"Let me see your hands."

He held out his hands. Shivers skittered up his spine as she traced over his palm.

"Your lifeline is deep. You're in good health."

"You see that?"

"I see two loves."

"Only two?"

"Only two, mon ami."

The urge to squeeze all the sadness out of her filled him. Brendon spotted a cell phone buried in a glass bowl filled with trinkets and keys. "Is that yours?"

Angelene dropped his hands and sighed. "Walter said I needed one. I'm trying to figure it out."

"You've never owned a phone? How did people ring you?"

"They called Lisette. Yasmine used to love running to my apartment to tell me I had a call."

"I'm going to put my number in it. If you need me, I'll come."

The voices in his head screeched at him. He shooed them away and swiped open her cell.

"Do you want a picture on your lock screen?"

"I don't understand."

Brendon dug out his cell and tapped it. The Dortmund logo lit up the screen. "Maggie wasn't impressed. Bloody Troy has a picture of Charlie, made me look like a dolt. What's a painting you love?"

"*The Witches Sabbath* by Goya."

Brendon typed, and the painting appeared. "You sure do like some interesting paintings."

Angelene took her phone, stared at the screen, and slid it into her pocket. "I'll see you Saturday."

"You're coming to the match?"

"Walter says I must watch you play."

Angelene looped her arms around his waist and pressed herself against him. He held his arms at his sides. A voice warned him, *she'll steal your light, run home.* Another cackled, *hold her.*

"I can stay, make you something to eat. I'm not the best cook."

"We have something else in common besides football."

"Text if you need anything."

He jingled his car keys and took one last look at her.

The doorbell echoed through the house. Brendon sprinted down the hall, slid across the marble floor and jerked open the door.

"What are you doing here?"

Maggie smoothed her pink hoodie and dug into her lip. After a few quick chews, she spoke. "I dropped Jack off at karate. I thought I'd say hello. You didn't text after the match."

Angelene jumped into his head. He pulled at his collar. "You don't care about my matches."

He led her into a room his mother called 'la mia magnifica stanza' and magnificent it was. The panelled walls were cream, leather sofas gleamed in the fire's glow. Handmade rugs in navy, ivory, and brown pulled the richness of the furniture together. Sofia had filled the room with luxurious fabrics and antiques, transforming it from depressingly dark and haughty to vibrant and cozy.

Brendon snatched the remote from within a baroque armoire. The sportscasters' lively banter filled the cypress and cedar scented air. He gazed at the television and cringed as the ball soared past the Dortmund defenders and blew into the net.

"Bloody hell, he should have caught that one."

"Can't you skip the highlights? It's just football."

Brendon bit down on the curse words. Football was the greatest sport on earth, and Angelene was coming to his match. The hug resurfaced. She had squished herself so tightly against him, there had been no space between them. What was he doing thinking about Angelene? His Nonna had once said, 'In God's eyes, the slate is clean if you make amends.' It was time to make amends. He clicked off the television and plopped beside Maggie.

"Mom will be home soon. We might as well make the most of it."

Maggie stared at him with a look of horror in her eyes. "Why didn't you tell me she was out? You know the rules."

Brendon slid across the sofa and parted his lips. A wave of heat washed over him. He eased her into the mound of throw pillows; her body was stiff under his. Maggie's face swirled, came apart like a jigsaw puzzle, reassembling into a green-eyed blonde. He slid his fingers under her shirt. The warmth of her skin sent pleasant shivers up his spine.

"I can't wait until July."

Maggie gripped the cushion and dragged herself from beneath him. "We've talked about this a million times."

"Eleven months is a long time to wait."

"I don't want to be up the duff like Camille Dunlop. Her parents made her go to school with that massive belly."

"I have condoms."

He slipped his hand into her sweater and cupped her tiny breast.

"Why do you have condoms? We aren't... are you? Did you meet a girl in Dortmund?"

Brendon scrubbed his hands over his face and groaned. "Troy gave me some. It was supposed to be my birthday present. Remember?"

Maggie shoved a chewed fingernail in her mouth. The words were muffled with each chew. "I'm scared."

Sparks crackled and buzzed around Brendon's stomach. "Scared of bloody what? People have sex all the time."

"Sweetheart, I'm home."

Brendon fumbled for the remote, switched on the television and imagined the sparks as snowflakes, melting away.

"Hello, my love," Sofia said, cupping his cheeks. "You're flushed."

Brendon pulled his face away and forced a smile. "How was lunch?"

Sofia unraveled a cashmere wrap and raised an eyebrow. "Exhausting. You know the rules."

"It's my fault, Mrs. Cook," Maggie said, frowning at her decimated manicure. "I took Jack to karate and when I didn't hear from Brendon, I thought I would stop by."

"I forgot to text. Blame me, Mammina."

Sofia laid her wrap over her arm and smiled. "I'm going to call your father. I miss him."

Brendon inhaled, counted to four and exhaled in one long breath. Liam taught him the yoga breathing, pranayama, after a red card incident. It was to calm the sparks before he reacted with cruel words or his fists. He counted his breaths, blew the ashy sparks away and took her hand.

"Mom's home now. You're safe."

"Every time we kiss, you turn into a wanker."

"Is it wrong to want to hump my girlfriend?"

Maggie screwed up her face and tore at a hangnail. "You've never pushed."

He stretched his arms overhead and clamped his hands together. "You keep promising. Bloody hell, we snog, my knob gets excited?"

"It was never important before. It's all you think about lately."

"I'm a guy. We think about humping."

Maggie whipped her purse over her shoulder. "Be patient." She dug her car keys from her pocket and stood. "I'm in a mood now. I hope Jack doesn't want to practice his karate on me or you'll pay for it."

"I promise to be patient."

He battled with the sparks and followed her to the foyer.

"Are you going to pick me up before the match?"

Brendon opened the door. Never ending black wrapped around the trees and moors. "Have Charlie drive you."

Maggie hesitated and stared at her mauled fingernails.

"Everything is fine." Brendon kissed her and patted her bottom. "I'll see you at the pitch."

He watched her leave, confused. He hadn't summoned Angelene into his thoughts. She appeared. He was torn between what was right and what was wrong. Maggie was right, springtime pretty and his. He had to get Angelene out of his head.

"Your father is leaving London early." Sofia marched out of the den and looped her arm through his. "He's excited about your match."

"He goes because it's what a dad is supposed to do."

"That's not true. He enjoys watching you play. It gives him something to brag about at work."

"The only thing he spews around the House of Commons is when I fuck up."

"Did you just use the king of curse words?" Sofia dragged her arm from his and gave him a gentle pat on the arm. "You're in a fine mood."

The evening churned within Brendon's head: the hug, reading his palm, Maggie squirming, asking for patience.

"I'm bloody fine."

"Swearing and brooding in my foyer is fine?"

"You wouldn't understand."

"I know what was going on."

"You mean what wasn't."

Warmth rolled over his body. He tugged at his hoodie and whipped it at the stairs.

"Why do you want to be like Troy and William sticking their pisello into every gnocca that walks by?"

"Troy sticks his pisello in Charlie. I don't give a shit who Will... Jesus Christ, mom."

He moved in long strides and flicked on the kitchen light. Brendon swung open the fridge and gazed around the immense box.

"Don't involve Jesus," Sofia said, flicking the charms dangling from her bracelet.

"Since when do you care about JC? You're angry with him and God. You have been for years."

He grabbed a container of roasted chicken and slid it across the counter. A tub of mixed greens ricocheted off the backsplash and into the sink. "Can we talk about this tomorrow?"

"We'll talk about it now. I don't want you grumbling around the house."

Angelene floated into his mind. He could feel her arms around him. Brendon cursed, shook her from his head and forked mixed greens into the container. Brendon sliced a tomato and placed the wedges on the salad.

"I think Kate still has a thing for Walter." Sofia grabbed a glass from the cupboard and poured herself some water. "I know her. She still loves him."

"She called him an arrogant donkey."

Brendon chopped a red pepper, dumped it on the chicken and sliced into a cucumber.

"Who hasn't called him cocky or pompous?" Sofia took a sip and stole a cucumber round off the cutting board. "They get along so well. It's a shame Walter couldn't see how wonderful Kate is."

"Did she tell you that, or are you making an assumption?"

He swept the cucumber into the container, poured on the dressing, and leaned against the counter.

"She beams when she talks about him. Sit, sweetheart," Sofia said, pulling out a stool. "It's better for your digestion."

Brendon dropped onto the stool and stabbed his fork into the lettuce. "Kate made it seem like she didn't care what Walt did." He crammed the salad into his mouth and wiped a splotch of dressing from his chin.

"Use a kitchen towel," Sofia said, tearing a section from the roll. "Simone called you dishy."

"I can't get past her nose. I would have asked for my money back." He ran a forkful of greens through a puddle of dressing and munched. "What did Kate think about Angelene?"

He studied his mother's reaction. Worry wrinkled her brow.

"She expected a glamazonian and got, well, Angelene."

"She's not that bad."

"You didn't see her at lunch," Sofia said. "She picked at her meal, kneaded her knuckles, barely said two words."

"I'd be nervous around Mrs. McGregor."

"Kate doesn't know what to make of her, and neither do I?"

Brendon smeared lettuce around the container and stuck the forkful in his mouth. He was having his own trouble trying to figure her out.

"I'm afraid if Walter pushes her too hard, she'll push back. There's a feisty side to her. I saw a hint of it today."

"You worry too much." Brendon rinsed the container and placed it in the dishwasher. "Uncle Walt wouldn't have married her if he didn't see someone worth marrying."

Sofia tilted her head to the side and flicked the B charm back and forth. "What about this feeling I keep having?"

"It's the same feeling you get when I fly to Dortmund, when Walter first brought Anastasia around, when Kate dated that guy from Wales."

"I spent most of lunch trying to calm Angelene."

"I'm proud of you for trying to make her feel comfortable."

Sofia's voice softened, and she reached for his hand. "What will I do when you're gone?"

"Fly to Dortmund every weekend."

A little quiver rolled in his belly. Angelene was harmless, consumed by her own fears and insecurities. She was just a girl trying to play a role she knew nothing about. The only thing Brendon questioned was how she got stuck in his head.

Angelene

Angelene loved the night. The rest of the world slept, everything was quiet and dreamy. Her love for all things washed in black evaded her. The forest was dark and distorted. The silence was intense and frightening.

'It was an exhausting day, God. I rehearsed what I would say and forgot. I begged myself to remember the rules, sit up straight, sip my wine. I was my bumbling self.'

Angelene lit a cigarette and gulped back streams of smoke. Lunch had been a dizzying pattern of colours. Victoria had been pickle green and just as sour. Simone had been turquoise and not the turquoise she dreamed of dipping her toes in, but boastful, 'I'm richer and prettier than you.' Sofia had been her usual elegant black and Kate, in her navy sheath and sensible pumps, was encouraging teal. It surprised Angelene Walter never dove into Kate's teal. She found it quite attractive.

The phenomena, seeing words in colour, started when Angelene was a child. Her teacher had asked her to spell the word apple, every letter had been a different colour, red, green, green, yellow, blue. She remembered the children laughing and her teacher yelling spiky red words. Veronique Hummel proclaimed her daughter a witch. Her teacher called it synesthesia. It was another thing that made her odd.

'God, forgive me for hugging Brendon. I cannot believe how bright his light is. It's not mine to have.'

She dropped the cigarette into the glass and drew the blankets to her chin. "Sleep, I beg you to come."

Her mind filled with the boy who looked like a man, the football hero, her boy in brown. A strange feeling fluttered in her belly, and she dug at her wrist.

'I'm supposed to be playing normal, being a wife, learning to love Walter. God, take Brendon from my mind. Forgive me for wanting his light. Forgive me for asking for forgiveness.'

7 Haphephobia

Brendon

Adrenaline electrified Brendon. It had been an intense first half. The play bounced between both ends, with a heavy attack coming from Taunton and Dorchester. There had been chances to score. Nothing had slipped past Brendon or Dorchester's keeper. It was the type of match Brendon lived for.

Brendon pushed open the dressing room door. Fans erupted in cheers and hoorahs. The stands were a living, breathing beast of humanity: foot stomping, whoops, chants, handmade posters, and flags waved; girls swooned and giggled; children clapped for their heroes.

He tightened his gloves, ready for battle.

"Still got dragons in your belly, or did you leave them in Dortmund?" Liam McMahon said.

"They never went away."

After years of being stuck in the middle of the standings, Taunton First began the hunt for a new coach. Word around Taunton was an ex-striker from the Shamrock Rovers was teaching physical education at Heathfield Community School. Liam McMahon had a reputation of driving the school team to success, making him a solid choice for the fledgling football club. Liam worked the team hard. He treated them like pro footballers and had a list of infractions in place to keep them focused. The team admired his winning spirit and for the hero he once was.

Liam tapped each player as they walked by and gave them an encouraging grin. "I didn't think I'd see you back here."

"Things didn't go as planned."

"Bets at the bookies have us taking the win."

Brendon took a sip of water and tossed the bottle toward the net. "There are holes in their defence. We need the opportunity to get the ball through."

"The keeper's good. Word is Tottenham is interested," Liam said.

"He's quick but gets out of position."

Liam zipped up his First jacket and stared down the length of the pitch. "Dorchester is putting up a strong fight."

"Their plays are weak. They're too focused on winning."

"I'm glad you're back."

"I'm not."

Liam chuckled and clapped Brendon's shoulder. "Get out there, eejit. Show them how it's done."

Brendon walked onto the pitch, got into position, and scanned the crowded stands. He spied Angelene squeezed between Walter and his father. There was no smile on her face. A rosy glow brightened her cheeks. Walter's arm was around her shoulders. His fingers lightly caressed her neck. A burning sensation swarmed Brendon's chest. Every visit to the farmhouse, Angelene had been his. She was Walter's wife again.

"Nice to see Mrs. Pratt out," Troy said.

The words sounded forced and fake, like he was happy to see Angelene but shouldn't be.

"She's a minger," William said.

"She's no arseface, pretty in a plain way," Troy said in the same odd tone.

Brendon breathed through the flickering sparks. There were forty-five minutes left to play. He had to forget about the jealousy and anger brewing inside him and concentrate on the match.

"Mom said she hid in the restaurant loo." William's tone was easy and arrogant. "She also said Mrs. Pratt was involved with a married man."

Sparks glowed hot and crackly. Brendon flexed his fingers and glared. "How does your mom know that?"

"She just does."

"Your mom's a bloody gossip."

The whistle blew, stirring the fans into a frenzy.

"Walter has got himself a slapper." William's laugh was so controlled it seemed artificial.

"Your mom should be concerned about what your dad gets up to in London. I've heard stories."

William twisted Brendon's jersey and scowled. "What are you going on about?"

"Ask your bloody mother. She knows everything." Brendon jerked his shirt free. "Get your fucking hands off me and take your seat on the bench."

Brendon took his position in net. He caught sight of Maggie nibbling her thumbnail. Resentment fuelled the dragons. A hand job would be nice, a quickie. He tore his eyes from Maggie, snagged the ball, and slammed it to midfield. Rachel was two rows up, waving a Cook #1 poster. An attacker approached. Brendon kept his eyes on the ball and grabbed it. The crowd cheered and stamped their feet. Brendon kicked it and glanced into the stands. Angelene smiled behind her fingers. Joy illuminated her face. Brendon followed the ball; it bounced off Troy's head. Dorchester picked up the rebound; Brendon dropped to his knees, skidded across the pitch, and cradled it. He rolled it back onto the pitch. Troy barreled in, kicked, and cleared it. Brendon wiped blood from his grass-stained knees, held his breath. First put the ball in the net.

"Keep it in their end. Push up," Brendon yelled.

The team listened. It was a victory for Taunton First.

The mood in the dressing room was euphoric. The season had started with a draw and a loss. Taunton First were back to their winning ways. Brendon ran a towel over the water gliding down his back. He had been quick, sharp, and Angelene had been there to see it. He never believed in love at first sight. The only thing he had fallen head over heels for was Signal Iduna Park. He believed in moments. There had been moments with Angelene—her finger on his palm, the kiss, the hug. Beautiful, wrong moments.

"You know that saying, 'undressing you with your eyes,' Rachel had you starkers all match," Troy said.

"I didn't notice. My eyes were on the pitch," Brendon said, drying his hair with a towel.

"I saw you looking." Troy dug in his shaving kit for pomade. "I'll meet you at the manor. Charlie and I have to celebrate."

Brendon tossed his towel into a rolling laundry cart and grabbed his shirt. "How do you know she'll be up for it?"

"We always hump after a win." Troy laughed. "Or a loss."

William zipped up his backpack and slung it over his shoulder. "You wouldn't know about that, would you, Cook?"

A ripple of 'oohs,' 'No, Brendon, stop,' 'I'm a good girl,' floated on the menthol-scented steam. Brendon flung his jersey in the laundry bin and shrugged the tension away.

"She's built like a girl," William said.

"I'd shut my mouth if I were you."

Brendon jabbed his finger into William's chest, knocking him into the wall. His temper had always been unpredictable. It had put him in the headmaster's office, parked him on the bench, and took his father back to a place he wanted to forget.

Do you know why you are here?

I pushed Freddy. He said I was a daft keeper. He said my house has ghosts and people died there.

Do you believe you're a bad keeper?

My Uncle Walt's friend Lukas watched me play. He called me a word that started with a p.

A prodigy.

Yes, sir.

A plaster isn't going to cover that gash over Freddy's eye.

I'm sorry, Mr. Oakes. I get these sparks in my belly and can't help it.

Walk away next time. One day, you're going to do more than cut someone's face.

"Knock, knock." Troy tapped his knuckles on Brendon's head. "You in there?"

Brendon breathed through the ashy aftermath. "Analyzing the match."

"You should have stayed in Dortmund, dickhead," William said. He ripped his backpack from the floor and shot up his middle finger. "Both of us should have a turn in net."

"Fuck off, Will."

"Breathe, mate. I'll meet you at the manor."

Brendon jerked on his clothes, snatched his keys, and left the dressing room. His father's Jaguar was gone. Maggie waited by his car, cell phone in hand, rapid fire texting.

"My parents didn't stick around?" Brendon unlocked the car and tossed his backpack in the rear seat.

"They had to go to Tesco for groceries. Walter is making a French dish called hachis parmenter."

"Dad needs to take notes," Brendon said. He slid behind the steering wheel and started the BMW. "That bolognese he attempted was dodgy."

"It was burnt," Maggie said. She sat, sent one last text, and shoved her phone into her pocket. "We ate it anyway."

Brendon pulled out of the car park. His mind tangled with all the things he shouldn't be thinking about—Angelene's lavender-scented hair, the little tears in her chapped lips. He glanced at Maggie and took her hand. The green moors passed in a blur of familiar images: apple orchards, fields of hay, forests of hornbeam, ash, and beech trees, Spence Farm, Walter's stone farmhouse. He veered onto the laneway and threw out an intention to anyone listening. Shoo Angelene from his head.

Brendon waved to Troy and turned into the carport. He brushed his lips over Maggie's cheek and grabbed his knapsack.

"You didn't get your hump in."

"Brian put me in a headlock."

Charlotte ran her finger along Troy's jaw and nuzzled his ear. "There's plenty of time for snogging, babes. Daddy said I could stay over."

"Your parents are letting you sleep at Troy's?" Maggie said.

Brendon led the pack to the door. It would be a cold day in hell before his parents allowed a girl to sleep over, even the virtuous Maggie.

"I promised my dad I would help Mrs. Spence with chores. He never says no."

"Not even your mom?" Maggie said.

"Mom likes to have romantic evenings with him. I can just imagine what they get up to when I'm not around."

"My dad was excited to have Mammina to himself when I was in Dortmund." Brendon opened the door and kicked off his shoes. "I ruined that for him, too."

"Charlie is the best egg collector in Taunton. The chickens love her, except for Lucy," Troy said.

"Any time babes is near me, that mangey bird pecks my ankles."

Brendon chuckled. "Pick a room. You can use the loo in the hallway."

"Can't I change with Charlie?"

"If my dad caught the two of you snogging, you'd be out on your arse."

"I'm not going to hump her with your parents around."

The girls giggled up the stairs. The Mediterranean-inspired room would be perfect for a poolside afternoon.

"You have no control when you see Charlie naked."

"She has a lovely body. There's a little freckle on her hip. It's the most brilliant thing I've ever seen."

"Better than her arse and jubblies?"

"I kiss it every time we get naked. Meet you in the pool."

Brendon seized Troy's arm and looked into his eyes. "You're being bloody lovey-dovey with Charlie, even more than usual. Did you do something to piss her off?"

Troy glanced at his feet and back up with a smile. "No way. Just love my girl."

'He looks guilty.'

Brendon shook the thought away and climbed the stairs. He flicked on his bedroom light, stripped out of his clothes, and dropped them on the floor. An ache ballooned and pressed into his ribs. He couldn't have Angelene. He shouldn't want her either. She was Walter's girl. He had his own, springtime Maggie with her blue blossom eyes and head full of knowledge.

Brendon grabbed his swim trunks off the bed and dragged them on. He wrenched towels from the vanity and with every step down the hall, he repeated, *'Maggie is my girl.'*

The front door burst open. He smiled at his mother's exasperated look.

"That store is just dreadful."

"It's not that bad, Mammina."

"Potatoes are potatoes no matter where you buy them," David said.

Sofia set down her purse and unzipped her Ferragamo riding boots. "I got you some fig bars. I know you like them at halftime. It used to be Smarties when you were little."

"I still like Smarties, only the blue ones."

"I hope you don't make Maggie pick out the blue Smarties," David said.

"Why would I do that? She saves them for me," Brendon said, reaching for the bags. "I'll help."

"Go to your friends."

"You sure?"

It could be a test, see if he ran from the code. His grin was genuine.

"Your mother can help, if it's not beneath her."

Sofia took a bag of vegetables. "Stai attento a come parli, David Richard. Remember who you are talking to."

"You played brilliantly, son."

David had never been an athlete. Academics was how he exercised. He tolerated football and would watch random Bundesliga matches to appease Sofia. It was not who David Cook was but it was a compliment. Brendon would take it.

"Think we can get a snog in before the Pratts arrive?" David said.

"That's bloody gross," Brendon called.

He made his way down the hall, past the great room and into the west wing. Along hallways painted midnight blue, woodwork illuminated rich mahogany by the sun that shone from the extension, and through the scents of lemon wood polish, roses, chlorine, and rosemary. Walls of glass soared to a vaulted ceiling of exposed beams. Modelled after a Tuscan farmhouse, the pavilion stretched into the forest. A stone wall housed a fireplace encased in mosaic tiles. Copper urns of ferns, teak lounges, and chairs cushioned in yellow and royal blue decorated the pool deck. Brendon tossed the towels onto a chair. His eyebrows rose, and he felt his cheeks warm. Charlotte climbed out of the water, adjusting the triangles barely covering her breasts. He turned away. Maggie lay on a lounge in a fuchsia one-piece- no cut-outs, no plunging neckline, no strings holding anything in place.

"Let's go in."

"I don't feel like it right now."

Brendon flashed her a knowing, pearly white smile and dropped into the lounge. "Is it Charlie?"

She glanced at Charlotte, took in the strings and triangles, noting she had curves in all the right places. Maggie was straight up and down, angles and, to most boys, invisible. If there was anything distinguishable about Charlotte, she was bouncy. Maggie had never been noticeable.

"There isn't anything to that bathing suit."

"You could wear a bikini. A little pink number with ruffles on your bum."

Maggie crossed her arms over her non-existent breasts. Her tone was sharp. "Where did you see a bathing suit like that? In the children's section at Debenhams."

"Last year's Sports Illustrated."

"I wouldn't look like those models."

Brendon leaned across the lounge and caged her in his toned arms. "You'd look like you."

The curtains covering the French doors fluttered. It had been hard keeping his eyes off Charlotte's 'barely there' bikini. Now Angelene. She was windswept, rosy-cheeked, and in awe of the glass room.

"La vache! I could live in here," Angelene said.

Walter chuckled. "By the pool?"

"I could paint, sit by the fire, float all day. How do you not spend every day in here?"

Brendon stared past the glass walls and into the forest. "I'm a busy guy."

"You should come in, Mrs. Pratt," Troy said. He flung his arm across his chest, shielding his nipples. Brendon swore Troy looked guilty or felt stupid for belting out the invitation. "Meet my girlfriend Charlotte."

"Bonjour."

Two voices duelled inside Brendon's subconscious. *Do the right thing. Stare at the pretty Mrs. Pratt.*

"You both played brilliantly today," Walter said.

Brendon's cheeks warmed. He lowered his gaze to the bruise forming around the abrasions on his knees.

Walter stood at the pool's edge, his arm wrapped protectively around Angelene's waist. "How do those scouts keep missing your talent?" he asked.

"I've been to every football trial. Still nothing," Troy replied.

Brendon stared at his knees, trying to drown out the voice whispering, *You want her. She's not yours.*

"I'll talk to Lukas," Walter said. "He knows a few scouts in London. I'll put in a good word."

He gave Angelene's hip a gentle pat as they walked away, and the truth cut through Brendon—she was Walter's wife.

Forcing her from his thoughts, Brendon turned to Maggie. "Come in the pool with me."

"Not yet."

Brendon swept Maggie into his arms. She kicked wildly and giggled. Her arms flailed as he tossed her into the pool. Brendon dove in, swam to her, and wiped her hair from her eyes. "I'm sorry."

"For staring at Mrs. Pratt again."

"I've never seen anyone react like that. It's a bloody pool."

He drew her close. She felt good and right. The tangled ball of 'what if's' and 'follow the code' intensified. Guilt was heavy.

A gasp tickled Brendon's ear. Maggie's arms tightened around his neck.

"What's the matter?"

"She's watching you."

There was nothing in the hall but a fading shadow.

"It was probably Richard the prick. He floats around the pool, pissed off mom had the extension built."

"Your grandfather didn't have blonde hair."

"Then it was one of the other ghosts that lurks around here."

The shadow was gone.

Brendon waved goodbye to Troy and Charlotte and shut the door. He wanted to believe Angelene had been staring at him. Maybe he crept inside her brain and hung out like she did his. Maggie's insecurity over Charlotte's itty-bitty bikini had to be the culprit of the mysterious shadow.

"Take this bottle to your mom," David said, handing him a bottle of wine. "I'm going to start the washing up. Walter's an excellent cook. He sure makes a mess."

"Have they gone through a bottle already?"

"Angelene can drink. Nervous habit, I think."

Brendon walked to the great room. He promised himself not to stare, not even a peek. The sound of the fire popping and crackling filled the silence. Brendon clutched the wine bottle and cursed softly. Angelene gripped the wineglass, her knuckles white. It had taken exactly five seconds to break his promise.

"Put that here, sweetheart," Sofia said, pushing aside an empty bottle. "Would you like a glass?"

Brendon shook his head and sank onto the couch beside Maggie. "Can I put the telly on?"

"That would be rude, sweetheart. We have guests."

"No one is talking."

"We'll talk. Let's talk," Sofia said. "I was thinking about your draw-ings, Angelene. They look like the illustrations from that old Grimm's fairy tale book Richard owned."

Angelene stared at the bottle like it was a decadent dessert. A line of desperation materialized between her eyebrows.

It was time for him to swoop in for the rescue before she downed another bottle.

"I hated that book."

"Richard used to shove the picture of the witch stuffing children into the oven in Brendon's face. You remember, sweetheart?"

"How could I forget? I still have nightmares."

"My grandpa read me Beatrix Potter. I loved Peter Rabbit," Maggie said.

"Do you get your inspiration from books?" Sofia said.

Angelene blew out a hefty sigh, poured wine into her glass, and gulped. "They come from my dreams."

Brendon raised his eyebrows. "Those are some dreams."

"I rarely bid on art at the auctions. Most of the paintings in the house belonged to David's father."

"Don't get too excited. They're bloody boring landscapes and creepy-looking people."

Angelene hid her smile behind her wineglass. He stared into his lap.

"I didn't know you were such a connoisseur, sweetheart. Would you prefer paintings of football pitches and Bundesliga logos?"

"I took art history."

"You attempted art history."

"I passed."

"I wrote your final essay," Maggie said.

"I did the research." His fingers tingled to steal the glass from Angelene. She could grip his hand instead. "It was that artist I liked. The poster was in the classroom. It was colourful, had all sorts of squares and circles. The couple was kissing."

Angelene sat up and clenched the stem of the glass. "Klimt?"

"That's it. I thought his name was funny. It reminded me of a girl's fanny."

"Oh, mio dio, you say the most inappropriate things," Sofia said.

Brendon grinned at his mother's displeasure and pointed to a darkened corner of the room. "We have one here."

Angelene sucked in her breath. Her voice was full of wonder. "You have a Klimt?"

"It's hanging over my Nonna's credenza. *Water Serpents*."

Angelene set her glass down and scrambled off the sofa. Brendon turned, dragging Maggie with him. Angelene touched her full lips and studied the painting.

"She looks like she's going to cry," Maggie said.

"Ms. Dolman said art should move you. She's been bloody moved."

The look on Angelene's face was dreamy, like she was floating with the women in the painting. The room blurred. All Brendon could see was her. Was it love, infatuation, limerence? He didn't know. The feeling marched through his insides, up his spine, making a home in his heart. Maggie leaned her cheek on his shoulder. Brendon blinked, refocused, told himself to pay attention to Maggie.

"What's everyone looking at?" David said.

"Mom told Mrs. Pratt about the Klimt painting."

"We should have sold it," David said.

"And not see Angelene's reaction?" Sofia kissed David's cheek and leaned into his ear. "Two and a half bottles."

Angelene grabbed her glass from the coffee table. "Why would you sell it?"

"It reminds me of my father. He paid more attention to that painting than he did Mom and I."

"Do you like it?"

Brendon fiddled with the clasp on his watch. Maggie's ragged fingernails dug into his arm; his mother arched her eyebrow. David looked impressed he had paid attention in class.

He cleared his throat and kept his eyes on his parents. "The women are beautiful. Klimt completed it during his golden period, where he used gold leaf. He's famous for that."

"Klimt loved women. Many of his paintings are erotic. Klimt was a rebel," Angelene said.

"My father was just like Klimt, a lover of women. He re-titled it, 'Those glorious lesbians.' He had a name for each of the women," David said. "Shall we? Chef Walter awaits."

Brendon jerked his arm from Maggie's grasp and rubbed the red indentations puckering his forearm.

"Bloody hell, you nearly tore into my skin."

"Do you believe me now? She couldn't take her eyes off you."

"She asked me a question. Was I supposed to ignore her?"

The glow of the fire brightened the midnight blue walls. The table had been set with David's grandmother's Royal Crown Derby dinner service and decorated with bowls of red roses. The crystal goblets and cutlery sparkled in the early evening sunlight. Warmed brioche, onions, and garlic scented the air. Brendon knew he needed to redeem himself with Maggie. He was guilty of falling into the *'I can't stop looking at Angelene'* trap again. Follow the code. Be a gentleman.

Brendon pulled out Maggie's chair and did his best to keep his attention on her, passed her a plate of Walter's French creation, filled her water glass. He was finding it difficult to focus on anything but Angelene.

"It tastes like shepherd's pie, Uncle Walt."

Brendon scooped up a forkful of potatoes, waiting for someone to reply. His mother and father nodded in agreement. Walter grimaced and covered the mouth of Angelene's wineglass with his hand.

"It's brilliant, Mr. Pratt. Just moreish," Maggie said.

"What is shepherd's pie?" Angelene said.

Brendon flipped his fork around his fingers with the dexterity of a drummer. The question floated around the dining room for anyone to answer. Her eyes were on him.

"It's, uh, like this."

The fork flew from his hand and clattered across the table. Sofia arched her eyebrow at the potato and beef Jackson Pollock created on the damask tablecloth.

"I'll make it for you sometime. It's similar." The veins in Walter's neck pulsed. "Put some food in your belly, peck, peck, peck like a little bird."

Angelene's hand shot out from beneath the table. She hooked her finger in her wineglass and polished it off. Brendon grinned. Klimt's rebel spirit had rubbed off on her.

Walter grabbed her glass, shoved his napkin in it, and tapped his knife against her plate. "Are you still going to university for teaching?"

"I'm hoping to be accepted at the University of Cambridge," Maggie said.

Brendon kept his glances subtle, hidden behind bites of food and sips of milk. The wine bottle had disappeared.

"Your parents will celebrate when I'm gone."

Maggie piled a scoop of potatoes on a slab of brioche and held it mid-air. "My parents like you."

"Since when?" Brendon dumped a pile of salad on his plate and stabbed into lemony rocket. "Your mom told me good riddance in August. She was happy I was leaving."

"How could they not like my baby? Look at that face," Sofia said.

His mother's cooing did not erase the line creased across Walter's forehead.

"Cambridge's education department is one of England's best," David added.

"Can you manage a long-distance relationship?" Walter said.

The ring Brendon had placed on Maggie's finger gave the impression he could. It had been impulsive and came with a lecture from his father about his habit of breaking promises. It seemed the right thing to do before boarding the plane to Dortmund. There was a part of him that wanted Maggie to join him in Germany; another part was unsure. As he stared at Angelene's wistful eyes, doubt resurfaced.

"We did." Sofia touched David's hand and looked at him with eyes of a love-struck teenager. "For two blissful years."

"Richard loved sending Mom and me to Milan. He was at his happiest when the taxi carted us off to Heathrow."

"Relationships are hard no matter where you live," Brendon said.

"If you play like you did today, they'll be no time for a relationship."

"Walter," Sofia said, shifting her gaze toward Maggie.

"We'll figure something out. That's what you do, right? Adapt, learn, and accept."

Brendon aimed the words at Walter. As far as he was concerned, Walter needed to do all three.

"Vous serez une grande star du football."

Held in her fervent, grey-green gaze, red heat stormed Brendon's cheeks. The flush rolled down his neck in slow waves.

"Finish your meal, sweetheart," Sofia said, her eyes and words steely.

"What did you say, Mrs. Pratt?"

Maggie dug her teeth into her lip and chewed. "She said you'll be a big football star."

"Don't tell me you're failing French," David said.

"He needs to learn German." Walter jammed his fork into a pile of potatoes and presented it to Angelene.

"He already tried German. The teacher won't have him back," David said.

Walter snorted. "Got a temper like Richard. A little fire in the belly never hurt anyone."

"Someone from school is helping me."

Brendon inventoried Walter. He smiled his crinkly smile, cheeks blazing crimson, knuckles white. If anyone knew about fire in the belly, it was Walter.

"Who?" David said. He laid his napkin over his plate and reached for Sofia's hand. "None of the teachers will have you. Your mother had to beg Madame Lafavre."

"I didn't beg, dear."

Maggie unlatched her teeth from her lip and scrunched her nose. "Rachel Jones."

"Miranda Jones's daughter? If she's anything like her mother, I'd watch out," Walter said.

"She's the tart..." Maggie said through a mouthful of brioche.

Brendon threw her a look and interrupted. "You're making the distance between Cambridge and Dortmund very inviting."

Sparks lit in fierce pops. Walter's knife tapped against Angelene's plate. Chewy mouth sounds came from Maggie. Disappointment furrowed David's brow.

"Brendon David, what a thing to say. What type of girl is Rachel Jones?" Sofia said, clicking through her silver bangles.

Brendon scrubbed at his ears- *tap, smack, click.* He closed his eyes, counted his breaths, and imagined the sparks as powdery soot.

"Dad thinks knowing a second language is important. I'm only doing what I'm told."

"If you had been doing as I asked, you would have kept your mouth shut last term and not ended up in Mr. Dawson's office. Every teacher in the modern languages department is afraid of you."

"I warned Mr. Lochmann the sparks were flying."

Brendon locked eyes with David. Silence swept through the dining room. He rocked the chair on its back legs, counting his breath with each tilt.

"We're working on his temper. Brendon knows the consequences if his grades slip," Sofia said.

David stacked his plate on Sofia's and kissed her cheek. "My apologies. We don't need to broadcast our problems. We have Victoria McGregor for that."

Walter dropped a forkful of mince on Angelene's plate and stood. "I'll help with the washing up."

"Maggie, come tell me about your trip to Paris," Sofia said.

"No more wine, little bird," Walter said. "I'll bring you a cuppa and a slice of Amelia's roly-poly. You might eat that."

Brendon dropped the chair to the floor, yanked the napkin from his lap, and tossed it on the table. The sound of Angelene scratching her jeans filled the silence. He knew he should be with Maggie. He couldn't pull himself from the dining room.

"You going to join Mom?"

"I want to go home."

"Do you have a headache? I do. The bloody conversation was daft. The constant tapping on your plate."

Angelene staggered to her feet, held a hand to her forehead, and wobbled.

"You're bladdered."

"If that means drunk, then I'm afraid I am."

She let go of the chair and swayed. Brendon hesitated and unglued his feet. It was the gentlemanly thing to do, help a damsel in distress.

"Take my arm."

"Get me another glass. Mother always said one more to straighten you out."

"Your mother was wrong." He flexed his arm as she leaned into him. "Walt's angry."

Angelene looked up at him, puzzled. "He's smiling."

"Last season, this punter waited for me in the car park. I let in two goals. He blamed me for the loss. Walter intervened, lifted him off the ground. He was smiling the whole time."

"Did he hurt the man?"

"Dad stepped in and stopped him. You never see Walt coming."

"Like you?"

"Everyone knows when I'm mad, I snap. I'll slam my fist into anything or say bloody awful things. Read Walt's face."

They stood in the foyer. Brendon surveyed the distance to the great room. There were ten steps to get her to the sofa, then she was Walter's problem.

"What do I look for?"

"His eyes turn icy blue. He's smiling, his eyes are crinkly, but there's no laughter in them."

"I mustn't make him mad."

"No more wine tonight."

She laid her cheek against his arm. "I'll have a cigarette."

"A cuppa and roly-poly. That'll make you feel better."

"What is rollee-pollee?"

"It's jam and sponge. We aren't fancy like the French, with your eclairs and those biscuits Maggie likes, macaroons."

"It's macaron. They're my favourite," Angelene said. "Vous êtes merveilleux."

Her breath, scented with wine, was warm against his skin. The expression in her eyes sent his heart racing.

"Merveilleux means wonderful. I only know that because Madame Lafavre said it when she learned I was in her class. I'm far from wonderful."

"You're my only friend."

He had been, when he wasn't supposed to be, when he went against his promise.

"Brendon David."

He jerked his head up and stared into Sofia's blazing eyes.

"Maggie and I have been waiting."

Brendon untangled Angelene's arm and placed a hand on her shoulder to steady her.

"It's my fault. I've had too much to drink. I'll go for a cigarette." Angelene teetered left and right. "The fresh air will help."

Angelene wobbled to the door. The scent of patchouli lingered in the foyer. Brendon took a step toward the door. Sofia stood in front of him.

"She's not your concern."

"Was I supposed to leave her at the table? Walter knows she's soused. He left her sitting there."

"I told you to stay away from her," Sofia said. "The feeling is back."

"Dad and I got into it. Your perfect family didn't look so perfect."

Sparks zipped; he brushed past Sofia. She snagged him by the wrist.

"This feeling has nothing to do with you and your father bickering. She couldn't take her eyes off you. Stay away from her."

Brendon wrenched his wrist free. "For fuck's sake."

"Stop swearing," Sofia said, her face softened and her tone was light. "I'm sorry, sweetheart. My stomach is in knots, and I don't know why."

"She's drunk. That makes you nervous. It reminds you of Uncle Gianni."

"Be a good boy, go to Maggie. I'm going to see if your father needs any help. Tell Walter he needs to take Angelene home."

Brendon rambled into the great room. Maggie stared at him with wide blue eyes and her best 'I'm-not-jealous' smile.

"Sorry I took so long."

"I understand."

"I didn't even tell you where I was."

He collapsed beside her and drew her into the crook of his arm.

"You were with Mrs. Pratt."

"She's bloody pissed."

"You did what you're supposed to do; be a gentleman. You held back Gemma's hair at William's birthday bash when she barfed."

Brendon's heart was warm and tingly. He wanted to be with Maggie. He wanted to be with Angelene. He liked the smell of Maggie's perfume. He didn't like the scent of wine permeating from Angelene. Maggie was his, smiling in that way that said, 'I adore you.' Angelene was drunk and married.

"You want to go to my room and snog?"

"No, I don't."

Brendon laced his fingers through hers and ran his thumb over the diamond solitaire. "I'm sorry about the dinner conversation. You knew about Dortmund before we started dating."

"It's been in the Taunton Times since you were seven, Taunton's hero."

"Just because I'm in Germany doesn't mean we have to break up."

"My cousin went to uni in Canada, and her relationship ended. The distance was too hard."

Brendon hadn't thought about the relationship's survival. All he wanted was to get to Dortmund.

"We'll try. Let's go to my room and snog."

He kissed her softly; his gaze shifted to the arched doorway. Angelene walked in precise steps to the painting, fell to her bottom and hugged her knees. He was falling for her again. The voices in his head battled. *Do the right thing. Sit and stare.*

"You want to play FIFA 18? I promise no snogging."

"Can we play something else? I never win that football game."

"Sure, you can pick."

"Should we tell Mrs. Pratt we're leaving?"

"I'm not sure she knows we're here."

Troy

Unlike most families who ate between five and six, dinner at Spence Farm happened after seven. The animals had been fed and put to bed. The coop locked. Suppertime was not a napkin in the lap, elbows off the table affair. It was noisy; food slopped from serving dish to plate; laughter, conversation layered over conversation. Harrison spoke about wanting to buy more cattle. Evelyn shared Victoria McGregor visited the stall complaining William wouldn't get time in net now that Brendon Cook was back. Brian and Callum had a day's worth of wrestling moves to boast about. Charlotte bragged about Troy's assist. Troy took it all in. The only thing he spoke about was Charlotte's teeny-weeny turquoise bikini.

The tabletop looked like an abstract painting: gravy splattered from Grandma Spence's Lancashire hotpot, green peas, dotted splotches of butter, a random slice of potato, a dash of orange carrot. Troy heard his parents chatting in the kitchen; Gavin was acing his classes. Evelyn was slicing apple pie. Harrison was warming the Devon custard. Troy's belly was full and his head stuck on an 'in awe' Angelene Pratt. That was twice now Troy had witnessed her wide-eyed, childlike reaction to something. Unlike most people who got excited over a footy match, new clothes, or a vacation, it had been the farm and an indoor pool that made her smile. Not that Troy had seen her smile. She always hid it behind her fingers like it didn't belong on her face. He had hoped a snogging session with

Charlotte would bump Angelene out of his, or his mom's famous apple pie or talking to his dad about the Man U match. She was lingering again.

A loud burp tore Troy away from his thoughts. Brian guzzled his soda and released another belch, this one a deafening boom.

"Geez, Bri, there's a lady in our presence." Callum crumpled a paper napkin and pitched it at Brian. "What a pig."

Charlotte grinned at a younger version of Troy. While Brian had Evelyn Spence's sandy blonde hair and serious grey eyes, Callum, Troy, and Gavin inherited Harrison's chocolate brown hair and twinkly cobalt blue eyes.

"Like you don't burp, dolt." Brian let out a series of melodic belches, varying in tone, and smiled proudly. "You're just trying to impress Charlotte. Be a gentleman."

"Isn't *SmackDown* on?" Troy stacked his plate on Charlotte's. He kissed her cheek, hoping the touch of his lips against her skin would shoo Angelene from his head. It didn't work. "Can't you both go away?"

"Looking to have some rumpy pumpy," Callum said. He gathered the utensils and dumped them into the casserole dish. "I heard you in the hayloft. The poor cows having to listen to that."

"Jealous," Brian said.

"Babes was giving me a wee tickle, that's all."

"I know what he was tickling." Brian pushed back his chair and serenaded them with a resounding burp. "Are you coming, Cal? We need to snag the telly before dad puts on *Gangs of London*."

Callum scraped the chair across the scarred hardwood floor and raced around the table. He pecked Charlotte's cheek, laughing as he dodged Troy's fist.

"Don't let Callum bother you, babes. You're my sweet little crumpet."

Troy pushed his chair back. He stacked the rest of the plates, potato, gravy, and leftover peas squished from between them.

"I doubt you'll leave me for a fourteen-year-old."

"Why so glum, babes?" Charlotte grabbed the serving bowls and followed Troy into the kitchen. "You've been quiet since we got home. Is it Brendon? I saw him sneaking a peek at me in my bikini."

"Nothing is wrong. Other than my pain in the arse brothers."

Custard simmered on the stove. Huge wedges of apple pie oozing with filling sat by two mugs and a pot of tea. Troy set the plates on the counter and opened the dishwasher.

"I don't blame my mate for looking. You have an amazing body, just brilliant."

Charlotte slid the dishes across the counter and wrapped her arms around Troy from behind. She rested her cheek against his back and held him so tightly, he was afraid his dinner might come up.

"What did you think of Mrs. Pratt?" The question slipped out before he could stop himself. It was a good time to ask the question. Charlotte was in a lovey-dovey mood, and he could avoid looking into her eyes. He knew his cheeks were red. His heart felt like it was about to thud straight through his chest. He didn't have time to react to Charlotte's pinch. Her fingers crawled up his chest and latched onto his nipples.

"Why are you asking me that?"

Troy tugged at her fingers and placed her hands on his stomach. "You must have an opinion."

Charlotte lifted Troy's T-shirt. Her fingers danced over his skin, from his belly button to the top of his jeans.

"Don't try to distract me. I want to know."

"Ah, babes, I don't know."

Troy noted a strange tone to her voice, brittle, like the words would break and little tears would fall from the pieces.

"I can see why Mr. Pratt was interested in her." Charlotte's voice cracked. She held Troy tighter; her words blew into his back. "She's like a naïve woman-child, you know the type; men want to rescue her. There's something fragile about her, but..." Charlotte hesitated and shivered. "She'll tear you to shreds."

Troy grabbed Charlotte's hands and spun her around. He lifted her chin and stared into her ocean-blue eyes. He could have sworn she felt threatened, and it lashed at his heart.

"She doesn't compare to you."

"You think she's pretty, don't you? My sweet little crumpet has a crush."

"I do not."

Troy winced as Charlotte's fingers twisted his nipples.

"Troy Alexander, tell me the truth."

"She has lovely eyes."

He batted her hands away and drew her in for a hug. Troy kissed the crown of her head and held her like he was afraid she might slip away.

"I had a dream, babes. After we had some bouncy-bouncy in the hayloft, I drifted off in your arms." She trembled against him as she spoke. "I saw blood on Mrs. Pratt's hands. It ran down her wrists and forearms. She stood there staring at me. I tried to wake you. I tried to wake everyone. Mrs. Cook, Mr. Pratt, Magpie, Brendon, no one would wake up. Then Mr. Cook came along and whispered, 'She'll make a lovely corpse.' It reminded me of the Dickens quote Ms. Hudson shared in English last term. Then, when you finally woke up, you were hollow, like someone sucked all the sunshine from you, and you told me she only wanted a small piece of your light. You said you loved her."

"It was just a dream. I don't love Mrs. Pratt."

"Promise me, babes. I couldn't bear to lose you." Charlotte smiled and patted his bottom. "I'd have to date Callum."

Troy lifted her into his arms and kissed her. "You don't have to worry about Mrs. Pratt or any girl. I'm in love with you." Troy set her down and turned on the taps. "You fill the dishwasher and I'll start the pots.

We have pie to eat and that movie to watch. Did you bring sexy knickers to wear to bed?"

Charlotte lined up the plates in the dishwasher. "I brought those lilac boy shorts you like."

"They show the perfect amount of your bum."

Troy dunked a potato-crusted pot into the sudsy water. He stared out the kitchen window. Dusk had settled over the moors in shades of blue, purple, and grey. He didn't love Mrs. Pratt. He didn't even like her. She was Uncle Walt's wife.

"I doubt anyone will try to pull Mrs. Pratt. No one in Taunton messes with Walter Pratt. The man is a legend."

Charlotte set a serving dish on the rack and gave a little half-shrug. "My daddy did."

Troy shook the water from the pot and set it on the drying rack. "When?"

"Mr. Pratt took my mom on a date. It was after he joined the Royal Navy. He came home to see his mom and bumped into mine at Ball's Fish and Chips. They went to the pub."

"I thought your parents met at uni?" Troy swirled the dishcloth around a pot and dunked it in the water. "Aren't they the love of each other's lives?"

"When mom came home for Christmas break, daddy came with her and told Mr. Pratt to bugger off."

"I wouldn't want to piss Walter off. He almost punched out that punter who went after Brendon in the car park. Luckily, Mr. Cook was there."

"I doubt anyone will try to pull Mrs. Pratt. She's pretty; a makeover will surely turn her into a ten but without a personality to back it up, she'll rate about a five." Charlotte lined the utensils in the basket and started placing the glasses on the top rack. "I'm not going to let Mrs.

Pratt own a space in my head anymore, despite Maggie's feeling. Magpie needs to worry about Rachel Jones, disgusting ginger tart."

Troy pulled the plug and squeezed out the dishcloth. He hooked his toe under the lip of the cupboard and opened the door, tossing it into the 'to-be-washed' bucket. He'd do the same as Charlotte, close off all areas of his heart and head from Angelene.

"So, you're okay with me helping Mrs. Pratt if she needs something?" He'd try one more time to come clean.

"Stay away from her. Broken people do broken things. Let Mr. Pratt fix her."

Troy opened the drawer and grabbed two forks. He placed one on each plate and shut off the burner. Troy poured custard over each slice and set the pot on the stove.

"I promise."

I hope you know what you are saying. Breathe me in. Be my friend. Unfold me and stitch up my scars with your sunshine thread. The devil has spoken.

"Babes, you're spilling custard on the floor."

Troy dropped the plate on the counter, reaching for a tea towel. He mopped up the custard and tossed the cloth in the bucket.

How had Angelene slipped into his head?

"Babes, were you thinking about..."

Troy silenced her with a kiss. He touched his forehead to hers and forced his sunshine smile. "I got an assist today. Pretty good for a centre back."

"Footy, footy, always footy." Charlotte grabbed his plate and licked the custard before it dripped to the floor. "Come, my sweet little crumpet, the movie awaits. I chose the *Devil's Advocate*. Mom said it's one of Keanu Reeves' best."

Troy thought it was a fitting movie to watch.

Angelene

Angelene dragged on a cigarette and blew smoke towards the ceiling. She pictured herself chin-deep in Brendon's glow. A little pang struck her belly. God spoke; she was doing a lousy job being a wife.

"I made you another tea."

Angelene dropped the cigarette and cranked the window closed.

"I told you I get anxious around people."

Walter grabbed a can of linen-scented air freshener and aimed it in Angelene's direction. "A group of strangers I can understand. Those are my friends. Your friends."

Angelene wiped the spray from her cheeks, bowing her head. Explanations, expectations. The shot to the belly was stronger, fierce. God was furious.

"Why aren't you wearing one of those nightgowns I bought you?" Walter sniffed and drenched the air with spray. "Do you suffer from haphephobia?"

"Why must you use big words? I don't understand."

"Do you fear me touching you?" he said, setting the can down. "You squirm, roll away. An old pair of boxers will surely deter me."

"They belonged to my friend Roman Krieger. I don't have much to remember him by. I won't get rid of them."

She studied Walter's face, looking for icy eyes, a façade of a smile. Overindulging fogged her brain.

"Another lover?"

Angelene groaned and slid off the nightstand. She thumped to the bathroom and slammed open the medicine cabinet, *act this way, wear this, sit up straight, eat, no more wine.* A different emotion clung to every word. The beehive of electricity was dizzying. Angelene bit into her tongue, grinding until she tasted blood. She brushed her teeth and spit a crimson blob into the sink. The buzzing softened to a hum.

"Next time we go to dinner, you'll watch the drink. You didn't even join us for tea and pudding, just stared at the painting."

"Have you looked at it? It's exquisite."

She tossed the toothbrush onto the vanity, scrambled across the room, and tucked herself under the blankets.

"Give me a kiss."

Angelene flicked his lips and curled into a ball. "Go away."

Walter finished her tea, walked to the bathroom, and grabbed his toothbrush. "Haphephobia, little bird."

"I don't kiss. You taste a person's breath, their teeth."

"Kissing is lovely; makes you feel like a teenager again."

She tugged the blankets around her neck; memories collided around her head. "A boy tried to kiss me once. He said it would taste like lemon macaron and champagne. Kissing is disgusting, spit dripping in your mouth."

Walter switched off the bathroom light. The mattress creaked as he lay on the bed. "Plenty of women would be thrilled to have sex with me."

"You've told me before."

"I suppose you have a headache."

Angelene drew the blankets over her head. "We have a party to prepare for; you'll want me on my best behaviour. Let me sleep."

Walter grumbled and thumped to his side.

She would try normal again. Be the perfect host, present a beautiful home, mingle, and shine.

'With what light? I lost mine years ago.'

8 Plucking Feathers

Walter

Beams of sunlight stabbed through the clouds, illuminating a black silk dress.

"Isn't it lovely?" Walter said. His gaze shifted from the smoke dangling from her mouth to the one flipping between her fingers. He took the unlit cigarette and slipped it into his pocket.

"I'll look like the nuns outside Sacre Coeur."

Angelene slumped on the edge of the nightstand and lit the cigarette "Must you be so incorrigible?"

Grey smoke curled around the words as she spoke. "I don't know what that means."

"You don't want to reform, improve."

"There's nothing wrong with me."

She inhaled deeply and blew out a mouthful of smoke. Walter grabbed the air freshener and squirted it at her.

"That dress isn't me. I should be able to pick out my own clothes."

"It's a Stella McCartney."

Angelene ran her arm over her face and raised her chin defiantly. "Who's that?"

"A popular fashion designer, Paul and Linda's daughter." Walter pulled the cigarette from her mouth and smashed it in the ashtray. He pulled a Tiffany blue box out of his pocket and snapped it open. "Would these make you feel better?"

Angelene stared at the Tahitian pearls. "Always wanting to hide my wrists."

"My friends aren't daft. I won't give them anymore to talk about."

"Why are you trying to change me?" Angelene slid her foot into a black pump. "These shoes impressed Victoria. What is it about red soles?" She kicked it off; it shot like an expensive bullet and landed at Walter's feet.

He picked up the shoe and placed it beside the other. "I'm not trying to change you, just the way you dress."

"I'm going to read."

Walter marched behind her. He had convinced himself over a round of scotch with colleagues, he would make a good husband. He had sown his wild oats, been the envy of the House of Commons. The defiant mood was making it difficult to enjoy matrimonial bliss.

"Two glasses of wine tonight."

"I'll be a good girl."

"I almost forgot." Walter handed her a black silk bag. The contents clicked and rattled. "For you."

Angelene stared at the bag. "What's this?"

"Makeup. I don't know what any of it is. My secretary Juliette said it was all the essentials."

Angelene tossed the bag onto the island and scrunched her eyebrows. "I don't wear makeup. I wouldn't know how to put it on."

"You're an artist. Paint your face as you would a canvas."

"It's not the same."

"You'll find some magazines in my briefcase. Study the models."

Angelene filled the kettle, set it on the stove, and clicked on the burner. "I don't want to look like a clown."

Walter rubbed her back and brushed his lips over her hair. "Poor little January girl, always so wintry."

"Hello, friend." Angelene kneeled on the window bench, touched her lips, and smiled.

Walter fetched olives and cheese from the fridge, placing them on the counter. "Who are you speaking to?"

"A rabbit."

He grinned and grabbed two knives. "Will you help?"

Angelene bounced off the bench and joined him. "You're smiling. You're not angry anymore. I asked God to make you happy."

"I wasn't angry. I was annoyed." Walter unscrewed the lid and handed the jar to her. "I'm trying to help you feel comfortable. Has someone told you you don't deserve nice things?"

"My mother," Angelene said, dumping the olives into a crystal bowl.

"You look the part; people will stop talking." Walter sliced through a brick of cheddar. "Taunton will see an improved Angelene Pratt."

"Why are you going to so much trouble? Planning a party, buying me a fancy dress?"

Walter arranged the cheese on a tray and positioned a wheel of brie in the middle. "I want my friends to know I'm happy."

"You want a perfect wife," she said, swiping a piece of cheddar and pecking at it. "I doubt it's in me. However, I'll try normal again. It's a little ill-fitting."

Walter chuckled and tossed a tea bag in the pot. "We'll be the power couple of Taunton."

Angelene folded the cheese in two and ate it. After she finished chewing, she spoke. "Not the Cooks?"

"You'll have more influence than Sofia." Walter poured water into the pot and scrutinized his little bird: tangled waves of blonde, delicate fingers, pale skin. Pluck a few more straggly feathers and she'd be perfect.

"I've never fit, not at school, at work, not even as a daughter."

"Everything I touch turns to gold."

"Shall I call you King Midas?" A shadow of a smile haunted her mouth. "Golden fingertips."

Walter stretched a sheet of plastic wrap over the bowl. It was a fitting nickname. Things had always worked out for Walter. Whatever he set his mind to, he achieved. After finishing A-levels, he joined the Royal Navy in the warfare branch. He couldn't be James Bond, but he could be close enough—sail the seven seas and defend his country. Walter told David before leaving Taunton he would work his way through the ranks, and he did just that, from officer to midshipman to Lieutenant Commander. Walter still hadn't finished. He was determined to join the Special Boat Service and led a team of highly trained men on classified missions. When England was looking for a Secretary of State for Defence. The only person qualified to do the job—Walter Pratt. He hadn't failed.

Walter poured tea into a cup and handed it to his latest project. Doubts had surfaced but he was Walter Pratt; failure was never a choice.

"Just how you like it, black."

"No milk or sugar? You aren't trying to change that?"

Walter grabbed his mug and followed her to the garden. They sat on the stoop, warmed by the sun. Anxious Angelene averted.

"What have we learned about each other today?"

Angelene watched the rabbit hop along the grass, stop and nibble at a patch of clover. "You like the Rolling Stones, cheddar cheese, and you want an elegant wife. Now you."

"You love Dickens almost as much as Victor Hugo, Psalm 51, and you made friends with a rabbit." Walter nodded towards the remains of the barn, beams and stone. "He's moved over there. Should I have the barn demolished?"

"It looks like it has grown from the soil. Leave it."

"I have some splendid memories in there."

Angelene propped her elbows on her knees and cradled the mug in her hands. "Share them with me."

Walter rested against the door frame and grinned nostalgically. "David and I smoked and drank in there, talked about girls."

"You smoked? And David?"

"We thought ciggies made us look cool. It lasted a week."

Angelene swallowed a small sip, her eyes moved along the golden horizon and up the hill. "Why wouldn't you sit at the manor? All those rooms and gardens?"

"Richard." Walter took a long sip of tea, set the mug on the stoop, and wound his arm around her. "The expectations he put on David were ridiculous, and the temper. The man was a brute."

"Where's David's mother?" Angelene said, leaning her cheek against him.

"Elizabeth passed after David got married. She hung on long enough to know he would be safe. That used to be her room," Walter said, pointing to Brendon's bedroom window. "She would sit and knit, waiting for David to come home. Elizabeth was a kind woman."

"Your light has dimmed. King Midas has a heart," Angelene said. "How did she pass?"

"Years of abuse and neglect took her before cancer did. That house, as beautiful as it is, has seen more sadness than happy times."

"What happened to Richard?"

Walter grabbed his mug and swallowed his tea. "He got what was coming to him." He moved his gaze to the barn, and his eyes brightened. "I lost my virginity in the barn."

Angelene hid her smile and snuggled into his chest. "With the animals watching?"

"Her name was Prudence. Everyone called her Pru."

"How is Prudence?"

Walter chuckled. "She's about three times the size and has six nippers."

"What a horrible thing to say."

"It's the truth. I saw her at Tesco pushing two trolleys. One full of groceries, the other packed with kids."

Angelene sipped her tea and looked at Walter. "Your mother and father. Will I ever meet them?"

A warm breeze ruffled Walter's hair. He gazed around the garden with a head full of memories. His father had been no better than David's. Geoffrey Pratt's abuse came in the form of silence. His mother, Audrey, had been quiet and dutiful, doing all the things a wife should do. All it got her was a cheating husband and a wild son.

"My father left us when I was ten. Followed his heart and a woman to Canada. I haven't heard from him since he sent me twenty quid for finishing A-levels. Mom lives with her sister and the ten cats they adopted in Bath. I'll take you to meet her sometime."

Walter hooked his thumb through the mug handles and pressed his lips in her hair. "Shall we?"

"What are we doing now?"

They walked into the farmhouse. Walter set the mugs in the sink and pointed to a recipe in a worn cookbook. "This. It's a favourite of mine."

Angelene whispered the recipe title and tilted her head quizzically. "Potted cheese? Do you serve it on the stove like fondue?"

Walter stared at the girl who was nothing like the others.

You think there's a heaven in her; she's all devil.

Douchette's warning hijacked him. The hair on the back of his neck rose. After wishing Walter good luck, Pierre Piedmont had something else to say. It blasted through Walter's head like a red warning light.

Loving her would be like a slice to the throat. Quick and fast.

Angelene ran her hand over his and pulled him out of his reverie. "I thought the ghosts lived at Rosewood Manor. You're spooked."

"Haunted by memories, little bird, back to the potted cheese."

"Do you plant it like a seed and wait for something delicious to grow?"

"You blend the ingredients and spread it on baguette."

"Your words are green."

Walter would have coloured himself cowardly yellow.

Brendon

Four on four at the pitch, not a goal scored, not from the corner or on a rebound, he had been on fire. Brendon was happy.

"Do you have your suit?" Sofia said.

David turned down the corner of the newspaper and grinned at the disdain on Brendon's face.

Brendon slid onto a stool, poured a cup of coffee, and scratched at the stubble on his chin. "You've asked a hundred bloody times."

"Are you going to shave that stuff off your face?"

"I don't have time. Maggie's waiting."

Sofia dunked toast into a poached egg. "You look scruffy like that riffraff we saw hanging around the docks in Clevedon,"

David spoke from behind the newspaper. "Leave him alone. Isn't it enough he's giving up an evening socializing with his parents?"

"You have such a lovely face. Why hide it?"

"It doesn't look that bad."

Brendon studied himself in the toaster. The dark stubble disguised his lovely face.

Sofia took a sip of coffee. Her gaze transfixed on him. "You can't see the cleft in your chin."

"No one cares, Mammina."

Brendon grabbed a slice of toast, rose, and draped the garment bag over his arm.

"I do." Sofia set down her cup and rattled the newspaper. "Isn't there something in that code of yours about appearance?"

"Don't get me involved," David said.

Brendon stuffed the toast in his mouth; crumbs dusted his hoodie.

"Where are your manners lately?"

"I'm saving them for tonight." He chuckled at Sofia's displeasure. From within his hoodie pouch, his cell phone buzzed.

"Wipe your mouth. Then give me a stubbly kiss."

Brendon stared at the screen. Every contact had a Bundesliga team logo attached to it, except Troy; he had the Premier League lion. He ripped a paper towel off the roll, swiped it across his lips, and shoved it in his pocket. His phone rang again.

David folded the newspaper and reached for a pitcher of orange juice. "I'd give her a kiss, or you'll be stuck here all day."

He brushed his lips over Sofia's cheek, puzzled by the mysterious caller.

"If your mother asks. You want to go to Burnham," David called.

Brendon shoved his feet into his trainers and swiped his finger across the phone. "I can't understand you... stop crying... I'll be right there."

He ran to his car, hung the suit bag, and slid behind the wheel. Puffs of sand blew up around the tires. Brendon turned onto the farmhouse lane, texted Maggie an apology, and rambled up the walkway. He pushed open the front door; lemony cleaners masked the fresh paint smell. The floors sparkled; banister glistened. The house was tidy and deathly quiet. Brendon walked towards the mudroom. The door was ajar. He stumbled and jammed his heels into a line of wellies. Angelene clutched a rabbit to her chest, her face washed in tears.

"There's a goshawk." She trembled and fell against his chest. "My rabbit... it's dead."

Brendon could feel the heat of the animal through his hoodie.

"I couldn't find anything to scare it away."

Brendon scanned the sky, following the wisps of clouds. There was no bird, just endless blue.

"It's gone."

"Are you sure? Check the trees."

A thump hit his chest. Another whack knocked his stomach. Its black nose twitched.

"The rabbit is alive." Brendon ran his fingers through the animal's fur. "There's no blood."

Angelene sniffed and nuzzled its tawny neck.

"Put it down. It'll hop to its den."

Angelene knelt; the rabbit stretched and bounced from her arms. They walked into the house. She sagged onto a stool.

"Where's Walter?"

Angelene snuffled and wiped her eyes with the back of her hand. "He's gone for bits of bob."

Brendon stifled his laugh. "It's bits and bobs. He must be excited about the party."

"It's all he's talked about."

"Why did you ring me?"

Her shoulders drooped, her mouth full and pretty, pouted. Brendon tucked the moment away with the others.

"I'm not sure. You were busy."

"I was listening to Mom complain about my stubble."

A dribble of snot filled the bow of her lip. Brendon reached inside his pocket and dabbed her nose.

"Walter wouldn't have come home to help."

Brendon handed her the crumpled napkin. "Not for a rabbit. He hunts."

"He doesn't understand how precious God's creatures are. The peacocks, pigeons, even Victor Hugo was my friend."

A pang struck Brendon's heart. "Who's Victor?"

"The statue at the Sorbonne."

"You were friends with a statue?"

"It's Victor Hugo," Angelene said, in a tone that suggested everyone would make friends with a statue. "*The Hunchback of Notre Dame* is one of my favourite books. I would sit at his feet every day. Hugo never judged."

"He isn't real."

"He was real to me."

Brendon stuffed his hands into his hoodie pocket. Friends with a rabbit, a statue. She gave new meaning to the word lonely.

"I've had very few friends. Most have gone away." Angelene propelled the magazine across the island. "Look at that girl. Do you think she's pretty?"

Brendon glanced at the cover model. "Too much makeup."

"Walter wants me to look like that."

The model was attractive in a 'made-up' kind of way. There was nothing special, nothing interesting or unique. Nothing captivated his attention quite like the wistful girl sitting in front of him.

"I think you're pretty just the way you are."

Angelene looked up at him with watery grey-green eyes. "You don't think I need makeup?"

"I don't, but if Uncle Walt asked, then it's best you wear it."

"Your mother wants you to shave, and you don't."

"I've always done as I was told. It feels good to go against Mammina."

"Your light is incredibly bright today."

"I don't get this light you're talking about. Most people would say I'm a moody arse."

"I don't believe it."

"I get in my head, brood as Mammina says."

"Brooding or not, you're beautiful."

Brendon cursed. The attempt to downplay his looks kept failing.

"My agent got me an ad campaign for a protein powder. He said it helps get you noticed. It got me seen in the wrong way. I want to be known for being ace on the pitch."

"You are and you will continue to be."

"Not if girls keep putting lists on Facebook. They never say the best keepers in the Southern League, just the dishiest."

"Beauty is more than a handsome face. You fought for ninety minutes yesterday, the determination and passion." Angelene twisted her hair into a braid. "I wish I had light like yours."

Brendon breathed in the moment. Her slight smile, her clear eyes.

"You sure see the world differently."

"There's beauty in everything. The leaves on the tree, a cloudy sky, the prickly thistles, you."

Her honesty swept over him. Guilt stepped in and knocked him back to reality.

"I should get going. I was supposed to be at Maggie's over an hour ago. It isn't right to keep her waiting."

It was wrong to allow Angelene to sink into his head. It wasn't right to find her so beautiful.

Maggie's house was in the middle of a row of terraced homes. The stamp sized lawn was overgrown. Ivy looked like it was sneezed from the short brick fence that framed the front of the property.Candy wrappers fluttered on the sidewalk. Evidence that a hyper little boy lived in the aging home cluttered the walkway and a sunlit patch of grass: Batman action figures, toy cars, and random blocks.

Brendon leaned against the car, preparing himself for an afternoon of babysitting. He glanced into the bay window. Jack jumped on the sofa, still in his pyjamas, hair sticking up like he'd stuck his finger in a light socket. The first time Maggie introduced Jack; Brendon asked if he liked football. The response was a spray of spit and a karate kick to the shin.

Brendon grabbed his garment bag and sauntered up the walkway. Yarrow and grass sprouted between the cobblestones. He opened the smudged door and kicked his shoes into a mountain of overturned wellies and shoes. The scent of sweaty socks and fabric softener wafted around him.

'There's beauty in everything. Find the bloody beauty.'

"Jack, come eat, or you can go to your room."

"Brendon the dolt is here."

A whoosh of black fabric blew past Brendon. Jack skidded to a stop, swirling his cape. He stuck out his tongue and sprayed a mist of spit across the hardwood.

Brendon hung the garment bag from a coat rack and tried to take the edge off his voice. "Listen to your sister. Go eat."

"You can't tell me what to do," Jack hollered. He slid into Maggie, ripped a box of cereal from her hand, and laughed maniacally.

"I hate Sundays," Maggie said, swiping her hand across her forehead.

Crumbs crunched under Brendon's feet as he followed her to the front room. Newspapers and magazines covered the coffee table. Toppled buckets of blocks covered the battered hardwood. Brendon swiped a half-eaten biscuit onto the floor and sank onto the threadbare sofa.

"Will Walter's party be as posh as your mom's?"

"Don't expect caviar and champagne. Think lager and sausage rolls."

"I tried caviar at your mom's do. I didn't like how it burst in my mouth."

"You wouldn't."

"Gosh, Brendon, what else did you learn in Dortmund other than football, dirty wanker." Maggie pushed an assortment of books to the floor and flopped beside him. "What's Walter celebrating?"

"He wants to do things married couples do, have dinner parties and stuff."

Maggie pulled at a pill on a throw pillow. "I hope Mrs. Pratt is covered up this time. You'll be gawking at her again."

Brendon shoved his hands into his armpits and dropped his head against the tattered cushion. "I wish you would stop obsessing over Mrs. Pratt."

The voice in his head spoke, *so should you.*

"Do you think she's pretty?" Maggie said, winding her hair around her finger. "Troy thinks she has lovely eyes. He got a pinch for saying that."

"Not really." He pressed his mouth against hers, silencing her with a kiss.

"Yuck. I'm telling Mom you were snogging." Jack arched his arm, pressed his tongue against his upper lip, and whipped Batman across the room. Brendon shot out his hand and caught it. Jack dashed from the room. Wet, bubbly laughter exploded through the house.

Maggie smiled. "Sorry."

Brendon didn't know if she was smiling an apologetic 'I'm-sorry-my-brother-is-a-dolt' grin or an amused 'That's-what-you-get-for-fancying-Mrs. Pratt' smile.

"Sunday wouldn't be Sunday without getting drenched in spit or having toys chucked at my head."

He scooted across the couch and leaned in for a kiss. Maggie placed her hand over her lips.

"No snogging."

Brendon breathed away the frustration. He reached for the remote, flicked through the channels, and stopped at the football highlights.

"Do you want a brew?"

"I can think of something better than tea."

Maggie giggled and slid off the sofa. "You're such a wanker."

"I wouldn't be if you'd do it for me."

"I heard that, Brendon Cook." Maggie broke into song, *Sandra Dee* from *Grease.* She had been a shoo in for the part. In more ways than one.

Brendon settled into the couch and winced as a toy car jabbed his back. He whipped it into an explosion of coloured blocks and analyzed an Arsenal goal.

"Bloody hell. Why didn't he move to the left? He would've made the save."

"What are you going on about?" Maggie said, handing him tea.

"The keeper. He didn't read the play. No wonder Tottenham scored."

"Football, football, that's all you *ever* talk about."

"It's the greatest sport on earth." He sipped the tea and made a face. "You put sugar in it."

Maggie nestled into the corner of the couch and folded her leg underneath her. "Milk and sugar, right?"

"We've been together two years, and you still can't get it right. Just milk."

A heavy bounce and thump stomped overhead. To Brendon's amazement, silence swept through the house.

"Is Jack getting some kip?"

A crash and thud kicked hope out of Brendon.

"He barely napped as a baby. Why would he start now?"

"To give me a bloody break. Bouncing out of bloody bed, bouncing around the house."

"Jack is a spirited child."

A block flew from the foyer. It spiralled through the air and plunked into Brendon's mug, splashing tea on his hoodie. Brendon set the mug down and dabbed at the stain. Jack fluttered his cape and flung himself into a karate stance, inches from Brendon's face.

"Hi-ya." He spun around and punched the air. "Why can't Charlie come over?"

Maggie hid her smile behind her mug. "I'll see if her and Troy can come next Sunday."

"I don't like Troy. The last time he was here, he kept kissing Charlie and smiling that daft smile of his." Jack wiggled his tongue at Brendon, flapped his cape and charged from the room.

"Jack fancies Charlie. The only time he sits still is when she's here. He stares at her with this look on his face."

"You better tell Troy he has competition."

"Jack looks at Charlie like you do Mrs. Pratt," Maggie said, staring into her tea.

"I'm trying to figure her out like everyone else."

"Do you think she has lovely eyes?"

Brendon clenched his hands, sparks lit. "I'm going home if you don't quit. I'd rather listen to Mom complain about my stubble than you droning on about Walter's wife. I repeat, *Walter's wife.*"

"Answer the question."

"I think… bloody hell, can you drop it? I've missed the Premier League highlights. Troy and I will have nothing to talk about in English."

"You could discuss the novel."

Brendon scrubbed his face and groaned. Rule seven: honesty.

"Sometimes I think she's pretty and sometimes she looks like a girl I'd pass on the street."

Maggie slurped her tea. "I get a strange feeling when she's around."

'*Me too,*' Brendon thought. "Mom said the same thing."

"It's like something bad is going to happen and I won't be able to stop it, like someone is going to get hurt."

"Don't be daft. Mrs. Pratt is awkward and shy; that makes people uncomfortable."

A thunder of footsteps boomed above their heads. Brendon clicked off the television and tossed the remote onto a stack of crinkled magazines.

"Would you like to go for ice cream? The place on Sycamore Close has gelato."

"You sure you want to take Jack for ice cream?"

"I want to stop him running around the house."

It wasn't how Brendon wanted to spend his afternoon. If it meant he didn't have to listen to Jack's bouncing or about Maggie's strange feeling, he'd do it.

Brendon fixed his tie and smoothed it against his chest. The voices in his head had awakened from their slumber, hissing, stretching through his mind and thoughts, entrancing him under a spell of anxiety. Leave *Mrs. Pratt alone. Sneak a peek. Look at your girlfriend, pretty, springtime Margaret. Pure, virginal, good little girl.*

"How do I look? Mom did a great job with my hair. It's a braided low bun, so sophisticated."

"You look beautiful."

It wasn't a lie. She looked pretty, typical Maggie pretty in a ruffled, capped sleeved dress.

"You behave yourself with my girl," Kevin Thornton said, slapping an overworked hand on Brendon's shoulder. "I worked on your mom's Maserati. The parts are as expensive as the car."

"Another bash?" Rosie said. "Is that all you toffs do?"

"Yup, Mrs. Thornton, every bloody night."

Outside, the air was fresh and wonderful. It snaked through Brendon's lungs, warm and clean. He opened the car door for Maggie, curious if Angelene could pull off being a host.

"You'd think it was our first date," Maggie said.

They coasted past the moors darkened by night's arrival. His mind was cluttered with thoughts of Angelene. Had she slaved all day, prepped for the party, planned the perfect menu, a signature cocktail? It would take a level of comfortability to prep and plan. Brendon grinned. Comfortable, and Angelene went together like vinegar and bleach.

"Your mom's proud to be middle class. She works hard, which makes her better than my mom who comes from money. She doesn't stop and think my Nonno built the textile mill from nothing. She thinks footballers are egotistical womanizers."

"It doesn't matter what my mom thinks about you. I like you."

Brendon parked alongside the ditch. The farmhouse was alive and bright. He grabbed her hand and led her up the walkway. Wisteria drooped overhead. Brendon opened the door and was greeted by the upbeat tempo of the Rolling Stones.

"What's that smell?" Maggie said, fanning her nose.

'It doesn't smell like bloody feet.'

"Incense."

Maggie stood in the doorway of the front room, plugged her nose with her fingers, and gazed around it. "What did she do to Walter's front room?"

"Decorated it."

"It's... I don't know how to describe it."

"I like it. The blue wall is nice."

Maggie took her fingers off her nose and exhaled. "You would."

Aromas, buttery pastries and cider, drifted from the kitchen. The display of artisanal cheeses, crudité, and hors d'oeuvres was grand and decadent.

"At least the sitting room looks normal," Maggie said.

The walls were chalk white, splashes of shamrock green livened the curtains and throw pillows. A monstrous sofa had taken up residence in the once barren space. It was dull compared to the colours and patterns in the rest of the house.

"Sweetheart, over here."

Women smiled in that way that said, '*What a good boy.*' He mumbled polite hellos and edged through the crowd.

"This is some turnout."

"Free food and drink, more opportunity to gossip." Sofia fiddled with his lapels that did not need to be adjusted and brushed away imaginary lint. "Why wouldn't they come?"

Brendon searched the sea of faces. Victoria grinned at him from behind an overfilled plate. It was as artificial as she was. Simone winked and mouthed a sultry 'hello.'

"Where's Uncle Walt?"

"I haven't seen him since we got here," David said.

Brendon rubbed his finger under his nose. "No Mrs. Pratt?"

"She's getting ready," Sofia said.

David grinned and patted Sofia's hip. "If she's anything like you, we'll be waiting all night."

"It takes time to look this good."

The absence of host and hostess raised a prickle of uneasiness in Brendon. Everywhere he looked, guests smiled, ate, sang along with Mick Jagger. This was Walter's time to shine—*look at me, look at my beautiful home, my perfect wife.* Brendon's stomach twisted. Something was off. The thread that tied him to Angelene was drawing him from the room.

"I'm going to the loo." He tossed a sausage roll at Maggie and flashed her a dimply smile.

"Stay away from Mrs. Batra. She's as bad as Rachel Jones," Maggie said.

Brendon slipped out of the room. The stairs creaked, a muffled '*Put the damn dress on*' seeped from under the closed door. Heavy footsteps approached. The thread strangled him.

Brendon ducked into the bathroom. A groan floated down the hall, followed by thumps and Walter apologizing for Angelene's tardiness.

'*Go back to Maggie, eat, talk football, get ogled by Mrs. Batra.*'

Something pulled him toward the bedroom. The strangling thread? The sound of whimpers?

Angelene sat on the edge of the bed, little bits of torn tissue at her feet.

"We had a wonderful day. I was doing normal things. His eyes changed to icy blue so quickly."

Brendon wiggled his tie and peered over his shoulder. Conversation, Van Morrison, laughter. He stepped over the threshold and froze. He was in Walter's room, with Walter's wife.

Angelene walked to the full-length mirror and dabbed the mascara staining her cheeks. She gripped handfuls of chartreuse silk and shook the fabric.

"This dress is me."

"Walt means well. He used to pick out clothes for Anastasia. She bloody loved it."

"He throws names at me like I'm supposed to know who they are." Her face went slack. She slashed at her thighs. "I want to wear *my* clothes. It would be easier to do normal things if I were comfortable."

"If it makes you feel better. Mom picked out mine and Dad's suits."

He had checked in, made sure she was okay, promise not broken. It was time to get back to his normal.

"I hate that dress. I hate Walter demands I wear it."

"You want those women to stop gossiping, don't you?"

Brendon glanced into the hall. The conversation had turned to Brexit; Tom Jones replaced Van Morrison. He lifted her chin and brushed his thumb over a smudge of mascara. "Put the dress on. They'll have nothing to talk about."

"Those women won't stop talking whether I wear this or that hideous dress. What's wrong with what I'm wearing?"

The slip of chartreuse skimmed over her body, highlighting her curves and pert breasts.

"I wish you could see what I do. You'd understand how bloody wrong it is."

"I thought Walter would want to show me off. He rambles on and on about his reputation and image."

"He wants you to look as posh as he does. That's how Walt makes an impression."

Brendon yanked a tissue from the box and dabbed her cheeks.

"I don't look like that girl in the magazine anymore. It took over an hour perfecting my makeup."

"Not quite."

Angelene jerked the dress from the hanger and tossed it on the bed. "I will wear the McCartney. She's the daughter of people I should know." She scrunched her nose at the white satin lapels. "I have this persistent knot in my belly, reminding me how out of place I am. My zipper, please."

Brendon's gaze drifted down her spine to the swoop of her bottom. Creaks and rattles came at him from every corner. He tugged at the pull. The dress fell around her feet. Black lace panties, no bra.

"Will you do me a favour?" Angelene said.

"Don't turn around, please."

"Will you keep your lamp on for me, so I know you're always there?"

"I promise."

Angelene

Angelene stared at the glow in Brendon's window. Walter's soft breathing filled the room. The night had been long. She listened to Simone prattle on about her love of Paris and Sofia talk about antiques. It had been a dizzying day of emotions, mourning the rabbit that was not dead, feeling something for Walter, then despising him. Washing herself in Brendon's light.

'Is it wrong, God, to be Brendon's friend? I could break a pattern this time.'

She had been an okay wife for part of the day. Normal sort of fit.

'I promise to continue to do wife things, keep a clean house, practice cooking. If I can do that part of normal, then I can be a friend too. I'll try again, God. This time I will get it right.'

9 Verschlimmbessern

Brendon

English had not been on Brendon's mind. He bumbled through French and fell asleep in the dining hall. The promise to leave his lamp on had him dragging his ass through training and classes. Brendon stripped off his school uniform and threw it onto a pile of clean clothes. He rummaged around the closet for his typical outfit: T-shirt, hoodie, jeans and dressed.

"It looks like Burnham-on-Sea won. We're off to Bridgwater Bay," Sofia said.

"I thought you liked that house. You're always going on about old bones and Edward."

He picked up a notebook, flipped through the pages and tossed it onto the dresser.

"The house is Edwardian, and it's lovely. The Pratts are joining us."

An ache bounced up Brendon's spine and coiled around his shoulders. He dug under a stack of football magazines, grabbed a notebook decorated with Dortmund logos and jammed it into his backpack.

"You haven't given her a chance. No one has."

"There are things in her past that are..." Sofia paused as if searching for the right word and rattled her bangles. "Questionable."

"You sound like your friends."

"Do you know why she was late for the party?" Sofia fluffed the throw pillows, adjusted them, and rearranged them again. "She refused to wear the dress. It was a McCartney."

"Who cares? She should be able to wear what she wants."

He yanked a textbook from a teetering tower. The stack toppled and banged onto the floor. Sparks lit and sizzled.

"Walter has certain expectations. Slinky dresses don't fit them."

Brendon snatched the book off the floor. He bit down on the words floundering around his tongue, sorting through what he wanted to say and what he should.

"She must have dressed like that in Paris."

"Why are you so concerned with how people treat her? It's about respect for her husband."

Brendon brushed past Sofia. He swiped a pen off his dresser and shoved it into his backpack. "People should respect her."

"Sexy isn't about letting everything hang out. Sexy is leaving things to the imagination."

"I doubt Angelene is trying to be sexy. End of conversation."

Sofia grabbed a hanger from beneath the mountain of clothes and hung his blazer. "Why are you in a mood? School's over."

"I ignored Margaret at Walt's do. She's making me study." He tore his backpack off the bed and marched to the hall with Sofia in tow.

"If you weren't cornered by Simone, you were gawking at Angelene."

"I wasn't gawking at Mrs. Pratt, bloody hell, Mammina," he said, pounding down the stairs.

Amelia scurried into the foyer, an apple and protein bar in hand. "Don't forget your snack."

Brendon counted his breaths: one... two. The sparks crackled.

"Thank you, Ame."

She patted his arm and smiled warmly. "Breathe. Breathe the entire way to Maggie's."

"No kiss?" Sofia said.

"You accused me of gawking at Mrs... No."

He left the foyer and breathed through the sparks. Guilt twisted around his throat. Had it been that obvious? He had mingled, talked to Kate about football, entertained Simone's flirting. Brendon sank onto the seat and started the car, cursing himself and Angelene's lace knickers.

Dense grey clouds dominated the sky. Taunton was brooding with him. Brendon drove down the crumbling tarmac. The world transformed from fields of green to rows of brown. The aging terraced homes sagged into one another, joined by brick-fenced gardens. Maggie's cat, Suki, lay across the bricks, her paws crossed, keeping a watchful eye on the street. Brendon parked alongside the curb and imagined fat raindrops, pummelling the sparks. One plunk, two.

The door opened. Maggie leaned into the frame and tapped her thigh. Suki jumped from the fence and plodded up the walkway behind Brendon.

"I booted up my laptop."

"No hello."

Suki purred and rubbed around his ankles. He ran his hand over her fur and threw his backpack into the entry.

"Your mood hasn't changed."

Brendon brushed past Maggie, wiped crumbs from the cushion, and dropped onto the sofa. He could come clean, tell her Angelene has a heart-shaped bottom, confess he had followed the hills and valleys of her spine. He leaned across the sofa and kissed her.

"You taste sweet."

"I ate a bag of jelly cherries."

Brendon held her cheek in his hand and kissed her just how she liked it, gentle and slow. A different kind of spark, the one he had gotten good at ignoring, ignited. He tugged her hand towards his crotch.

"Homework," Maggie said between kisses.

"Soon."

"Will you quit it," she said, pushing at his chest. "What's got into you?"

'Black lace knickers.'

Brendon blew out a sigh and raked his fingers through his hair. "Do you know what Troy and Charlie did today?"

Maggie unzipped his backpack, grabbed his notebook, and tossed it on his lap. "They did *it* in the custodian's cupboard."

"Tilly thought it was funny. She almost peed her knickers; she was laughing so hard."

Maggie wiggled the mouse. A picture of her and Brendon sitting in the rose garden at the manor flashed on the screen. "Matilda sounds like a pig when she laughs, squealing and snorting. It's as annoying as her gum chewing."

Brendon folded open his notebook and stared at the question, 'Find a quote that shows Werther's love for Lotte.'

Maggie opened a file titled 'Old Assignments I Aced' and clicked on the A+ report. "I heard something else today."

"Dawson will expel me before first term ends."

"Rachel gave you an origami envelope filled with blue Smarties?"

Brendon groaned and pressed open the novel.

"Did she?" Maggie dug her tooth into her lip. After a few chews, she spoke. "Your ears are red."

The stuffy, sock-smelling air was scorching and smothering. Maggie's whingeing about Rachel and Mrs. Pratt lit the sparks he was trying to avoid. Brendon thumbed through the book, and a quote jumped from the page.

'I have so much in me, and the feeling for her absorbs it all; I have so much, and without her it all comes to nothing.' Bloody hell, Goethe, you hit the nail on the head.'

"I gotta go."

A war began in Brendon's head. A gentle voice whispered, *go back to Maggie and apologize.* The other, which he had named Padre Diavolo, pushed him to the farmhouse and willed his hand to knock on the door.

"Bonjour, mon ami."

She looked as sad as her voice, holey black leggings, his hoodie, hair in a messy ponytail. She rubbed the cuff over her bloodshot eyes and tugged his hand. Brendon followed her up the stairs. Paint cans and rollers littered the hall. She had painted the walls chocolate brown.

Brendon froze at the bedroom door. Clothes lay like dead bodies over the floor and bed. "Bloody hell, if Walt sees this." He picked up a beaded camisole, folded it into a square, and placed it on the dresser.

"Walter can fuck off." Every syllable was set to a piercing frequency. "I've disappointed him, embarrassed him. Your mother will take me shopping for clothes."

"What can I do to help?"

"Stay and have tea. I need to sort through this mess. I'm scared of what I might do to myself."

Brendon glanced at the faded scars on her forearm. "I'll stay."

"Tea first." Her tone softened. The darkness swept from her eyes. "Milk, oui?"

"You remembered, bloody hell, Maggie still can't get it right."

She touched his chin; his belly fluttered. "How do I take mine?"

"Black."

"Always remember how to make a girl's tea or coffee. It's as important as remembering a birthday."

Brendon dragged a box to his feet, then grabbed a piece of jade chiffon. He couldn't tell whether it was a skirt or a shirt. He tossed it into the box and held up a spaghetti-strap dress. He heard the shuffle of feet and looked up. "You can't keep this?"

Angelene put the mugs on the nightstand. "I'm afraid not."

Brendon grabbed the mug and stared over the rim. How could Maggie accuse him of fancying Angelene? There was nothing special about her. She was plain, dishevelled, with bloodshot eyes and colourless cheeks.

"That's too bloody bad. Does it all have to go?"

Her presence took over the room, snatched his breath, disarming his defences. She had spilled her disaster at his feet. Her vulnerability was beautiful. She was beautiful.

"I can only keep what he bought me in Paris and London."

"These are your things. It's like he's asking you to throw yourself away."

Angelene held up a beaded slip. "Mrs. Secretary of State for Defence would not wear something like this."

"You could if you were my wife. I wouldn't care what anyone thought."

Angelene grinned behind her mug. "You wouldn't want me for a wife."

He unravelled a slinky raspberry chemise and beamed. "Are you bloody kidding? If you were in this."

"Once you get to know me, you'll change your mind."

"Walter says he wants to improve you. He's making things worse by wanting to change you."

"There's a German word for that. Verschlimmbessern," she said, scooping up an armful of clothes.

Brendon tossed a shirt into the box. "I think you just smiled. If you'd move the clothes out of the way, I could see."

"Mother used to grow angry when I smiled. If she wasn't full of joy, I had no right to be happy." She moved across the bed and brushed her lips over his cheek. "Thank you."

"I said I would be here for you. I meant it."

"You have a beautiful face. I could paint you."

Brendon stared into his tea. A flush spread over his cheeks. "I'm trying to get away from that, remember?"

"You shouldn't be upset about some silly list. At least you aren't ugly."

He looked at her tangled hair, wistful eyes, and wrapped an arm around her. "You don't think you're ugly, do you? There's beauty in everything. You said so."

"I struggle to see it in me. Sometimes I stare in the mirror and wish my face would change, my body."

"I wish I had spots and a receding hairline."

Brendon set down his tea, took her hands and walked her to the full-length mirror. "Don't you see it? You smell like cigarettes but you're beautiful."

Angelene leaned against him and drew his arms around her. Brendon's gaze swept over the anchor alarm clock, a Royal Navy hoodie. Walter was everywhere.

"I'll help you finish." He bent down and picked up a low-cut cocktail dress. "This is brilliant."

"In the box, mon ami."

He held a lacy blouse against his chest. "This, too?"

"Throw it all in. It'll be less painful."

He grabbed an armful of denim and silk and dropped it in the box.

"How will I ever learn to be the wife he wants?"

Brendon tossed the remaining items into the box and closed the flaps. "I'm sorry Walt was a dick."

"Your mother will help me. I'll be a better version of me."

Brendon picked up the box and rested it against his hip. "Where should I put this?"

"By the front door. Your mother and I are dropping the clothes... what did Walter call it?"

"A charity shop."

"That's it."

Brendon walked down the staircase and set the box by the door. Her thumbnail scratched and pulled at the thin polyester leggings. Soft cracks and pops clattered behind the walls, leaves rustled, and somewhere among the trees, birds chirped.

"Don't do that."

"It's another bad habit."

He folded the cuff around her fingers like a mitten and held tight. "Is there anything else that makes you feel better?"

Angelene stared at the stucco ceiling and sighed. "Booze, cigarettes."

"Healthy things."

"A bath." She fell into his chest and inhaled. "You, your brown."

Breathless, heart hammering. The thread wound around them, fused her to him, electric, sparkly.

'Bloody hell, I feel dizzy.'

"If you were in Parc Floral and you saw me, would you want to speak to me?" She rubbed his back, meandered to the stairs, and dissolved onto the step.

"I have a feeling you would have run away."

"I might have. I do an excellent job at running."

"Healthy things tonight."

"I'll have a bath and eat."

Brendon fished his car keys out of his pocket and twirled them around his finger. "Don't let Mammina pick out your clothes; she wears a lot of black. You're more of a colour kind of girl."

"You're a sweet boy."

"Black tea, yellow, and Victor Hugo."

"Borussia Dortmund, tea with milk, and a dislike of school." She tugged on the sleeves and wound them around herself like a scarf. "Visit me again?"

Mammina's warning pulsed in his head. Padre Diavolo cackled.

Maggie

Maggie studied the timeline in her agenda, all her assignments mapped out in in pink and lime green ink. She placed her chin on her hand and cracked open the chemistry textbook. She enjoyed doing homework at Charlotte's. The house was quiet and smelled glitzy, like champagne and orchids. Charlotte's bedroom was glam, and there was no Jack to contend with.

"Thanks for letting me come over."

Charlotte wound a towel around her hair like a turban, grabbed pyjama bottoms and a T-shirt from her closet. "I thought you were hanging out with Brendon?"

"He barely spoke." Maggie put her thumb in her mouth and skillfully bit around her nail. "We didn't even get to his homework. He rushed out the door, said he had to go."

Charlotte rubbed a towel over her legs and pitched it into the laundry basket. "Do we have to do homework?"

"We can talk about Rachel giving Brendon Smarties. She picked out the blue ones, daft cow."

Charlotte wiggled into the T-shirt and dove onto the bed. "That feels better. I had a bit of babe's love goo on my bum. It itched all day."

"You're disgusting. Mr. Dawson could have suspended you."

Charlotte peered at Maggie's notebook and copied an answer. "When the mood strikes."

"You could open your textbook. The answers are on page 221."

"I can't concentrate when I wear one of babe's T-shirts. One smell and I miss my crumpet horribly."

"You've got a collage of pictures on the wall. You can't stare at it then look for the answer?"

Charlotte dropped her pen and rolled to her side. "What else has got your knickers in a twist, muffin?"

Maggie tapped her pen against her lip. A few seconds passed before she spoke. "I haven't slept in days. I get a chunk of sleep, then I'm awake."

"Did you dream about humping Brendon and now you feel guilty?"

"I dreamt he cheated on me."

"Mr. I-do-everything-mommy-and-daddy say."

Maggie tossed her notebook and textbook to the floor and lounged against a pile of velvet and glittered throw pillows.

"He was snogging Mrs. Pratt, and he was ready to, you know, my mom walked in and called him a wanker. Then I failed all my classes."

Charlotte grinned an 'you're-a-nutter-but-I-love-you' grin and snuggled next to her. "Brendon would never cheat, and you're the smartest person I know; there's no way you'll fail."

Maggie blew her bangs from her eyes and sniffed. "He's been distant. You should have seen him at Walter's do. He was making the Charlie face at Mrs. Pratt."

"Is that like the O-face? I asked my crumpet if I made one and if it was cute."

Maggie poked Charlotte with her pen. "It doesn't have anything to do with that. It's the face Jack makes when he sees you."

"Ooh, does he have a crush?"

"Don't let on you know. He's a handful as is."

"Brendon is a nice bloke." Charlotte glanced at the collage of Troy and smiled dreamily. "Brendon signs autographs for the little footy players. He volunteered as a goal coach for the youth team."

"He's always around Mrs. Pratt or sneaking a peek. He doesn't know I've caught him." Maggie shoved the pen in her mouth and chewed. "Didn't you find Mrs. Pratt weird?"

"What do you mean by weird? Like nutter weird or like the swots in physics? One of their paper airplanes got stuck in my hair."

"I've accepted girls stare at Brendon. I just bite my lip and hope the jealousy goes away. The day we swam at Brendon's, Mrs. Pratt was hiding behind the curtain watching at him."

Charlotte yanked at the collar of Troy's t-shirt and took a whiff. She looked briefly at the collage then back to her Man U-inspired manicure. "You need to worry about Rachel, not Mrs. Pratt."

Maggie studied Charlotte's face. The weird feeling flitted around her stomach; it was a brush-off.

"I told Brendon she was staring at him, and he didn't believe me. She was there, I swear."

"Have you forgotten she's married? Mr. Pratt is ace for an old bloke. His eyes crinkle when he smiles. He looks like Sean Bean, more Ned Stark than Boromir."

"Will you be serious?" Maggie said, tapping Charlotte on the cheek with her pen. "Mrs. Pratt is the worst kind of pretty. She's dangerous like she doesn't know she's beautiful."

"Give Brendon a pinch when he gawks. Babes will never look at her again."

Something cold sliced through Maggie, and she shivered. "It's like she has a scream stuck in her throat."

"Mrs. Pratt is one of those introverts I read about in psych. They make people uncomfortable because they're quiet."

"I'm not sure."

"Ah, Magpie, maybe you need to hump Brendon."

"My mom would cut off Brendon's thing if he came near me."

Charlotte reached across Maggie and snatched a framed photo of her and Troy off the nightstand. "It's brilliant how two people fit together." She kissed Troy's face and cradled the picture. "Babes and I are a perfect match."

"I'm sure that's what Mrs. Spence was thinking. Please God, give me a boy to fit perfectly with Charlotte Donovan."

A tickle crawled up Maggie's spine and prickled the hairs on her neck. She had come to know this feeling over the past few weeks. It whispered, *she's there, stealing breath, watching, waiting.*

Angelene

Angelene sifted her fingers through the dirt. The smell of damp earth enchanted her; she moved on. Upturned soil turned velvety green. She stumbled onto gravel and Spence Farm. The coop door squeaked open. Angelene kneaded her knuckles, excuses danced around her head, '*I have trouble sleeping. I lose track of time when walking.*' Her anxious gaze met Troy's. The words tumbled from her mouth.

"I went for a walk and ended up here. I'm sorry."

"Do you always walk around at night?"

"I don't sleep well. I've been meaning to explore the property." Angelene swallowed, flexed her fingers, and shook them out. "Now seemed like the right time."

Troy closed the gate and stuttered. "It's late…. I should probably walk you… I'm supposed to call Charlie… bleeding heck, Mrs. Pratt."

"Sorry for troubling you."

"I'll take you home. Dad has seen some foxes around here the last few nights."

Angelene hesitated. Troy's presence was luminous, golden yellow. It filled the laneway and glowed against her. Could he hear her heart pounding?

A door slammed, and a boy who looked like a younger Troy swung from the door frame.

"Troy, I've perfected my pile driver. I want to show you," Callum yelled.

"Show Brian."

Feelings, colours, words electrified Angelene like an overloaded circuit board. *'Always stumbling into things, tripping over your feet, anything to drench yourself in their light.'*

Angelene pressed her fingers against her forehead, *buzz, crackle, buzz.*

"Mom said no more wrestling, Troy."

Troy secured the coop and tucked the keys into his pocket. "I'll be back in a minute."

"Who's the girl?"

He smiled awkwardly, eyes dropping to the ground before flicking toward the house. "Head inside. I'll run back. It'll take less than a minute."

"Your house sounds hectic."

"Four boys. Gavin's at university, and Brian and Callum think they're pro wrestlers. Busy doesn't quite describe it."

"I don't have any siblings." Angelene plucked a feather from a patch of clover and twirled it between her fingers. "Family might have meant something to me. We could have protected one another."

"Sometimes I wish I were an only child. I never get a moment's peace. Brian threw me over the ropes after dinner. The sofa, in case you were wondering."

"It sounds wonderful to me."

The buzzing hummed. The crackling stopped. Troy's glow calmed the noises. She liked his smile; every part of his face twinkled. When he spoke, the words shot from his mouth in vibrant, sunburst yellow. Angelene looped her arm through his, touched the spot on her throat where her cross used to sit, and asked God to forgive her.

"Blimey, Mrs. Pratt, it took days to stop thinking about you."

"I like your sunshine. It radiates through your skin."

"That's my heart racing. If Charlie finds out, I'll get a horrible pinch."

"I don't mean to make you uncomfortable. Your smile is contagious."

Troy cleared his throat and stared beyond the farmhouse. "You get stuck in my head, and it makes me feel like a wanker."

"Do I annoy you? I do that often, annoy people."

"That day Brendon and I worked in your garden; I kept asking myself what is it about you? It was hard to look at Charlie."

Angelene tightened her grip. She had heard it before. She wasn't entirely sure how it happened.

"You're in love?"

"Charlie was meant to be my girl."

Roman Krieger told her love was a wonderful thing, like sunshine, peace, intense, home. Love had been none of those things, just black, chaotic, and messy.

"It must be an amazing feeling. My mother said love makes you crazy."

"It does, but it's the good kind of bonkers."

"Is Brendon in love with Maggie?"

She tried to stuff the words back in; it was a stupid question. She didn't know why she asked it.

"I thought he was. Before he left for Dortmund, they were all over each other, as much as Maggie can be. Since he came back, he's... I don't know, different."

They ducked under a gnarled hornbeam branch. Angelene glanced at Rosewood Manor, touched her lips, and smiled. His lamp was on.

"I would say Brendon is in like."

"Charlotte is lucky to have you."

"It's the other way around. It's not often a girl like her wants to be with someone like me."

Angelene cocked her head to the side and studied his profile. "I don't understand what you mean, a guy like you. You're special."

"You're doing it again, giving me those eyes. I'll be thinking about you when I fall asleep."

"What is one thing you love about Charlotte?"

"That's a hard one. I love so many things about her. She knows what to say after I mess up a football tryout. She smells like jasmine and coconut."

Angelene followed a pattern of stars and dived into the midnight blue sky. "You make love seem easy. If love were a colour, you and Charlotte would be pink. If love had a look, you both wear it."

"You'll fall in love with Walter and see how simple love is."

"I'm trying my best to trust love and fall deeply into it. I need to get normal right first, be comfortable playing wife."

"Think about all the things you like about Walter. It'll be easy then."

"I'll start tonight." Angelene opened the door and grinned. "Thank you for walking me home."

"Bonne nuit, Mrs. P."

"Bonne nuit. Petit à petit, l'oiseau fait son nid, des grandes choses peuvent être réalisées."

Troy stared at his feet and smiled. "That sounded pretty, whatever you said."

"Little by little, the bird makes its nest, great things can be achieved. Never give up on your dreams. Au revoir."

Angelene slipped into the house and slid the deadbolt into place. She enjoyed walking arm in arm with Troy, loved the scent of hay on his clothes. She liked it, and it wasn't right. With each step up the stairs, she recited a '*Hail Mary.*' She knelt by the bed and clasped her hands.

"God, please forgive me for falling into Troy's sunshine. It's my patterns. I fall into them before I realize I have. Please forgive me. Amen."

Angelene stripped off her clothes and burrowed under the mussed blankets. She scrunched into a ball and imagined herself in a field of green filled with the bluest cornflowers and prettiest buttercups. God shone his love down, and every scar on her body disappeared. Her heart was whole, and all the lost pieces fit into place. Sleep came in a wave of golden yellow.

10 Cacoethes

Brendon

Cacoethes: the uncontrollable urge to do something inadvisable.

Brendon left the engine running and sprinted to the door. He could hear soft whimpering coming from somewhere within the farmhouse. He peeked into the kitchen and frowned at a clutter of dishes, eggshells, and the smell of burnt toast. He followed the sound to the bedroom. Clothes covered the unmade bed. Price tags gleaming in the sunlight.

"What the bloody hell are you doing sitting in the walk-in wardrobe?"

"I'm supposed to be hanging up my clothes. They've been lying on the bed for a few days now."

"Mom nags about the shit on my floor. I don't cry."

"Walter and I got in a horrible fight." Angelene sniffed and reached for his hand. "He let me decorate the house; I must wear the clothes. I told him I want to be me, and he said he didn't like me. He hates the brown walls."

Brendon helped her to her feet and brushed damp strands of hair from her cheek. "What a dick."

"He changed his tune when I cried." She wiped her eyes on her sleeve and poked at her belly. "I need a church. I fell asleep after the argument and dreamt about mother. She was screaming at me, calling me ugly and stupid. I... it's a terrible habit."

Brendon ran his thumb over the red scratches. "I told you not to do that."

"Please take me to a church," Angelene pleaded. "I need to feel God. I need Him to know I'm sorry for hurting myself."

Brendon snatched a wrap from the bed and draped it around her shoulders. "I told you healthy things."

"Please, no lecture. I've heard enough from Walter about my drinking and smoking."

Brendon placed his fingers on the small of her back and led her towards the stairs. "You should have called me before you cut yourself. What did you use?"

"A hanger."

Brendon grabbed her keys from the little table by the door and tossed them at her. At school for just over a week, and he was cutting classes already, and for what? A desperate call. Saving the damsel in distress. A woman he hardly knew.

Brendon climbed into the car and reversed onto the road. Clouds swept in, swallowing the blue. Rain fell in steady plunks, turning the street slick black. The thread that tied him to her strangled him.

"What else is the matter? Walter's been a dick before. You didn't cut yourself."

"Nobody has ever liked me, not my mother, the kids at school."

"I like you."

It took Brendon exactly ten minutes to zoom past the moors and into civilization. His mother could be anywhere. She ruled Taunton. Mrs. Lord Chancellor had her hands in everything that made the town tick. Amelia could be running an errand. She rarely deviated from her routine. Sometimes she slipped out to Tesco or the butcher shop. He needed a church away from the town centre. The unimpressive building with the red doors was perfect. He was sure God would be hanging out, arms outstretched to receive one of his flock.

"What's this?" Angelene twisted in the seat and pressed her nose against the window.

"St. Theresa's."

"Where are the statues and stained glass?"

Sparks flitted around his belly. "I bunked off school and you're upset there's no bloody stained glass?"

"Will you come with me?"

"I'll wait here. I'm liable to burst into flames for all the bloody, terrible things I've done lately."

Brendon relaxed and tapped open the Champions League app. He studied the match predictions. Odds were in Dortmund's favour. He dropped his phone in the cup holder and watched wood pigeons peck at the grass. Cutting, picking, scratching, little scars hidden behind bracelets and long sleeves. There had been a girl in Year Six, caught in the art cupboard, digging a chisel into her arm. He never understood what made Tabitha Harper cut herself. Rumour was, she felt dead inside and cutting made her feel alive. His heart hurt. Did Angelene feel the same way?

Voices mingled with the steady plunk of rain.

'God works fast,' Brendon thought. 'Angelene must be a good Catholic. Mom has been waiting for years.'

"God forgave me." Angelene's face looked brighter. "I felt it in my belly. I'm deserving of His love again." She laced her fingers through his and exhaled, long and slow.

"You're worthy of lots of things."

He backed out of the car park. Her hand was warm in his.

"Is your mother angry with me? I tried on everything she passed over the fitting room door."

"She didn't mention anything."

"Her style intimidates me."

Brendon chuckled. "Her fashion sense or her?"

Angelene leaned her cheek against the window. She traced her finger along the telephone wires. "She's so elegant and sophisticated. Those shop clerks ran right over to her when we walked in."

"They make bloody good commission, that's why."

"Everything was so expensive. The skirt she insisted I buy, a pencil skirt, cost more than a month of groceries."

A strange comfort settled over Brendon. His heart steadied, and his fingers relaxed in hers. The thread that bound them together loosened. Bunking off school—worth it to see her smile.

"She has extravagant tastes. Did she make you buy Italian? Mom swears Italian designers are superior."

"I think so. She got very excited about a jumpsuit by Miu Miu. I thought there was a cat in the store." Angelene placed her fingers against her throat like she was searching for something. "My mother once said, if I were a cat, she would have drowned me."

She seemed happy enough. The tears had dried; the splotches had faded from her cheeks. He was okay to leave her. Madre Innocente, the other voice he had named, stabbed him with her staff of guilt, reminding him of the poor choice he had made. Padre Diavolo pushed Madre Innocente away.

"I have an outfit for a cream tea, high tea. I never knew there were so many ways to have a tea party."

Brendon pulled onto the farmhouse laneway and parked beside the walkway. Rain misted the windscreen.

"No ciggies, no wine and no bloody hangers."

"I'll paint, read, soak in the tub, pretend I'm floating in the ocean."

He had never seen her eyes shine so brightly. He blinked; it wasn't a hallucination. There was a twinkle of a smile.

"You've danced with the devil, mon ami. I can see him flickering in your eyes."

"I've got to know him quite well. His name is Padre Diavolo."

Angelene stared into her lap and pinched a knuckle. "Are you in love with Maggie? I'm trying extremely hard to fall in love with Walter. Love scares me."

"I'm in like."

"She has a ring on her finger." Angelene turned to face him, pinch, pluck, pinch, pluck.

"I was leaving for Dortmund and thought it was the right thing to do. I jumped before thinking."

"I have a habit of doing that, too."

Brendon laid his hand over hers. She stopped plucking and leaned her cheek against the leather seat. They sat silently. His heart took on a crazy rhythm as she stared into his eyes. After a few beats, he spoke. "Have you always been quiet?"

"The less I say, the less I get noticed."

"The quiet ones get noticed the most."

"You think."

"People don't know what you're thinking. It's scary."

"I never know what to say," she said tracing over his finger. "I practice for hours. The words stick in my throat."

"I'm the same." A little shiver travelled up his spine. Her touch was electric. "If I fail a test or screw up, I'll spend the entire day thinking of something to tell dad."

Brendon found himself staring at her mouth, at the tiny cracks in her lips. *'One kiss, a peck, just to say I hear you and I care.'*

Madre Innocente's attack was swift, straight into his heart. He shook the thought away. Kisses were powerful. So much could be said in a kiss.

"I wish it were the end of the day. We could watch the Dortmund, Barcelona match. I could tell you the difference between a cream tea and high tea."

"Go to school. I should have called a taxi," Angelene said. "Promise to give me a kiss on my brow when I am dead. I shall feel it."

"Bloody hell, that's depressing."

"It isn't. It's Victor Hugo, *Les Misérables*. Au revoir."

Brendon waited until she was inside the house, then drove away. *'You're going to hell, Cook.'*

"Sorry I'm late. I had to pop into Boots, headache; the queue was long."

Rain splattered the classroom window. The smell of Rachel's tuberose perfume and the last cigarette she smoked hung in the stuffy air. Outside, the sky was ghostly grey. The leaves on the trees were just beginning to turn around the edges: bronze, red, and yellow.

"Du bist der Mann meiner Träume," Rachel said, glancing up from her phone.

"Bloody brilliant, what did you say?"

She smiled and flicked her tie at him. "You're the man of my dreams."

Brendon loosened his tie, releasing the heat tingling under his collar. He looked at the gallery of photos on her phone, amazed at the array of boys. "That's the attacker from Wellington."

"He was fun for a while. Movie dates and pints at the pub got boring."

"Edwin Bellingham, the swot?"

"He tried to dazzle me with his knowledge of subatomic particles."

Brendon recognized the goalkeeper from Truro, the clerk from the sweet shop. The infamous list had to be true.

"That's me."

Rachel enlarged the photo and kissed it. "You look dishy in your black kit. The green one makes you look like a giant grasshopper."

"Have you been with all those boys?"

"Not all of them." Rachel glanced at him, slowly crossing her legs. "Dawson is going to have you by the goolies if he finds out you bunked off French."

"He isn't happy I'm back."

Brendon looked away from her freckled thighs, eyed a water bottle decorated in a red rhinestone tiara and nodded towards it.

"Go ahead, knuddelbär. Du hast schone Augen. You have beautiful eyes."

"Why do I need to know that?"

"In case you meet a fit German girl," Rachel said. "Say something about me."

Brendon took a sip and sorted through the German words floating around his head. He had heard different things from his teammates in Dortmund, Schön, hübsch. He didn't want to give Rachel the wrong idea. He scraped his fingers through his hair and took another sip.

"Ich mag deine hare."

Rachel twirled a curl around her finger. "Boys never say they like my hair. Most tell me they like my tits or arse."

"Both are bloody brilliant. I'm trying to be a gentleman."

"The rumours are true; *you are* a good boy."

"Depends on who you ask."

"Would you like to be a bad boy?" The buttonholes stretched as she slid towards him. "I think you secretly want to be bad."

Brendon tore his gaze from her breasts. She had a way of lighting his insides on fire.

"I brought us something. Mittagessen." Her tone changed from sultry to bubbly. "Ready, knuddelbär?"

She leaned over the desk and dug into a monogrammed bag. Brendon tilted the chair back and peeked under her kilt. Black lace Brazilian panties.

"A German feast for German lessons." She laid an embroidered table-cloth over the desks and handed him utensils wrapped in the same floral fabric.

"You didn't have to do that."

"I wanted to. Mom was out with her latest victim. I was bored."

Brendon took the stack of containers and opened the lids. "Chef let you into the kitchen to heat it up?"

"I gave him a pack of Marlboro Gold," Rachel said, setting out plates. "Königsberger Klopse, Gruen Bohnen, and Gurkensalat."

"It smells better than it sounds."

Rachel laughed and filled him a plate. "Meatballs, green beans, and cucumber salad."

"You went to a lot of trouble."

"You're worth it."

Brendon jabbed his fork into a meatball and popped it into his mouth. "Bloody hell, that's good."

"I'm glad you like it. I volunteer at the old age home on Trinity Road, helping in the kitchen and delivering meals. The cook is German," Rachel said, nibbling a green bean. "You should come round to mine. I'll make you schnitzel."

"Can we start the lesson?" He stabbed into a cucumber round and smeared it through the sauce.

"Welches Bier wurdest du empfehlen."

Brendon munched on the cucumber and raised his shoulders.

"I said, which beer do you recommend? Give me your notebook and I'll write it down for you."

He couldn't tear his eyes off Rachel. Her mouth looked pillowy and full of promise. She was pretty in a made-up kind of way. Madre Innocente pierced his heart, and he looked down at his plate.

"Is Thornton following you to Dortmund?"

"She's going to uni in Cambridge." Brendon stacked a meatball and green bean on his fork and spoke around chews. "She might transfer. Who knows?"

"Does that make you sad?"

Rachel slid closer to him. A flurry of tingles rippled through his groin. He tried to squash them. She was the tart of Taunton. Rumour was he was top of her list. Pulling number one would give her bragging rights. Guilt ripped through him. She wasn't a slapper. She was a 9.25.

"I'll try to manage a long-distance relationship."

Rachel finished her lunch, wrapped the napkin around the plate, and set it in her tote bag. "I had a boyfriend in Lisbon. Miguel. He was a striker, ace at putting the ball in the net."

If Brendon weren't trying so hard to be a gentleman and please Madre Innocente, he would have licked the plate clean. The girl could cook. He smeared the last meatball through gravy and draped the napkin over his plate. "What happened? By the look on your face, you really liked him."

"He moved to Turin," Rachel said. She took his plate and placed it in her bag.

"Does he play for Juve?"

"The youngest on the the team."

Brendon handed her an empty container and leaned back in the chair. "Bloody hell, you should have held on to him."

"Italy is further away than Portugal. It wasn't meant to be," Rachel said. She put the containers in her bag and folded the tablecloth. "I found a prettier boy to fancy."

"Who's the lucky guy?"

Rachel edged closer, pressing her breasts against his arm. "Sitting here."

"Ahem."

Maggie's voice swept into the classroom. Her shoulders sagged under the weight of her bookbags, cheeks mottled bright pink.

Brendon fumbled with the utensils and passed them to Rachel. "Hey, Mags."

"I'll see you in Latin, knuddelbär."

Brendon nodded and stared at his feet. "Thanks for everything."

Rachel smiled the flirtiest 'you're welcome' smile he had ever seen. He tore his eyes off her wiggling hips and flashed his best dimpled smile.

"You look ace today, Mags. Did you do something different with your hair?"

Maggie crossed her arms over her chest and shoved her thumbnail into her mouth. She ripped at a hangnail, kicking his shin. "Don't try to flatter me. I've been texting you. Gemma said you weren't in French."

The compliment didn't put a smile on her face. Brendon bent down and kissed her cheek.

"I drove into town, Headache."

"You could have gone on dinner break and missed German with the tart."

Brendon wiggled his tie. The pristine wood-framed walls shrunk around him. Kisses and compliments weren't working. It was time to pull on her heartstrings.

"Remember that time at the pitch when my head was pounding, and I barfed. It's that kind of headache."

He walked away, longing for fresh air. The pungent wood polish, vanilla and tuberose perfumes were stuck in his nose.

"Why can't she tutor you like a normal person? Not have her jubblies pushed up to her chin."

"She *is* tutoring me like a normal person. What she wears has nothing to do with it." Sparks simmeed in his belly. "Did you know she volunteers with old people?"

"She's a slag and a saint, brilliant. Why were you thanking her?"

Brendon slammed his hands against the door, welcoming a blast of cool, wet air. The lie was not a lie anymore. An ache crept through his skull. Padre Diavolo orchestrated a symphony of sparks, and Madre Innocente shamed him for being a liar.

"She made me lunch."

"Was it German lessons or a date?"

"Bloody hell, will you quit it. I didn't ask her to do it."

Brendon barged past a group of students. He needed Padre Diavolo to put down his baton, or Madre Innocente to stab him with her staff. It was hard to get a breath.

"It's part of her tart plan, flatter you, do wonderful things. She'll be checking you off her list soon." Maggie grabbed the sleeve of his blazer. Her book bags battered her hips. "Will you slow down. My legs are shorter than yours."

Brendon tugged his arm free and wiped a film of drizzle from his face. "I'm trying to get away from you."

Maggie sniffed and trudged behind him. "You're a dolt. Can't you see she's flirting with you?"

Every molecule inside Brendon screamed at him to stop and hug her. He didn't have it in him.

"Rachel flirts with everyone. I don't think she knows how to act any other way."

Maggie stormed past Michael Collins, her acting partner, bashing him with her overstuffed bag. "She tried to pull Mr. Torres last term. He left his position in the science department."

"That was a rumour. He had to go home to Valencia. His mother was sick."

"Rachel wants her number one. She wants to... you know."

"I enjoy being her number one. It makes me feel good to know someone fancies me in that kind of way."

"That was a daft thing to say." Maggie jerked a tissue from her pocket and rubbed it under her nose.

Brendon didn't know where the comment came from. Frustration, guilt, Padre Diavolo? He scraped his fingers through his hair and contemplated what to do: hug her, rub her back, call himself an arsehole. It wasn't in him to do any of those things. The day had been a roller coaster. Up, down, worry, frustration, joy. There had been more climbs and dips than he could manage.

"Don't bloody cry. People are staring."

"I fancy you." Maggie kicked his ankle, blowing her nose. "It shouldn't matter that some slapper who can't keep her hands off anything in a football kit likes you."

"Can you please stop crying. I need to take a few breaths. Who knows what I'll say to Mr. Clark."

"You don't care what you say to me, but God forbid you act like an arse to our teacher."

Heat rippled over his body; Maestro Padre Diavolo was at it again. Sparks blasted like a firestorm.

"Aren't you going to say sorry?"

"It's better if I keep my fucking mouth shut."

"Mr. Cook, language," Mr. Clark said, yanking open the door. "Tuck in your shirt. Must I remind you of the dress code every day?"

"Will everyone give me a fucking minute."

The words flew from his mouth. Students froze. Mr. Clark tut-tutted loudly. Mr. Dawson snuck out from behind the privet hedges.

"Strike one, Mr. Cook."

"You've got to be bloody kidding. I asked for a minute so I could breathe. No one fucking listened."

"Is that strike two?"

"No, sir."

"Go to the room beside my office," Mr. Dawson ordered.

"It smells like bloody barf in there."

"Plug your nose."

Brendon whipped his backpack over his shoulder and groaned. Damn Maggie for crying, Angelene for being needy and Padre Diavolo for stirring up the fire.

'*Do as you're bloody told. Go to Latin and gawk at Rachel's boobs, payback for Maggie's whingeing.*'

He jerked open the door. The secretary glared at him and pointed her pen at a room no bigger than a cupboard. There was nothing but a desk and a chair. No windows to look out, nothing but ivory walls and the overwhelming scent of vomit. Brendon dropped into the chair. His backpack landed with a thud on the floor.

Mr. Dawson flew into the room, flipped his combover back into place, and laid his bony hands on the desk. He wore the dreaded 'don't-mess-with-me' headmaster stare. His voice cut into Brendon.

"Henry VIII's wives, where they were born, how the marriage ended, and if they had children. I suggest you start." He left, banging the door shut.

Brendon dug into his backpack and threw the book on the desk.

An irritated disembodied voice raged from outside the door. "I heard that. Get that temper in check, or I'll ring your mother."

"You'd love that. You get a bloody biggie every time you see her." Brendon thumbed through the pages and folded open his notebook. "Who was your first victim, Henry?"

He wrote Catherine of Aragon and listed the facts. A soft ping came from within his blazer pocket. His bad mood lifted. Angelene was sorry for acting like a brat. Brendon turned his attention back to the assignment. Bullet point after bullet point filled his notebook until he got to Catherine Parr. Fifty minutes were up.

Mr. Dawson opened the door, splayed his hand on Brendon's book and twisted it towards him. "I'm sure Mr. Clark would have preferred paragraphs, but you've finished it. What have you used instead of dashes?"

"It's the Borussia Dortmund logo."

"You're an artist," Mr. Dawson said. "How's your temper?"

"Concentrating on Henry's wives helped."

"What have you learned?"

"Henry was a prick like my grandfather." Brendon sighed and stared at the watermarked ceiling. "Is that strike two? Sometimes curse words just fly out of my mouth."

"Pay attention in Latin and you'll start back at three."

"I promise."

"No football highlights, and tuck in your shirt."

Brendon jammed his shirt into his trousers, burst through the door and gulped fresh air, clearing the smell of puke from his nose. Bolting across the lawn, he ripped open the door and raced down the hall, grinning at Mr. Campbell. He could be a model student for fifty minutes. Some of his dad's love of academia had to be in a gene or two.

"I heard you had to sit in that room." Rachel moved her chair closer. Her hair tickled his fingers.

"News travels fast."

"They were making all kinds of bets in maths. Not me, I like when you get all fired up."

"It's got me a red card, suspended and back in Taunton. It's a pain."

"You've had quite the day, knuddelbär."

An assignment floated onto the desk. Brendon glanced up at Mr. Campbell; 'I-have-my-eyes-on-you' glinted in his steely grey gaze.

"Look at the list of nouns and decide which meaning is right, then divide the nouns into declensions. Why is the end of a noun crucial?"

Rachel flung her hand up in the air. Brendon's eyebrows lifted at the sight of her bouncing breasts.

"I hope you are going to give us the answer and not ask what's under Brendon's toga again."

Brendon stifled a laugh. He liked Rachel's wit. She was fearless and owned an abundance of lace bras. She was a 9.75.

"It tells us whether the noun is singular or plural and what role it plays in the sentence."

German, Latin, Rachel was smart too. Despite his disdain for school, he found smart girls attractive. There was more to Rachel than a round bottom and full breasts. A little stir flickered in his belly. Rachel Jones was a ten.

"Psst... Brendon. Look under the desk."

Brendon leaned back and peered into her lap. She had pulled up the Dortmund, Barcelona match on her phone.

"Dawson forgave the swearing. I need all three strikes to get me to July."

"Copy my answers. If Campbell comes around, just shove my phone up my kilt."

Brendon swallowed. Padre Diavolo snickered. Her legs were creamy white.

"You want me to put my hand up your kilt?"

She nibbled the end of her pen. Her eyes flickered. "I dare you."

Brendon stood the textbook up on the desk and stretched his legs into the aisle. "Can I ask you something?"

"Will I go to dinner with you? I'd love to, knuddelbär."

"Are you being nice to me because you're trying to conquer this list I keep hearing about?"

She reached for his tie and ran her fingers over the silk. "I don't need to act nice to knock you off my list."

"Really."

"I see you staring at my jubblies."

Brendon scratched down an answer and glanced at the screen. It was 0-0. He liked when Rachel touched him or played with his tie. He liked it too much. It was bad enough he struggled with the warm, buzzy feeling around Angelene; now he had to contend with flutters in his groin. Padre Diavolo whispered, '*It's just harmless fun.*' Brendon put some space between him and Rachel. It went against the code, and despite feeling annoyed with Maggie, she was his girl. Brendon pushed Padre Diavolo out of his mind. It was easier to concentrate without him snickering in his ear.

Walter

Walter pulled out a leather stool and settled onto it. "Isn't this pub a little trendy for you?"

David pushed a pint of lager towards Walter. He unfolded his napkin. "Beatrice said the steak and mushroom pie is the best in London."

Walter cradled the pint and glanced at the young crowd. "Your sixty-year-old secretary dines here?" He took a hearty slug and plunked the glass down. Walter studied the menu, deconstructed dishes, reinvented British classics. It intrigued him. How does one deconstruct fish and chips? It would be a sin not serving it in a paper-lined basket.

"My party was a complete disaster."

"Everyone had a wonderful time."

"I was hoping Ang would come out of her shell and mingle. Put on that frock and be damn normal."

David picked up his spoon and cracked open the pastry. Rosemary and peppery scented steam escaped the bubbling stew. "You could have let her wear what she wanted. She might have been more comfortable."

Walter pointed to the fish and chips and laid the board on the bar. "Go through the same humiliation as last time. It's a damn dress. I didn't ask her to cut off her arm."

"The day you saw her in broken sandals and an outfit you said came from a charity shop, did it bother you?"

"I assumed once she got a taste of Chanel and Louboutin, she'd be a new and improved Angelene."

David blew on a spoonful of pie. "Did you make the right decision? Marrying a project."

"I love a great project. Maybe I was meant to be a bachelor."

"You're navigating your way through marriage," David said, washing the mouthful down with a swig of beer. "You're adjusting."

The bartender set a basket before Walter. Malt vinegar wafted into his nose. He was happy to see they had not deconstructed the fish and chips.

"Have I told you about her moods? One minute she's happy, as happy as Ang can be. The next, she's pouting. She's messy, incorrigible, shy."

David dunked a wedge of pastry into the gravy and held it above the bowl. Little droplets of sauce plunked into the stew. "Sofia is headstrong and smothering. I wouldn't want her any other way."

Walter stared into his pint. Single had been a choice for him. Random dates, the occasional steady girlfriend. He had been okay with nights alone on the sofa. Marriage was the ultimate project. He couldn't fail. He wouldn't.

"Ang is an unusual girl, no moral compass, no fixed personality. I see so much potential in her. Have you looked at her face?"

"I have, but not in the way you mean."

"She's a mix of Claudia Schiffer and a young Brigitte Bardot. Under that mess of hair and charity shop clothes, she's stunning."

"Have you told her this?"

Walter shook his head and sliced through the crispy batter. "I've been focusing on the negatives."

"Give it time. You'll accept Angelene's quirks and fall madly in love."

"The shopping trip didn't go well," Walter said between bites.

David laid the napkin over the bowl. "Have you shopped with Sofia? It would make anyone miserable."

"Is it so bad wanting her to look classy and respectable, not like those slappers we see at our local?"

David chuckled. "It depends on your definition."

"The other day she was attempting to make me an omelette. A bird landed on the windowsill, there went brekky."

"Accept all the parts of Angelene, the weird, wonderful, and give her some time to settle in before you demand so much of her."

"Even the parts that make my hair stand on end?"

David swilled beer around the mug. "I don't understand."

"Neither do I. We were having a pleasant moment and then..." Walter pierced a chunk of fish and waved it at David. "It doesn't matter."

Walter pointed to their empty mugs and relaxed onto the stool. Caterpillar to butterfly. This was a challenge he liked, the fight to see it blossom into something beautiful. It had only just begun.

Angelene

She was angry, spiky red.

'*You shouldn't have asked him to leave school. You shouldn't be holding his hand. You're a needy, desperate girl. Shame on you, Angelene Greta Hummel.*'

Angelene ran her fingers over her faded yellow T-shirt, praying the colour would bleed into her red and she'd be vibrant orange. She lit a cigarette, pressed dial, and paced.

"I'm red, Lisette."

"I better sit then."

"Sofia and I went shopping. It was a painful experience. I miss myself even more."

"Did she pick out your clothes?"

"She suggested things," Angelene said, smoke twisting around the words. "Black, everything black. Walter said, 'black is a powerful colour.' I told him black is not a colour; it is absent of light. True black doesn't exist. He hung up."

"I told you to wait. You had to run off to England."

"I'm tired of following the rules. The only time life is simple is when I'm with Brendon and Troy. Troy's sunshine is intoxicating, and Brendon comes at me in electric sparks."

"Angelene, you promised God you would stay away from men. You married a stranger and now, two more."

"This time will be different. I'll remember things like boundaries and rules."

"You're not good at being friends with men. You've tried, it failed horribly."

Angelene stared into the colourless night, the cigarette dangling between her fingers. "Sofia goes into protection mode when I'm around."

"I take it one of those boys is her son. Haven't you learned anything?"

"I'll prove to God I can break the pattern and be a friend."

"The price will be hefty, being this boy's friend."

A pang of déjà vu so strong squeezed Angelene's chest. She knew this feeling—the strangling suffocation. Something had led her to Taunton. Not the rock-like hands of the dashing Lieutenant Commander, now Secretary of Defence. Something stronger, powerful.

Little electrified arrows pointed to the place she swore she had visited before. The glow in his bedroom window was intense. The cigarette fell from her fingers. She walked away from the light's power. The backs of her knees buckled against the bedframe, and she stumbled onto the bed.

"Angelene."

She forced the words out of her mouth on a ragged breath. "I've known him before, Lisette."

"It is your pattern. Call your husband. Do it now. Before it's too late."

11 Fish and Chips

Brendon

Brendon sprawled along the sofa and laid the newspaper across his lap. His plan for the day, analyze his match, watch a Dortmund game, enjoy an empty house.

"No one in the house," Sofia said.

Brendon clasped his hands, reached overhead, and stretched his muscles. "Yes, Mammina."

A smile teased Sofia's ruby-red lips. "I spoke to Mr. Dawson. You were watching football again."

"He'd find any excuse to give you a bell. He's got a biggie for you."

"Who's got a biggie for my wife?" David kissed Sofia's cheek and patted her hip.

"Mr. Dawson. The prick told me mom has a lovely shape."

David glanced at Sofia's curves and smiled. "You sure you don't want to come?"

Brendon tossed part of the newspaper on the floor and spread out the sports section. "Antiquing in Yeovil, I'll pass. Dortmund and Bayern play today." He scanned the headline and grinned. *'Taunton's hero is back and at the top of his game.'*

"Here's another for your scrapbook."

"Put it on your father's desk," Sofia said, wiggling his chin. "You look older in the photo. Shave for Mammina, please."

"Leave him alone," David said, gently tugging her arm. "You want to join us for dinner? We're meeting Kate at that Italian place on Eastgate."

"There's a freezer full of food. Football and quiet, sounds like the best day ever."

"Kate's bringing a date. He's from Dublin. Wouldn't you like to meet him?" Sofia said.

"You can tell me about him when you get home."

"Suit yourself." Sofia kissed his eucalyptus-scented hair and sniffed. "I'm going to miss this smell."

"I'll leave you the bottle."

"Stop teasing. I hate the sound of that. It makes it seem like I'll never see you again."

"You might not if you don't stop," David said.

"Maybe I'll start hunting for homes in Dortmund."

"Isn't it time you got on the road? The M5 is crazy on a Saturday."

"We're not buying a home in Germany," David said, rubbing her arm. "Enjoy your quiet."

"See you later, arrivederci, ti amo."

Brendon relaxed into the sofa and studied the football standings. His phone vibrated; he shot up his middle finger and went back to the paper. It buzzed again. Brendon grabbed it and stared at the Paris Saint-Germain logo. If he kept the conversation short, Padre Diavolo could not rise and convince him to visit. He pressed speaker and flung the phone on the sofa.

"Were you ignoring me?" Her voice was raspy, untroubled, almost joyful.

"I was reading the newspaper."

"Watch football with me."

The better choice, join the Thornton family outing to the Wookey Hole Caves, play the devoted boyfriend. If he went round to Walter's, the door would open again, Angelene would be stuck in his head, and Maggie would be an afterthought.

"I'm supposed to go to Maggie's for dinner."

"I don't want to be alone."

Brendon leaned into the cushions and gazed at the ceiling. He clutched his phone and tapped it against his forehead. He would talk football, give her his own play-by-play, nothing more than Brendon the commentator. It was just a match, like watching it with Troy.

Guilt swept through him as he swiped his keys off the umbrella stand. Angelene was a friend, and that was all. He locked the house, trudged through the grass, and flicked the pull on his hoodie. A list of reasons why this was a bad idea raced through his head: where was Walter; his parents might decide a walk around the roses would make for a nicer afternoon, Troy could show up looking to play one on one. Brendon was so immersed in his thoughts; he didn't hear the door open.

"Why are you standing at the end of the laneway?"

He raised a reluctant hand, his heart knocked about. Pink cheeks, cherry red lips, he couldn't tear his eyes away. Brendon pushed guilt aside and rambled up the drive.

"The Dortmund match is about to start," Angelene said.

He slipped out of his shoes and followed her to the sitting room.

"It's bloody boring in here. White, green, and grey, a little plain for you."

Angelene bristled and yanked two bottles of beer from the fridge. "Walter does not like my colourful walls or the patterns I picked out."

"You're a better decorator than him."

"Tell him that." Angelene held up a bottle and wiggled it. "Join me."

"I'm not a big drinker. I barf when I have too many, which is like three, maybe four."

Angelene passed him a bottle. "Don't make me drink alone."

"One, and that's it."

Brendon was crazily uncomfortable. He wasn't sure where to sit: the ottoman, the barrel chair, beside her.

"Isn't the sofa wonderful? Two people can lie on it," Angelene said, running her fingers over the plush pewter velvet. "We can stretch out."

An uproar of cheering fans and overjoyed commentators diverted Brendon's attention from the gigantic sofa—goal for Dortmund. Brendon swallowed a mouthful; he was supposed to be watching the match, not cuddling. Annoying flutters stormed his belly. The heat from the fire penetrated his hoodie. Angelene's eyes bore into him with that 'I-need-to-be close-to-you' stare. He eased onto the oversized cushions and stretched out his legs, his gaze darting nervously to the doorway. Walter could come home and catch them snuggling on the sofa for two.

"Can you hold this?" He passed Angelene the bottle and swiped his cuff over his brow. A great furnace door opened inside him, and his neglected sexual fire roared to life. His skin flushed, his hands and eyes were hot.

"I can't relax."

"Are you worried about Walter?"

"I'm having a cuddle with his wife."

He concentrated the match and pushed his body deeper into the cushions. '*I'm worried I'll feel something I shouldn't.*'

"Walter won't be home until tomorrow. He's going to something called a stag for a Monsieur Huntington."

"Dad mentioned something about that. He's our MP."

She looked at him, puzzled. Her expression was adorable.

"Taunton's Member of Parliament."

A little wrinkle formed between her brows.

"He's getting married. A stag is a party."

Angelene handed him the bottle. She took a hearty gulp of beer and wiped her mouth. "Your father isn't going?"

"He's hunting for treasures with Mammina."

Brendon swilled his beer and finished it in three gulps. He set the bottle on the floor and stared at her thin shoulders, her clavicles and graceful neck. The thread that tied them lassoed him. He didn't know what it was, but it was as if he already knew her, as if they had been friends or soul mates in a previous existence. It was easy with her. It might be something in her face, her eyes. She just seemed to know, to understand.

"He loves your mother," Angelene said wistfully.

Her voice, raspy yet dulcet, pulled him back to Walter's sitting room and the sofa for two.

"They're like a couple of teenagers. It's awful."

The roar of the fans exploded into the room. Brendon smiled. Could the day get any better— another goal for Dortmund.

"The keeper should have saved that one," Angelene said.

"He had no chance. No defence out front."

Angelene finished her beer and set it on a book about Cubism. "I'll be watching you on television, remembering the day you kept me company."

Something stirred within Brendon. The 'in love' feeling, 'limerence.'

'*We're friends, nothing more, just mates watching football.*'

"You'll be busy going to charity galas and discovering the world with Walt. You'll forget about me."

"I forget to take out the garbage or put the milk back. I don't forget moments. I have a head full of them: good, bad, stinging, strangling, smothering, joyful, yellow, angry red."

He held her gaze; she looked as if this might be their final moment together. Time stretched thin, sounds faded to a hush, his heart fluttered. at him like it was the last time they would see one another. He leaned closer; applause and cheers shattering the silence, brought him back to Uncle Walt's sitting room.

"Bloody hell, what a save."

Brendon pushed himself deeper into the sofa. Angelene didn't seem fazed by what he thought was an attempt to kiss her. She looked only at him as if committing him to memory.

"His dive is as impressive as yours. Does Maggie watch with you?"

"She sits with me. Football isn't her thing."

"Oh my goodness, it's the greatest sport."

"Can you be anymore perfect? You're pretty and you love football."

Brendon didn't know where the words came from. They spilled from his mouth carelessly. It was the truth and not right.

"Walter wants me to go to auctions and lunch with those nasty ladies. I won't do it."

"You'll make him angry."

"You have beautiful eyes. A little Mephistopheles, a little Archangel Michael. You are the knees of bees."

"I have no idea what you mean but it's the bee's knees."

She laid her head on his arm and dragged her fingers over his. Every nerve in his body stirred and tingled. The beer, courage, Padre Diavolo, pushed him closer to her.

"Mephistopheles serves Lucifer. Michael is a warrior angel who carries an exquisite sword of light. You have both in you."

Brendon rested his chin on the crown of her head. "Are you saying I'm the bloody devil?"

"We all have the devil in us; it's how you choose to play with him."

The roar of the fans thundered off the walls. She gripped his hand, flutters gently floated.

"Did you ever watch PSG play?"

"We didn't have money for tickets. Sometimes my friend Francois and I would sit outside the Stade de France and pretend we were in the stadium."

Sadness flooded Brendon. He had been to Chelsea matches with Walter. Manchester United with Troy, Dortmund, Bayern, the list went on.

Angelene's voice was faraway. "I'm glad you came. You're my sign."

"Charlie is into that stuff. She was chuffed to know Scorpio and Taurus were a brilliant match. I'm a Leo, and Maggie is a Pisces. According to mystic Charlotte, Mags and I aren't."

"No, silly." Angelene traced along the veins in his hand and looked at him. "I asked God for a sign that I made the right decision moving to Taunton. I saw your face when I prayed, and then your lamp turned on. As for astrology, I'm a Cancer, to some, literally."

"Bloody hell, who would say that?"

"Just know that Leo and Cancer are a match."

The promise to stay away dissolved. He would never forget this afternoon, watching his favourite team with the most attractive woman he had ever known. His perfect match.

"How come you never talk about your mom?"

"She was not like Sofia, any mother."

"Do you look like her?"

He pictured a taller, blonder version with hopeless green eyes.

"Mother had dark hair. She was obsessed with old Hollywood, a bitch like Joan Crawford and aloof like Greta Garbo. There was always someone adoring her."

Her voice was small and tight. She let loose his hand and dug her fingernails into her forearm.

"Please don't do that."

"I told you, it's a habit."

Brendon moved her hand away and ran his thumb over the indentations. "Break it."

"There's another game on."

"Bayern and Leverkusen. It'll be brilliant."

"Stay, please."

Maggie's dinner invitation flashed through his mind. Madre Innocente rammed her staff of guilt into his ribcage. Padre Diavolo snickered delightfully.

"No more talk about Walter or your mom. We're going to watch the match, and you can help me analyze the plays so I can persuade Troy the Bundesliga is better than the Premier League."

Angelene buried her nose in his neck; his heart sputtered. "I love the way you smell."

"Have you eaten?"

It was a stupid thing to ask. The flutter of her eyelashes on his throat was heating his furnace again.

"I've smoked and drank that beer."

"Bloody hell, you take lousy care of yourself. What do you want? I can make a decent fry-up."

"I would like fish and chips."

"You haven't had fish and chips. Bloody hell, it's a British classic."

"Walter has promised. We have yet to go."

"Would you like some?"

"You'll have to go into town."

Brendon grabbed his hoodie and wrestled his arms through the sleeves. A drive into town could be the remedy to escape the lingering 'in love' feeling.

"I'm not getting mushy peas, they're bloody disgusting."

"What is a mushy pea? Peas should not be mush-shee."

Brendon chuckled. "No, they shouldn't."

He watched her curl into the corner of the sofa. The urge to kiss her lingered. He enjoyed kissing. Maggie liked slow, gentle kisses without roaming hands. His first kiss had been with a girl named Bronwyn he met on the beach in Burnham.

Brendon climbed the hill and sprinted to his car. Angelene's lips were chapped but still kissable. *Stay, go,* weaved through his thoughts, innocent or led by his devil?

The smell of upturned earth and apple trees, heavy with fruit, drifted over the moors and through the car windows. The clouds had blown away, leaving the sky pale blue. Gold glowed over the town centre. Brendon parked out front of Ball's Fish and Chips and stepped onto the sidewalk. Everywhere there was something to tempt the Saturday shopper: a bakery with displays of pastries, clothes, shoes. The café was full. Mr. Lawson swept the street in front of his sweet shop, and Mrs. Morimoto watered the orange chrysanthemums surrounding the entrance to her boutique. A pack of teenage boys strolled down the cobblestones, chatting and passing a cigarette between them. Brendon swung the door open; brass bells jingled, releasing the scent of canola oil and beer batter into the breeze.

"I'll be damned. What's it been, a year, two?"

Diners looked up from feasting on fish and chips to see who John Ball was making a fuss over. Some nodded hello; a little boy hugged his football to his chest, eyes full of awe. A group of girls Brendon recognized from history giggled. His cheeks burned. He waved at the girls, which made them giggle harder and blurt out all sorts of things: 'OMG, he waved at us.' 'He's so dishy.' 'He's totally fire. Imagine snogging him.'

Brendon smiled politely at a couple annoyed by the incessant giggling and leaned into the counter. "Hey, Mr. Ball. Can I get two orders?"

"Salt and malt?"

"Is there any other way?"

He dragged a chair away from a table and sank onto it. With a quick swipe, he unlocked his phone and opened the Dortmund app, scrolling through the team news. The bells clanked. A random straw wrapper blew across the black-and-white checkered floor.

"Look who it is."

Brendon glanced up from the screen. "Bugger off, Will."

"What's the Prince of Taunton doing eating greasy food?" William slung his arm around Matilda and snickered. "Coach won't be happy with his favourite keeper."

"I could ask you the same thing."

"I don't follow that daft diet Liam recommended."

"Where's Gemma? Did you forget you have a girlfriend?" Brendon said, sliding his phone in his pocket.

"Working. Tilly and I are just friends."

"Is that what you call it?"

Madre Innocente gave him a quick jab. He was as bad as William McGregor.

Tilly wound a string of gum around her finger and smirked. "Rachel's having a bash tonight. You should come."

"I'm busy."

She blew a bubble the size of her head and popped it with her finger. "Margaret got you on a short leash?"

Mr. Ball grinned and plunked a brown paper bag beside the register.

William glanced at the counter and back at Brendon. "Two orders? Who's the lucky girl?"

"None of your business."

Brendon kicked the chair under the table and rambled to the counter.

"On the house," John Ball said. "The way you've been playing, you deserve free fish and chips for a year."

"I haven't played better than anyone else," Brendon stated, tossing twenty pounds on the counter.

"You're a good kid. Glad you're back on the pitch. I was worried about the team," John said, throwing a look in William's direction.

Brendon smiled. If Mr. Ball knew what he was up to, he might change his mind.

William stared at himself in the straw dispenser, fixed his hair, and grabbed a handful of napkins. "Rachel puts on a brilliant party."

"Are you taking Gemma or this tart?"

"You're having dinner with that girl from the pitch. She *had* to have your autograph," William said.

"Nope, now fuck off."

William jabbed a straw through the plastic lid. "Poppy McKenzie? She's been trying to get into your knickers since primary."

"Ellen Barker from French?" Tilly said.

"Bets at school say you've gone off Thornton," William said.

"Have a fantastic time at Rachel's."

"Maybe he's a poofter, Willie."

Brendon ignored Matilda's comment and waved to Mr. Ball. The door jingled behind him, and the sparks fizzled. Brendon climbed into the car. His mind filled with excuses in case one of them opened their mouth. He could deny being at Ball's. Maggie would believe him over William and Matilda. He could be honest and tell her Angelene was alone, or say Walter begged him to check in on her. Brendon turned down the farmhouse lane. He'd watch the Bayern match, eat, and go home, call Maggie, be attentive and listen about her adventure at the Wookey Hole Caves. He might even throw in an 'I love you.' Brendon grabbed the bag; who was he kidding, he was 'in like.'

"The commentators said this would be the match of the day."

Angelene looked away and smiled her sometimes smile, no hand covering it, no trembling fingers. He watched the smile quirk at the corners of her mouth like she was fighting against it. It grew and faded, then grew.

"Fish and chips."

He rolled his eyes at his lame remark and dropped onto the sofa beside her.

"We'll eat out of the box. No utensils, no napkins."

Brendon ripped open the grease-stained bag, releasing the warm scent of malt vinegar.

"You're being a rebel today, Mrs. Pratt."

She puffed out her chest, scrunched her brow, and wagged a finger. "All I hear is no, no, no. You'll get fat; ladies don't do that. I go into town and it's hello Mrs. Pratt, no Angelene, just Mrs. Pratt."

"You should have kept your maiden name."

"I don't like Hummel either."

Brendon chuckled and handed her a box. She held the carton to her nose and inhaled the malty steam.

"Who's in net for Bayern?"

He opened the carton and grabbed a chip. "Neuer. He's among the top keepers in the Bundesliga."

"Better than you?"

"Bloody hell, yes. I still have a lot to learn."

Angelene tore into the fish, crispy bits of batter scattering across her lap. "You'll be better than Monsieur Neuer."

"Thanks for the vote of confidence."

"Your passion for the game will take you far. People notice you."

He wanted to ask her if she noticed him but kept it to himself. Why ruin a perfect day when he knew the answer?

"I'll come to Dortmund to watch you play," Angelene said. She piled a chip on a piece of fish and spoke before she had finished chewing. "I will be one of the 80,000 fans watching you."

"Walter will want to see Lukas. They were in the Royal Navy together."

"Not with Walter, just me."

Brendon clutched the box. The idea of her sitting in the stands at Signal Iduna Park was incredible and silly.

"You think Walter allow you travel to Germany alone?"

"I'll tell him I'm visiting Lisette and Yasmine and then take the train. I might go to Switzerland and find Roman."

Brendon nibbled a chip. A burning sensation tingled in his chest. "Who's Roman?"

One point for stupidity and one for jealousy.

"Roman was one of mother's lovers."

"You were close?" he said, dropping his half-eaten dinner on the table.

"Roman was my hopeful papa."

"Did you not know your father?"

Angelene licked salt from her fingers and tossed the empty carton into the torn bag. Brendon glanced at the box, then her, amazed she had finished it. Peck, peck, peck. Anytime she had come for dinner, she would play with her food, take a small bite, peck away. She had consumed the colossal mound of chips and devoured the fish.

"When I visit Dortmund, you can take me on a date. Imagine me, Angelene Hummel, out with a handsome football player."

"Why are you changing the subject?"

"It would be my fairy tale, like I've been asleep for years and finally woke up."

Warmth spread over his cheeks. He forgot the 'who's your father' question. It sounded wonderful. Angelene in Dortmund, the two of them discovering the city. It was a fairy tale, a story about a girl rebelling against her demanding husband.

"Did you forget you're married?"

"Who would know?"

Brendon took her hand and ran his finger over the enormous diamond. "The rock on your finger might give it away. If I were taking you out, I wouldn't want it to be a secret."

"I've always been someone's secret. It would be normal for me." She laid her cheek on his palm; a surge of electricity swept through him. "It's a beautiful story, you and me in Dortmund. I would trip into my old ways."

"I'd have the prettiest girl on my arm."

She smiled the tiniest smile. Brendon ran his thumb over her lip. Twice now she had 'sort of' smiled. It was a moment to keep. Angelene and her sometimes smile.

"Mother and I used to clean for the Dupont's; it was my job to straighten their travel brochures. Once the Duponts had planned their adventure, it was never a trip or vacation, always an adventure, they would give me them to me." She reached under the newspaper for her cigarettes and lit one. "I covered an entire wall with pictures. When mother was entertaining one of her lovers, I would go to my room and stare at it."

Brendon waved at a plume of smoke. Her eyes were far away, like she had transported herself to one of the countries she longed to visit.

"I dreamt of the Serengeti Plains, walking through the tulips in Tivoli Gardens. Neuschwanstein Castle, picking wild cornflowers."

He grabbed the cigarette pack and tossed it on the island. Something told him this was a two or three cigarette story.

"Walter can take you to all those places. He loves to travel." Brendon scrunched the bag, stood, and stuffed it into the garbage. He went to the stove and set the kettle on the burner.

"They're just dreams," Angelene said wistfully.

"Dreams come true. I wanted to play for Dortmund since I was five. They signed me."

He dropped a tea bag into the pot and leaned against the counter. Smoke rings danced around her head like a vapoury wreath; she remained far away—Holland, the Alps.

"You want to see the world? Tell Walt. All it takes is money, and he has plenty."

The kettle whistled. Brendon tipped water into the pot. He dug in the fridge for milk, the entire time his eyes were watching the ball move around the pitch.

"They're going to pick up the rebound if the defence don't get it out."

The commentators sang praises for Bayern and the striker that slammed the ball into the net.

Angelene looked at him. Her mouth shaped into an O, eyes bright and wide. "You knew Bayern would score."

"I'm good at reading plays. It's like a sixth sense. I feel the players' vibes. I can see where the ball is going to go. When I walk onto the pitch, I know whether we'll win or lose. I feel it in my stomach," Brendon said, handing her a mug.

She smashed out the cigarette and peered into the cup. "It's black."

"I remembered."

"Maybe I don't want to see the world with Walter."

"Are we back to that?" Brendon sat beside her and took a sip of milky tea. "He's your husband. Mom and Dad travel somewhere every year. They went to Morocco last spring."

Angelene drank a slug of tea. Her voice was defiant and bitter. "It wouldn't be fun with Walter. He would tell me how to act, dress. If we went to Italy, it would be all your mother's favourite places. I swear he secretly loves her."

"Then you'll have to go by yourself or with your friend Lisette."

He sipped his tea, studying Neuer as he moved about the net.

"I'll start my travels in Dortmund."

"Why not the Czech Republic? You can visit Prague Castle."

She set her cup down, crawled across the couch, and snuggled into his side. His mother said there was power in a hug; a person could communicate by saying nothing. He had mastered the mom hug, the friend hug. Maggie liked to be smothered in his arms. He had a hug for everyone in his life, but this hug, how she tucked herself close to him and clutched his shirt like she was afraid he might slip away, was the best.

"You would pick me cornflowers. You would let me wear my shortest skirt. We would drink as much beer as we wanted."

"Now you *are* dreaming."

"It's a beautiful dream."

A sting tugged his thundering heart, and even though Madre Innocente was scolding him, he wound his arm around her.

"It would be bloody brilliant if you were in Dortmund. I'm terrified to join the first team. What if I'm bollocks and forget everything I've learned? They'd toss my contract away."

"You won't fail." Angelene snaked her fingers through his. "You're a star, a bright, beautiful star. I see it and it's incredible."

"You make my heart feel like it's going to explode. I like it. I like how you make me feel."

"You've been there for me, so I'll be there for you. I'll take a train, run, swim. I'd even get on an airplane; it frightened me horribly but I would do it so I could hold your hand."

Padre Diavolo whispered, 'Kiss *her*.' She glanced up from his chest; he pushed guilt aside and parted his lips. A knock echoed off the walls. Brendon pulled away; his gaze darted nervously around the sitting room. The knocking grew louder.

"Answer the bloody door before they break it down."

Brendon rubbed his hands on his jeans, trying to digest what had happened. They had been talking; she would be there for him. She would fly, swim, run. Madre Innocente was relentless. He was her friend. He had told himself no more visiting. This was more than a visit.

The knock was persistent.

"Go see who it is?"

Angelene dragged herself from the sofa, tiptoed to the doorway and peered into the foyer.

"Bloody hell. Go look out the front window."

He listened to her shuffle across the hardwood. She gasped and rushed back. "I feel like I've been buried alive. I can't breathe."

"Taphephobia," was all he could say.

"It's a terrible fear." Angelene clawed at her knuckles. Panic dripped from the words. "It's why I avoid funerals."

"What's going on? Did you not hear us?" David said.

An excuse, he needed something sharp, believable. Nothing came.

"I stopped him." Angelene twisted her shirt around her hands and stared at her feet. "I went for a walk, and when I got back, I heard noises."

"The house is old," David said.

Brendon glanced at his mother. She was assessing the room. What little he had eaten churned in his stomach. The highlights lit up the sitting room, two cups of tea, mussed throw pillows on the sofa for two.

"What do you mean you stopped him?" Sofia said.

"I heard a car, and I ran outside. I was scared."

"Perfect timing, sweetheart," Sofia said, cooly.

"I was keeping Troy company at the stall. I drove by, saw Mrs. Pratt..."

Sofia cut him off before he could finish. "It's time you went home."

"I should look around. Maybe someone is in here."

"Go home, Son. I'm sure it's the pipes or mice."

"What if it's a machete-wielding nutter?"

"Do as you're told." Sofia surveyed the room and tapped her lip. "Why are there two cups of tea?"

"Wasn't I supposed to go home?"

Angelene finally looked up from her feet. "I offered him a cup. It's my fault."

"I'd be more upset if it were candles and wine. Home, now," David said.

Brendon drove into the carport, switched the car off and shuffled to the front door. It had been a confusing day, a lovely day. He walked across the dark foyer and climbed the stairs, longing for his bed.

He stripped off his clothes, sprawled onto the mattress, and jerked the blankets over his head. He heard the door close and Sofia's footsteps. Brendon shut his eyes and lay as still as his raging heart would allow. He held onto his laughter as Sofia tsked the clothes he had dropped on the floor. She pulled back the blankets and ran her fingers through his hair.

"I can't lose you. What would I do?"

'I'll always be there, Mammina. I love you, now go away so I can dream about everything Angelene said.'

Sofia switched off the lamp; he shot out his hand and touched her wrist.

"Turn it on, please."

"How do you sleep with it on?"

"Richard the prick has been visiting again."

Brendon snuggled the pillow. He closed his eyes and imagined Westfalenpark, a park bench, and the prettiest girl sitting upon it.

Sofia

The 'something is going to happen' feeling fluttered in Sofia's stomach. From within the manor, the sound of tinkling piano keys danced down the hallway. She recognized Fur Elise. It had been Elizabeth's favourite piece to play.

"We need the house blessed again. Brendon's been sleeping with his lamp on. Richard the prick has been visiting."

David played a haunting melody, his fingers gentle on the keys. "I made you coffee. I know you prefer it over tea."

"Thank you, darling. Why did you stop?"

"Music hasn't sounded the same since Mom died," David said. "I can feel her hands on mine when I play, smell her lily of the valley perfume. I wish you could have spent more time with her."

"Elizabeth was a good woman. She deserved better than Richard."

"Do you remember the summer you stayed here?"

Sofia's breathing slowed as the memory swept through her. "How could I forget? My father pouted for days."

"It was the best summer of my life. Richard had flown to Copenhagen for business or a lover. Mom was her old self."

Sofia snuggled into David's arm. Her heart swelled with memories. "Mother promised Poppa, you'd be a perfect gentleman."

"And I was."

"We ate in the garden. Elizabeth talked about planting roses. She'd be happy."

"Mom played *Fur Elise*, we danced."

"You stepped on my toes."

David laughed. "The number of times I squashed your foot under mine, you still smiled, even with bruised toes."

"We've been through a lot, haven't we?"

"We've faced many storms."

"What do we do about hurricane Angelene?" Sofia sipped her coffee and placed it on the saucer. "I looked into her eyes tonight. There was this desperate need to be forgiven."

"You haven't liked any of Walt's girlfriends."

"Only Anastasia. She couldn't keep her hands off Brendon."

"There's a childlike quality about Angelene, like she doesn't feel safe in the adult world."

Sofia had always loved David's intelligence. It made her feel secure knowing he had all the answers to the world's problems. There was no bravado in it. He was modest about the law degree from Oxford, his rise to the top. Sofia loved the way his mind worked. He broke any crisis down into logical chunks. Some research, a discussion, more research. From the moment she spotted him eating stracciatella gelato on Via Spadari, she had been hooked. Her mother Nicola teased her, 'the boy was pale, skinny, British.' Sofia felt his eyes on her and a minute later he was buying her another bowl of blood orange sorbetto and her mother a coffee. Something clicked. She loved his accent, his handsome features, and his mind. The way he saw Milan was fascinating. He was a gentleman at sixteen. The quality that stuck with David about her, besides her beauty, was how unjaded she was. She exuded happiness and love. Sofia knew at sixteen David Cook would be her husband. They married at eighteen. First love, first kiss, first lover.

"Sofia? Are you worrying about this mysterious intruder or something else?" David's warm tone pulled her back to the ballroom.

"I was thinking about the day we met." The feeling twisted around her belly. Intruder, Brendon, the lost little bird. "You feel sorry for her, don't you?"

"Sometimes."

"What does Walter know about her family? What if her father was worse than Richard?"

David closed the cover, picked up his cup, and sipped. "I don't think she knows who her father is?"

"Even better, daddy issues. Don't you see the incredible sadness?"

"All the more reason to welcome her and ease her into that group of women you choose to be friends with." David finished his tea and wrapped his arm around her. "I'm tired. All this talk of Angelene and ghosts has exhausted me."

"Too tired for romance?"

"I'm not that tired." David grabbed his cup and glanced at the piano. "I wish things could have been different for Mom."

"All Elizabeth wanted was for you to be safe and loved. She died knowing her wish had come true."

They walked hand in hand. Sofia rubbed David's arm as he shivered against her.

"Has Richard moved from Brendon's room to the foyer?"

"Every room in this house holds a chapter of my life; few are worth reading."

"There must be a happy memory somewhere. The ballroom where we danced. What about here? Think."

David scanned the foyer. "All I can hear is Richard calling me a brat."

Sofia wiggled his arm. "Think harder."

"Signal Iduna Park, 80,000 fans sitting in the imaginary stands."

"Every time you came home from work, Brendon was playing football here."

David smiled. "He'd trip over his Dortmund jersey."

"You see, not every room holds a terrible memory."

"Some are good, like the ones in our bedroom."

"Cheeky, Lord Chancellor."

"You saved me, Sofia. You made this place a little less frightening," David said. He nuzzled her neck and tightened his grip on her hand. "Sei il grande della vita mia."

"You're the love of my life."

The feeling fluttered in Sofia's chest. If the walls could talk, Rosewood Manor would have quite the story to tell. She was sure Angelene had one, too.

Angelene

"There are no ghosts, no ghosts lurking in the attic. The ghosts are in me."

Angelene paced.

12 Sehnsucht

Walter

Morning came at Walter, hard and forceful like the thump in his skull. He dropped a duffel bag of dirty clothes by the staircase and followed the scent of brewed coffee. The kitchen sparkled; floors were polished. If there had been an intruder, he had been neat.

Walter filled a mug, sipped, and made a face. The brew could burn a hole in one's chest. He sighed and glanced up the stairs at the brown walls. Angelene had called it chocolate; he called it mud. Plumes of sandalwood and cigarette smoke trickled down the hall. He gulped the coffee, erasing the pungent smells from his throat.

"Your fag has burned to the filter."

Angelene stood in front of the easel, paintbrush in hand, cigarette dangling precariously from her mouth. He turned his attention to the canvas. A cloaked figure with bony hands clawed at a girl in a yellow dress. Alarm bells rattled in his head.

"Can't you paint cheerful things?"

He dragged a spindle-back chair across the scarred parquet and settled onto it.

"It's all I know." She tossed the cigarette into an overflowing ashtray and swirled the paintbrush in crimson paint.

Walter sipped and coughed. "Look around you. The view is lovely."

Angelene dabbed crimson paint across the child's fingers; the blobs ran onto the wilting flowers.

"Are you going to tell me about the intruder?"

"I went for a walk. When I came home, I heard scratching and rattling. You have ghosts."

"They live at Rosewood Manor. Could be rats."

She dunked the brush in a jar of cloudy water and sorted through a can of brushes. "It sounded like footsteps. I got myself all worked up."

"If you painted happier things, you might not have imagined a nutter roaming around our home."

"What I paint has nothing to do with the sounds I heard."

He watched the slow rise of her chest, locking his inquisitive gaze on her unimpressed stare.

"Why are you staring at me?"

"I learned about kinesics interrogation from a friend."

"Was her name Dominique? Madeline?" She chewed on the end of the paintbrush, tilted her head from side to side, then dipped her brush in grey paint. "Do you think I'm lying, Admiral Pratt?"

Walter pressed his lips to the mug and sucked down the syrupy, acrid brew. "I wasn't an admiral. I was Lieutenant Commander with the Special Boat Service."

"Did you sail magical ships?"

"The Special Boat Service is an elite counter-terrorist unit. The operations I took part in were highly classified. We were the best of the best."

Angelene swept grey paint through the cloak. "Should that impress me?"

"Most people are, then again, you aren't most people."

He cradled the mug against his chest and walked to the table cluttered with canvases and tubes of acrylics. Walter shuffled through drawings of smirking gnomes and wicked fairies.

"Back to the intruder."

Angelene groaned, swishing the brush in the water. "Enough talking. You're giving me a headache."

"Why Brendon? Why not call David or me?"

"I ran outside. Brendon drove by." Angelene stepped back from the easel and studied the painting. "They could have killed me."

"Rats? Rusty pipes?"

"The stag was more important than me." She threw up her hands and rushed from the room.

Walter tossed a sketch onto the pile and followed her. "I'm here now. Give me a kiss."

"I don't kiss when I'm angry."

"You don't kiss at all. Stop running and show me you're happy I'm home."

He met her halfway down the stairs, cupped her chin and kissed her hard on the mouth. "You need to be kissed. You'll like it."

"Should I call you Rhett Butler?"

"You're familiar with *Gone with the Wind*?"

"I didn't like the book. Scarlet O'Hara is a brat."

"Does she remind you of yourself? Paint something pretty while I'm at the pub," Walter said. "I'll check for rats when I get back. You can hold the ladder."

"Aren't you afraid I might leave you in the attic to rot?"

Walter rinsed his mug and set it in the sink. "Pretty things, trees, the moors, the roses up at the manor."

"You can control what I wear, not what I paint. It helps me."

"Bloodied creatures, terrified little girls?"

"It's a release."

That unsettling feeling prickled the hair on the back of Walter's neck. "What have you seen in your twenty-five years to make you paint such horrific things?"

"I don't want to talk about it."

"One more kiss and I'll leave you alone."

"Hurry before I change my mind." She pursed her lips together so tightly they disappeared.

Walter grumbled under his breath and hastily brushed his lips over hers.

"I was Lieutenant Commander, Mrs. Pratt. Think about that when I'm gone."

Brendon

Brendon wandered into the kitchen in rumpled shorts, a sleeveless T-shirt, his hair more mussed than usual. The air held the warm odours of coffee and toasted ciabatta. Sofia buttered toast and stared thoughtfully out the window. Muted gold flickered through the forest canopy, casting a glittering sheen across the bark. The forest looked pretty, not the formidable monster she had steered him clear of.

"Jeans and a pullover, how pedestrian, Mammina. It suits you."

"Flattery will get you everywhere."

Brendon grabbed yogurt and berries from the fridge. He removed the lid, dumped the berries over it and flopped onto a stool.

"Why did you stop at Walter's? I don't believe the intruder story." Sofia poured coffee and shoved the mug towards him.

Brendon dropped his spoon. It clattered against the container, flinging a blueberry across the island and onto Sofia's plate. "I just woke up. Maggie's been blowing up my phone. We'll talk later."

"Don't get angry." Sofia popped the blueberry into her mouth and looked at him. "It was strange, don't you think?"

"Maggie ringing my phone and texting obsessively?"

Sofia picked up the toast and pointed a triangle at him. "Who would wander around Taunton Road at night?"

"Walter's house is bloody creepy."

"Let your father and me worry about Angelene. She drinks too much. Smokes too much. You don't need to be around a woman like that."

Brendon pushed the container away. A slow grumble emerged from his throat. "You should be concerned about the girls hanging around the pitch."

"I was at the salon the other day. Rosie Thornton calls them the tarts of Taunton."

"I don't know any tarts."

A series of chirps rose from the depth of his pocket. He fumbled for his phone and grumbled. "This is the fifth time Maggie's called. There's about a hundred texts."

"My goodness, you're grumpy," Sofia said, dropping the half-eaten piece of toast. "What's the matter?"

"Your questions. Bloody Maggie. I'm about to explode."

"Do that breathing thing. I can't have you exploding all over my kitchen."

He took a small breath, wrestling with the tie on the bread bag. "Jesus Christ."

"Give it here," Sofia said, tugging the bag from his hand. "Call Troy, kick the ball around until you simmer down. Eat your yogurt."

Brendon dragged the container back with his spoon. He didn't know what was causing the sparks. Madre Innocente and her staff of guilt. Padre Diavolo and his pitchfork of temptation, the incessant beeping, his mother's questions.

"You don't like Mrs. Pratt, do you?"

"I'm finding it hard to get to know her. She flits about trying not to draw attention to herself; all she's doing is drawing attention to herself."

"You didn't answer the question."

Sofia set down the plate, walked to the fridge, and poured him a glass of milk. "I can't get past this feeling you and your father dismiss."

A muffled ping filled the air; Brendon bit into the toast and grimaced.

"I can see why you're annoyed. Your phone has beeped five times in the last ten minutes."

"Maggie invited me to dinner."

"You hung around the Spence's stall instead? That wasn't nice."

Brendon chugged the milk and ripped a paper towel from the roll. "You've never had dinner at Mags. Jack pings food at me. Mrs. Thornton glares and Mr. Thornton takes the mick out of me for being a toff."

"I've told you a hundred times, you accept the invitation and tolerate it."

His phone chirped. Brendon dropped his toast. "Jesus Christ."

"Will you stop saying that."

"Since when do you care about insulting Jesus?"

"It's God I have a problem with. He gave me you, although it could have been Satan with that mouth of yours."

"I think Dad might have had more to do with it than God. You can thank Richard the prick for my mouth."

"I wish you had inherited Richard's love of learning and not his temper." Sofia snuggled his neck and embraced him. "A hug used to calm you. Your shoulders are tight."

"I do have a love for learning. Ask me about Dortmund, the Bundesliga, what it takes to be a great keeper."

He reached out from beneath Sofia's arms and took a bite. "You're making it very hard for me to finish my brekky."

"Promise me you'll leave Angelene alone."

"No more Mrs. Pratt."

As he said the words, Madre Innocente jabbed his heart. Padre Diavolo patted his back. He would try.

"She scares me."

Brendon swirled his spoon through the yogurt. "Nothing scares you."

"The forest frightens me. I hate flying."

"I can understand the forest, but flying, you've been all over the world."

Sofia tightened her embrace. "Your temper scares me. Those horrible things Angelene paints."

"She's just an odd girl you didn't get to meet before Walt married her," Brendon said. He ate some yogurt, pushed the container aside, and gobbled his toast in three bites.

"What's that supposed to mean? I have no control over Walter."

"You would have done everything in your power to prevent him from putting a ring on her finger."

"You're a cheeky thing."

"And you're bloody squishing me."

The lovey-dovey animated tone vanished. Sofia spoke in a voice that was taut and sombre. "Every time you walk out that door, I can't breathe. Please, no more visiting Angelene."

"Bloody hell, Mammina, I won't visit her or go in the forest. I'll practice my breathing, use a bloody condom."

"Do you know how happy you make me?"

"Even when I'm cheeky?"

"You were meant to come into my life. You filled all my empty spots." Sofia squeezed his shoulders and dropped onto a stool. "Ti amo."

"Ich Liebe dich, Mammina."

"You'll pay attention to some girl, not Madame Lafavre. Ruby danced in the Paris Opera Ballet."

Brendon scooped up a spoonful of yogurt. "Rachel looks better."

"I suppose you told me you loved me."

"I did. Rachel is teaching me all sorts of important stuff."

Sofia arched an eyebrow and poured coffee into her mug. "I love you is important?"

"Rachel is always telling me she loves me." He scraped up the last of the yogurt and tossed his spoon into the sink. "She taught me another word, sehnsucht."

Sofia opened a Moleskine journal and clicked her pen. "I'm afraid to ask what it means."

"It's an intense yearning for something."

Brendon rinsed the container, opened the cupboard, and dropped it in the recycling bin. The sofa for two, her eyelashes tickling his neck, her love of football. '*I wonder if she's thinking of me.*'

Madre Innocente struck his heart. She was probably enjoying breakfast with her husband, spinning a tale about the mysterious intruder.

"Make sure you apologize to Maggie. No wonder Rosie doesn't like you."

Brendon glanced at Sofia's agenda: aperitivo, antipasti, formaggi e frutta, and dolce.

"Planning an afternoon tea?"

"It's my turn to have the girls over." Sofia listed prosecco and olives, tapped her pen against her mouth and added mascarpone. "Your phone beeped again. You best be on your way."

"See you later, Mammina."

Sofia looked up from her notebook and pointed at his rumpled shorts. "You haven't showered."

"I brushed my teeth. If I don't get over to Mags, she'll have either chewed through her lip or gnawed her bloody fingers off."

Sofia's gaze moved from him to the forest. She shivered. "Put a hoodie on."

"I set it on the banister."

His mother, the most intimidating woman he knew, feared Angelene. The only feeling he got from Angelene was a pleasant simmering in his belly. Angelene was more afraid of herself.

Suki crouched on the bricks. Her tail swished little whirlwinds of sand into the air. The cat took a cautious step, wiggled its bottom, and pounced on a bug.

'Be like the cat, tread bloody lightly.' He'd need a handful of compliments, kisses, and his dimpled grin to avoid an aggravated Maggie. He raised his hand to knock; the door swung open. Brendon dragged her into his arms. Her chewed fingers were damp against his back.

"I didn't think you were going to show. You never answered a text or rang me."

Brendon soaked in the silence. Sehnsucht blossomed, glowed, expanded, suffocated him.

"Where's everyone?"

Maggie pulled away and stared up at him with sad, blue blossom eyes. "Mom and Dad wanted to take Nanna for fish and chips before she went home. I should be there. We should be there."

"We'll bloody go then."

Brendon sagged against the wall. His keys dug into his palm. The pain distracted him from the sparks.

"If you had answered your phone or come round for dinner, you would have known."

"I'm sorry. I watched football and fell asleep."

Brendon counted the shoes at the door. Twelve pairs. The smell, or guilt was strangling him.

"You couldn't text to say you were having a kip." Maggie sniffed and bit her bottom lip. A few seconds passed before she spoke. "Have you gone off me?"

He searched for the words she wanted to hear. He loved her; he fancied her; she was pretty. The urge to run tingled through his limbs. He could tell her he had to meet his dad and Walter at the pub or Troy at the pitch. Aching heat crawled down his back. He tore off his hoodie and bunched it in his hands.

"Charlie says when boys act distant, they want to break up."

"I haven't gone off you."

Brendon left her standing among the shoes and scent of feet. He walked into the front room, flung Batman to the floor, plunked onto the flattened cushions, and reached for the remote.

Maggie dropped beside him, cradled a throw pillow against her chest, and stared at the remote.

"I can't watch football highlights."

"I want to talk."

Brendon dropped the remote on a crumb-covered magazine and stretched his legs across the cluttered coffee table.

"The Dortmund match was bloody brilliant. I'd like to study the keeper's saves."

"They loop through the daft highlights all day." She hesitated and stared at her decimated fingernails. "Do you fancy a snog?"

"What if your parents come home?"

"Charlie says a snog is the best way to end an argument."

He drew her into his arms; her lips tasted like cotton candy; her body, warm. There were no stirrings in his belly, no heat in his groin.

You would pick me cornflowers. Imagine me with a handsome football player.

Angelene's voice whispered through his mind, the almost kiss. He peeled open Maggie's blouse and slid his hand over her cotton-clad breast. Gripping the collar of his shirt, Brendon yanked it over his head and tossed it to the floor. Tingles took over the sparks and invaded all the ignored parts of his body. Troy had instructed, one afternoon in the dressing room, he needed to kiss Maggie gently, add a bit of tongue and slowly dry hump until she was panting and begging for it. Maggie was not panting or begging. There were no moans. She wasn't clawing him in the throes of ecstasy.

Brendon pulled his mouth away. Her cheeks were bright red. She blinked as if something was stuck in her eye. Brendon tugged at the button on her jeans, just like he expected, pink cotton.

"Do you have a condom?" Maggie said.

"Why would I bring one? You're never up for it. I'll pull out."

"How will you know when you're, you know?"

"A guy knows when it's going to happen. Stop bloody talking or I'll lose my biggie."

He shifted the waistband of his shorts and smothered her mouth with his.

Maggie pushed on his chest. Her voice was soft and scared. "That's how my mom got pregnant."

"Don't fucking do this again."

"My parents will be home soon. You know Jack can only sit for so long before he's bouncing all over the restaurant."

"Can we go to your room?"

Maggie wiggled from beneath him, hunkered into the arm of the sofa and dragged her blouse over her chest.

"You're not allowed upstairs."

"Bloody hell, I'm about to explode. Can't you give me a wank?"

"Go to the loo and do it."

All the lovely warmth puddled at his feet. He was empty, unsatisfied. A different kind of heat rushed through him, blazing with sparks.

"How can you be gagging for it, then say no? Charlie told me she gets tingly, don't you?"

Maggie struggled with the buttons on her blouse. "I wasn't gagging for it. You don't even have a condom."

"You can't keep saying no," he said, jerking his shirt on.

"You want it so bad. We'll go to Vivary Park and do it in the rear seat of your car."

He dragged his hoodie from between the cushions. Sparks whizzed through his body. It was hard to breathe.

I would fly home and take a train... We would walk hand in hand.

He could feel Angelene's hand in his, smell her perfume. He missed her.

Sehnsucht.

"Before you leave for Germany."

"Should I ask Kate to write up a contract?"

He ignored her sigh, raised his hands above his head and rapped his knuckles on the wall.

"We can try in Burnham," Maggie pleaded. "I'm more relaxed away from home."

"Family only. Mom's rules."

The lie slipped out, smooth and easy. He stared at his hands, his muscles tensed. What was he thinking? Angelene would be with Walter. There would be no walks on the beach or time alone. Maggie might be an excellent distraction.

"Can't you stay home?"

"Walt and Angelene are coming. She's having a hard time settling in. Dad thought a weekend away would help her feel part of the family."

"Is it because I said no again?"

Brendon placed his hands behind his head and gazed at the ceiling. The sparks settled, his breathing slowed, Angelene resurfaced, smiling her sometimes smile.

"I'm going to go."

He shoved off the sofa, wincing as he stepped on Batman's arm. He hooked his toe under the toy and flung it across the room.

"My nanna wants to see you."

"She doesn't like me anymore than your parents. She greets me with hello numpty."

"You can watch the daft highlights."

"I'm not in the mood to get stuff thrown at me."

Maggie sniffed. Her lips twitched into a smile. "Will you give me a bell?"

Brendon kissed her cheek and flashed her a 'please understand' smile. He flung up his hand in a meager wave and grabbed his cell. She would make him feel better.

Angelene

Angelene stood at the mouth of a tree-lined road that led to a pond. Years of tire tracks had made permanent indentations in the dirt. The breeze carried the smell of wild mint and damp leaves. The branches of the beech and poplar trees bent into a natural arch, knotting and twisting into a magnificent green canopy. Angelene stepped under the claustrophobic tangle of branches, followed the fresh tire tracks, and jumped into the car.

"I came as fast as I could."

Brendon gripped the steering wheel and stared beyond the trees at the pond. "I couldn't breathe."

"I'm feeling the same. Walter has been hovering around me, complaining about my paintings." Angelene ran her sweater over her face and clasped her hands. "Did you argue with Maggie?"

"I got frustrated, and she started sniffing, which means she's going to cry."

"What's troubling you? We're here for each other."

"I don't want you to think I'm a bloody pig."

Angelene dragged his arm across her lap and laid her hand over his. "It would take a lot for me to think of you as anything other than beautiful."

Brendon leaned back and flicked the Dortmund keychain back and forth. "I need to respect the bloody code. I shouldn't be pushing Maggie into doing anything she isn't comfortable doing."

"Are you talking about sex? I'm the last person you should talk to."

"If we were a couple, would you, you know, want to..." Brendon shifted in the seat. "Do that."

"Is Maggie a virgin?" Angelene touched his crimson cheek and smiled. "Are you?"

"Will was thirteen. Troy was sixteen. Troy's bloody brother Callum lost his on his fourteenth birthday."

"You think sex will make you a man?"

"It'll stop my friends from taking the piss."

His words were soft brown and jumped at her in a way that dazzled her. "Your light is more beautiful now."

"My light isn't getting me humped."

"You must respect her. Don't force her."

"I'm going to bloody burst."

Rain fell through the webbed canopy, tapping a soothing rhythm on the car. She traced a vein in his arm, her heart wrenched as old wounds opened.

"Don't dim your light because you're horn-nee. Stay away from temptations, like that flirty girl at school."

"Be patient."

Angelene placed his arm back in his lap. Her voice was wistful, coated in regret. "Wait for Maggie. It will mean the world to her."

"We both needed to escape from someone today."

"We're so different, yet so similar." Angelene followed the outline of his tattoo. "Instead of a *Tale of Two Cities*, we're a tale of two people. Au revoir, mon ami."

"I'll drive you home."

"I enjoy walking in the rain. I would hate Walter to question why we're together."

"I was driving home from Mags' and saw you. Mention the code. He'll understand."

His words shimmered around her in sparkly brown. She had only seen that kind of glow once before. It wrapped around her heart and squeezed.

"Do you feel better?"

"I'm bloody randy but yes."

"Mon Dieu, think about football."

"I'm just being honest, mon chou."

Angelene giggled softly and touched the nape of his neck. "Where did you learn that?"

"An exchange student. She called me mon chou. Her friend, Raisa, used to yell mon petitou every time she saw Troy. He had bruised nipples for weeks."

Déjà vu overwhelmed her again. The fleeting moment of alignment was perfect, eerie.

"I wish we could watch the highlights together. You really watched the match, not pretended."

Angelene opened the door and held her palm out to catch the rain. "My friend, the boy with liquid blue eyes, told me a person knows they're in love when they can't experience anything without wishing that person was there to see it. He showed me all his favourite places in Paris."

"Are you saying I'm in love with you? Bloody hell, I don't love Maggie."

"I don't love Walter, so we have something else in common. Hold on to your light. Once it's dim, it doesn't take much for it to fade out. See you soon."

A prayer of forgiveness screamed in Angelene's head. She wandered down the road, looking for pretty things. Prickly brambles poked at her; all around her was misty grey. The wisteria wept as she hurried along the walkway. Walter greeted her at the door with a towel in hand.

"How was your walk? Did you find pretty things to paint?"

Brendon surfaced in her mind, her belly churning. God was upset with her.

"The air here is lovely." She rubbed the towel over her hair and slid out of her wellies. "I can smell autumn coming."

"Would that be Spence farm?" Walter kissed the crown of her head and handed her a cup of tea.

"No, silly, I can smell the apples and soil."

Angelene patted her face and neck, tossed the towel into the mud-room, and trudged into the sitting room. She sat on the sofa, breathed in the scent of tea, and prayed silently.

Walter picked up the remote and flicked through the channels. "*Goldfinger* is on. Would you like to watch it?"

Angelene sipped her tea and smiled her practiced smile. "Is it a documentary about you?"

Walter chuckled. "It's a James Bond film with Sean Connery. The true James Bond."

"I know the books. I've never seen a movie."

She twisted Brendon into a mixture of colours so she could be Walter's wife, play normal and appease God. She had a habit of twisting things, squeezing tight until they strangled.

"David said Brendon's been having some trouble with Margaret." Walter rambled around the kitchen, opened the cupboard, and grabbed a plate. "Daft giving that girl a ring."

Angelene knew the answer but refrained from saying it. Conversations she had with Brendon could slip.

"Do you not like Maggie?"

It was an odd question. Angelene studied Walter's face. He was neither puzzled nor surprised.

"It doesn't matter whether I like her. Margaret is a bit of a bore. Brendon would do better with a girl with fire in her belly, someone wild."

A strange numbness tingled down Angelene's spine and lashed at her heart. The weird prickles marched through her body and settled into her fingers, yearned, itched for Brendon's light.

"A femme fatale?"

Walter laughed, placed lemon macarons on a plate, and set it on the coffee table. "Pardon me?"

"A seductress. You want a girl who uses her parts to entice and enchant?"

Walter settled on the sofa and dragged her against his chest. "Why would you want pleasant and innocent when you can have a wildfire blazing at your fingertips."

"Maggie is a nice girl, respectable."

"Now that I think of it, nice girls can come in some incredibly sexy packages."

Angelene shook the tingles from her fingers and plucked a cookie from the plate. "So can Satan."

"You're the most devout person I know, and you mention the devil," Walter said, snorting. "I have yet to see a horned red monster impaling the sinners of Taunton. The devil doesn't exist."

"He is always present," Angelene said. She touched the tip of her tongue against the lemony filling. "Sometimes he is extremely attractive, the most beautiful thing you've ever seen. Other times, he wears a disguise of magnificent light. I have seen Him. I have watched Him fall."

Walter sipped his tea and ran his hand over her thigh. "This is why I don't put faith in religion; too much storytelling and condemnation. It's about making choices. Not the devil made me do it. It's an excuse to appease guilt."

"The devil lives in all of us. He speaks through us. I believe that."

"You have lived through some terrible things, little bird. Your memories are your devil. It's the voice in your head, not Satan."

The voices in her head were her saboteur and ruled by Lucifer. The devil was real and alive, burning to get out. She had seen him hovering over Brendon and in herself when she looked in the mirror.

"You have to stop listening to your inner voice. Have you not looked at yourself? You're beautiful, little bird."

'It's my disguise. My devil playing dress-up.'

Angelene snuggled into Walter's chest. All the talk about Brendon, Maggie, the devil, had exhausted her spirit., tangled her thoughts and drained her yellow to grey.

Walter rested his chin on the crown of her head and held her tighter. "Has all this talk of the devil frightened you? You're shivering, little bird."

"Please don't call me that. It used to mean something; it doesn't anymore."

"It suits you. You sound like a little bird when you talk. You peck away at your food and flit about like you're learning to fly. It's endearing."

Angelene breathed in the peppery scent of his cologne and pointed to her tea. "I don't want to talk about me anymore. It makes me uncomfortable. Tell me more about James Bond."

"He is highly intelligent and cunning," he said, handing her the mug. "One may consider him arrogant, manipulative, or hot-tempered. I see him as a man who pushes himself to the limit, sets goals, and is very loyal to his institutions. I admire that."

"In other words, you are James Bond, Monsieur Secretary of Defence, Lieutenant Commander."

Walter laughed. "We have similar qualities. Bond is a lone wolf. I'm a people person."

"We are the extrovert and the introvert."

"What's wrong with that? I can bring the best out in you, and you can rein me in a little."

Angelene smiled softly. It was an interesting concept. He would have to dig deep to find the best in her, and she doubted anyone could rein him in.

Angelene placed her mug on the coffee table and took his hand. She stared at the lines and crevices in his palm.

"You know I don't believe in that stuff."

There were breaks in the main line slicing through his palm, islands, and chain structures.

'What do I see? Fortune, success, golden fingertips,' Mere de tous les diables thought.

13 Stealing Light, Stealing Breath

Maggie

Maggie handed Charlotte a basket of clothes and flopped onto Troy's bed.

"Troy has more photos of you than Man U posters. It must be nice rating higher than a football club."

"Doesn't Brendon have pictures of you in his room?" Charlotte said, sliding a stack of jeans into the dresser.

"He has one. It's usually knocked over."

Maggie enjoyed visiting Troy's house. It made her feel better about the crumbling terraced home she lived in. The house was just as noisy when all the Spence boys were there. It smelled like freshly baked bread and a mixture of three different colognes: woody, citrusy, and musky. Each boy had their own distinct smell, and it wasn't manure like Troy thought. Maggie had always felt at peace in Troy's house or hanging out in the hayloft. Today, she was a bundle of nerves. Alarm bells rattled her brain and gave her a terrible case of the collywobbles. Charlotte had convinced her to skip classes to watch First play. The other thing that had her stomach spinning and on alert—a dream. Over and over, it played in her head like a movie. Charlotte, Troy, the Cooks, Walter Pratt, and Brendon were asleep. The world was dismal grey and bled great rivers of red. She tried to run from the blood. She drowned, screaming for help. She woke with a horrible feeling that her life was going to change.

"Shall I ring Mr. Dawson? Let him know you didn't barf," Callum said. He grinned mischievously and pointed at Maggie. "You don't have cramps."

"This match is important to crumpet. He expects me there," Charlotte said. She picked a T-shirt off the floor and held it to her nose. "I'll phone Parkfield Primary and ask to speak with your mom. Maybe give the Somerset Wildlife Trust a ring, tell your dad something tall and weaselly has been roaming around his cattle."

"I guess all three of us faked stuff today," Callum said, leaning towards her. "You want to stay here and be my ring girl?"

Maggie grabbed her purse and chuckled at Callum's red cheeks. "Are you chatting Charlie up?"

Callum stared at Charlotte and smiled, opened his mouth to speak, and closed it.

"I adore you," Charlotte said, ruffling his hair. "Take it easy on Brian when he gets home."

Maggie hooked her arm through Charlotte's and dragged her from Troy's bedroom. Callum was on their heels.

"Are you coming for dinner tonight?"

"Your mom is making pie and mash. I never miss that."

"Can I sit beside you, like you be in the middle... between Troy and I?"

"What would your girlfriend think?" Charlotte said.

"I broke it off. She smelled like cough medicine, tasted like it too."

Maggie stuffed her feet into her Mary Janes and rolled her eyes. "I thought my brother's crush was bad."

"Chloe Burton was talking about you." Charlotte swiped her car keys off the half-moon table by the front door and checked herself in the mirror. "She likes that you're taller than the other boys, just like my little crumpet, tall, lean, and twinkly."

"Are you telling me a porkie? She smells like blackcurrant jam."

"I heard her," Maggie said, giggling into Charlotte's shoulder. "She said you have a dishy smile."

"Blooming brilliant," Callum said dreamily.

They left Callum and his crimson cheeks and skipped to the car. Maggie flopped onto the seat and blew out a heavy breath. The collywobbles were back. The dream flashed through her head.

"Can you tell me why we drove all the way out here again? We could have hidden in the town library until the match started."

Charlotte started the car and slowly backed up. She flipped down the visor and examined her reflection. "I promised babes I would put his laundry away. I'm practicing being a wife. Mrs. Spence is going to teach me how to bake a pie and crochet." She pursed her lips and turned her head from side to side. "I need to put some lippy on. Acting ill does nothing for my looks."

Maggie tossed Charlotte a tube of lip gloss and gasped. "Charlie, stop."

Charlotte jammed the car into park. They scrambled out of the car.

"Mrs. Pratt, are you okay?" Maggie studied Angelene's petite frame. No bruises or red marks. She seemed to smile.

"I didn't hit you, did I?" Charlotte said.

"It was my fault," Angelene said. She gazed longingly at the cows grazing in the pasture. "Walter told me we are going to Burnham-on-Sea. I was daydreaming about the house on the sea that's really a bay."

Images from the dream flicked through Maggie's head. She flashed an uncertain smile and touched Angelene's arm. "You aren't hurt, then?"

"Daddy would kill me if I dented his car." Charlotte examined the bumper and swallowed. Maggie was having a hard time reading her face: scared, nervous.

"I'm fine," Angelene said. She glanced over Maggie's shoulder at the cows, gazed at the chickens, and back to Maggie. "Were you visiting the animals?"

Charlotte squished herself close to Maggie. "I was doing some laundry..."

"Charlie felt ill, and I have cramps."

"Il est mon soleil."

A chill prickled Maggie's skin. She pulled her blazer tighter around herself. "Who is your sun?"

Angelene plucked a feather from the gravel and swished it over her palm. "Troy's smile lights up the world, painting everything gold."

"Babes has a dishy smile." Charlotte licked her glossy lips and crossed her arms over her chest. "He's my sunshine. I sing that song to him when he feels down."

Angelene tilted her head and stared at Charlotte's mouth. "Your words are pink, and you, Maggie, are cherry pink and white."

Maggie laughed nervously and took two steps back.

"It's the way I see people," Angelene said. "When Charlotte talks about Troy, the words are pink; that's love."

Maggie knocked her elbow against Charlotte's arm. "We've missed kick-off."

"What does love feel like?"

A strange flash struck Angelene's eyes. A tingle rushed over Maggie's skin, cold and sharp. Something felt wrong, but not wrong all at the same time.

"Don't you love Mr. Pratt?" Maggie said, trying to mask the quiver in her voice.

"I love Walter's hands. They're powerful, and not in the sense they're big, more like they build beautiful things. He smells like cardamom and pepper, like a man who has travelled, like a man I once knew."

Maggie hooked her arm through Charlotte's; the prickles rippled down her spine. Angelene was smiling a pleasant 'we're-friends-aren't-we' smile. Her presence was snowy and bracing.

"I may have felt something once. It was odd and made me extremely uncomfortable. I ran from it to Sacre-Coeur Basilica and asked God to help me understand. You both should know what love feels like."

Maggie yanked Charlotte's arm. "You tell her, Charlie, so we can go."

The words trembled from Charlotte's mouth. "It f... feels like home, s... safe and comfortable. You miss them when they aren't around, like right now. I miss crumpet."

Brief flashes of the dream, grey, blood red, sliced through Maggie's mind. She was breathless, like someone had covered her head with a blanket and twisted it around her neck. "I wish we could stay and talk, but we have to get to Taunton Park."

"Does Brendon feel like home?"

Maggie stumbled into the bumper, '*she wants something of mine.*'

"You take care of Troy's sunshine. You hold the key to his light. J'espere que vous n'allez pas faire du mal..." Angelene paused. The sunshiny tone to her voice sounded fake. "A bientôt."

Maggie gripped Charlotte's hand and they scrambled back to the car, dove onto the seats, and slammed their hands on the locks.

"Did she just threaten me? You're brilliant in French."

Maggie watched Angelene walk down the road. Her heart thundered against her rib cage. Questions swarmed her head. Why would Mrs. Pratt worry about Charlotte hurting Troy? Was she threatening her? Did Mrs. Pratt have a crush on Troy?

"She said something about, uh, how brilliant the cows are."

"She's a bleeding nutter, Magpie."

The drive to the pitch was quiet. The expression on Angelene's face haunted Maggie: longing, desperation, sadness. She couldn't put a finger on it.

"Babes is going to be so upset I missed kick-off."

Maggie tugged her purse over her shoulder and grabbed a blanket from the rear seat.

"I doubt Brendon even noticed."

They slid their tickets under the glass, smiled shaky smiles, and edged their way to their seats.

"I'm freezing. Share the blanket with me."

Maggie shook it out and wound it around them. "I feel the same way; it isn't even cold today."

The look in Angelene's eyes lingered, *'stealing light, stealing breath.'* One look from Angelene and she had come undone. It was scary to think someone so tiny could have so much power over her. Maggie snuggled closer and focused on a bigger problem.

"If my mom finds out I told a lie to get out of classes, she'll murder me."

"Margaret Thornton would never tell a porkie. Poor little muffin with cramps."

"I saw Ms. Haversham's face. She didn't believe we were both ill?"

"That old prune. She needs to retire." Charlotte wiggled her fingers at Troy then blew him a kiss. "I had a prop."

"What did you do?"

"I asked Edwin Bellingham for some of his fish pie and dumped it in a Tesco bag. I mixed in some milk. It looked just like sick. The smell was vile."

Maggie closed her eyes and breathed away the flutters upsetting her belly. "I'm done with this month's Cosmo." She pulled the magazine out of her purse and handed it to Charlotte. "I didn't read the whole thing. The last few pages were stuck together."

"It's babes' spunk. We read the article, 'Twenty Positions to Blow His Mind.' I gave him a wank."

Two men sitting two seats over chuckled into their cups of coffee. Maggie scrunched her nose at them and groaned.

"I touched that disgusting stuff. You could have warned me."

Charlotte pressed open the pages and pointed to a pink silhouette on her hands and knees, a blue silhouette behind it. "Wouldn't you like to try that?"

"Not very romantic. Your bum stuck up in the air."

"It's not my favourite. This one is."

Maggie studied the pink silhouette straddling the blue one. She glared at the two men who were more interested in their conversation than the match and lowered her voice.

"Do you just sit on it? Doesn't it hurt to have his thingy shoved all the way up there?"

"You're the sweetest muffin; it feels brilliant. I can look at my crumpet the whole time. He has the cutest 'O' face."

"I've seen 'O' faces in movies. They look daft."

"You don't know what you're missing."

"I forgot to do the quiz." Maggie hooked a ragged fingernail under the page and flipped it over. 'Are You Toxic?' jumped out in vibrant red writing.

'Stealing light, stealing breath, stealing Charlie's sunshine' seared through Maggie's brain.

"You're not toxic. Toxic people have deep wounds. Nothing bad has happened to you, unless you count Jack."

Maggie glanced at the first question, *'Do you discover people's weaknesses and use them against them? You know Charlie loves Troy. You knew if you threatened her, she'd buckle. I saw Charlie's face. You scared her.'*

Maggie rooted around in her purse for her glasses, putting them on. '*Do you regularly play the victim? Brendon's always running to you, falling for the pathetic, poor-me pout.*'

"Stop. You need to read the article on sexual positions. Start with missionary, you'll love it."

"Cheers to that, luv," the two men said in unison, tapping their cups together.

'*Do you always have something sad, pessimistic to say?' She's a spiritual vampire.*'

"Maggie." Charlotte closed the magazine, tucking it in her bag. "You're not a toxic person. You're the sweetest muffin. Which I'm sure Brendon would love to dive into."

Maggie held up the corner of the blanket and shielded her face from the amused men. "I thought I was ready on Sunday; I couldn't do it. Brendon got mad, then I got mad at myself for thinking I should just do it to make him happy."

Charlotte scrolled through her gallery on her phone, tapping on a picture of Troy. "It shouldn't be that confusing. Do you want my advice?"

"If it involves me getting on all fours, no."

"Wait until the Cooks have gone to bed and sneak into Brendon's room. You'll hear the bay outside his window. It'll be very romantic."

Maggie dropped the blanket and snuggled closer to Charlotte. "I'm not going to Burnham."

Charlotte held up her phone, aimed it at Troy, and snapped a series of photos. "You always go."

"Not this time."

"That attacker is going to run right into my crumpet." Charlotte dropped her cell in her lap, covered her eyes, and peeked through her fingers. "Not his hair. Do not ruin his hair."

The whistle blew, and the referee waved a yellow card at the Hayes player.

"Mrs. Cook wants a family weekend. Brendon told me the Pratts are going," Maggie said. Her eyes grew wide at Charlotte's gallery. "How many photos do you have now? A thousand?"

"You're one to talk. Your bedroom is filled with pictures of Brendon," Charlotte said, snapping a photo. "Here comes that attacker again."

"Brendon will make the save," Maggie said soberly. "Don't you think it's weird, Mrs. Cook making Brendon go?"

"Hayes has been in our end for twenty minutes now. Babes will be too exhausted for a snog."

Maggie took off her glasses and placed them in her purse. She rolled her eyes and tugged Charlotte's hair. "Are you listening to me?"

"Of course, luv. Babes is playing brilliantly; I'll be in Manchester yet."

"Mrs. Cook likes when I come. We go shopping and have lunch at a posh restaurant. You know the type where there's nothing on the plate but a leaf of lettuce and a blob of sauce." Maggie gnawed at her nails, tugged, and pulled on the loose cuticles.

"You know what I think," Charlotte said, jerking Maggie's hand away.

"I'm not sure you're entitled to an opinion. You haven't taken your eyes off the pitch."

"The next eleven months are going to be horrible. Mrs. Cook has been clingier since he got back."

"I keep asking Brendon why she's so overprotective. He won't discuss it."

"Some moms are just like that. Did you say you were up for a hump on Sunday?"

Charlotte held up her cell, tapped her fingernail on the camera, and smiled at the photo.

"I'm trying to have a serious conversation, and you're back to taking pictures. I think he's gone off me."

"If you don't stop whingeing, Brendon will run as fast as he can. Put a smile on your face and let's go meet our men."

"I wish I were half as confident as you."

"I have bad days, too. Remember when I tried DIY blonde highlights, and they turned orange. I felt ugly for weeks."

Maggie folded the blanket and tucked it under her arm. "I couldn't tell."

"I'm a better actor than Miss. Baxter thinks. I cried on Troy's shoulder every day. Act, Magpie, you're the best actress in drama."

Maggie followed the flow of fans leaving the bleachers. She glanced at Brendon. The team surrounded him, celebrating the win. "You sound like Mrs. Cook."

"You're always going on about how so and so looks, if their boobies are bigger or their clothes are nicer. People only put the good stuff on social media. They don't put pictures of themselves with spots or in their jimjams."

"Bets at school are we're on the outs."

"Brendon's been on his best behaviour. It's all they have to bet on."

Charlotte unlocked the car and tossed her bag onto the rear seat. "Should we mention almost running Mrs. Pratt over?"

"I don't want to talk about it. I'll get the collywobbles again."

Maggie placed her thumb in her mouth and chewed. Monsters came in all shapes and sizes. This one was tiny and helpless.

Troy

Troy turned into the pub car park. Charlotte ran her hand over his thigh; he twisted his mouth and pecked her lips.

"Thanks for letting me drive your dad's car. I feel proper posh in his Mercedes."

"Ah, babes, I like your Fiesta."

He parked the car in the farthest parking spot away from the door, switched off the engine and leaned back in the seat. Adrenaline raced through his veins. It was another win for First and rumour was scouts from Newcastle United and Tottenham had been at the game. He had played with dragons in his belly and fire in his feet, got an assist and almost scored had the ref not discounted it. He had to get off the farm, and he hoped today's performance was enough to spark an interest.

"Do you think Maggie's pretty? She's feeling down."

Troy unbuttoned his jeans and pushed the seat back. "Will it get me a pinch? That attacker ran into me, bleeding hard. I have a bruise on my hip."

"It'll make her feel better," Charlotte said, unzipping his zipper.

"Michael Collins is always following her around. Ask him."

"I'm asking you." Charlotte slid her hand into his jeans and leaned towards his lap. "Tell me, babes."

"She's pretty in that scrubbed-clean kind of way."

"Do you think she's a minger?"

"I think she's sweet like a fairy cake and smells like one, too." Troy smiled down at her. His eyes on her mouth. "She's too smart for me."

"Are you saying I'm dumb?"

A moment passed before Troy spoke. Charlotte's mouth was warm. Her tongue teased him. It was hard to concentrate. She was gentle fingers, moist lips and fearless.

"You're smart at the right stuff." Troy gasped and moved his fingers through her hair. "Like who plays for Man U and how to pick out my outfits for posh parties. I'd take that over the scientific method any day."

A warm, tingly sensation surged through Troy's body. "It's going to happen."

"Hold my hair back."

Troy's belly muscles contracted, and he gripped the grab bar. "There's a napkin in my pocket."

Charlotte wiped her mouth, reached into the console, and shook out a piece of gum. "Did you like it, babes? You deserve a treat after that match."

"It was brilliant, just brilliant. Are you sure you want to go for a drink? Will asked Tilly and Rachel."

Troy glanced out the car window. Brendon and Maggie had arrived and were standing toe to toe. It looked like WW3 was about to happen.

"Those tarts don't bother me."

Troy zipped and buttoned his jeans. If there was one thing he prided himself on, other than his footy skills, he was an amazing boyfriend. It irked him that William ran around with Matilda Morimoto instead of his devoted and oblivious girlfriend, Gemma. Troy had been over the moon happy when Charlotte agreed to go on a date, and he had been determined to put all his boyfriend skills into action. He had his own code: honesty, loyalty, show Charlotte off as his girl, guard her secrets, respect, miss her when she wasn't around. He was consistent and patient, gave wonderful hugs when she was down. Someone once told him he would eventually betray Charlotte, whether the peek at a girl lingered too long or he spilled the secret that she still slept with her blankie, it would happen. It had with Mrs. Pratt. He was as guilty as William. He had broken his code.

"We can finish watching that Netflix series."

"By the looks of things, Magpie needs me."

Troy watched Charlotte tousle her chestnut hair and apply lip gloss. He would choose her over and over again. He couldn't picture himself without her, so he couldn't tell her he had fancied Mrs. Pratt for a minute or two. It would destroy her. Charlotte was fiercely loyal and expected the same from him.

"My mate needs a hump."

"Is that it?"

"Is that *it*?" Troy said. He flipped down the visor and smoothed his bangs. "Brendon hasn't really touched a set of jubblies yet."

"If he weren't so obsessed with football. He might have humped sooner."

"Maggie doesn't do anything."

"What if I wanted to wait until marriage or was scared, would you get all whingey?"

"You've always been up for it."

Charlotte's mouth dropped open. She raised her fingers and pinched the air. "Are you saying I'm a slag?"

"You're not a tart if you've only been with one bloke. I could touch your jubblies and put my hand down your knickers."

"You do that tickle from the inside thing."

Troy snapped the visor and kissed Charlotte's neck. "Tell Maggie how good it feels. Brendon can give her a tickle too."

Charlotte twisted in the seat and leaned against the door. "Brendon's been spending time with Rachel. Does he fancy her?"

"I have a theory. You can't say anything."

"Hurry, it looks they're going to kill one another."

"He fancies Mrs. Pratt. He gets this dreamy look on his face whenever she's around."

'Like you do, dolt.'

"Her eyes lit up when she spoke about him."

Troy tossed the keys into her purse. It was hard to read Charlotte's face. He was good at knowing when she was upset or angry. When she needed him to be quiet and hug her, or when she wanted to snog. He didn't know what she was feeling, but if he were to take a guess, he would say something, or someone threatened her.

"What are you going on about?"

"Nothing," Charlotte said, gripping his nipple. "She's anorexic, needs a tan, and has a crooked tooth. Plus, she's a nutter."

Troy batted her hand away. "Bleeding heck, she's not that bad. You have to get a good look at her."

"Have you been hanging around Mr. Pratt's house?"

"No, uh, I saw her and Walt out walking."

A little jab pierced his heart—rule break.

Charlotte held her fingers over his nipple and glared. "You look like the two of you shared a moment."

Troy wrestled into his hoodie and planted a kiss on her cheek. "There's something about Mrs. Pratt that creeps up on you."

"Like the flu."

"She loves football. Of course Brendon would have a crush."

"If he sticks his knob in anyone. I'm not sure what I would do," Charlotte said. She touched his cheek, and for a moment, Troy thought she might cry. "You stay away from Mrs. Pratt. She steps inside you and sticks like glue. She's creepy."

"Has something happened?"

"It's a feeling I get when she's around, like she's preying on my spirit and energy."

"What is she? A bleeding vampire?"

Charlotte pushed open the door. She was avoiding the question.

"I've been craving your mom's pie and mash all afternoon. I promised Callum I'd sit between the two of you."

Troy hadn't felt anything but guilty the night he walked Angelene home. It had taken a while to knock her out of his head, but he hadn't felt drained. No one knew Angelene Pratt. She was a stranger with strange habits and strange things to say. Something twisted in Troy's stomach.

Brendon

"Are you going to tell me what's bothering you?"

Sparks whizzed through Brendon's body. They had lingered over porridge and berries, through his school day and onto the pitch. The plus side of the nagging sparks, he played a feisty, no-fear game of football.

"I'm not going to stand in the car park all night. Bloody talk."

The setting sun washed the horizon in sweeps of melancholy pastels. A battle raged inside him, *run to little bird. Console Margaret Grace.*

"You looked bloody miserable throughout the entire match."

"I'm worried the school called my mom," Maggie said.

Brendon crossed his arms and leaned against his car. "If they gave out awards for attendance, you'd win."

Maggie bit her bottom lip, chewed and spoke between nibbles. "You've been acting dodgy since you were at mine. We've barely said two words to each other."

"I'm trying not to lose my temper."

William and Tilly strolled towards the pub wearing 'we-know-something-you-don't' smirks.

"Lover's quarrel?"

"Fuck off, Will."

"Why isn't he with Gemma? Are you hanging around cheaters now?"

"I don't hang around with Will."

"Are you going to tell us who you were buying fish and chips for?" William said. His 'try-to-get-out-of-this-one' grin accentuated his overbite and fuelled the sparks dipping in and out of Brendon's turbulent stomach.

Maggie licked at the tiny tear in her lip. "You told me you were knackered and fell asleep."

Brendon's hands tingled with sparks. Maggie was too smart for excuses.

"I grabbed one for my dad."

"He was in Yeovil with your mom."

"He had a craving when he got home."

William laughed like he was hatching an evil plan. "Sounds like a lie to me."

Brendon shook out his hands, hoping the sparks would fly out his fingers. Every inch of him was on fire. The lie was easy but wrong, wanting to kiss Mrs. Pratt and run from Maggie, wrong.

"Get in the car, Maggie."

"You not coming? Rachel will be so disappointed her knuddelbär went home," Tilly said.

Maggie stuck out her tongue at Tilly and scrambled into the car.

"You look guilty, Mr. Football. Adios."

Light flooded the car park. Troy flung up his middle finger at William and jogged to Brendon. "You coming inside? Rachel keeps asking where you are. Charlie's going to slap her."

"I'm liable to punch Will in the nose."

"Maybe that's what the wanker needs."

"Dad and I have been getting along lately. I don't want any aggro, smooth sailing until July, that's my plan."

"What's up? We won, you played brilliantly."

The secret was eating a hole in Brendon. He had a crush on Angelene and a crazy voice by the name of Padre Diavolo pestered him to do things he shouldn't. Spilling everything would undo the knots but it would get back to Charlotte, who would tell Maggie. There was only one person he trusted. She understood expectations and lived with a set of strangling rules. She would take a train and hold his hand. The girl who wasn't his.

Brendon glanced at Maggie texting furiously and stepped away from the car. "Maggie's my problem." He picked up a stone and whipped it towards the road. "You're getting a bloody BJ and I'm listening to her whine about bunking off school."

Troy jammed his hands into his pockets and looked at a wad of gum stuck to the pavement. "Charlie and I were snogging."

"I may be a fucking virgin, but I know what was happening."

"Don't tell Charlie you saw. She'll never do it again."

"Your secret is safe with me."

"Have you gone off Maggie?"

"Why does everyone keep asking me that?"

"You used to carry her book bags, text her after a match."

Brendon imagined a violent wind battering the sparks, silencing the raging fire.

"Do you fancy someone else? Rachel? Mrs. Pratt?"

'*The truth will set you free. The truth will get me a bloody blubbering Maggie.*'

"Don't be daft."

"I'm just asking, mate. I say her name and you get this look on your face."

"I feel sorry for Mrs. Pratt. People treat her like shit."

"Rachel?"

Brendon chuckled and kicked a stone across the car park. "No one fancies Rachel. She's jubblies and an arse. Both of which I like, but never in my lifetime would I fancy her. She doesn't even rate."

"What would you give her out of ten?"

"Two. One for her arse and one for her tits."

"Be nice to Maggie. She loves you. See ya."

Brendon strolled to the car and plunked onto the seat. "Don't ask about the fish and chips."

Maggie shoved her hands between her thighs and gnawed her lip instead. "I wasn't going to."

"I don't want to talk either."

"I took a quiz today about toxic people."

"Not talking."

Brendon gripped the wheel. Madre Innocente scolded him. He hurt Maggie, lied, allowed William to get under his skin, and all for a girl he couldn't have.

"Toxic people are emotionally manipulative. They get you under their control. You bend over backwards for them."

He switched on the radio. A poppy tune filled the silence in the car. "No more talking."

"They take your time for granted," Maggie said, turning down the volume. "They expect you to drop everything."

Angelene's voice whispered through his mind. *What is this? Where are the sculptures and stained glass?* She had complained about the church and didn't seem to care he had bunked off school. She needed him, and that took precedence.

"Toxic people need your help to get through things." Maggie's eyes were wide, vibrant blue.

Brendon clutched the steering wheel, sweat gathered in his armpits. Maggie's brain was in overdrive.

"Do you know what Charlie did in the car park?" He stopped alongside the curb. It seemed like an excellent strategy, avoid conflict by changing the subject, fling some dirt in her direction, make her feel guilty, *'toxic Brendon, manipulative prick.'*

"It's a nasty thing to do in front of everyone's local."

"I bet Troy didn't think so. I'm sure he enjoyed it."

Maggie hooked the plethora of straps over her arms and tore into a jagged fingernail. "I'm sure he did."

Brendon didn't understand how feelings could change from 'I'm in serious like, here's a ring' to 'I'm falling for Uncle Walt's wife.' He hadn't spent much time with Angelene. All he knew was the moments shared meant something. If anyone was toxic, it was him.

Shadowy darkness veiled the farmhouse; the dormer windows glowed sinister yellow. He told himself to go home, call Maggie, and apologize for being a prick. Despite his best intentions to follow the code, he needed to see Angelene.

Brendon parked under the willow tree, jerked on his hood, and rambled up the walkway. The door opened as if she had sensed his arrival.

"I was going to text and ask if you would stop by." Her voice was raspy, sparkling with happiness. She peeked around the door, smiling a rosy pink smile.

This was not toxic. This was paradise.

"You should have seen the save I made today. The ball slammed into my chest and bounced into the Hayes player's foot. He tried to put it in the right corner. The dive I made, bloody brilliant."

"I wish I had been there." Angelene grabbed two plates from the drying rack and pointed her chin towards his head. "Take your hood off so I can see your face. Are you hungry?"

He yanked at his hood. The island was a mess of lettuce, green beans, boiled eggs, and potatoes. An opened tin of tuna and black olives sat on the cutting board.

"I thought you were a terrible cook."

"You can't mess up a salad. Will you join me?"

The voices in his head argued, '*Go home. Stay.*' The battle continued with Madre Innocente leading her army of guilt and Padre Diavolo charging through with his pitchfork of pleasure.

"I'll eat at home. I don't know why I came."

"For someone who played an amazing game, your light is dull. Stay and talk. We're here for each other, non?"

'If she were toxic, she wouldn't want to hear about my day or wonder why I was upset. She'd tell me about a fight with Walter or one of her sad stories, deflect the attention back to her. Toxic, my ass.'

"What are we having?"

"Niçoise salad. I had it at a café with Roman. I thought I was special dining with a handsome financier. The server thought we were father and daughter. We played along."

"Can I help?"

"Grab the salad dressing from the fridge. Bring me the tuna and olives."

"You made the dressing?"

"Mother was so mad Roman took me to lunch. He had to make her one for dinner. Olive oil, lemon juice, Dijon and Roman's secret, honey."

"Your mom was a bloody cow."

"She didn't like when her men paid attention to me," Angelene said and sliced into a tomato. "I'm done talking about my mother. Tell me what's wrong so your light brightens. Peel the eggs, please."

"William gives a whole new meaning to taking the piss. He never shuts his bloody gob, always digging at me."

"He's jealous. He'll cast a shadow over you because your light is so bright and his is dull. What else?"

He rolled an egg over the counter, cracked the shell, and peeled. "Maggie was whingey all day."

She grabbed the eggs, sectioned them, and arranged the halves on the plate. Brendon was both happy and sad. The simple enjoyment of constructing a salad together made his insides tingle and his heart hurt.

"Why is Maggie upset?"

"She bunked off school."

"We'll sit on the sofa. I have a bottle of wine open."

"Have you been drinking all day?"

"I had one glass after my walk, honest."

Brendon plopped onto the sofa. Loose sheets of paper, stubs of charcoal, and smudged tissues covered the coffee table. The ashtray was empty, the bottle almost full. Her mood—the glorious, sunny yellow mood—was all her.

"Has Maggie never lied before?"

"Once. She told her mom she was sleeping at Charlie's so she could stay at mine. Worst night of my life. She slept in mermaid pyjamas, felt guilty. I had to drive her home."

Angelene set down her plate and shuffled through the drawings. "I drew these today."

Brendon nearly dropped his fork. "Bloody hell, those are me. What will Uncle Walt think?"

"I'm going to give one to your mother. Maybe she'll like me."

Brendon studied each illustration. Every detail was right, from his widow's peak to the cleft hidden beneath the stubble.

"Walter isn't going to like this."

"Other than the one I'm giving your mother; he'll never know."

Brendon didn't know what to think: flattered, embarrassed, panicked.

"Why did you draw me?"

"I enjoy sinking into your light."

"What about your light?"

"I lost mine years ago and have struggled to find it."

Brendon shovelled in the last bites. He set his plate on the floor, lacing his fingers through hers. "Who hurt you?"

"I knew a boy who was a lot like you. His passion was architecture. He saw the world in lines and shapes. He knew the history of every famous structure in France."

"What happened to him?"

"He loved Casa Batlló, the House of Bones in Barcelona. I'm sure he is daydreaming on one of its balconies."

Brendon slumped into the cushions, wiggling his fingers within hers. For a tiny girl, her grip was unbelievably strong.

"You need to know maths and physics to study architecture."

"Be creative, a visionary, a dreamer. He put triangles, arches, and squares together to make incredibly beautiful things."

"I failed geometry."

"School does not make you smart. Life and God are your best teachers."

She dug under the illustrations for a book wrapped in Van Gogh's Starry Night. Angelene thumbed through the pages, stopped, and tapped a charcoal-stained fingertip on it. "This is *The Nightmare* by Fuseli."

"That's a perfect title."

"What do you see in the painting?"

Brendon nuzzled against her and studied the picture. "She must be having a bad dream with that thing sitting on her chest."

"Go on."

"She should be scared. She looks like she's enjoying the dream, like the girls in the videos Will's shown us in the dressing room."

"What kind of video was that?"

Brendon ran a finger around his collar and swallowed. "An inappropriate one. She gives the impression, bloody hell, of being satisfied by that thing."

Angelene grinned and touched his cheek. "The creature is an incubus, a demon. They have their way with women."

"Good thing she's asleep. If she saw what she was humping."

"Does the painting scare you?"

"She looks at peace." He slid his arm around her and buried his nose in her hair. The day's tension unravelled and burned away. "I hear you're coming to Burnham."

Angelene closed the book and set it on the coffee table. "Walter is excited. Will you be there?"

"Mom wants me to go."

"You don't want to go to the house on the sea that's really a bay?"

"I'd rather have a break from my parents. Since I came home from Dortmund, things have been tense." Her touch was gentle. No one toxic could have fingers this soft. "Mammina is clingier. Dad's pretending to be over it."

"What did you do? Walter said it happened twice."

Brendon laid his cheek against the crown of her head. Just as she didn't want to talk about her mother, he wanted to forget the day his world blew up.

"It was the opportunity of a lifetime that came with a list of expectations and promises."

He buried his nose in her hair and closed his eyes. The scent of lavender and the slow beat of her heart lulled him.

"What are you thinking about, mon ami?"

"You and me in Westfalenpark."

"We could go to Oktoberfest, eat potato dumplings and bratwurst, drink until we can't stand."

"You'll be cleaning up barf."

"I'll wipe your chin like you do my nose."

Brendon opened his eyes and grinned sleepily. "I better get home before Mom sends out a search party."

He stared at her mouth, memorizing the shape of her lips.

"I'm glad you came over. You make Taunton a little less frightening and normal,slightly easier."

Brendon stretched, yawned, and strolled to the door. "I hope that bloody incubus doesn't pay me a visit."

"It would be a succubus."

"Are you telling me there is a female version of that thing?"

"There's a seductress in the Dead Sea Scrolls, with horns and wings full of sin. Someone said I carried my sins on my broken wings and stole light like a succubus."

"Whoever said that was a dick."

"Get home to Sofia before she worries herself sick and her elegant black turns grey."

"Have you always seen people in colour?"

"All my life," Angelene said. "When someone speaks, their words come at me in colour and then surrounds them. I know all about a person just by their colour."

"I'm boring brown."

"Brown is wise and grounding, like the mighty oak. Sweet like chocolate. What colour am I?"

"You've been a bit of a chameleon tonight. You were yellow when I got here, then sad greyish blue, then faraway purple and now I'd say you're pale yellow, kind of happy."

"I am kind of happy. Sweet dreams, my boy in brown."

He walked away immersed in her yellow.

Angelene

Angelene stared at Fuseli's *Nightmare*.

'I am a succubus. Stealing light. Stealing breath. Stealing their wings.'

14 Stuck

Brendon
He followed a trail of feathers; gnarled branches tore at his skin. He dropped to his knees and cradled her. Blood spilled from her wrists. Wake up, little bird.

"Wake up, knuddelbär."

Brendon blinked and opened his eyes. Rachel grinned at him. Her mouth was the colour of raspberries, the buttons on her blouse—ready to burst.

"What are you doing at school so early, meine prinzessin?"

"Ah, knuddelbär, that's sweet. I've never been anyone's princess." Rachel undid her braided hair and shook it out. "Mom and I had a meeting with Dawson. If it isn't my shirt, it's my shoes. I need to tie my hair up, lower my kilt, wear tights or those itchy trousers."

Ask her to sit or don't. Brendon stretched out his legs and contemplated the question. A group of Maggie's drama friends walked by and gave him questioning eyes. First's striker, Nigel Davies, made a gesture with his fingers and snickered. Madre Innocente told him to shoo Rachel away. Padre Diavolo enjoyed the view.

"You ready for your lesson today, knuddelbär?"

"I've been practicing all morning."

"Really?"

"With every box jump, eins, zwei, drei. I got all the way to twenty-nine. I forgot how to say thirty."

"Dreißig." Rachel unwrapped a Double Lolly. She placed the powdery lollipop in her mouth and licked the residue off her lips. "Why didn't you come into the pub? Was it Will? I don't know what Tilly sees in him."

Brendon gave her the easiest excuse. "I was knackered."

"That's not what I heard." She flicked her tongue around the lollipop. His mind took him to a place it shouldn't. "I heard you and Thornton were arguing."

"We were debating stuff."

Rachel tugged at her blouse buttons. Her breasts sprang from their cotton restraint. "That's better."

A bloom of heat painted Brendon's cheeks red. "You could have warned me."

Rachel laid her tie over her cleavage and grinned. "Is that better?"

It wouldn't matter if she tugged down her kilt or wore trousers. There was something about Rachel that made his insides flutter.

"Was it because Tilly and I were sitting at the table?"

"We were discussing toxic people."

"They're insecure." Rachel bit the lollipop. She slowly licked sugar from her lips and tossed the stick into a garbage pail hidden beside an immense glass case of trophies. "It makes them feel better to make people miserable."

"Like when you call me knuddelbär. You don't think that upsets Maggie."

"I can't help it. I bet you give great cuddles."

Brendon liked how her eyes shined like polished amber, and she wore Converse high tops instead of flats. She was different, and he was curious. Did she own a battery-operated boyfriend like William said? How long was the famous list?

"Did your private chef make your lunch today? I've seen you in the dining hall with a bagged lunch."

"She's our housekeeper and yes, Amelia did. I've got a sandwich, salad, nuts, fruit."

Rachel lowered her gaze, her voice softened. "You're brilliant, you know that."

"If you'd like me to share my lunch, just ask." Brendon patted the spot beside him. "It's the least I could do after you cooked for me."

Rachel looked at him quizzically. "You want me to sit? Boys never want to talk to me, like really talk to me." She peeked into the classroom and wiggled her fingers. "Troy's in there with Emelia Bunton. Poor thing. She's the worst tutor, smells like mothballs and cabbage."

"Ms. Hudson wants him to apply himself." Brendon tapped the floor again. "Sit. I enjoy talking to you."

The hallway filled with students. Brendon flicked the end of his tie between his fingers. He ignored the prying stares and raised eyebrows.

"Tell me how to say red in German."

Rachel sat; her kilt ballooned around her as she stretched out her legs. "Rot."

He touched a curl and twisted it around his finger. "Your hair is rot."

"Dein haar ist braun."

"How do you say beautiful again?"

The vent whirred, showering him with heat. He loosened his tie and undid a button. Her exposed cleavage and perfume, doubled the temperature in the hallway.

"Schon." Rachel pulled two lollies from her blazer pocket and dropped one in his lap. "Indulge, knuddelbär. I know you like blue Smarties. I wasn't in the mood for chocolate this morning."

"I haven't had a Double Lolly in years. My dad used to hide them in his briefcase. When he came home from work, I would carry it to the den. There was always one stuck between his pens." Brendon unwrapped it and tucked the crinkly plastic into his pocket. "He started buying buckets of them and hiding them from my mom. I'd get one if I finished my homework."

"Why did he hide them?"

"Mom didn't want me eating candy. I overheard her telling him I was hard to settle at bedtime. She had an excuse for everything."

"Has she always been protective of you? I'm lucky if I get a good night."

Brendon stuck the lolly in his mouth; the tart cherry flavour tingled on his tongue. "From what I ate, where I could play. Even the bloody sheets I slept on. Dad and I can't say goodbye. It's, see you soon. How do you say delicious?"

"Lecker."

"And brilliant?"

"Brillant or hervorragend," Rachel said, unzipping her purse.

Brendon's eyebrows raised at the collection of lollipops stashed amongst the lighters, packs of cigarettes, and makeup.

"Take a couple."

"Don't tell Liam. He'll fine me for each one." He took a handful of lollies and shoved them into the front pocket of his backpack.

"Even your coach is protective of you."

"As Mammina says, I'm a commodity. Liam's protecting Dortmund's investment."

"I won't tell."

"You didn't buy all those sweets, did you?"

"You know the sweet shop across from Ball's?"

"It sells jelly unicorns. I bought Mags a bag for her birthday. I've never seen anyone so happy over bloody sweets."

"The owner, Mr. Lawson, calls me his strawberry muffin. He gives me handfuls."

"Bloody creepy, don't you think?"

"He doesn't stare at my tits or anything. He feels sorry for me."

"Why?"

"He knew my dad before he ran out on us," Rachel said, grabbing her phone.

"Bloody hell. Did he just up and leave?"

"Last I heard, he moved back to Liverpool. Bleeding scouser."

Brendon glanced over her shoulder at a photo of her and Tilly. "Can you tell Tilly to stay away from Will? It isn't helping my situation with Maggie."

"William isn't even her number one. Mr. Walker is. Keep that to yourself."

"The physics teacher? He's bloody married."

"Tilly doesn't care about that stuff," Rachel said, tapping the camera icon.

"Do you have any married blokes on your list?"

"I may be a tart, but married guys are off limits. My mom got involved with a barrister. He had a whole life in London, a wife, daughters. I hated my mom the two months they were humping."

"I'm on your list. I have a girlfriend. Troy too."

"Girlfriends come and go, but a wife, that's supposed to be forever. Once you make those vows, you respect them. My dad had a few slappers on the side. I think that's why my mom lost faith in commitment."

"My dad takes his vows bloody seriously. One time we were at the pub with his best friend Walt and these women came in."

"You're talking about Walter Pratt? His crinkly smile and that 'I sailed the seven seas' vibe is brill. Mom thinks he's dishy. Anytime he's on the telly, she stops whatever she's doing to watch him."

"He told us to have a look. All my dad said was they looked like nice ladies."

"I've seen your mom. He'd have no reason to look." Rachel flicked through the photos and stopped at a picture of Brendon coming off the First team bus. "My mom says she's a stuck-up cow."

Brendon took her phone and scrolled through a series of pictures of him. Rachel was as bad as Charlotte. "People think that about her. She isn't. Nonna raised her to command a room, take no prisoners."

"I wish my mom were like that. Every time a relationship ends, she's a miserable cow. She fills the freezer with ice cream, doesn't leave her room until the next one comes along."

Brendon had seen his mother rattled. The worry on her brow had Angelene attached to it.

"My mom stresses when things aren't perfect. She likes everything, including dad and I, to be just so."

"I'd like my mom to fuss over me," Rachel said. She held up her phone and scooted closer. "Let's take a pic together."

A cacophony of laughter and voices echoed down the hall. Some of Maggie's classmates glared. Boys looked at him like, 'What are you doing with the slag?' Someone bet he'd have her in the rear seat of his Beemer.

It was just a photo between friends.

"Just one, and don't be bragging about it. Maggie will kill me."

He laid his cheek against hers. Her reflection was pretty, a softer Rachel.

"When I say Dortmund, smile."

She counted down from three; as she said 'Dortmund,' Brendon crossed his eyes and stuck out his tongue.

"Oh, bollocks. I wanted to remember this moment."

"You want to remember these musty halls?"

"You're the first boy who hasn't tried to chat me up."

A feeling of 'I like you' bombarded Brendon. One simple thing like a photo meant the world to her. She wasn't a tart. Taunton had labelled her like they had Angelene.

Brendon leaned against her and flashed his best dimpled smile. Her hair smelled like the sweet peas Amelia grew on the kitchen windowsill.

"You look dead gorgey. When you're famous, I can brag I knew you. Can we take another?"

"I'm getting the evils from Maggie's friends."

"So, what?" Rachel said. "Something silly this time, like duck lips."

Brendon pursed his lips together. Someone said, 'They've been taking pictures together,' and then the clunk of bags and buckles.

"What are you doing?" Maggie said, kicking his foot. "Is this why you didn't pick me up? You wanted to spend time with the tart."

He pushed himself off the floor and extended his hand to Rachel. "Bloody hell, relax."

Rachel dusted off her kilt and hooked her bag over her arm. "I'll see you at dinner break."

"No, you won't, daft cow."

"What have you got in these bags?" Charlotte said, heaving the totes at Maggie's feet.

"Stuff," Maggie said. She stuck her tongue out at Rachel and sniffed. "No German today, no German ever. Auf weidersehen."

Rachel smirked a 'just-try-and-stop-me' grin and wiggled her hips. "See you, knuddelbär."

"He's not your cuddle bear."

Bets flooded the hallway. 50p Thornton was going to cry. Two pounds Cook would end up in Dawson's office.

"You're a dolt," Maggie said. She jabbed her fist into his belly and grabbed her bags. "A wanker and a git."

Brendon rubbed the sting in his stomach and battled with the sparks. "Has Jack been teaching you karate strikes again?"

Students stood in doorways, teachers strolled past and tapped their watches. Sparks flickered and soared like firecrackers.

Charlotte wrapped her arm around Maggie and rested her chin on her shoulder. "You can give him an ear bashing at lunch."

"Why were you early for school?"

"I needed to get away from Mammina. She was going on about me leaving for Dortmund in July."

The temperature in the hallway rose another ten degrees. Sparks crackled and whirred like a Catherine wheel, unleashing a spray of crimson lava. Brendon loosened his tie and took a shallow breath.

"You didn't text or give me a bell."

Charlotte pecked her cheek and picked up Maggie's laptop bag. "Let it go, muffin."

"Did your crumpet ring you after training?"

"I promised to help with geoggers. I never got to tell him the importance of river hydrographs. Callum put him in a headlock."

"Listen to Charlie and go to class before I lose my temper. I'll wind up in that room that smells like barf and down a strike."

Crack, whir, inhale, exhale.

"You're not meeting the ginger tart."

"It's just a photo. Babes took one with a girl at the pitch a few weeks ago. The only photos that matter are the ones of you and him," Charlotte said. She tugged at Maggie's arm and glared at Brendon. "You're a wanker. You need to talk to your best mate. He's a lovely boyfriend. He could give you some tips. Poor wee crumpet had to meet with his tutor this morning. He'll be miserable today."

"You better be at the dining hall, twelve sharp," Maggie said. She hiked her bags over her shoulders, wobbled under the weight, and stomped off.

Brendon practiced his breaths with every angry step to the classroom.

'I am calm. I am as bloody cool as a cucumber.'

"What did you do this time, mate?"

"Where do I start?" Brendon squeezed behind the desk and released his backpack to the floor with a thud. "I didn't call her. I was talking to Rachel. I didn't pick her up this morning."

Tilly skipped into the room, chirping an exuberant, 'Bleeding tart, you did what?' into her phone.

Ms. Hudson stood in front of her, held out the yardstick, and stopped her in her tracks. "Matilda Morimoto, put your phone away and spit out that gum. It's a disgusting habit."

Matilda leaned over the bin and spat a wad of magenta goo into it. She grinned at Ms. Hudson, slid her phone into her pocket and dropped onto the chair. "You made Rachel so happy this morning. She'll never delete the photos."

"Turn around, Matilda, or it's off to see Mr. Dawson."

"You better do it, or you'll end up in the room Camilla Barton was sick in. The scent sticks in your nose all day," Troy said.

"If Charlotte doesn't want to live on the farm with you. I'm more than willing. I love cows and chickens," Tilly said.

Ms. Hudson tapped the yardstick against the desk; quiet flooded the classroom. Brendon stretched his legs into the aisle and sagged into the chair.

"So far, we have concentrated on Werther's love for Lotte. Today, we'll look at his sorrow. Mr. Spence, a quote."

Brendon hid behind his book and smiled at Troy's flushed cheeks.

"Have you read the book?"

"I've tried, but it's depressing. Werther is always whingeing about Lotte. There must be other girls in Walheim. He did a lot of walking around the place."

A small burst of air expelled between the gap in her teeth. "I'm sure there were, Mr. Spence but that wouldn't make a good story. Matilda, a quote?"

"I haven't been focusing on the sad parts. I'm with Troy, it's terribly depressing."

Brendon glanced at a page and read a few sentences. Out of the ashes, a pathetic spark lit and stung his heart. He slowly raised his hand.

"Why, it's a miracle. Dazzle us, Mr. Cook."

Brendon cleared his throat, stuck his hand under the desk and shot Troy the finger. "'I have so much in me, and the feeling in her absorbs it all, I have so much and without her it all comes to nothing.'"

Werther yearned for Lotte and could only be a friend. He, too, was nothing more than Angelene's friend.

"She gets stuck."

"Pardon me, Mr. Cook."

Heat flickered across his face. Troy stifled a laugh, and the rest of the class stared at him in disbelief. The kid who made it perfectly clear he hated Taunton College had suddenly become a model student.

"It's the book. Poor bloody guy."

Ms. Hudson wedged her ample bottom on the corner of her desk. "I'm curious what you're thinking. There's five minutes left of class. Why not continue to impress me?"

"Sometimes you meet someone and even though you know it's not right, you fancy them anyway. When they aren't with you, they're stuck in your head. You go about your day, wanting to see them. You know it's wrong, but they're there, stuck."

Tilly held a hand to her heart and gushed. "I'm telling Rachel. You're the sweetest."

"Thank you, Mr. Cook, for making the girls swoon. Quotes, I want quotes."

"What was that?" Troy said. He shoved his notebook into his backpack and hiked it over his shoulder. "You're a footy player. Not a swot."

"Don't you love Charlie like that? You couldn't get her out of your mind the first time you saw her at the pitch."

His phone buzzed. Brendon read the text, pinched his lips together, and edged through the mob of students.

"Slow down, mate."

Brendon stomped to a stop. A misty breeze cooled his cheeks. "I'm going to throw my phone into the hawthorn bushes if Maggie doesn't stop whingeing."

"You got the sparks in your belly?"

"It's a bloody fire. I've got to get out of here."

"Not a good idea. You bunk off and you'll be down a strike."

"There's Miss. Morrison from the Career Centre."

"She's looking fit today. What are you going to do?"

Brendon strolled across the lawn, massaging his forehead. "Miss. Morrison, do you have a minute?"

"Of course, Brendon," the willowy blonde said. "What can I do for you? You already know where you're headed."

"My head is bloody pounding. I feel like I could honk. Can I leave?" He gave her the eyes he used when he needed Mammina to forgive him.

"I can't give you permission to leave."

"I'll make an appointment to see you. You like Leverkusen, don't you? I can tell you all about the team. They're fifth in the standings," he said, touching her arm.

"I'll get into trouble."

He held a hand to his stomach and wobbled. "Talk to Madame Lafavre. I've seen the two of you eating together."

She leaned into him and rubbed his back. "Do you promise to schedule a meeting?"

Brendon nodded and clutched his stomach.

"You best get home."

"Did you do something different with your hair?"

"I asked for beachy waves and caramel highlights. Do you like it?"

"It's beautiful."

"Come on, mate, you don't want to honk all over Miss. Morrison's shoes," Troy said. He tugged Brendon's arm and nudged him towards the car park. "You only have three strikes."

"If I don't go, I'll lose all three and Mammina may follow through on that daft rule her and dad made."

"This isn't you."

Troy was right. It wasn't him. Sure, he hated school; he loathed the long days, the jail sentence. He went out of duty, respect. It's what a good boy does.

Brendon watched Troy walk away, rattling the keys in his hand. He needed to breathe. He needed her.

A frog hopped from within the bullrushes to a lily pad. Brendon counted the ripples that moved over the water. He ran through a list of all the things he had done wrong. He enjoyed spending time with Rachel. He was ignoring Maggie. He had manipulated Miss. Morrison, gave her a desperate look, complimented her, promised a meeting he had no intention of keeping. Butterflies tripped out of their cocoons, churned his stomach, filled him with sweaty waves of nausea. He was getting good at making poor decisions.

"I found some feathers."

A smile tugged at Brendon's lips. Her hair was windblown, cheeks vibrant pink, and tucked into the pocket of her denim shirt were three white feathers. The list disappeared. Madre Innocente shrank away. Padre Diavolo whispered, '*She's beautiful.*'

"Have you had a good morning? Mine was bollocks."

"Walter called. He could not find his notes. He had me searching all over the house. It was my fault because I hadn't tidied," Angelene said. She peeled his hand off the steering wheel and placed her fingers into his. "Your light is dim."

"The day started well. I was ace at training and didn't get frustrated with William. I got to school earlier than usual. I even dazzled Ms. Hudson."

"It sounds like everything is okay."

"Maggie and I got into a fight again. She's pissed off I was talking to Rachel."

"Stay away from Mademoiselle femme fatale. She's a troublemaker. The Salome of Taunton."

Brendon agreed. Rachel made him think all sorts of inappropriate things. Nice or not, Rachel would jump all over him if given the chance.

"The novel we're reading in English really got to me. That bloody guy is in love, like the world stands still kind of love. He can't be with Lotte because she's married, and it made me think about you." He locked eyes with Angelene; butterflies stormed his stomach. "I can't stop thinking about the things you said."

The words came, the butterflies flinched and crawled into their cocoons, frightened by his honesty.

"Would you come to Dortmund?"

He searched her face. It was expressionless.

"Maggie should be the only person on your mind."

"You just pop into my head. I could be at the pitch, watching telly, when I can't sleep. You're there."

"We're friends. My only friend. Please don't make me repeat the pattern." She let go of his hand and wove strands of hair between her fingers.

"All those things you said meant nothing?"

He unravelled her hair and rubbed the red marks. She had a look on her face like she had run to a far-off place—from the pattern, from him.

"Truth or one of your fairy tales?"

"Think of me as your friend. I need to please God and show him I can break the pattern."

The desperation in her voice tugged at his heart. Reality slapped him. He hated Walter for bringing her to Taunton.

"Please help me keep my promise to God."

"I guess being your friend is better than nothing."

"You must help me break the pattern. Go back to school, apologize to Maggie."

"Arse lick you mean."

Angelene pushed open the door and stared into the grey sky. "Apologize. She's a good girl."

"For you. I'll drive you home, it's starting to piss down."

"I'll walk."

"If you came to Dortmund as my friend, would you go to the Football Museum with me?"

"Only if you visit the Museum am Ostwall."

He took her hand and ran his thumb over the dots of paint on her fingers. "I'd go anywhere with you."

"And I with you. Go tell Maggie you love her."

"Right. Maggie. Apologize."

"There's a quote from the book *Paris Spleen* by Charles Baudelaire. 'La plus belle des ruses du diable est de vous persuader qu'il n'existe pas.' The devil's finest trick is to persuade you he doesn't exist.' He is here, and he is in all of us. Protect your light."

"You're too pretty to have the devil in you."

"I have the worst kind. I hope you never have to meet them."

Brendon peered through the sweeps of rain. The devil was wandering down the road. He slowed the car, opened the window, and smiled at Rachel's soggy kilt and high tops. "Get in."

She tossed a waterlogged cigarette in a puddle, climbed into the car, and rubbed her goose pimpled thighs.

"Am I glad to see you."

"There's a hoodie on the rear seat."

She stretched over the console, his gaze shifted to the rear-view mirror, orange lace knickers.

"You had the same idea as me."

Rachel bounced onto the seat and laid his hoodie over her thighs. "Thornton and her swot brigade have been giving me the evils all morning. Michael even told me to stay away, cheeky bugger. This is sixth form, not primary."

"Since when do you care?"

"It's frustrating. You'd think we snogged or something. I guess Thornton has banned me from teaching you German."

Brendon turned into the Taunton College car park and parked beside Troy's Fiesta. "I should be able to talk to who I want without Mags getting pissed off."

Rachel squeezed her hair between the folds of her blazer and relaxed against the leather seat. "She needs to write to an agony aunt."

"How about you teach me now? I'll share my lunch with you." His fingers brushed over her legs as he reached to unzip his backpack.

"You'll get more aggro from Thornton."

"I'm already in trouble."

He opened a brown paper sack and pulled out a sandwich. Brendon unfolded the waxed paper, passed half, and bit into the tower of chicken and spinach.

"Is that Branston pickle?"

"Amelia says it makes a sandwich." He set it on the paper, dumped a container of dressing over the salad, closed the lid, and shook it. "I only have one fork."

"This is enough. Wir sollten morgen frühstücken"

Brendon raised his eyebrows and jabbed his fork into a mound of kale and rocket. "I'm supposed to understand that."

"We should have breakfast tomorrow."

"You *do* have the devil in you."

"I'm just a girl who knows what she wants. Satan isn't telling me what to do." Rachel licked pickle off her finger and took a bite. "I'm going to quiz you, knuddelbär, you up for it?"

Brendon nodded and cracked open a can of sparkling water.

"How do you say yes?"

"Bloody easy, ja."

"And no."

"Nein."

"How do you say please?"

"Bitte."

"Kann ich einen küss bekommen?"

Brendon stashed the container in the bag and tossed it into the rear seat. "I thought you were quizzing me?"

"Do you know what I said?"

He shook his head and bit into his sandwich. "Nope."

"I asked for a kiss."

"You don't give up, do you?"

"I bet you're a brilliant kisser."

Padre Diavolo snickered. '*Time to come out and play.*'

"We better head in. Maggie's waiting for me. I should apologize for being a prick."

"Sit beside me in Latin? I downloaded the Bundesliga app. I'll have the news feed ready for you."

They stepped out into the pounding rain. Brendon reached for her hand, and they raced across the lawn. He opened the door and his eyes shifted from Rachel's rain-soaked shirt to Maggie.

"Miss. Jones, I thought I told you to tie your hair up. Button your shirt, young lady."

Rachel winked and ducked into the washroom. Brendon stared at the ceiling and cursed. Mr. Dawson marched towards him, slinging his long, elastic arms.

"You missed French."

"I told Miss. Morrison I was feeling iffy."

Mr. Dawson tapped his finger against his lip and studied his face. "You've made a miraculous recovery."

"I pulled over on the way home and honked. My head bloody hurts, but I'm here."

"Next time you feel like missing class, talk to me. Miss. Morrison believed that rubbish."

Brendon glanced at Maggie and wiggled the knot in his tie. "I guess that's a strike?"

"I spoke to Ms. Hudson. Your insight into the novel impressed her. Take that enthusiasm to history."

One bullet dodged, onto the next. He tossed the intention 'wish me luck or have the roof cave in' into the air and plastered on a grin.

"Headache again?" Maggie said. She scrunched her nose at Rachel and swatted his arm. "Why were you with the ginger tart? An impromptu German lesson."

"I was driving back to school and saw her walking. It's pissing out."

"I've been texting you, gave you a bell twice. You could have answered."

Sparks glided through his body. Entertained students walked by, whispered, and grinned at Maggie's sour expression.

"Can we talk later? I haven't finished the homework."

"You're going to the pitch with Troy. You wouldn't want to break your promise to him."

"I'll take you to that café you like. I promise."

"Of all the people you choose to spend time with, it's a girl you would never speak to."

"I'm getting bloody irritated."

"You're irritated? I told you to stay away from her."

"What are you, my bloody mom? I can talk to whoever I want."

"Be nice to me. You're leaving for Burnham on Friday. I want your full attention for the next two days." She whipped a bottle of paracetamol at him. It bounced off his chest and rolled into the wall. "Nice save, Mr. Football."

Brendon snatched the bottle off the floor and swore no more thinking about Rachel or Angelene. He'd revisit the Gentlemen's Code and ask Troy what it took to be a wonderful boyfriend.

Angelene

Angelene poured a cup of coffee and walked to the kitchen island. She studied the treasures she found on her walk: the feathers, a pebble, a bouquet of wildflowers tied with a stem of mint. She picked up an oak leaf, twirled it in her fingers, and grinned at a box she had discovered buried in the barn. She had a plan for the old box: clean it, paint it, add all the treasures she had found. She'd title the assemblage, 'the day the pattern fell apart.'

The oven timer pinged. Angelene slid the leaf into the box. She grabbed an oven mitt, opened the door, the warm scent of garlic and simmering chicken blew across her cheeks. It was picture-perfect. She set the dish on the stove and swiped open her phone.

"You'd be so proud of me."

"No hello. What are you doing, little bird?"

"Hello, husband. I'm plating my dinner. There was a recipe in that book of yours for cassoulet. I did it. I made dinner."

She scooped beans and chicken onto her plate; his laughter was gold and shimmery.

"That's wonderful. You'll be a chef yet."

"I can feel the pattern breaking. For the first time in my life, things are falling into place, into a new pattern with normal things."

"I wish I were home with you."

"I wish you were here, too. You could try my cassoulet. You'd see the floors are spotless and the loo, as you call it, is sparkling clean."

"I'll book you an appointment at the salon to celebrate."

The smile fizzled from her lips. "What is wrong with me now?"

"Nothing. Women like going to the salon."

"I'll do it for you because wives are supposed to look pretty for their husbands."

"Would you like Sofia to join you?"

"I must do it on my own. I will take a taxi and discover Taunton."

She was yellow, bright, shining from the inside, yellow. The pattern would be different, strong, solid, unbreakable yellow.

15 Edwardian Dreams

T roy

    Troy sulked into his tea. The smell of bacon sizzling and eggs frying on the griddle was drowned out by the early morning rush. All Troy wanted was to escape the madness of his house and enjoy a greasy fry-up with his girl. He got a noisy restaurant and a whingeing Maggie Thornton.

"Does Bronwyn still live in Burnham?" Maggie said. She squirted a blob of ketchup on her plate and smeared a piece of toast through it. "Brendon had the nerve to tell me her lips tasted like strawberry sponge."

"Can we talk about something else? The entire drive here, I miss Brendon. Why hasn't he texted?"

"I bet he doesn't miss me. I'm gutted, just gutted."

Charlotte poured tea and dropped a sugar cube into the cup. "I'm sure he misses you, muffin. Babes, text Brendon and remind him how important it is to keep Magpie happy."

"I'm not getting involved," Troy said. He piled bacon on toast, took a huge bite, and got the words out as he chewed. "He doesn't need to know you're pouting."

"You're my mate too. Text him *for me*," Maggie pleaded.

Troy swallowed and sipped his coffee. "He'll be gone for a weekend. He's been away longer."

"I knew he wouldn't be in Dortmund long after his dad laid down all those rules."

"You're a bleeding nutter," Troy said.

"I'm in love."

"Love makes you do crazy things," Charlotte said and slurped her tea. "Ollie Grant shaved his head last term when he heard Miss. Morrison fancied Jason Statham."

Maggie propped her elbow on the table and leaned her cheek on her palm. "Do you know anything? We've had a fight almost every day."

"What do you think babes knows? He tells me everything, then I tell you."

Troy smiled an 'of-course-I-tell-you-everything' smile and shrugged. "Sixth form. His friend Andreas called from Germany. The keeper who took Brendon's place is bollocks. Dortmund's U19 team dropped from first to fourth. My mate is devastated."

Maggie slipped her pinky into her mouth and nibbled her fingernail. "It's more than that. I talked to Gemma last night, and she said she's been feeling the same way about William."

Troy dipped his toast into an egg, golden yolk spilled across the plate. "He hasn't said anything to me."

"Do you think he fancies Rachel?" Maggie pulled out her pinky, examined the nail, and shoved it back in her mouth. "Gemma thinks William fancies Matilda. I don't know why. Her gum chewing is incredibly annoying."

"So is your whingeing."

Troy dropped his fork and flung his arm over his chest as Charlotte's fingers dove in for the pinch.

"Troy Alexander, what a nasty thing to say."

"See what you did? I'm not her little crumpet now."

"Don't get angry, babes. After school, we'll have a cuddle. I'll tell you about this dishy footy player named Troy Spence who outshines Beckham and Ronaldo."

"More famous than Messi?"

Charlotte ran her finger along his jaw and wiggled his chin. "Of course, babes. Now, tell Magpie Brendon doesn't fancy anyone but her."

"I swear he doesn't like anyone."

"Then why is he being such a dolt?"

Troy wiped his mouth and dropped the napkin onto his plate. "You could always give him a wank."

Maggie groaned, picked up her toast, stared at it, and tossed it back onto a pile of beans. "It always comes back to that."

"Now, muffin, it's not that bad. Put a little Durex Play Perfect lube on your hands. A gentle, twisty motion as you go up and down. You'll be a pro or have a peek at Brendon's face while you're doing it. You'll know if he's enjoying it."

"I don't want to look at his face. That's revolting."

"What about Mrs. Pratt, babes?"

"Did you have to mention that?"

"Charlotte Elodie Donovan, you're supposed to be my bestie."

The server strolled over to the table and left the receipt. Her perfume smelled familiar, woody, spicy. The hidden smile. Her arm looped through his.

Maggie gasped and pointed an accusatory finger. "Oh my gosh, you're making the Charlie face."

Troy stuffed his hands in his pockets and slid down the booth. "I don't even know what that is."

"It's the face Jack makes at me. You *have* a crush on that nutter."

"Brendon fancies Mrs. Pratt. I knew it," Maggie said.

"No, I don't and neither does Brendon."

"You said it after I gave you a special treat, which you'll never get again if you like her."

Troy didn't know what it was or how to describe it. Angelene popped into his head and swarmed his insides. He was sure Brendon got warm and gooey inside, too.

"Mrs. Cook is fit, but I don't fancy her the way Mr. Dawson does."

"Brendon has gone to the Pratts to work in the garden, move furniture. Any opportunity to talk to her and he's there."

"You fancy Mrs. Cook?" Charlotte said.

Troy groaned and laid thirty pounds on the receipt. "I'm her meatball."

"You're *my* little crumpet," Charlotte cooed.

"All I'm saying is Brendon had a crush; it's over. He only has eyes for you."

"Remember when we sat in the hayloft?" Maggie said. "Remember that brilliant spiderweb?"

"There are spiders in the barn all the time. What's your point?"

"We called her Penelope. It amazed us how long and hard she must have worked on her web. She was there every day, looking beautiful, waiting for her prey. She devoured that poor fly."

Troy smiled at Maggie, guiltily amused. "Are you comparing Mrs. Pratt to a spider?"

"The deadliest."

"I'll admit she's odd but dangerous... you're losing the plot," Charlotte said. She wrapped her fingers around Troy's. Her face looked like it did when they went on the ghost tour of the Wookey Hole caves, unnerved.

"You okay?"

"I hate spiders, you know that."

"Are you sure it was a crush? I swear Brendon's gone off me."

"He fancied her for like a day."

"Do you think she's the devil? Regan in The Exorcist could speak different languages."

Troy laughed. "For a smart girl, you're awfully stupid."

"Babes, let's stop by the sweet shop and get some jelly unicorns, so Magpie stops worrying."

"Can I come over tonight? I don't want to be alone," Maggie said.

"No, you may not. I'm tired of talking about Brendon."

Troy could have sworn Charlotte had been uneasy, and he was sure Brendon still had a crush on Mrs. Pratt. She could be a devil, tempting boys with her pretty disguise. A black widow, quietly stalking her prey. A girl looking for her lost pieces. A girl carrying too big a load. Something stirred in Troy's belly. She had done it again, snuck into his head.

Brendon

Shades of green and brown flashed by Brendon's car window. The sun bobbed behind the clouds and flickered through the trees. There were a million smells along Taunton Road: sweet clover, apple trees heavy with ripe fruit, curing hay. The world around him was fresh, new, and gorgeous, especially the woman waiting by her front door. Walter had texted, asking him to drive Angelene to Burnham, poor little bird had been pacing all night.

Brendon backed the BMW in, left it idling and strolled up the walkway.

"Have you been waiting long?"

"About a minute. I had to finish packing. Walter said the weather could be fickle like me."

"He told you that?"

"He says my affection bounces all over the place."

Brendon grabbed her luggage and shoved it into the trunk. "Your husband is bloody charming."

"He can be," Angelene said. She twirled her ponytail around her finger, relaxed into the seat, and tucked her purse at her feet.

"The lie-in did you good. You look pretty and different." Brendon shut the trunk and rambled to the passenger side. He closed the door and glanced at her. "You got your hair done."

"Walter wanted me to look like Brigitte Bardot." Angelene blew her bangs from her eyes. "The stylist called these curtain bangs. I call them annoying."

Brendon pulled out of the farmhouse laneway and pressed the top down. "Was she fit? Bardot, not the stylist?"

"She was a beautiful woman. I couldn't believe what I saw in the mirror. It didn't look like me."

"What kept you up all night? Your new hairdo?"

"God. I needed him to tell me the pattern was breaking. I paced until he finally gave me a sign."

The paradise of the English countryside faded into a low urban sprawl. Brendon zipped around the roundabout onto the Toneway and headed towards the M5.

"Pacing isn't good. You should have given me a ring."

"Drag you into my crazy thoughts? You needed your rest."

"How come you didn't wake Walt?"

Golden light washed over her pale skin. Delicate—too perfect for the world. She had a grip on his heart. It wasn't right harbouring a crush on Walter's wife.

"He'd be grumpy if I disturbed him. I need him happy. I'm yellow and I don't want the feeling to leave."

The traffic bunched up. Brendon eased up on the accelerator. The moment was flawless. While drivers cursed and gripped their steering wheels, he savoured how peaceful Angelene looked and how calm his heart was.

"Tell me about your mom."

Angelene wiggled in the seat, reached for her cigarettes, and dropped them back into her purse. "I don't like to think about Veronica, 'I'm changing my name to Veronique because it sounds more exotic,' Hummel."

"Don't you have any happy memories?"

"My memories, even the bad ones, are precious to me. I prefer to keep them hidden."

A precision of cars snaked down the motorway. Exhaust fumes perfumed the air. Brendon slowed the car and tucked a strand of hair that had fallen from her ponytail behind her ear.

"You can trust me. You should know that."

"I promised Walter no more sad stories."

"I'm asking you to share. We're going to be stuck in traffic for a while."

The pink faded from her cheeks. She became one of her paintings, colourless, pained, and haunted.

"My mother was a beautiful, empty shell." Angelene pulled the ends of her sleeves over her trembling fingers. "She loved looking glamorous; the makeup didn't hide her poor decisions. She wore them better than the old Hollywood looks she tried to mimic."

"Your father?"

"He might be the boy from Berlin. Maybe the man from Spain who spoiled her with gifts of turrón and vermouth. It could be the traveller from Istanbul. I may be parts of all three."

Brendon dug under the wool cuff and held her hand.

"Mother wanted to leave me at the hospital, God convinced her to keep me. She said I was punishment for the madness she felt with those men." She continued between shaky breaths. "Mother wanted a life where she could flaunt her beauty and be free. I stole her freedom. I need a cigarette."

"Don't let go of my hand."

"Men circled her like wolves, hungry for their prey. It was mother who devoured them."

"Roman Krieger was one of those wolves. You made it seem like he was a nice man."

"He courted mother. He could have been the man who saved us."

The traffic thinned. Brendon put the pedal to the floor. He had seen the same stretch of trees and moors for fifteen years. It had always been a boring drive; stuck in the rear seat, flipping through football magazines with nothing but the M5 to look at. The sky was bluer, the air sweeter, the highway could go on forever.

"Mother didn't like when her men paid attention to me, especially Roman. She never said, but he was her favourite."

"Maggie's mom was up the duff at fifteen. She never regretted being a mom."

"Gustav, her Danish lover, asked mother if he could make love to me, like it was normal to seduce a child. I thought I stepped into a chapter of *Lolita* by Nabokov." Angelene paused and shrank into the seat. "Gustav's favourite quote from the book was 'I knew I had fallen in love with Lolita forever, but I also knew she would not be forever Lolita.' It resonated with him. I never wanted to read that book."

"What did your mom do? Mammina would have killed him."

Angelene's smile was close-lipped. "She left."

"How bloody old were you?"

"Thirteen."

Brendon breathed in the briny air. He was dizzy with disbelief. How does a mother leave her child?

Angelene dragged his arm across her breasts and brought his hand to her mouth. Her lips danced over his knuckles as she spoke. "My only refuge was the Victor Hugo statue. He was my saviour. Please, Brendon, one cigarette."

"Keep holding my hand. I'll tell you about my life, the Dortmund training camp, the U19 squad, bloody school."

"What were you like as a child?"

Brendon flicked the indicator and changed lanes. "Richard the prick would have said a brat. Mom calls me her miracle, and dad... he's never really said."

"Did you always want to play professional football?"

"I wanted to be a pirate for a while."

Angelene twisted in the seat and smiled. All the colours that made her shine overtook her pale cheeks. She was pink, sparkling green, and brilliant yellow.

"Did you search for buried treasure?"

"Walt, Paddington, and I would sail the seven seas. Walt was a brilliant pirate. He planned the best adventures."

"You keep talking about this Paddington. He must be special."

"He was my best friend, other than Troy. One of the greatest defenders in history. I'll introduce you sometime."

Heat danced on his cheeks. Little flutters took flight in his belly. He wasn't supposed to be feeling this way. She was a friend. A beautiful, wounded friend.

"You must have had some happy times."

Angelene gazed at a gull, screeching and soaring through the streaks of white clouds. She hung her arm out the window, catching handfuls of peaty, algae-kissed wind.

"When Roman visited."

"What was one of your favourites?"

"He took me to Notre Dame. I wanted to meet Quasimodo. Did you know his name means half-made? I identified with Quasimodo. Like Paddington, he was a special friend."

Brendon touched her cheek. The warmth from her skin seeped into his finger and he held onto the moment.

"Are you happy now?"

"The blue sky, salty air, wind in my hair. I'll remember every second of this drive and how you made me glow."

Brendon turned off South Esplanade onto a dirt road lined with oak and walnut trees. She had shared parts of her story and held his hand so tight; he couldn't feel his fingers. She had been his for forty-five minutes.

It was time to tuck the butterflies away. They were friends, and no matter how lovely the time was, he had to respect her wishes.

"Is that the house?" Angelene unbuckled the seatbelt and bounced to her knees, gazing at the Edwardian home. He had never seen her so happy, sunshiny liquid gold.

"It's wonderful. A sign too, Cook and Pratt, extraordinary."

A stacked fence framed the property. September wildflowers poked between layers of glimmering stone. As a child, Brendon would balance along the top of the wall, walking the entire length to the shoreline. He could picture Angelene, arms outstretched, doing the same.

"The porch is a work of art." Angelene traced her finger in the air around the outline of the wooden frame. "Look at the decorative windows and stained glass. I thought Rosewood Manor was impressive. I prefer the house by the sea that is really a bay."

She leapt from the car, held her hands to her mouth, and gazed with childlike wonder.

Brendon stood and stretched. He had happy memories in Burnham. This would be his happiest.

"Little bird, you're here." Walter wore a pleased with himself smile, towel around his neck, his sandy brown hair damp. "Sofia can finally breathe. You've arrived one piece."

"One of these days, she's going to faint. I'll pop the boot."

Brendon plunked the suitcases on the ground. Angelene jumped into Walter's arms. An ache filled Brendon's chest. The drive had been sweet. He had chipped away at her wall and digested her story. The sunshine left him. Hers glowed.

"This is quite the welcome. You're positively radiant this morning," Walter said.

"The drive was lovely. I've never driven in a convertible before."

Walter grabbed her suitcase and looked at Brendon. "What did you talk about?"

Brendon hid his nervousness behind a grin. "Football, what else?"

"You're a saint, listening to this one prattle on about footy."

Angelene hooked her arm through Walter's. She wore a look on her face that said she told herself to do it. "I know all about the Bundesliga now."

"You're impressed with the outside. Wait until you see the inside," Walter said.

Brendon heaved his backpack over his shoulder, collected his Dortmund duffel bag, and shuffled to the door. The sun shone through the stained glass fanlight, casting a rainbow of colours across the tessellated floor.

"You made it." Sofia swooped towards him with outstretched arms. "How was the drive?"

"The usual. Heavy traffic."

Moments of the drive circulated around Brendon's head. He tried to stop his heart from shrivelling. It was stupid to think he meant anything to her. He was a friend like the Victor Hugo statue.

"Did she fill your head with sad stories?"

"We talked about football. I'm going to take my stuff upstairs."

Brendon climbed the stairs and shut out Angelene's 'ooh's' and syrupy, 'c'est beau.' The walnut floor glimmered like a golden pathway leading Brendon to a narrow door. When he was little, the doorknob was an enormous diamond, and the claustrophobic, creaky staircase led him to the belly of a pirate ship or the dressing room at Signal Iduna Park. It had always given him joy to hide away in the attic turned bedroom. He dropped his bags on the floor, nothing about the room spoke to his tastes other than the framed photo of him in his Borussia Dortmund kit. The furniture was ostentatious; the walls painted subdued blue. Brendon leaned against the dresser. His fingers wrapped around a fuzzy pink cardigan. Guilt crept in and knocked around his head. He had done it again, dived into hope, dismissed Maggie, and struggled with being Angelene's friend.

"We're going into town to have lunch on the pier."

Sofia's voice transported him back to his bedroom. He pulled off his ball cap, tossed it on the bed, and scratched out his flattened hair. "I'll stay here."

"It's that restaurant you like. We can share a bowl of Eton mess."

"I fell asleep before I finished my homework. I'll sit in the conservatory and work on it."

"Is everything all right? You're smiling, but there's no twinkle in your eyes." She held up her palm. Brendon took hold of her hand, stopping the dreaded 'Oh my goodness, he's ill' swipe to the forehead.

"I swear to God I'm fine. I worked myself too hard at training."

"Don't swear to Him. He's an awful listener. I'll make you a cup of tea," Sofia said, rubbing his arm. "I brought some fruit. There are crisps in the pantry."

Brendon moved to the circular window, heartsick. The water moved as peacefully as the memories floating through his mind. Elaborate sand-castles housing pretty princesses, driftwood pirate ships, his first kiss. They were together in his imagination, him and Angelene, walking hand in hand along the beach. She was glowing bright yellow and all his.

If Brendon had a paintbrush, he would have created a masterpiece ti-tled 'Edwardian Dreams.' Sofia had researched the era to ensure the sitting room stayed true to its charm. The built-in fireplace was white. A sequence of photos telling the story of David and Walter's friend-ship was displayed on the ornate mantel. The walls were pistachio with white crown moulding. White shears framed the windows. The furniture—pebble grey. It was clean and functional, Sofia, but not Sofia. The memories Brendon had in the room were long and happy.

Brendon gazed from Walter to his parents and decided a more fitting title would be 'Bedtime.' The only person who didn't look like they had taken a dose of sleeping pills was Angelene. She sat on the edge of the sofa; her legs bounced as if she were powering up to fly. The nervous energy spilled across the floor and took hold of him. New title, 'The Caged Bird.'

"That was a pretty heated game of Scrabble," Walter said. He laid his hand on Angelene's knee and squeezed.

Brendon scratched his head at words like fozy, zaxes, and zek. He had a feeling he knew who ruled the Scrabble board.

"Who won?"

Sofia smiled sleepily. Her head rested on David's shoulder. "Your father. He's the only person I know who can make words with X's and Z's."

"Did you play?" Brendon said.

Angelene pried Walter's hand from her knee and gently rocked. "Non, je me sentais stupide."

Walter draped his arm over her lap and clinked the ice around his glass. "You could have used French words."

Angelene pushed Walter's arm off her legs and bounced to the end of the cushion. Brendon rubbed his lips to hide his smile.

"Did you enjoy the bubble and squeak? It's a favourite of mine and Walter's," David said.

"I liked the potatoes." Angelene rocked and bounced, lifting herself up and down. Brendon's smile faded. Walter wound his arm around her, gripping her shoulder.

"Ang eats more potatoes than that Irish bird I dated. What was her name?"

"Branagh," Sofia said.

Walter's eyes were piercing blue. Sparks lit inside Brendon, hot and fiery.

Bounce, grip, bounce, grip.

"Are you coming to my match on Sunday?"

Steer the conversation to football before he dove across the sitting room and snagged Walter by the throat.

"Beatrice told me I needed to get out to more matches, show my support," David said.

"We'll go, sweetheart. I'd like to see the new extension to the dressing room."

Brendon rolled his neck, trying to ease the tension that bound him like a noose. *'Walter should hold her hand or take her for a walk.'*

"I spoke to Lukas the other day."

"How's my friend?" Walter said.

"He was in Stuttgart, got his eye on a sixteen-year-old midfielder."

Walter braced Angelene's shoulder. Curse words slapped against Brendon's mouth.

"Lukas has an eye for talent. He saw it in you, and here you sit."

David knocked back his scotch and set down his glass. "Twice, dear friend, he's blown it twice."

"He could do a hell of a lot for the Bundesliga. Every damn team was begging for him," Walter said. He loosened his grip on Angelene's shoulder and rubbed his brow. "Sit still. You're making me uncomfortable."

An awkward silence fell over the room. David stared out the window, disappointment darkening his face. Sofia ran her hand over his neck, transfixed by the relentless bouncing.

"Can we go out?" Angelene's voice was small and taut.

Brendon grinned at the sleepy, 'are-you-serious' expression on Walter's face.

"Does anyone in this room look like they could venture into town?"

"New places make me nervous. I need to get out."

"Tomorrow."

Brendon glanced from her bouncing to the harried look in her eyes. He had to do something before she a had a tantrum or jetted herself through the roof.

"I could take her into town."

Sofia twisted her bangles round and round her wrist. "I don't think that's a good idea."

"I'm not tired."

"The pubs close at eleven," David said, glancing at his watch. "It's 10:00. They opened that dance club, not really Walter's thing."

The conversation was over. Silence.

"I'm going to call Maggie and finish my homework."

A chorus of 'good night' followed Brendon as he shuffled from the room and climbed the stairs. He trudged up the hidden staircase, stripped out of his clothes, and buried under the blankets. Brendon heaved his Latin text onto the bed. A sheet of paper decorated in hearts and 'fancy a snog, knuddelbär' fell onto his lap.

'Break the pattern, friends helping friends.' He repeated the mantra. Sleep kidnapped him and took him to a place he didn't recognize.

Run, run fast. Quick, a kiss to the forehead before she slips away.

He slammed into a golden birdcage and gripped the icy bars. A little bird swung back and forth, her wings clipped and frayed. Feathers floated around him, tickling his nose and neck.

"Are you awake?"

Brendon rubbed his eyes and grinned. "Your wings are fixed."

"Get up, hurry."

He shot up, frantically clutching the sheets. "Bloody hell, what are you doing?"

Angelene tossed jeans and a black thermal shirt on the bed, her eyes wild. "Quick, get dressed."

"Is everyone asleep? What bloody time is it?"

"Midnight. Your jeans."

"Uncle Walt said no."

"To hell with Walter. I'll smother him if I don't leave."

Brendon tugged on his jeans and socks. He rushed to the bathroom, splashed water on his face and scrubbed his teeth, his mind whirling.

"This isn't a good idea."

"I need out. I can't breathe."

Brendon dropped his toothbrush in the holder and wiggled his arms through his shirt. "Mom has insomnia. Dad usually gets up for a snack."

"Do you want to play with your devil tonight?"

A fire raged in her eyes. Intoxicating green scorched his heart. The adventure was dangerous and not him.

"Padre Diavolo is a dickhead."

"Père Satan, meet Mère de tous les Diables."

Shadows followed them down the hall. Every creak and rattle bellowed and boomed in Brendon's ears, his heart thrummed louder and louder. He glanced at Angelene—jeans, V-neck Henley, the famous red-soled shoes. He didn't see a pitchfork or horns hidden beneath the waves of blonde.

"Can we walk?"

Brendon covered the deadbolt with his hand and slowly turned the latch. "It would take about an hour."

A blanket of grey clouds hid the moon. There were no nighttime sounds, no crickets, no owls hooting, no sounds from the water, just quiet. Cold sweat prickled Brendon's skin, the world was too quiet.

"If dad finds out I took you into town after Walt said no, he'll have me by the goolies."

He took a few breaths to steady his heart and shaky limbs.

"Let's play with the devil. Lucifer has a lot of suppressed anger. We don't want to upset him."

"If I keep saying yes to him, I'll like it too much."

Brendon gently twisted the key in the lock and nodded towards the BMW. "Have you ever driven a car?"

"Pierre tried to teach me. He gave up when I kept stalling it."

"Just shift it into neutral," Brendon said, tossing her the keys.

She snatched them from the air and jumped inside the car.

"There's a keeper in you. I'll get you out on the pitch."

"I would love that."

Brendon put his hands on the hood. They slid across the gleaming black paint. He wiped his palms on his thighs, cursed Padre Diavolo, and pushed. The BMW rolled onto the road. He knocked on the roof and scrambled into the car.

"Aren't you afraid?"

"Non." She ran her hand over his, eyes chaotic green. "This is what friends do. They help one another, and I need you."

Brendon tapped his fingers against the steering wheel. The rhythm was as relentless as his thundering heart. "We could have a cuppa in the garden and talk."

"You must stop smoking," she said. "Watch the bread, but he devours a loaf. All his fucking rules, you understand."

The town unfolded in front of them, a jumble of century-old shops and modern boutiques. Streetlamps lit the pavement in an amber glow, illuminating the side street. Brendon maneuvered around crates and flattened cardboard boxes. Thumping bass bounced through the white brick walls.

"You ready, mon ami?"

"I should be in bed. I was dreaming when you woke me. I'd like to know what happened."

"You can go back to your dream later. I'm finally able to breathe."

Every part of him was alive. Electric music thumped and chugged, late-night smells of coriander and cumin laced the brackish air. He rested his palm against a red-painted door. The music pulsed through the wood. A blast of hot, stuffy air scented with hops, perfume, and desperation hit his face. White, blue, and pink strobe lights ignited the dance floor. The chugging rhythm bounced in his chest. Brendon tore his gaze from a couple entwined like snakes to the scarred and sticky bar. Dim globe lights barely illuminated the empty cocktail glasses scattered among bowls of lemons and limes. The bartender chewed on a toothpick, flexed his muscles, and flirted with two scantily clad women.

"Two pints of whatever and a bottle of wine," Angelene said slipping two fingers in her pocket. "Make it two."

Brendon pulled out his wallet, Angelene wagged her finger, and tossed fifty pounds on the grungy bar.

"Where did you get the money?"

Brendon grabbed the mugs and followed her through a maze of white melamine tables and silver pedestal stools.

"Walter's wallet."

"Won't he know it's missing?"

They found a white lacquered booth and slid onto the zebra-print bench.

"Walter shoves wads of euros and pounds into his wallet. He thinks it makes him look important."

"There's a lot of alcohol on the table. I don't really drink."

A steady stream of fog puffed from hidden smoke machines. Brendon coughed. Laser lights blasted the crowd with rays of vivid red.

"Did you forget who we're playing with?"

"Padre Diavolo wants to get me into trouble."

"How do you feel?"

An image of Sofia running through the house searching for him battered his brain.

"Nervous, terrified, alive."

He chugged back the pint in a series of throat quenching gulps. Rebellion flickered in Angelene's eyes. Lucifer had disobeyed and revolted against God, so had the woman sitting across from him. Her god was six feet tall with rock-like hands.

"You're yellow right now, mon ami, not pretty yellow, but scared yellow."

"Shouldn't I be red like the devil?"

"The devil isn't red. He's white, cold, and empty." Angelene moved her finger around the rim of the mug then took a slug. "Lucifer doesn't like when people ignore him. He does things to get their attention. No one listened to his side."

"For someone who loves God so much, won't He be upset you're sympathizing with the devil?"

"I have empathy, and that's a good thing. I understand how Lucifer must have felt, never having a voice."

Brendon held up his mug and shook it at the bartender. He fixed his eyes on Angelene. The glass was cumbersome in her hand. The rebellious look had morphed into something he had never seen before, like she was searching for something, her missing pieces, freedom, a scream that had been stuck. He thanked the bartender, handed him ten pounds then took a long sip.

"You look beautiful."

He sipped his beer and relaxed into a mess of feathery pink pillows.

"Is that Father Satan talking? He's a liar."

"He's also a thief and a tempter. It's me, not the devil or the beer."

She drank the lager and poured wine into the lingering froth. "Do this. Don't do that. Wear this, speak this way."

Brendon finished the beer, filled it with wine and sipped. It tasted of vinegared berries. "Get good grades, be respectful, lead by example."

"You do the last naturally. The boys on the team gravitate towards you."

"Did you see the look on my dad's face when Walt told him I should be in Dortmund?"

Angelene laughed. "David puts a lot of faith in education. I can just imagine what he thinks about me."

"With knowledge comes power, my dad lives by that motto."

"Genuine power comes from growing, using the knowledge you have, and challenging yourself. It comes from the heart, not filling your head with information."

"Richard used to lock my dad in his room and force him to study," Brendon said through a mouthful of wine. "Richard didn't want a dolt for a son, neither does David Cook. I'm not the son he wanted."

"How could he not want someone as gifted as you?"

"I'm not supposed to talk about it."

The glow of black lights shone on the packed dance floor. Gigantic warehouse fans showered Brendon in sweaty, perfumed air. He had held tight to all the rules and the code—yes, Mammina, no, Dad, I'll be a good boy and do good things.

'They're not made of stone. Break the rules. It's one night.'

Madre Innocente spoke. *'Break one, say fuck you to the code and its so long good boy.'*

Brendon licked his lips, chugged the wine, his throat remained dry.

Stay, go, apologize, face the consequences.

"I'll take you home. The music is giving me a bloody headache."

"Can we go to the beach? I'm not ready to end the evening yet."

'Break free, slip through the bars that have penned you in for so long.'

"I'll grab us another bottle."

"Padre Diavolo is back."

"He's a fucking prick."

Brendon slid out of the booth, found his feet, and pushed through the crowd. He laid thirty pounds on a stain of something sticky and pointed at a bottle of red wine. He left the change and took her hand.

"Am I still scared yellow?"

"You're maroon, fiery red, slashed with white."

A sliver of moon cut through the clouds. Silver streaks lit a path, leading them to the street. No one would believe the adventure he was having. He titled this chapter, 'The night I played with Satan.'

"If we walk far enough down the beach, we won't have to hear that bloody music. You'll see the Low lighthouse."

"I know the way."

She led him down the road, past a whitewashed pub with bright green shutters and a convenience store. The shore was a few steps away.

"How did you... how..."

"I don't know. Everything seems so familiar, like your hand in mine."

They trudged through the sand, littered with pebbles, ropes of marram grass and bony driftwood limbs, until the techy boom-boom was a whisper. A breeze swept in from the shimmering black water. Angelene unscrewed the cap, took a long sip, and passed it. Brendon drank, took another sip, and flopped onto the sand.

"Tell me more about Paris. You."

"Why? Do you like sad stories?"

Brendon picked up a pebble, the pink and ivory stripes glimmered in the moonlight. It would look nice in Mammina's bowl of treasures. A reminder of the night he met the mother of all devils.

She passed the bottle and draped her arm around his waist. He nuzzled her hair, breathed in lavender, and shoved the bottle into the sand.

"I want to understand where your light went."

"You make it very hard to break the pattern."

"I know all about Charlie. She loves every shade of blue. She lives off sweets, and if you asked her to choose her favourite, she'd tell you five different things. She loves Troy and Spence farm. I could go on."

"No one has cared to ask."

"What about Lisette?"

He unscrewed the cap, held the bottle to his nose. It smelled like the chocolate-covered cherries his Nonna loved.

"Lisette thought I made poor choices."

"What about that professor you worked with?"

"The men I've known wanted to fuck me, that's all." She gulped a few mouthfuls, handed him the bottle, and rested her cheek against his arm.

"Not me." Brendon hiccuped and grinned a tipsy grin. "I wouldn't know what to do. Troy tells me things, but honestly, I'm bloody scared."

"It isn't all it's cracked up to be."

"Troy said it's as brilliant as stopping someone from scoring."

"It's not that exhilarating." She dug in her purse, tossed a pack of cigarettes and a silver monogrammed lighter onto the sand.

"He doesn't want you to smoke, but he buys you a lighter?"

"At least I'll look classy."

It was as if he had stepped onto the pitch at Signal Iduna Park. His heart climbed to his throat, butterflies tiptoed out of their cocoons and began a nauseating dance. The feeling was back. He drank another mouthful. The wine *had* to drown the butterflies.

"When you were dreaming of playing football in Dortmund, I dreamt about surviving."

Brendon pressed his lips against Angelene's temple. She leaned into him and melted against him.

"Imagine if my parents were visiting Paris, and they found you, thirteen years old, sitting at Hugo's feet. They could have brought you to Rosewood Manor."

"You would have been six years old."

Brendon took a long sip and passed her the bottle. "You could have played football with me and Paddington. Mom might have let me play in the forest."

She would have been a sister if his parents had rescued her. He told himself to think of her as a sister. It would be easier to follow the code and be her friend.

"Imagine me growing up at Rosewood Manor. I would hold my teacup properly, say the right things. My scars would disappear. I wouldn't be afraid of mirrors."

Brendon drew a heart in the sand. He was about to draw the letter A but smudged it out instead. "You'd have to study and get good grades."

"I wouldn't mind sitting behind that big old desk, learning about the world from David. I would have been someone."

Tears swarmed her eyes. Brendon rested his chin on top of her head. "I wish you could see what I do."

"What you see is not what you get."

"I don't want you to cry. I want to finish the wine and talk about daft things, things that make you beautiful yellow."

"Sometimes the tears just sit there and blur my eyes. Sometimes it's harder to breathe."

"Which is it now?"

"Breathe."

She took a deep drag, her eyes focused on the water. Smoke slipped from between her lips, spiralling through the air like a ghost. Her mouth was full and pretty. The smoke was magical. The smell, mingled with her perfume, captivating him.

"Fuck. These damn butterflies."

"What butterflies? There is nothing but water and sand."

"The butterflies are in my belly. It could be the wine. It tastes bloody awful."

"Sofia has spoiled you with luxurious food and wine. It tastes fine to me."

Brendon shimmied his phone out of his pocket and swiped his finger across it. "Can we take a picture? We'll always have this moment."

"Have proof we snuck out? It must be Father Satan speaking to me right now."

He tapped the camera, adjusted it to selfie and held the phone in front of them.

"I don't like it. Turn it off."

"Move your hands."

"You see my crooked tooth when I smile."

He held the camera at arm's length and rested his cheek against hers. "Grin then."

A whisper of a smile brightened her face. The photo was perfect.

"What time do you think it is?"

Brendon squinted at the lock screen. "Three."

"The devil's hour."

"Bloody hell, you really put a scary spin on things."

"This is the hour when Satan is most powerful." She dropped her cigarette into the wine bottle and pushed herself up.

"Let's hope Satan uses his power to get us home."

Brendon staggered towards a cement embankment and braced himself against a damp pillar. He unzipped his fly, showering the stone. She fell against his back and snaked her arm around his waist. Her fingers pressed into his belly, sending a flurry of flutters through his body.

"Did the devil tell you to hug me while I was going wee?"

"I'll ask God to forgive me."

They climbed the concrete steps and deposited the bottles in an over-flowing garbage bin. There was no life on the streets. Sludgy light glowed from the streetlights.

"Our Lord Chancellor will be pissed off if I'm caught driving drunk."

The pavement bent and bobbed under his feet.

"We can't leave your car here."

"I don't know what's worse. Driving home drunk or confessing we snuck into town."

"Drive slow."

Brendon gripped her hand as he swayed left and right. "Watch the barf."

He guided her around a technicolour puddle and opened the car door, his insides twitched. He'd drive slowly, keep his focus on the road and hope Padre Diavolo and Uncle Gianni the Reckless would help guide him home. Brendon eased his foot on the gas and somehow found the end of the street.

"I needed this," Angelene said.

She traced along his neck; each tiny hair stood on end. Her touch was intense, like she had reached inside, wrenched his heart, scooped the breath from his lungs.

"Stop touching me. The butterflies are fucking out of control. I'm going to barf."

He wasn't about to vomit. Uncle Gianni the Reckless and Padre Diavolo were going to coax him to pull over and kiss her.

"I thought it might relax you."

"It feels *too* good."

He switched off the headlights and racked his brain. Had he parked beside the Aston Martin or the Jaguar? He was sure he had parked beside Walter's car. He remembered staring at the license plate. It had always amazed him that the random set of letters assigned to Walter's plate were his initials, W.A.P. Brendon parked, relieved. He didn't know how he did it, but they were home.

Brendon held a finger to his lips. The staircase looked a mile away.

Her body weaved and bobbed. She clasped the heel of her shoe and collapsed into the wall.

"You need to get to bed."

"I don't want to disturb Walter. He might think it's an invitation for sex."

The floor shifted, and the walls tilted like he was back in the funhouse in Blackpool. He led her to the sofa and they tripped onto the cushions. Every creak and rattle rising from the vents stirred his insides.

"I'll remember this night."

"Me too, mon ami."

He moved toward her and rested his hand on her cheek. His body tensed. It was dangerous and stupid. It was just a kiss. Angelene pushed on his chest, her eyes wide.

"Please, I can't breathe." She burrowed into the pillows and dragged a throw over her shoulders.

Brendon staggered to his feet and bumped his shin on the coffee table. He cursed, clutched the armrest, and placed his lips on hers. Angelene squirmed deeper into the corner of the sofa and touched her lips. His brain stuttered. He had kissed her.

Angelene

Angelene stared at the hulk of a man tangled among the sheets. She tiptoed into the room and dropped her shoes on her suitcase.

"You're awake, little bird."

She froze. A cold prickle crept over her cheeks and neck. "I couldn't sleep. I was going to go for a walk."

Walter scratched his hair and yawned. "It looks like it's going to rain."

Angelene stared at the steely grey clouds. "Mother said God was crying when it rained. I need to feel God."

Walter tore away the blankets and stretched his arms to the ceiling. "I'll come with you."

Angelene dug through the mound of clothes, cringing at the pain in her temples. She picked up a wrap and wound it around her trembling shoulders.

"The promise is broken."

"Did you promise God you'd take a stroll?"

"I need him to help break the pattern."

"You're talking nonsense this morning," Walter said. He pulled on his jeans and grabbed a hoodie hanging on the back of the door. "We had best be on our way before God sheds his tears."

'*He's already crying.*'

16 Déjà-Visité

S ofia

Wind blustered through the walnut trees. Rain tumbled from the clouds and tapped a cacophony of plunks and clacks against the window. The kitchen was the only room in the house Sofia had remodelled. Barn beams ran along the length of the ceiling. The oven was built into a wall of stone, and an island, the size of a small country, occupied the middle of the room. The inspiration, her aunt's Tuscan estate.

Sofia stared into her coffee cup. She had always envied people who slept well. When she first moved to Taunton, the battle over Rosewood Manor kept her awake. Over the years, party plans, the transformation of Taunton Park, stories to keep Brendon out of the forest, the ghosts, took precedence over sleep. Last night had been no different. Walter prattling on about Brendon staying in Dortmund had rattled through her brain. She could have sworn she had heard footsteps around four o'clock.

"It doesn't look like the rain is going to let up." David pulled out a beechwood stool, sat and reached for the coffeepot.

"I was hoping for tea in the garden."

"Scones and posh sarnies. Angelene will love that," David said, pouring himself a coffee.

"She might."

"Do you think she ever settled down?" Sofia topped up her mug, sipped, then spoke. "I thought I heard footsteps this morning. I was going to get up and see if it was her, but the house was cold, you were warm."

"Angelene paces when she can't sleep."

"I can't imagine being that anxious."

"You play with your bracelets, wear my old jumper." David spooned sugar in his mug then grabbed the cream. "Everyone does something to ease the nerves."

"Even you, Lord Chancellor."

"I fly through my speeches. Beatrice writes 'slow down' on my notes to remind me."

Sofia sipped her coffee and rested her hand on his. "You're incredibly charming when you give a speech. You look so confident."

"I hide it very well."

Thunder rumbled, and rain splattered across the window. Last night's conversation played through Sofia's mind.

"Should we have let Brendon stay in Dortmund?"

"Walter has made you doubt we did the right thing."

"It was a dream come true. We took it away."

"We've been through this. We let him go; we brought him home. He punished us by calling the entire modern languages department pricks," David said. "He promised again at the start of this term."

"Some professional football players start at sixteen."

"And some at eighteen." David swirled more cream into his coffee and stirred. "You weren't ready to say goodbye. You were smiling when we walked into the house."

"I was happy to see him."

"You were over the moon he was home."

Sofia had always wanted to be a mother. She loved the idea of showering someone in love, someone she had created with the love of her life. Brendon had been the perfect little boy. Dark hair, dark eyes. God got it right for once. He had listened. What Sofia hadn't expected was a prodigy. A boy wonder. Taunton's hero. Men from all over England and Europe had their eyes on her boy. He would be the next star goalkeeper. They were ready to steal him away at seven years old. She fought fiercely to keep Brendon in Taunton. They could have him at sixteen. When sixteen came and Dortmund offered Brendon a contract, she fought again. She let him go at seventeen, eighteen, and hated to admit she had been happy when David brought him home. Her biggest fear was not the temper Brendon had inherited from Richard Cook. It was losing him.

"I contacted the Professional Football Scouts Association after Lukas set his sights on him. I hoped to keep him in England."

"Clubs in France, Italy, wanted him. Dortmund won. He broke his promise and now he'll do his time at Taunton College."

Sofia ran her finger over her bracelets. The trees swayed against a grey sky.

'*Shift your worry, Sofia, there are bigger issues.*'

"Do you think Walter and Angelene are going to make it?"

"I don't know."

"I know Walter likes a challenge. I'm concerned."

David pressed his lips against the wrinkle on her brow. "Worry about Brendon finishing sixth form."

The door burst open. A spray of cool, wet wind followed Walter and Angelene. Walter pulled off his hood and shook out his damp hair. He unwound Angelene's soggy wrap; puddles of water pooled under their feet.

"Hand me a kitchen towel, Davy boy, these tiles cost a fortune."

David tossed the roll and grinned. "Where have you two been?"

Walter dropped a strip of paper towel on the floor and ran his foot over the puddle. "The farmer's market. We got all sorts of goodies: blood sausage, fresh goat cheese. We'll have a fry-up like no other."

Sofia rubbed David's arm and slid off the stool. She grabbed the shopping bags and plunked them on the kitchen island. "You cooked last night. Why don't you let us make it?"

Walter chuckled. "Have you had one of David's fry-ups?"

Sofia flicked through her bracelets. Angelene hadn't shared in Walter's joy or laughed at their drenched clothes and hair. Her breathing was shallow and raspy. She scrubbed at her wrist as if trying to remove a stain.

"Did you enjoy the walk?"

Angelene bowed her head and wiggled out of her wet sneakers. "It was nice until God cried."

"My mother used to tell me God was playing a game of bocce when it stormed."

"God is crying. Excuse me."

Sofia stood next to David and snuggled against his arm. The hair on the back of her neck prickled. Wintry. Disconnected. Shame. If Sofia was as observant as her mother, she might have read Angelene better.

"Why would God cry?" Sofia left David's side and walked to the cupboard. "He doesn't weep. He gets pleasure watching people suffer."

"Ang didn't sleep well," Walter said in a disconcerted tone. "This weekend is exactly what she needs. I'll change and start brekky."

Sofia grabbed a stack of plates and set them on the island. "She couldn't look at me."

"You intimidate her." David gathered the cutlery and laid it in a pile next to the plates. "Even Liam shudders when you're at the pitch."

Sofia positioned a placemat, aligned it precisely with the stool, and moved to the next. "She'd better get used to me if you and Walter expect us to be friends."

Sofia floated around the island, centred each placemat, then the plates. The utensils were next, lined up perfectly on either side. She studied the soapstone countertop and grinned. Everything looked perfect.

"I'm not sure she'll ever be comfortable with you," David said. He grabbed a bowl of oranges and the juicer. "I'm going to start squeezing. Why don't you see if sleeping beauty is awake?"

Sofia stepped into the foyer, gasped, and flung her hand to her chest. "Oh, mio dio."

Angelene pushed and pulled on her knuckles. An uneasiness stole Sofia's breath.

"I'm on sausage and bacon duty. Roman used to say blood sausage was the heart and soul of the United Kingdom. It sounds disgusting to me."

"I agree. We'll stick to bacon."

"I'll put extra slices in the pan."

Sofia released an exasperated breath and climbed the stairs. Walter's rendition of *Brown Sugar* mingled with the rain pummelling the roof. She opened the door to the secret staircase; laughter from five-year-old Brendon haunted the tiny space. She couldn't count the number of times she had chased him up the staircase, Paddington dangling at his side, his Dortmund jersey hiked up around his ankles. Memories ran in slow motion. She wanted to be there again, climbing into the belly of Queen Anne's Revenge, or heading to the dressing room at Signal Iduna Park. Sofia reached the top of the stairs, and a distinct memory invaded her mind—her brother Gianni. Her smile dropped. The room smelled of booze and vomit. Sofia's gaze moved from the clothes scattered on the floor to the lump hidden under the blankets. Angelene could barely look at her. She had been twitchy, lost in thought; God was crying for her.

'*You're being silly, Sofia.*'

She backed out of the room; sweat tickled her back. She followed the sound of laughter and froze in the kitchen doorway. Angelene touched David's arm and stared up at him. Sofia questioned her motives.

'*Looking for what? Approval? Love? Flirting?*'

"Angelene and I are shopping after breakfast. You can get your son up."

Sofia tied a scarf around her neck, applied her signature red lipstick, and tossed the tube on the vanity. She grabbed her Prada bag and walked down the hall. Angelene stood in the middle of the bedroom in her underwear and a grey jersey pullover, beads strung around her wrists, clothes strewn across the bed.

"Is something the matter?"

"I can't put an outfit together," Angelene said, throwing up her hands. "I don't understand the rules."

Sofia sighed softly and marched into the room. "Stop fretting over something as silly as an outfit."

"Sometimes normal fits, and other days, it's too loose, too tight."

"Today, it's going to fit right," Sofia said, handing her a pair of jeans. "Can you look at me?"

Their eyes met, and a shiver trickled down Sofia's spine. Guilt, longing, sadness, a mixture of all three. *Forgiveness, she wants me to forgive her.*

"Now what?" Angelene said. The words came out on an exasperated breath. "This doesn't look fabulous."

Sofia hid her worry behind a grin. "Accessories. Hand me the indigo and white wrap."

She snapped it open, tied it, and pulled waves of blonde from beneath the layers.

"Bracelets, check. Your Vuitton bag, lipstick."

Angelene pointed to the dresser. Sofia paraded across the room and dug through the bulging makeup bag. Classic red, tawny pink, and nude.

"Not the red. I haven't worked up to that colour yet. I'm feeling pink today and not in the way Troy looks at Charlotte."

"What are you talking about?" Sofia said, choosing the pink.

"I'm feeling emotional and timid."

Sofia applied the lipstick and took a step back. "You look lovely. Riding boots or booties?"

"What are you wearing?"

"My ankle boots. You ready?"

"I don't want to disappoint Walter. God is disappointed. That is enough for today."

"I wouldn't worry about disappointing God. He has a terrible habit of letting people down."

"God is always beside me. Today he's weeping for me."

They walked down the stairs. Sofia put on her boots and grabbed the keys from an antique washbasin. She opened the door, popped an umbrella, and studied the dismal sky.

"Looks like God is going to cry all day."

She took hold of Angelene's hand and led her down the soggy walkway.

Angelene slid onto the seat and fumbled in her purse. "May I?"

Sofia lowered the window down an inch. Her fingers struck the steering wheel in a series of staccato taps. She found herself distracted as she drove towards the town centre. Her Prada boots felt too tight. The smell had stuck in her nose, reminders of Gianni, her father blaming himself for his reckless behaviour, her mother furious he was drunk again. Guilt or shame flickering in Angelene's eyes.

"You're worried. Is something troubling you?"

"Brendon's room stunk of wine. He doesn't drink. He might have a glass with dinner."

Angelene took a long drag and tossed the cigarette into the rain-soaked wind. "He wants to be in Dortmund."

Sofia angled the Jaguar into a spot out front of a row of shops. "Why talk to you? Why not Troy or me?"

"Je suis désole. I'm upsetting you."

Sofia opened the umbrella, walked around the car, and took Angelene's hand. "You think Brendon drank because he's still upset about Dortmund?"

"Sometimes people turn to unhealthy things to cope."

Rain pummelled the pavement. Sofia tugged open the door. The tiny shop shone as if built from gemstones and glass, ammonia lingered in the air. She set the umbrella by the door and turned to adjust Angelene's scarf.

"Beautiful things can make a person reckless." Sofia reached for a silver and gold cuff bracelet. The lacy pattern shimmered under the track lighting. She slid it onto her wrist and rotated it left and right. "Do you agree?"

"Beautiful things always get me into trouble."

The look on Angelene's face shifted like a kaleidoscope, endlessly changing from one emotion to the next.

"Drinking his troubles away doesn't sound like Brendon."

"You know your son better than me," Angelene said, clenching her hands together. "Or are you asking because you've watched me drink the nerves away?"

Sofia wiggled the bracelet off and handed it to the salesclerk with her charge card. "It's an opinion."

"People do all sorts of things when they can't control their emotions. Walter told me Brendon has a temper."

"He broke a boy's nose. David had to work some magic so the family wouldn't press charges. He pushed a boy on the playground, split Freddy Chaney's forehead open."

"Isn't it better he drank?"

"You seemed upset Walter wasn't in the mood to go into town," Sofia said. She tucked her charge card into her wallet and moved to a display of rings. "It's silly of me to think you and Brendon would sneak out."

Sofia tried to distinguish the look in Angelene's eyes: shame, disappointment?

"It's hard for me to settle in unfamiliar places. I've hardly slept since coming to Taunton."

Sofia held up a gold charm bracelet and wiped the thought from her mind. Brendon was a good boy. The charms tinkled in her fingers. A good boy who would do anything for a friend.

"This would look lovely on you."

Angelene shrank away and hid her arms behind her back. "No bracelets."

"You should buy something. The rings are exquisite."

A tray of baubles locked beneath the glass winked and glittered under the bright lights.

"Can you bring out the display so she can have a better look."

The salesclerk unlocked the cabinet and placed it before them. Angelene picked up an oblong ring set with jade and diamonds.

"It reminds me of my mother."

"Really?" Sofia said, perplexed. She hadn't answered the question. It was a simple yes or no. She avoided her eyes, twisted the subject.

"My mother loved Greta Garbo." Angelene's finger shook as she slid the ring on. "She loved the scene from *Grand Hotel* where Garbo says, 'I want to be alone.' She said it to me often and in such a way, it made my insides scream. Garbo wore a ring like this in a picture mother had framed."

"Buy it as a tribute to your mother."

Angelene handed the clerk the ring and fumbled within her purse for her wallet. "I'll buy it in honour of Roman. He thought Garbo was beautiful."

"Shoes are next. We'll get you some sensible pumps. You can work your way up to the stilettos Walter wants you to wear."

Sofia popped open the umbrella and guided Angelene onto the drenched pavement. They walked side by side. A steady stream of rain pinged against the black monstrosity. Angelene pushed the door open with her hip. Sofia patted her upper lip with her scarf, stunned. *'How did she know this was the store?'*

"Did Walter tell you... how..."

"I don't know, déjà-visite. It's happened before."

"Is it like déjà vu?"

"Similar. I knew we had to walk precisely ten steps from the jewellery shop."

The salesclerk, in a pinstriped suit and shined Zanotti shoes, swirled his lacquered pompadour and grinned handsomely at Sofia. "It's twenty-five and sunny in Milan."

"Where is the nightclub?"

"Looking to go dancing, Mrs. Cook?"

"Is it close by?" Sofia said. Her fingers danced over her bracelets. *Click, click.*

'How did you know? Unless you drove by. You saw it on the way to the club with my son.'

"It's a two-minute drive, Pier Street, then Esplanade," he said.

'Brendon would have driven the other way. He would have.. no he wouldn't sneak off with her. He's a good boy. I told him to stay away.'

"Who's this?"

The salesclerk's voice brought Sofia back to the boutique.

"You must have snatched her off the runway."

Angelene glanced over her shoulder. The store was empty.

"He's talking about you. Stephano, meet Angelene Pratt."

"As in Walter Pratt? Why, that cheeky bugger. He never said a thing the last time I saw him."

"It happened rather quickly."

"It's nice to meet you. We just got the Gucci winter collection in. You two sit." He pointed to a burgundy chaise that looked like a giant pair of lips and snapped his fingers. "Eloise, champagne for Mrs. Cook and Mrs. Pratt."

Sofia settled onto the curved sofa. Her eyes fixed on Angelene's knitting fingers. "Walter never told you about this store?" She passed Angelene a flute of bubbly; her chest grew tight.

"He talked about River Parret, the Bristol Channel. I know Burnham. I feel like I've been here before."

Sofia could feel the emotions roiling through Angelene, with every fidget and slurpy, panicked sip.

'*It could be me. My thoughts are racing, so many questions.*'

"This store isn't me." Angelene's voice was tiny, shaky, drawing Sofia out of her thoughts.

"The last pair of shoes I bought was from the Marche aux Puces de la Vanes for ten euros."

Sofia took a small sip. A wall of boxes formed in front of them. Déjà-visité, the stink of stale wine and vomit. It had to be memories of Gianni that had her rattled.

After a brief silence, Sofia spoke. "Walter expects you to play the part. You need props. A fabulous pair of shoes is the best."

"I don't belong in these stores. I can't breathe."

"You have every right to shop here." Sofia held up a strappy crimson stiletto. She slid her foot in and angled it from side to side. "Brendon uses a breathing technique when the sparks light. That's how he describes his anger, fiery sparks. Try it, breathe in, and slowly exhale."

Angelene laid her hand on her chest, breathed in, and quickly released it. She didn't have the gumption to stand up to Walter. Sofia doubted she'd have the courage to persuade Brendon to sneak out and get drunk.

Sofia set the stiletto back in the box and reached for a peep-toe slingback. "Try this on. It looks like something Garbo would have worn."

"Teal is an introverted colour. It suits me. They say people who like it appreciate things that are different and don't want to fit in. I've never belonged anywhere."

Sofia lifted a wedge sandal and examined the wooden heel. "Where do you get these ideas?"

"I see letters and numbers in colour. I read palms. Mother hated it. She said I needed an exorcism to rid the devil."

Sofia tilted her head, set down the shoe, and held out her hand. "What does mine say?"

"You have breaks in your lifeline, trauma, and loss. Three, no, I see four."

Sofia steadied her hand. Her heart raced. "Go on."

"Your heart line curves upward. You're passionate. You have a sun line, no wonder you're so confident."

"Are you sure you see four breaks?"

Angelene ran her finger along Sofia's palm. "I'm positive about three. The fourth, I'm not sure it's happened yet."

Sofia tugged her hand away and smiled nervously. "Who knew you could see so much in a person's hand."

"People say eyes are the window of the soul; it's a person's hands. Touch is a language all its own. I shy away from it."

Sofia stared at her palm. "What do you see in Walter's hands?"

"He has golden fingertips."

"Are you happy?"

"Sometimes I feel yellow and sometimes I'm a jumble of colours waiting to come together, like a kaleidoscope."

"How are we making out here? More champagne," Stephano said.

"No, thank you. I'm ready." Sofia ran her thumb over her lifeline—three losses, maybe four. She shook her hand as if to flick away Angelene's touch and handed him two boxes. "Angelene?"

"I'll take these. Teal suits me."

"Nothing beats a good pair of shoes. I'll set them by the register," Stephano said.

"Does Walter make you happy?"

"I'm learning to be a wife. My friend Lisette made it look easy. You do."

Sofia handed her charge card to Stephano. She had never considered herself a wife. She was a partner. Marriage took work. Sofia wasn't sure Angelene had it in her.

"David and I married at eighteen. It hasn't been easy. You saw it in my lifeline."

"You're in love. That's all you need."

Sofia thanked Stephano and grabbed the umbrella. She studied the pewter sky; rain fell in fat plunks. God hadn't finished weeping.

"Love is not enough. You need to see each other as equals."

"Walter will never see me as his equal. That's why he married me."

"He's learning to be a husband. King Midas will surely turn you into gold." Sofia unlocked the car and sagged behind the steering wheel, drained.

"Do you believe that?"

"It isn't about changing who you are, just the props, like choosing accessories."

"A boy told me I didn't need to change. He likes my messy hair and holey jeans. I'm patched, stitched together. My clothes are a representation of that."

"Was that boy Brendon?" Sofia clung to the silence.

"It was just a boy, a boy surrounded by beautiful brown light."

Sofia parked beside Walter's Aston Martin. She was home. She needed a fix of David, joy to overtake the heaviness.

"What are you wearing to dinner? I must start thinking about it, so I don't keep everyone waiting."

"A black wrap dress and my new red shoes."

"I'll wear black too, with my teal shoes. I'll channel my inner Sofia and dazzle King Midas."

"Have you read Walter's palm?" Sofia grabbed her purse and shopping bags. She didn't bother with the umbrella. She needed God's tears to wash away Angelene's sorrow that had stained her skin.

"He thinks it's nonsense. I studied his palm one night while we were watching television. He has one break in his lifeline, only one true love."

A chill swept over Sofia. She hurried up the walkway and stepped into the house. "I'm home."

"You didn't buy the store out?" David said.

"I was tempted. Italians make the best shoes."

"Shoes, clothes, purses, shall I go on?"

"Where's Walter?"

She could feel Angelene's presence. It was as cold and cloudy as the day.

"Upstairs. We stopped at a football shop before coming home. He purchased a Chelsea shirt and wanted to try it on. He bought one for you too, Angelene."

Angelene fumbled through a shaky smile and left the foyer. Sofia collapsed against the door.

"Tired?"

"Exhausted. Where's Brendon?"

"Did you know Miranda Jones's daughter does his Latin for him?"

"It wouldn't surprise me."

"He's in his room finishing his homework. I made a pot of tea. Join me in the conservatory?"

The bags clattered to the floor. Her movements were sluggish, like she was wading through quicksand. Sofia sagged onto an ivory and azure floral club chair with heavy eyelids.

"She didn't mention anything about love. She skirted around all my questions."

"Were you prying again?"

"She isn't in love with Walter. Her eyes lit up when she mentioned a boy with brown light."

David sat on the edge of the chair and ran his hand under her hair. "I'm not sure Walter loves her."

"What are they doing together?"

"Walter has a way of dazzling women."

"He has golden fingertips."

"Angelene has an interesting way of seeing things."

"She reads palms." Sofia slid her fingers over her bracelets. "She saw four breaks in my lifeline. Has Walter told her anything?"

"I told him not to. Not yet."

"Four. Doesn't that concern you?"

David wrapped his fingers around hers and squeezed gently. "There's no truth behind any of that stuff. You've had a long day. You're tired."

"It's a strange kind of exhaustion. I feel empty, drained, dry."

"Angelene's melancholy wears on people."

"How was Brendon?"

"He stared into his ginger ale. Walter went on again about the fuss they're making in Dortmund. He couldn't look at Walter or me."

'The boy in brown, the boy who likes her as she is, messy, stitched together. Who does she mean?'

"Let's go cuddle. I need to rest."

"Can we snog?" David said.

"Can we kiss? Yes."

Sofia looped her arm through David's, tucking herself close to his side. The feeling overwhelmed her, no love, golden fingertips, a boy with brown light. Questions flitted around Sofia's head. She would lie down, concentrate on her husband, and hopefully see things a little clearer over dinner.

Brendon

What are we going to do today, Uncle Walt?

Do you see the driftwood? What does it look like?

A ship with a mermaid on the bow.

Then we're pirates in search of treasure.

I love you. Mommy says you should always tell someone you love them just in case something happens.

I loved you before you were born. I held my hand against your mother's belly and introduced myself as your Uncle Walt; you kicked. I said, Sofie, you've got yourself a footy player.

Brendon jerked and blinked his eyes. The Latin text clunked onto the floor. There was no beach, no driftwood pirate ship, no Uncle Walt. Shoving his notebook off his lap, Brendon swallowed, moistening his parched throat. He groaned at the pain throbbing in his temples. He couldn't remember whether he had kissed Angelene or she had kissed him. What he did remember- she had pushed him away.

Brendon closed the door to his room and made his way downstairs. He peeked into the sitting room and braced himself against the door-frame. Angelene dipped a paintbrush in a jar of water, swirled it in a beige-pink paint pod, and gently stippled small dots on the paper. Madre Innocente shouted instructions, '*Leave, call Maggie or Troy, go back to your room.*'

"I see you standing there."

Brendon blew out a heavy breath and perched himself on the edge of the sofa. He glanced at the painting, admiring the waves and tiny shells. "That's nice."

Angelene dropped the paintbrush in the water. Her eyes were as grey as the day. "Last night was special. You ruined it. I need God to forgive me."

"He needs to forgive me, not you."

"Your mother asked if we went into town."

He had no memory of getting into bed. All he remembered was waking, covered in sweat, and stumbling to the bathroom to vomit. He was sure Sofia had tried to wake him for breakfast.

"What did you say?" Brendon's voice was thick and unsteady.

"Our secret's safe. That's why God won't stop crying."

"You bloody begged me to go. I'm sure that's why He's pissed off. You and your fucking devil. I told you Padre Diavolo is a prick."

Angelene smeared brown paint over the painting and groaned.

"What about..." Brendon lowered his voice and picked at his fingernail. "The kiss."

"We were drunk. You spoiled everything."

"Did you enjoy kissing me?"

She crumpled the picture and tossed it onto the coffee table. "It made me uncomfortable. I can't trust you."

Brendon picked up the painting and smoothed it across his lap. Memories of the beach flooded over him. She was a tease, worse than Rachel. At least he knew the intention behind Rachel's tickling fingers. Angelene had sucked him in, made him have the feels, then spat him out.

"I didn't try to hump you. You touched me like you wanted me to kiss you."

"You should have had your way with me. It was what you wanted," Angelene said, gruffly.

"Not everyone has bad intentions. You looked at me like Charlie does Troy."

"That wasn't me."

"What if I told you I loved you."

"You're stupid. Things happen to people who fall in love with me."

Sparks whirred. He tossed the painting at her and jammed his hands in his pockets. "Walter would have liked that."

Brendon stormed from the room. His thoughts were as crumpled as the painting. He slumped onto the stool and unlocked his phone,

Maggie's number glowing back to him. His fingers drummed a restless rhythm against the counter before he shoved the phone away, mumbling a string of spark-infused curse words.

"Having an argument with Margaret?"

Madre Innocente pointed an accusatory finger at him. '*Look at Walter. Look at the man who loves you like a son. Make your amends and leave his wife alone.*'

"Have you ever tried to be friends with a girl?"

Walter reached inside the fridge, grabbing two bottles of water. "I'm friends with Kate."

Brendon ran the bottle over his warmed cheeks and forced himself to face Walter. "You've kissed Kate. Doesn't that make you more than friends?"

"Kate and I tried; it didn't work out."

"You stayed friends, doesn't it make things awkward?"

"Have you kissed Miranda Jones's daughter? I won't tell your dad. Just because I helped write that code doesn't mean I've always followed it."

This was his way out. Confess he had snuck out, got drunk and kissed Angelene. Brendon practiced the speech, his head flooded with memories. Walter had been there for him, supported him, defended him.

"I kissed her."

"That Jones girl is fit, eighteen going on thirty."

Brendon swallowed, chugged the water, and swallowed again. This was his chance to do the right thing, release the guilt, and brace himself for the beating of a lifetime.

"I didn't mean for it to happen."

"Do you feel sorry for what you did?"

"At first, no. Now I feel like a bloody dolt."

"Monogamy is tricky."

"Mom and Dad love Maggie."

"If there ever was a girl, you took home to your parents, it's Margaret Thornton. Do you love her?"

Angelene stormed Brendon's brain. He clamped his fingers around the bottle and squeezed. "I thought I did. I can't stand her."

Walter laughed. "I understand. Ang can drive me completely mad some days."

"What if I want to snog her again?"

"Then you need to ask yourself if you want to be in a relationship with Margaret."

"I know one thing I want. Maggie has made it perfectly clear she doesn't want that."

"I feel your pain. Ang is reluctant to do anything intimate, even kiss. Who doesn't like to kiss?"

The words hovered around Brendon. Her resistance made sense. A kiss was no different from sex. He had forced himself on her.

"I broke her bloody trust."

"Don't beat yourself up." Walter finished his water and chucked the bottle into the recycling bin by the door. "Just don't do it again."

"I hear footsteps. I better get ready. Mom will expect me in my suit."

"We can't have a simple getaway without Sofia wanting us to get all dolled up."

"I'm sorry."

Walter smiled his crinkly grin. "For what"

"I was a dick when I came home from Dortmund, an arse to you."

"I would've been pissed off, too. You're a good kid." Walter patted his shoulder and left.

She didn't kiss Walter. When he could get her alone, he would apologize and promise not to do it again. He would keep his lamp on and be her friend.

"Brendon, our reservation is in forty-five minutes."

He looked at his mother. The queen of Taunton was doing a decent job hiding her worry.

"You look nice, Mammina."

"I came to wake you this morning and your room..." There was hesitation in her voice, like she was wrestling with the words. "It smelled like..."

"I argued with Maggie and drank some wine. Daft."

"Bottles?"

"Enough for me to barf, Mammina."

"Five minutes and do something with your hair."

The bottle crinkled in his hand. He had a two-hour meal to get through with no Charlie face or guilt etched on his brow. He would become the dutiful son, consume himself in the character, the sweet prince of Rosewood Manor.

Dinner had gone as Brendon expected. Angelene had downed an Old-Fashioned, five to be exact. Walter talked about past conquests, how Sofia was the perfect politician's wife. Brendon didn't have to use any of his acting skills. Walter and his drunk wife had taken centre stage.

Brendon loosened his tie and strolled into the sitting room. He swiped the remote off the nest of books and clicked on the television. Walter's hushed and displeased voice travelled from the foyer. He tiptoed to the doorframe and pressed his back to the wall.

"Can you make it up the stairs, little bird?"

"You and your women. Kate, Branagh, the Russian princess, even Sofia. Does David know you lust after her?"

"Bed now, before the whole damn house hears you."

"Enculer."

"Fuck you. What about you and your married men?"

Brendon hands clamped in tight fists. He could use the Gentlemen's Code as an excuse and step in front of her, save the damsel in distress.

"I need a cigarette."

"Go on, little bird. Your words become very sharp when you drink. It's no wonder people leave you."

Brendon exhaled the sparks and flopped onto the sofa. His first instinct was to protect her, something—a flutter, Madre Innocente—warned him to protect himself. He heard the door close. Angelene hobbled across the floor and plopped beside him. Patchouli permeated from her skin, spicy and musky. There was a snag in her stockings. She was drunk, pouting, and beautiful.

"Pour me a glass."

"I thought you didn't like scotch?"

"Just fucking pour it."

"Bloody hell, don't be a bitch to me." He pulled the stopper from the decanter and filled a glass. "I was a good boy tonight. No elbows on the table, chewed with my mouth closed, napkin on my lap."

"Did you hear that ridiculous conversation?"

"Unfortunately."

"Walter is a playboy, oui?"

Brendon contained his laugh. "He loves women."

"He has made love to all of them."

"Not all of them. Kate wouldn't have anything to do with him until he promised her a commitment."

"She's more wonderful now, smart and classy, not some gutter girl from Paris."

She downed the scotch and slid the glass across the table. It ricocheted off the books and fell at his feet. Brendon picked it up and ran his foot over the spill.

"Why do you call yourself that?"

"You don't know what I've done. All the bad decisions and stupid patterns I trip into."

Brendon's gaze darted around the room. He nervously moistened his lips. "Speaking of poor decisions. I'm sorry for kissing you. I made you uncomfortable."

Angelene poked her finger into the run in her stocking and dug into her thigh. "It was a strange kind of uncomfortable. I can't describe it."

"I'd love to find those pricks that hurt you and punch them in their fucking mouths."

Angelene glanced up and grinned wistfully. "My hero."

Brendon held his hand over hers and hesitated. She was calm; a hurricane raged in her eyes. Deciding it was worth the risk, he grasped her fingers. "Who hurt you? Who made you hate yourself so much, you can't see how brilliant you are?"

"You sound like Roman."

"You can't listen to that voice in your head. I never should have listened to Padre Diavolo."

"He's a prick, oui?"

"Just as bad as the mother of all devils."

Her fingers wrapped around his.

"Sometimes I blame myself when we lose. I'll analyze every move and criticize myself. Self-doubt is a bloody confidence shaker."

"I've felt nothing but shame and guilt. God must be so annoyed with me, asking for forgiveness all the time."

"That's his job, right?"

"I must exhaust Him."

"Probably."

Angelene sighed and stared at the ceiling. "Can you pour me another?"

"No bloody way. I'll make you a coffee."

Brendon clicked off the television and helped her from the sofa. They walked silently to the kitchen. He pulled out a stool and patted the cushion.

"Where are David and Sofia?"

"They went for a walk on the beach. Dad likes to hold Mom's hand."

Brendon filled the kettle and clunked it onto the stove. He opened the cupboard, pushed aside tins of soup, and grabbed instant coffee. "I apologize for kissing you. You need to know that." He spooned a heap of coffee into the mug and leaned against the counter. "I'm sorry for telling you I love you. I don't love you, that is, I fancy you but love, no way."

"I don't like the word."

"I said fancy, which is a strong like."

The kettle boiled. Brendon tipped water into the mug, turning off the burner. He added cream and set it before her.

"How come you frown every time Walt calls you little bird?"

"I was Roman's little bird. It meant something different when Douchette called me his that. It took everything sweet and pure away from it. I've asked Walter to stop."

Brendon moved her bangs from her eyes and grinned. "What colour are you right now?"

"Weepy blue, staticky red and grey."

"Then we need to make you yellow. A happy memory."

"Schellen-Ursli."

"What the bloody hell is that?"

"A book Roman used to read to me. We used to chase winter away like Ursli."

"Some of my best memories is Mammina reading me the Paddington stories."

Angelene stared into the creamy coffee. "I bet you looked sweet curled up beside her."

"I'd have on my Dortmund shirt, Paddington in my arms. She was the best storyteller. Yellow yet?"

"Grey."

"You better tell me something else."

"I loved when Roman spoke about Switzerland. He used to tell me about the edelweiss and alpine aster. I used to dream about running through the fields, listening to the cowbells. Roman said I would surely find my wings. Switzerland is magical." She gulped back the coffee, rose, and rinsed the mug in the sink. "Please be my friend."

"Whenever you need me, I'll be there."

"I'm a hint of yellow."

"Keep thinking about running through the fields in Switzerland with Roman, you'll be yellow by morning." Brendon held out his hand and tried his best to cover his sadness with a grin. "When I turn my lamp on tomorrow night, I want you to turn yours on, too. I'll know you're yellow. Deal?"

"Deal."

They walked hand in hand to the foyer. Angelene glanced at her feet.

"I wanted to tell you how handsome you look tonight."

He leaned into her ear and whispered, "Don't. I'll want to kiss you again."

"My mother liked a man in a suit. It was one of the few things we agreed upon. You were meant to wear suits."

"Mammina says the same thing."

"Will you help me?"

"I'll always be there."

Angelene

Angelene slipped on a lacy nightgown; it was scratchy and uncomfortable. The weekend had turned into an alcohol-soaked tangle of memories, some to remember and others she couldn't wait to forget.

Normal had been difficult. God was angry with her. She was willing to try to play wife again, to see if it fit. This was her fourth attempt.

"You're wearing a nightgown. You look lovely," Walter said. He drew the blankets over himself and kissed her shoulder.

Angelene inhaled deeply. Sex was part of normal. She gazed out the window, his lamp was on.

"Do you mind if I turn the lamp on? I'm not sleepy."

"Not at all, little bird. All that fresh air made me tired."

"Are you too tired for that?"

Walter eased her onto the bed and kissed her. "That, as you call it, will make me sleep like a baby."

He raised her nightgown. She turned her head, staring at the glow coming from Brendon's window. Angelene gripped the sheets and squeezed her eyes shut. She painted herself yellow and shut out Walter's moans.

"I'm trying, Walter."

"I know, little bird."

Angelene swallowed through her rattled nerves, pecked his cheek, and pulled down her nightgown.

"It'll be the lips next time. Fais de beaux rêves."

Angelene reached for *Tale of Two Cities* and flipped to a dog-eared page.

"'I wish you to know that you have been the last dream of my soul.' Did you write that about Brendon, Mr. Dickens? If there ever was a sweeter dream. Fais de beaux rêves, mon ami. Déjà-visite, I've been here before.'

17 Tu Me Manques

Troy

Chickens clucked and pecked at the feed surrounding Troy's feet. He dug under a feathery belly, smiled, and tossed an egg at Charlotte.

"What if I missed? Mrs. Nutter is making a special trip for these eggs."

"Be nice." Troy pressed his tongue against his lip and pilfered under a plume of tawny feathers. "That should be twelve."

"How come you have to do this and not Brian or Callum?"

"I skipped chores yesterday to meet Brendon for a pre-pre-match warm-up."

Troy peered down the laneway, flicking the pull on his Manchester United sweatshirt. Angelene approached, daydreamy and golden. She was a different Mrs. Pratt than the one who stumbled into the coop, polished but not entirely comfortable. Angelene smiled a tiny, 'I-won't-say-a-thing' smile. It was as if she had slipped into his mind and read his guilt.

"Your eggs," Charlotte said, shoving the carton at her.

"Did you gather them?"

Charlotte flung out her hand and grasped Troy's nipple. "Babes did. He's gentler than me. *Babes*."

Troy sucked in his breath and unclamped her fingers. "What did you think of the match, Mrs. P?" He draped an arm over his chest and tugged Charlotte to his side.

"I thought that corner kick would've gone in. You were right there."

Troy pressed his mouth against Charlotte's hair. Heat swept over his cheeks.

"Walter mentioned scouts were at the match," Angelene said.

"I've got my fingers and toes crossed."

"I'll put you in my prayers," Angelene said.

Troy felt thirteen again, crushing on a woman who was nothing like he fancied. There was an aura surrounding Angelene. It struck him like a viper.

"Still two pounds ninety-five?"

'She isn't a spider. She's a witch.' Troy shook the thought away. She was Walter's wife and here to buy eggs.

Charlotte dug her elbow into his ribs. "She asked if the eggs were still..."

"I heard her."

Angelene had done it again, worked her magic, cursed him with a love spell.

"Mom said to give them to you."

Angelene stepped closer and examined his face. "Are you feeling ill? You're pale."

"He's suffering from the Charlie face," Charlotte said.

"Is that some kind of disease?"

"It's inflicting the boys around Taunton. Nothing a snog can't cure."

Troy rubbed the back of his neck and forced a grin. "I was thinking about how I can prove myself to those scouts."

"I see the spark. God sees it and He will make your light shine."

Troy licked his lips nervously. Only a witch could turn the pleasant tingles into excruciating knots.

"You have it. It's in your heart and those miraculous feet." Angelene waved, gave a slight smile, and walked away.

"She sees a spark. That gobby cow, no one sees a spark in my little crumpet but me."

"I didn't have the Charlie face."

"You did, babes. And she was looking at you like you were a bag of Jelly Babies."

"She wasn't."

"I heard Mr. Pratt call her little bird at the match. He should call her little cat."

They walked towards the house, which was once a regal manor. The relic of sombre stone and weathered wood was as tired and ancient as the moors.

"Why's that?"

"What's that saying, the cat that got the cream? She looked smug, proud of herself for something."

"Can we change the subject?" Troy said, scraping his boots on a cinder block. "I want to start the day on a good note."

"If you give Mrs. Nutter the Charlie face again, I'll give you a pinch you'll never forget."

Troy opened the door to a room smelling of oats and hay, cluttered with muddy boots and dusty jackets.

"I love you."

"I know, babes. I don't blame you for looking. A new hairstyle and mascara can do wonders for even the ugliest girls."

"That's all it was. I still think you're the prettiest girl in England."

The house was brighter than a big top and just as noisy. Brian stood on the sofa. Callum held out his scrawny arms, ready for the clinch. Brian jumped off the cushions, clutched Callum's blazer, grunting as he took him to the floor.

"Nice one, Bri," Troy said.

They entered the kitchen. Flour dusted the counters; scraps of pastry were stuck to a well-loved rolling pin.

"Mom made her treacle tart."

"I'm coming for dinner." Charlotte peeked into a bowl of filling and licked her lips. "Your mom's pastry is scrummy."

Troy took her hand. The feeling of never wanting to let go made his heart swell. It was just the gentle push needed to knock Angelene out of his head.

"Mom! Charlie's joining us for supper."

Evelyn Spence's voice came from somewhere within the house. "You have an hour before school. Don't be late."

"Brendon didn't send Magpie a text. Nothing all weekend."

They walked deeper into the house to a puny box which had once been the tack room. The window framed a picture-perfect view of the barn and coop. A constant reminder of where Troy had been born and where he might stay.

"He was getting game ready."

"All weekend?"

Troy flicked on the light; the wall of Manchester United posters cast a red glow over the mess of clothes creeping from the drawers.

"He didn't meet up with that girl, did he?"

"Don't be daft. He didn't talk about Burnham," Troy said. He yanked off his T-shirt and tossed it onto a mountain of laundry. "Brendon seemed distracted, like his mind was elsewhere."

"On the match? Dortmund?"

"Like he was lost in happy moments," Troy muttered, staring at his hands.

"He *met* up with that tart."

"No, he didn't. I'm going to shower."

"Come sit, babes. You know your brothers are going to burst in here. I haven't perfected my pile driver yet."

A crash and bang exploded from the sitting room; laughter rippled down the hallway. Troy stripped out of his grass-stained jeans, twisted the lock, and squirmed into the jumble of blankets.

"That'll be you on the cover one day." Charlotte slid a Match magazine off the nightstand and kissed Troy's cheek. "Troy Spence brilliant defender."

She dropped the magazine to the floor and scrunched her nose at a buxom blonde wrapped in a pink satin bow. Charlotte picked up the magazine. The centre page fell open in three swishes. "Look at the size of her boobies." She glanced at her own doctored breasts and sighed. "What are you doing looking at this?"

"Will passed it around the dressing room and stuck it in my rucky. He said I could compare your jubblies to hers."

Charlotte batted him with the magazine and dropped it in the bin.

"You're a million times prettier than that girl."

"You're just saying that so I don't give you a pinch."

Troy groaned and pressed against her to stop his heart from leaping from his chest. "I like the highlights in your hair. Your nail polish is ace."

Charlotte ignored his compliments and nuzzled his neck. "Are your parents going to the caravan soon?"

Troy ran his hand over hers. A purple rhinestone decorated her ring finger. "No, why?"

"We need to have a party. Maybe if Magpie has a few alcopops, she'll be up for it."

"Should you be plotting this stuff?"

"I think she wants to hump. She asks a lot of questions, turns a lovely shade of pink."

"I'll get Brendon to ask his mom. She never says no to him." Troy moved his fingers over her stomach and grinned. "Fancy a snog?"

"Your brothers will barge in here to put you in a chokehold."

Troy leapt from the bed and shuffled through the mess on the floor. "Mom, Charlie and I are doing homework. Tell Brian and Callum not to bother us. I need to finish English."

"You mean biology," Evelyn Spence hollered. "I'm leaving for work."

"Your mom knows we're having a hump?"

"She has four randy boys. She isn't daft."

He unbuttoned Charlotte's shirt and pressed his lips against her stomach. "You still coming to Manchester with me or London or wherever?"

Charlotte wiggled out of her shirt and dropped it on the floor. "Liverpool, Germany, France. Wherever, babes."

Troy ran his hands over her bottom and tugged at her kilt. He grinned at her cherry print knickers.

The old walls shook. Feet stomped down the hall, followed by peals of laughter.

"I've got to get out of here."

"You will."

He kissed a trail up her stomach and gazed into her ocean-blue eyes. "All I think about is playing football. There isn't anything else I see myself doing."

"We're going to Manchester. Don't give up hope."

"I don't know why you chose me." Troy unhooked her bra and kissed the space between her breasts. "You could have any boy in Taunton."

"The chickens make me laugh and you look dead gorgey holding a pitchfork." Charlotte slid off her underwear and wound her legs around him. "Even dishier in your football kit."

"Brendon looks like a proper footy player. He doesn't even have to try. Posh car, posh clothes."

"You don't need those things to be a brilliant football player. Be quiet and concentrate. You need to hit that spot that makes me tingle."

Fists hammered against the door and rattled it on its hinges. "Troy! I knocked Brian out."

"Go away, Callum. We're busy."

"Slow down, babes."

"I want to finish before he breaks the door down." Troy gripped her hands and turned his head towards the door. "We'll be out in a bit."

A fit of laughter erupted outside the door.

"When you're finished having some rumpy pumpy come to the sitting room."

Troy spoke between kisses. "If I'm not up to my knees in manure, it's those two bothering me."

"I know what will help."

She clamped her thighs around his waist, tossed him onto his back, and rose above him.

"You should wrestle the Inquisitor with a leg lock like that."

"Just close your eyes and let me do the work. Poor crumpet has had quite the morning."

You have it. I see the spark. God sees it, and He will make sure your light shines.

"How do you do it?" Troy whispered.

"Quiet, babes, you're making me lose my rhythm."

He blinked and stared. Charlotte was no longer Charlotte. She was blonde with piercing green eyes.

"Babes, your heart is going to beat out your chest."

Things that made other people scared like clowns and heights had never frightened Troy. There was not much in life that scared him. He didn't know what it was about Angelene, but he was afraid.

Brendon

Overexuberant chatter buzzed in the dining hall. Huddles of students exchanged the latest gossip over their designer lunches. The once executive chef had convinced himself a stint at Taunton College would be less stressful than the restaurant he captained. He spruced up the menu with French classics and gourmet twists. Over-salted chips and burgers sans the gastrique seemed to be the only items that dazzled the finicky teenagers.

Brendon studied the selections: fettuccine al a poulet et béarnaise, or Cumberland sausage.

"How was Burnham? You haven't mentioned anything?" Troy said.

"Boring."

"No walks on the beach? No kisses?"

"Who would I be kissing?" Brendon pointed to the fettuccine and grabbed a bottle of water from a dish of ice.

"You're awful twitchy. When Ms. Hudson asked you to describe how Werther's emotions govern his life, your voice cracked, like when we were twelve."

"Mom made me spend time with my dad. Happy now."

The memory of Angelene standing beside his bed unfolded in his brain like the pages of *A Bear Called Paddington*. The details were vivid. Every touch, the desperate plea in her eyes.

"Still being punished?"

They walked to the quietest corner and slid their trays across the table. Brendon hooked his foot around the leg of a chair, dragged it closer, and dropped onto it.

"Mom thinks I need to repair the relationship. I had to play chess, and uh, Scrabble."

Brendon dug around the pasta. He was positive there was chicken buried under the pool of sauce and even more positive, Troy didn't believe him. Brendon knew he was in the wrong, lying to Troy. Their friendship had been effortless. They could watch football, not say a word, and be completely comfortable in the silence. They didn't need to make a pact to be there for each other. It had been an unspoken rule since day one. He was lying to his best friend.

"Bollocks. When my dad and I spend time together, there's a Man U match on." Troy took a slug of water and wiped his lips on the back of his hand. "What did the Pratts do? Play chess and Scrabble too?"

Brendon shifted in the chair; heat rolled over his cheeks. The secret was eating a hole in him.

"Married people's stuff."

'Argue, make up, argue.'

"Spend anytime with Mrs. Pratt?"

"Don't be a wanker."

The dining hall doors squeaked open. Every boy in the room gawked at Rachel, hips wiggling, a coquettish smile. Brendon met her gaze. She was the distraction he needed.

"Hiya, number one and number three." Rachel dragged a chair along the parquet and dropped onto it.

"We have names," Troy said.

"Can't a girl have any fun. Hello, Troy, hello, knuddelbär." She slithered to the edge of the chair, lifted Brendon's cuff, and glanced at his watch.

"There's a bloody clock on the wall."

"I'd rather look at your posh watch. You smell dishy." Rachel ran her fingers over Brendon's knuckles and stared at Troy with a look that burned through his school kit. "Do you?"

"Do I what?" Troy said.

"Smell as dishy as knuddelbär." She leaned across the table and sniffed. "William's a dolt. You don't stink like manure, you smell delicious."

Brendon looked up from his lunch and nearly choked on his pasta. She wore lace knickers with ruby-red lips embroidered on them.

"Can you sit down?"

Rachel wiggled her bottom and laughed. "Like what you see?"

"The entire dining hall can see up your kilt."

"You're no fun. Neither are you, number three." Rachel pulled an apple out of her purse and crunched. "You want a bite, knuddelbär?"

Troy rolled his eyes and twirled pasta around his fork. "What do you want? You're going to get me a pinch if you don't bugger off."

Rachel ran a sticky finger over Brendon's ear. Her breath was warm and sweet against his cheek. "I saw knuddelbär and thought I'd say hello. Margaret is making things difficult."

Brendon shrank away and rubbed his sleeve over his earlobe. "Do you mind? Michael and the drama swots are two tables over. They're probably texting Maggie right now."

"You're blushing, knuddelbär," she said, whipping the apple core into the garbage.

"You're as red as that apple she just ate, mate."

Rachel pulled a tube of lip gloss from her pocket, pumped the applicator up and down, and layered it on her lips. "Thornton called me a schlampe."

"I don't know what that is."

"A trollop."

She leaned her breasts against his arm. The fork fell from his fingers. Her breasts looked the size of the cantaloupes Amelia had brought home from Tesco.

Troy pinched his lips and flicked water at Brendon. "Cool off, mate."

"Sorry, Maggie called you a trollop. Can you leave now?"

"Anything for you, knuddelbär. Kisses."

"Your phone beeped. It's probably Maggie giving you shit."

Brendon tapped open his phone, read the text, and deleted it.

"You sure nothing else happened in Burnham? No Bronwyn? You didn't stumble upon any other girls on the beach?"

Brendon grabbed his water bottle, spun the cap off, and chugged. "Just chess and scrabble."

'I kissed her. I told her I loved her.'

"You're looking awful innocent, mate, which scares me."

Sofia

Sofia flumped onto the sofa, her mind jumbled. Questions came home with her from Burnham and rode in the passenger seat to Kate's Victorian terrace. Kate's home had always been a place to take refuge when life got tough. While Sofia preferred dark colours, mixed antiques with contemporary design, Kate decorated her home in what Sofia described as 'shabby in a fashionable way.' Distressed wood, muted colours, vintage, relaxed. Sofia always felt at home among the dove-grey walls and scarred hardwood floors. Today, she felt nothing but a sense of dread. Had she imagined the smell? Had Angelene answered the question about love and the boy with brown light?

"Thanks for letting me come over. I know you're busy."

"I was tied up in court all morning. This is just the break I need." Kate set a plate of lemon madeleines on an antique steamer trunk turned coffee table and snuggled into the corner of the sofa. "What's up? You sounded upset on the phone."

"Every detail. The dimple on his left cheek is deeper than his right. The cheeky twinkle in his eye and all from memory."

"What are you going on about?"

"Angelene drew a portrait of Brendon." Sofia clicked her bracelets and took herself back to the kitchen at Rosewood Manor. She and Amelia were working on last-minute details for her tea party. They were sipping coffee and discussing the menu when the doorbell disturbed them. Sofia hadn't been expecting anyone or any deliveries, and she certainly wasn't expecting to see Angelene holding a gift for her. It was to apologize for ruining the weekend. The gift was wrapped in the prettiest paper and tied with a teal ribbon. Angelene was proud of herself for picking out the frame at an antique shop in town. Sofia asked Angelene in for coffee. She politely declined, spoke of finding her wings, and fluttered away, leaving

Sofia with more questions. Why a gift? What flickered in Angelene's eyes: guilt, shame, yearning for forgiveness? Why draw Brendon?

"Did Brendon have glowing red eyes and horns?"

Kate's voice pulled Sofia back from the memory.

"Have you ever heard of Tartini?"

"He was a composer."

Sofia flicked her silver bangles. The charms tinkled. "He had a terrible inferiority complex, was depressed."

Click, click, click.

"The devil appeared to him in a dream, and he wrote his most famous piece, *The Devil's Trill*."

Kate sipped her tea and shook her head in disbelief. "What are you saying? Angelene's mastery of art is because she made a deal with the devil?"

Click, click, click.

"Don't people usually sit for portraits? I don't want Brendon around her."

"What is she going to do? Put a hex on him? Perform black magic."

Sofia smoothed and re-smoothed her blouse. She struggled to breathe through the flutters.

"She looks at him in a way that makes me uncomfortable." A sense of dread, life spiralling out of control, caused Sofia's stomach to pitch. "Angelene frightens me. It's like she's constantly in a state of dying, like she gave up struggling to live and now floats, chin deep in the memories. There's a desperate look in her eye, help me, but let me die."

"Tough weekend?"

"It was a roller coaster. David and I took Brendon to Alton Towers when he was ten. It was my turn to ride it. I ended up in the lady's room."

"I certainly hope you didn't spend the weekend in the loo."

"One minute Walter and Angelene were laughing. I think she was laughing. You never can tell with her, then she's pouting, he's angry."

"It's bound to take some time. They're still getting to know one another."

Sofia stuck a fingernail between her bracelets, *flick, clack.* "You put the Bible box on the mantel."

Kate rested her hand on Sofia's. "What's the matter? You can't tell me a portrait has got you this upset."

"I think Brendon snuck out with Angelene."

Sofia stroked her eyebrow. Her throat was tight, clogged with questions. Brendon wasn't a liar. He wasn't a drinker, yet he smelled and looked like he had pickled himself in cheap wine. Angelene had worn the same look.

"Angelene begged Walter to go into town. I thought she was going to bounce through the ceiling she was that anxious. He said no, she pouted."

"What does that prove?" Kate said. She patted Sofia's hand and reached for a cookie. "You're upset over the portrait."

"I went to wake Brendon for breakfast, his room stunk of wine."

"Did you ask him about it?"

"I think she seduced him."

Kate bit into the cookie and smiled an 'you're-so-dramatic-but-I-love-you' smile.

"If he *did* sneak out, and that's a big if, he did it on his own accord. I wouldn't blame him," Kate said. "It must be hard doing as he's told all the time."

"She had her hands all over David."

"Since when are you a jealous woman?"

Sofia met Kate's gaze. A small frown creased her brow. "I'm not jealous. She needs to understand boundaries, always touching and flirting."

Kate finished the cookie and washed it down with tea. "I don't think she means any harm."

"I wish I were as observant as my mother. I might understand her."

"Did you ask Angelene?"

"I hinted, and she danced around it." Sofia picked up a cookie, stared at it, and dropped it back on the plate. "She's obsessed with my family."

"Your life is like a fairy tale. Rosewood Manor, the king and queen of Taunton, the prince. Who wouldn't want to be part of that story? What does she know about family?"

Sofia recalled conversations with Angelene. Neglectful mother, absent father. While Sofia was attempting to understand the girl from Paris, Angelene was trying to figure out what family meant.

"I told Brendon you still love Walter."

Kate glanced at a photo of her and Walter on the beach in Burnham. "I never loved Walter."

'*Neither does Angelene.*'

Sofia followed Kate's gaze, grinning softly. "Admit you love him."

"I'll always love him. Underneath all that bravado, he's a wonderful man."

"Angelene says he has golden fingertips."

"There's truth to it. Everything he touches turns to gold."

The unsettling feeling welled inside Sofia. It was too coincidental. Angelene begging to go out, Brendon hungover.

"Don't turn your back on Walter."

"Are you worried about him, too?"

"Their marriage seems strained, forced."

"She's more work than he expected."

Sofia ran her thumb over the breaks in her lifeline. "Angelene reads palms."

"A good Catholic girl."

"She saw things, things we don't talk about. She saw a fourth." Sofia pulled her cardigan tighter around her chest. Goosebumps prickled her skin. "Something is going to happen. I can feel it."

Kate tucked a wisp of her auburn hair behind her ear and grinned. "Give me your hand."

Sofia laid her hand on Kate's lap, her heart knocked wildly.

"I see a woman with a beautiful manicure who loves antiques like I do and worries."

"Something doesn't feel right."

"You're worrying for nothing. This is Walter's mountain to climb, not yours. Did you ask Brendon if he snuck out?"

"He got into a fight with Maggie and drank his anger away. Brendon doesn't do that, Angelene does."

"This weekend has opened old wounds. It's only natural you'd worry."

"Stay by Walter's side. Be there for him."

Kate wrapped her hand around Sofia's. "I'll always be there. No more worrying."

Sofia didn't know why the feeling lingered or what it meant. The look in Angelene's eyes haunted her, like an omen. Something bad was going to happen.

Angelene

"Do you think God heard my apology?"

The light inside the booth was dim. She could see the priest's silhouette on the other side of the screen. His holy presence was all around her, in the perfumed air and the melodic tone of his voice.

"You've confessed your sins and thanked Him."

"Why hasn't He given me a sign?"

"Sometimes they're subtle, and you're too busy or troubled to notice. Be patient."

Angelene scrambled from the confessional and allowed herself some time to collect her thoughts. She hoped once she left the church, God would let her know he had forgiven her.

Angelene pushed open the door. The September sun hit her face; it took a moment for her eyes to adjust. She rambled across the car park, no twinge in her belly, no flutter of her hair. Angelene tugged on the taxi door and dropped on the seat. The scent of brandy tobacco carried her back to the flat in Paris and Roman Krieger.

"Can you take me to the bookstore?"

The driver flicked the indicator and pulled onto the street. "Which one? There's one on High Street and East Street."

"I'm not sure. It's beside a patisserie and a clothing store."

"Is that the one that sells witchy stuff?"

"If you consider candles and crystals witchy, then yes. It was the only shop that could find the book I was looking for."

"You're new to Taunton?"

Angelene twisted her engagement ring around her finger. "I married a man from here. I'm sure you know him, Walter Pratt."

The driver smiled. His face reminded Angelene of the moon.

"I've driven him home from the pub a few times. You live in the farmhouse next to Rosewood Manor."

"Do you know the Cooks?"

"From one generation to the next."

"Their son."

"Footy star. Nice boy. Helped me change a tire once. I was stuck on Taunton Road."

Angelene studied the driver's face: chubby cheeks, sky-blue eyes, bushy white moustache, head full of white hair. His words came out vibrant green.

"What's your name?"

"Malcolm."

"How long have you lived in Taunton?"

"Sixty-two years, been driving taxi since I was twenty. I know Taunton like the back of my hand, the people too."

"May I call you when I need a ride? The taxi I took earlier smelled like spoiled milk."

Malcolm pulled alongside the curb. He turned and grinned. His moustache fluffed over his lip. "I'd be honoured."

"Can you wait? I'll only be a minute."

"I have to pick up Mrs. Mulholland from the salon."

Angelene slid her purse strap over her arm. The attempt at a smile pained her.

"I'll drop her off at home and come back."

"I'm still trying to find my wings. You've made me feel safe."

"Shouldn't that be your feet?"

"No, my wings. My feet lead me to all sorts of stupid places."

Malcolm chuckled. "You say some funny things, Mrs. Pratt."

Angelene pushed open the door and leaned into the car. "Please call me Angelene. Mrs. sounds strange to me."

The boy with liquid blue eyes would have admired the Tudor façade. The sign, written in Old English lettering, creaked back and forth on its wrought iron frame. 'Where the Raven Flies.' Angelene stepped inside the dimly lit shop, yet it was as bright as the Tibetan singing bowls vibrating in the air. Plumes of incense snaked around the shelves of books and tables of spell-infused candles. Angelene tapped a bell. A blood-red sphere with lacy white veins weaving through it caught her attention. She touched the stone and a tiny shock zapped her finger. She withdrew her hand and stared at her fingertip, amazed at the sensation.

The salesclerk, draped in a jade kaftan, appeared from behind a curtain of clacking beads.

"It's pretty, isn't it?"

"It made the hair on my arms stand up. What is it?"

"Crazy lace agate."

Angelene touched her lips, overjoyed. God had given her a sign. She picked up the crystal and rolled it between her fingers. The electricity tickled her hand.

"Agate has incredible healing powers. It makes you feel whole, less vulnerable."

"Do you think God has touched it?"

"If you're drawn to it then yes."

"It might help put me back together," Angelene said, setting the stone on the counter. "You found the book?"

The salesclerk slid the book out from beneath the cash register, presenting it like a sacred gift. Angelene's gaze darted over the illustration of Ursli and his cowbell. She drew a breathless sigh.

"I've never seen anyone so happy about a book."

"A book takes you places. A story is magic."

"It makes me feel good knowing you'll love it."

"This is more than a book. It's an old friend."

She pressed the book to her lips, breathed in the memories, breathed in Roman Krieger.

Angelene pushed open the door. A thin strip of sunlight severed the grey clouds and washed the street in pale gold. Angelene smiled; it was sign number two. She approached the black cab. Malcolm fiddled with his moustache. He had the newspaper spread across the steering wheel.

"Can you take me to Taunton Park?"

"There isn't a match today. The boys might be training."

"I like the energy there."

One by one, the streetlamps turned on. Angelene memorized which shops she would like to visit: a charity shop to rescue things, an antique shop to breathe in history, a bakery.

"You'll be my driver from now on."

Malcolm laughed. The sound sprang from deep within his chest, lifting his cheeks and jiggling his belly. "You're a sweet girl."

The scent of brandy tobacco seeped from the heat vents, invading her nose and mind.

Roman, why do you pay so much attention to Angelene?

Angelene needs love from you, her mother.

You're like Gustav, always staring at her.

I'm nothing like Mr. Jennsen. My heart breaks for her. She's going to end up like you, searching for love, receiving it, and running as fast as she can. Someone needs to love little bird.

"I thought you'd fallen asleep."

"I was daydreaming. It gets me into trouble," Angelene said. "Drop me off here. I'll walk the rest of the way."

"Call me if you need a ride home."

"Thank you, you'll make finding my wings much easier. See you soon."

Angelene stepped out of the car and walked along the sidewalk, fringed with pennyroyal and knapweed. The energy from the pitch swept over her like a million prickles. It frightened her and intrigued her. The atmosphere was golden and pleasant. '

'This is a test to see if I can be his friend. Please God, be with me.'

She crossed herself and smiled. Brendon paced, stopped to fumble with the pylons, then paced again.

"Are you nervous?"

Brendon batted the ball between his feet and grinned. "Where did you come from?"

"I had Malcolm drop me off at the corner."

"Malcolm the taxi driver?"

"He's the nicest man. I liked how his taxi smelled."

"They usually smell like armpit and kebobs."

Angelene laid her purse and the paper bag on the bench and grabbed the grass-stained ball. She looked at Brendon in rapt fascination. She thought God was beautiful and that beauty itself was an expression of God. God had done his best work creating Brendon Cook.

"You need gloves." He dug in his duffel bag for a pair of Puma Evodisk gloves and held them out to her.

His voice pulled her from her rapture.

"They're big and have your name on them." She held out her hands. He slid the gloves on and adjusted the Velcro. "My hands look like flippers. Why are they sticky?"

"It's latex. It gives them a good grip."

"Now what?"

"Get in net. It's coming straight down the middle, centre shot."

Angelene walked across the field and stood behind the white line, her stomach squishy. A strange feeling captured her. It was as if the pitch, the trees, and the ball were magic, and she had stepped into a dream.

"That was much too easy. Try again."

Brendon laughed at the serious look on her face. "You barely cover the net. What if I miss and I give you a black eye? I'd feel terrible."

"I'm waiting."

"Try to figure out where I'm going to put the ball."

She watched him pass the ball between his feet. He kicked it, she rushed to the right side.

"Easy again."

"I'm coming in for the rebound."

The ball soared above her head. She lost her balance and landed on her bottom. Angelene burst into unrestrained laughter. It shot from her mouth in beams of yellow and tickled her insides. A little hitch prickled her throat. She couldn't remember the last time she laughed.

"Shoot again."

"You sure?"

She dusted the back of her jeans and took position. "This time don't stop. Keep trying to score on me."

"You're asking for it."

"Dortmund against PSG."

"No bloody competition."

Angelene moved backward into the net; a car idled by the curb. Icy tingles snaked over her skin. She had learned over the years to trust her gut. It had always been right about Douchette, Gustav Jennsen.

"We have to go."

"What's the matter?"

The car waited a little too long at the stop sign, then drove off.

"It's getting dark. Your mother will wonder where you are."

"You afraid I'll get another goal?"

"There was a car. Someone was watching us."

"Was it Troy's Fiesta?"

She shook her head and followed him to his BMW. Angelene looked up and down the street. She yanked at the sleeve of her shirt, dabbed at the sweat above her lip, and imagined herself washed in yellow.

"This is a test."

"Did I fail?"

"We promised to try again. I wanted to see if I could be with you without adoring your light."

"Do you fancy me?"

"Be serious. I had a feeling. It took my breath away and made God angry. I need to learn to live with your light and not want it."

Brendon grabbed a bottle of water from the console, took a drink, and offered it to her. "I had a feeling, too. Maybe we can't be friends."

Angelene took a small sip. The mouth of the bottle tasted salty. "We're going to do this. I'm going to prove to God I can be friends with a boy, tell my devils to fuck off."

She carefully slid the book from the bag. Many nights, it had brought her comfort. Roman Krieger had grown up listening to the story of the brave little boy. The first time he shared it with her, the darkness of night lifted; she too could be brave like Ursli.

"You found your book."

"I gave my copy to Yasmine so she could chase winter away and welcome spring. I feel like I've put back a missing piece."

She reached into the bag and wrapped her hand around the crystal. It vibrated. God was pleased. She could do this, be Brendon's friend and not want his light. Golden warmth washed over her insides. The feeling was so powerful it stole her breath.

"Did I tell you Rachel made me lunch a while back? A German feast for German lessons."

"Mother would spend days planning a meal for a lover. It was the way to a man's heart, not that she cared. She stole their hearts and ran."

"Maggie said it was one of Rachel's tart tactics."

Dusk crept slowly behind the trees, around the bleachers, and surrounded the houses in shades of blue, grey, and purple. A thin strip of gold peeked along the horizon. God was still with her.

"My mother was an expert at luring men, their favourite foods, favourite sexual positions. Mother thought her vagina was gold."

Angelene squeezed the crystal and committed Brendon's profile to memory. She would never forget the day she had found her laugh.

"Mademoiselle femme fatale will tempt you. Padre Diavolo is strong in you."

"You sound like the priest Nonna made me sit with when I was ten."

"Why did she do that?"

"I was obsessed with jubblies."

Angelene shoved her fingers between her thighs. The blush on his cheeks was charming and tempting.

"Sofia's sweet boy, obsessed with breasts?"

"It started when we were in Italy and accidentally stumbled onto a topless beach, boobs everywhere," Brendon said. He took a long sip of water and screwed on the cap. "In year five, Matilda Morimoto told the headmaster I was staring at my teacher's baps. Mom was so embarrassed."

"I can't imagine how David reacted."

"He lectured me about objectifying a woman."

A strange warmth fluttered through her belly. She squeezed her thighs tighter to stop it from spreading.

"Padre Diavolo has been part of you for a long time."

"It wasn't my fault. Miss. O'Malley wore low-cut dresses and whenever she bent over, it's all I saw."

"Are you still obsessed with breasts?"

"Bloody hell, I love them. I've never really touched one, just ran my hand over Maggie's."

"Padre Diavolo has filled your head with lustful thoughts."

Brendon shoved the keys in the ignition and flicked the BVB keychain. "Can I tell you something?"

"Don't tell me you want to kiss me. You'll ruin my day."

"I missed you today, in a friend sort of way."

"Never say I miss you; say tu me manques, you are missing from me."

18 The Untea Party

Brendon

Brendon dropped an unfinished assignment on Mr. Clark's desk. Henry VIII hadn't been on his mind. He was bogged down with memories of Angelene's laughter. He could still see the look on her face when laughter exploded from her mouth, like it surprised her a laugh still lived inside her. The 'in love' feeling was relentless.

"Are you coming to my rehearsal tonight?" Maggie said.

Brendon launched himself through the door. The sun warmed his cheeks. He marched ahead of her, leaves were turning, wavering in the breeze, holding on stubbornly, like Maggie.

"I said I would."

"You used to like watching my rehearsals. We'd go out after. It's been our thing."

It had been a thing for two years, celebrating her getting the lead role and forcing himself to sit in the musty theatre. Afterwards, go to the nauseating pink café she loved. He went out of duty and loyalty to the code.

"Bloody hell, I'll meet you after class and we'll drive over."

"Don't sit beside the tart," Maggie warned. "I have spies everywhere."

"Enjoy theatre studies."

Brendon walked away. The 'in love' feeling returned, transporting him to the pitch and the joy that overwhelmed Angelene.

"Knuddelbär, wait up."

Rachel snaked her arm around his waist. Maggie's warning flashed through his head, and he spun out of her grasp.

"Dancing, are we?"

"Maggie has spies. They're probably watching me right now."

"I missed you today."

"It's tu me manques, you're missing from me."

Rachel lifted his blazer and smacked his bottom. "You have a brilliant bum, knuddelbär, it doesn't jiggle."

He tugged at his blazer and nodded towards the laurel bushes. "There's some of Maggie's friends. I bet they're texting her right now."

"I was enjoying German lessons. Thornton has ruined everything." Rachel shot up her middle finger at the group of girls and hooked her pinky through his belt loop. "Why don't you come round to mine? Thornton will never know."

Brendon unhooked her finger and marched ahead, putting some space between them. "Bloody terrible idea."

"Don't trust me?"

The oak doors to the science building groaned open. Troy waved and ran towards them.

"Are you bothering my mate again?"

"It isn't bugging if he likes it."

"I asked you to keep those covered." Troy folded Rachel's lapels over her cleavage and turned to Brendon. "It's time for a party."

"You're suggesting I have one."

"You have the biggest house."

Rachel smoothed her lapels in place and flicked her tie at Brendon. "I could finally see inside Rosewood Manor. I bet your bedroom is ace."

"You won't go anywhere near his bedroom," Troy said, lifting his cuff. "We've got ten minutes, call Mammina."

"It would be brilliant, knuddelbär."

Brendon grabbed his phone, unlocked it, and hit speaker.

"Shouldn't you be in class?" Sofia's voice was cool and curt.

"I have ten minutes. Did I tell you how beautiful you looked this morning?"

"What did you do?"

Troy laughed. Brendon clamped his hand over his mouth.

"You aren't going to get a call from Dawson."

"You're interrupting my party."

"Can I have a few people over this weekend?"

"Absolutely not. I'm flying to Brussels to see your father. I won't have my home turned upside down again."

"I'll keep everyone in the great room."

"You promised *a few people* last time. Five turned into fifty. Amelia found condom wrappers in my Nonna's majolica vase."

Troy and Rachel burst into laughter. Brendon shot up his middle finger. "I won't let anyone hump in the house."

"Can't you say make love?"

"We're teenagers, we hump. Please. I need this."

"You needed the last party. The answer is no. Let me get back to my friends. You get to class."

Brendon raised his shoulders and slid his phone into his pocket. "You heard her."

"Be a rebel, have it. Cheers, mate."

Brendon scratched at his tousled hair. He would need a foolproof plan. The list of rules would have to be extensive. He opened the door. Dust motes floated in the musty air. Should I or shouldn't I rolled through his mind. Padre Diavolo thought it was a smashing idea. Madre Innocente scolded him. He'd give himself until the end of Latin to decide.

"Both of you to the blackboard." Mr. Campbell's nasally voice snapped Brendon out of his reverie.

"I didn't have time to finish the assignment."

"You certainly find time to dazzle us on the pitch. Why not amaze us with your knowledge of Latin."

Brendon sent his backpack flying down the aisle and begged the sparks to go away.

"I will not tolerate your temper in my classroom," Mr. Campbell said. An arthritic finger poked Brendon's spine and pushed him into the ledge. His cheeks tingled and burned. Rachel grabbed a magnet and stuck her assignment to the board. She nudged Brendon and nodded toward the paper. Chalk fell in white flakes onto the pink and blue smudged tray.

"Very good, Mr. Cook. You can thank Rachel after class for providing you the answers."

Rachel shaped her fingers into a heart and winked. "Ich liebe dich."

Mr. Campbell tutted and fingered his bow tie. "I'm happy you love Brendon. Please go to your desks and start today's assignment."

Brendon dusted his hands and sauntered to his desk. A little paper crane dropped into his lap.

"What's this?"

"Cranes stand for success and good fortune. All your dreams will come true, knuddelbär."

He examined the folded paper and set it on the corner of his desk.

"Will you keep it?"

"I'll put it in my bedroom."

Rachel dug in her blazer pocket and placed a handful of Love Hearts on his notebook. He pushed a candy towards her. She smiled and popped it in her mouth.

"Kiss you, I would love to, knuddelbär."

He picked up a candy—the message, 'I love you.' Angelene was married, he had to respect that, even if it hurt worse than the time he got a football boot in the stomach. He'd let her be Mrs. Pratt.

Brendon shook Angelene from his head. A pink candy rolled across his desk, 'In love' written in white.

"Aren't you a love them and leave them kind of girl?"

Rachel glanced from Mr. Campbell and back to Brendon. She held her notebook in front of her mouth and lowered her voice. "Have a party. Show me around the manor."

"Get myself into trouble?"

"It isn't trouble if you want it to happen."

Brendon's cell phone vibrated against his thigh. He looked at Mr. Campbell, hid his phone under his desk and cursed at the angry emoji. Brendon scrubbed at his heated cheeks.

"Can I go to the toilets?"

Theodore Campbell aimed his pen at the door, his face twisted. "I expect a completed assignment."

Brendon strolled out of the classroom. He walked down the hall to the bathroom and surveyed the stalls before dialing.

"What the bloody hell are you doing?"

"I should ask you the same thing." Maggie's voice hissed through the phone. "Charlie said you may have a party."

"You got me out of Latin for this?"

"I know you've been eating sweets with the tart."

"Mammina said no."

"Your last party was a disaster. There was cigarette butts smashed in the carpet. You barfed in her roses."

Brendon scowled into his phone. To hell with her, the code, and the good boy. It was time to play with Padre Diavolo.

"Mom is going to Brussels. She'll never know."

"We can spend the weekend together. Go for a walk in the forest."

"You know I'm not allowed in there."

"You'll have a party but won't go in the forest."

Brendon knocked his phone against his forehead and sighed heavily. "It's bloody different. There are ghosts in the forest."

"There is no proof ghosts exist except the ones people create in their heads. Defying your mother is defying your mother."

"Mom has her reasons. It would bloody kill her if she found out I was in the woods."

"Don't have the party."

Brendon shook the tingles from his fingers, switched the phone and wiggled the sparks from the other. The plan would have to be rock-solid to protect the illustrious manor from hordes of rowdy teenagers.

"I'm having it. If Mammina finds out, I'll smile my best dimpled smile. She'll forgive me."

"What's the matter with you? Your dad is still upset about Dortmund. Don't you want to make things right?"

"Dad will lecture me. I'll tune him out. I'm getting good at that lately."

"You're getting good at lots of daft things."

The party was on.

Walter

Grey skies coiled around the Eiffel Tower as the wind drove the rain into a frenzy. Walter pressed his fork against the smeared remains of his tartelette a l'echalote confite. It had been a long few days in Paris. The UK-France summit was going as he thought it would. Discussing the security and defence partnership with his French counterpart was one of friendship and cooperation. Their plans—increase the interoperability of their joint defence capabilities and continue to support Ukraine. Tomorrow's agenda: the future cruise and anti-ship weapon programme.

Walter set down his fork, pushed the pillows against the headboard, and closed his eyes. Memories of Burnham slashed through his mind. He had seen many sides of Angelene. Some he adored, and some he could live without. Quiet Angelene held his fingertips on their walk to the farmer's market. Drunk Angelene hissed at him, and the other

Angelene—guilt-ridden or shamed- still lingered in his head. He still couldn't put a finger on which emotion had been eating her up.

From within the rumpled blankets, his cell phone buzzed. He had already spoken to her. They bickered over her attending Sofia's tea party. She had one of her stomach aches. After he had convinced her to go, the next argument was over her outfit. It had been a struggle not to throw his phone out the window. He told himself to be patient; the girl was delicate, emotional, with scary habits. It wasn't just alcohol he had to worry about. Sharp things, screams that had been stuck for years, poke, knead, twist, strangle.

Walter's phone buzzed again. He kept his eyes closed and fumbled around the mussed sheets. A few beats passed before he opened his eyes. Poppet. Endearingly sweet. He had meant to change it. He couldn't bring himself to do it. Kate Miller would always be his poppet.

"Afternoon, barrister. What do I owe the pleasure?"

"Just checking in. How was Burnham?"

He noticed a tone in her voice like she knew but wanted his take.

"Have you seen Sofia?"

"That's not what I asked."

"Burnham was lovely. I jogged on the beach, watched the sunrise. Ate some delicious food."

"Did Angelene enjoy herself?"

"She had a wonderful time." He tried to sound confident. It was difficult to lie to his friend. "She loved the house."

"You'd tell me if you were struggling, right?"

"Angelene has her moments. She's an anxious little bird. I'm trying to come to terms with it."

"I won't worry about you. I refuse to waste time worrying."

"The only thing you need to be concerned with is me surviving this summit meeting."

Kate laughed. "No one understands defence strategies and weaponry better than you, Lieutenant Commander. Sofia said some things..."

"Sofia is finding it difficult to relate to Ang. She's a strong woman. Ang is shy, in her head, insecure."

"Do you love Angelene?"

Love was a funny word. He loved the way Angelene painted: furious strokes, focused and guided by the subject. He loved how she could quote Hugo or Dickens. He loved her pert breasts and the curve of her back, how soft and pale her skin was, but her? He wasn't sure if all the parts he admired came together yet to form one big explosion of love.

"I admire things about her."

"Walter..."

"No lecture, poppet, and no worrying. I'll figure it out. I always do. I'm..."

"Walter Pratt, the man who conquered the world. Please don't make me worry about you."

"I assure you everything is fine." Walter glanced at the alarm clock. "I have a meeting in twenty minutes. I have to change into my suit and study my notes. Can I call you later? I miss talking to you."

"Call your wife. I'll have you and Angelene over for dinner soon."

Walter listened to the click of the phone. Rain pelted the window, blurring Paris from his view. He wanted to tell Kate everything, that he was scared, hesitant, afraid to fail. Maybe if he had talked to Kate before putting a ring on Angelene's finger, things would be different. Maybe he should have told Kate he was afraid of her strength, her independence, afraid of losing someone he loved. Walter looked at his wedding band and buried the feelings deep inside. Here he was, instead of there.

Angelene

Angelene's eyes drifted to the window. The sun hung low between the trees and cast a pale stream of grey gold across the gleaming parquet floor. She didn't know how long she had been at the manor or standing beside the credenza. The only things she had noticed were a wall of books, the extravagant display of food and Victoria McGregor's ritual: pick up a sandwich, sniff and place it on her plate- pluck, sniff, stack.

"Angelene, you haven't eaten a thing."

She tore her gaze from the window, a twitchy grin on her lips. "I ate before I came. I keep forgetting afternoon tea means there's food."

"I thought holding the party in the library would make you comfortable. You love books like a mother would a child."

"You've been very considerate. I've been friends with more books than people."

Sofia glanced at Victoria sniffing a beef and horseradish sandwich and Simone studying her reflection in a silver candlestick. "I imagine they could be."

"These sandwiches look like roses."

"That's herbed mascarpone with smoked salmon. There's Branston pickle and cheese, egg, watercress and, just for you, jambon-beurre. Walter said you liked ham and butter."

Simone stabbed an olive with a toothpick and jabbed the air. "You should get into event planning. It'll give you something to do when Brendon leaves."

Angelene took a plate off the stack, examined each tier, deciding on ham and butter, a triangle of egg, and Branston pickle. She grinned politely at Sofia and walked in light, precise steps to the sofa.

'How to sit like a lady. You read it this morning. Knees together, ease down gently, smooth my skirt, angle my feet. How do I do that and balance my plate? These ridiculous rules.'

Angelene flumped onto the cushion and cursed quietly.

"How's Brendon?" Simone placed the toothpick on her plate, pawing at her hair.

Sofia forced a smile. "He's fine."

"Eshana and I went to the last match. He was brilliant, so dishy in his black kit." Simone ran her fingers over her décolletage. Her voice took on a sultry tone. "Why hasn't he asked Eshana out?"

Sofia sipped her tea and narrowed her eyes. "You or Eshana."

Angelene couldn't wait to go home and put the afternoon in her sketchbook. Sofia's annoyed face, Victoria's sniffing, the look of lust in Simone's eyes. She would title it, 'The Untea Party.'

"Didn't you notice our William? He's just as handsome in his kit."

"He sits on the bench, Vic. What's to see?" Simone said.

Brown goo seeped from the corner of the sandwich. Angelene glanced around the room. Sofia and Simone had locked eyes; Victoria was studying the desserts. She stuck her finger in the pickle and licked it. It was sweet and sour.

"Eshana would be better suited than Margaret Thornton. Similar backgrounds, similar lifestyles."

"You'd be able to gawk at him all the time." Victoria shoved her nose in a Bakewell tart and sniffed. "Thank goodness Brendon is attractive. My William is smart. Smart gets you somewhere like Oxford. That's where he'll be next September."

Something stirred within Angelene. Brendon had been there for her. Now it was her turn. Little flutters moved in her belly. Her mouth was dry.

"Brendon sees things uniquely."

Victoria's crumb-filled mouth dropped open. Simone chuckled, "Oh dear."

Angelene met Sofia's cool gaze. Mere de tous les diables had found her voice.

"Thank you, Angelene. I don't pay attention to Victoria's opinion about Brendon. It's always a competition." Sofia jerked her silk cuffs and pressed her shoulders back. "You barged in, attached a price tag to the new chairs I bought David, inventoried the china, the fabrics, even the damn food."

"Well," Victoria poo pooed. "It doesn't take brains to kick a football around."

"C'est des conneries. It takes concentration, foresight."

She needed a cigarette, a glass of wine, something to keep up the confident charade. Sofia's questioning gaze was chasing the mother of all devils away.

"You seem to know a lot about football," Simone said.

Victoria lifted herself off the sofa, marched to the credenza, and helped herself to tea. "I could have sworn I saw you at Taunton Park. I finished handing out flyers for the gala. I'm still annoyed you asked me to do that, Sofia."

"Do you fancy Brendon too?" Simone said.

Angelene cleared her throat and picked at the black paint embedded under her fingernail. "I fancy, as you call it, my husband."

"You must have a doppelgänger," Victoria said. The seams on her paisley dress stretched as she dropped onto the chair. "You weren't in net?"

Angelene twisted her bracelets around her wrist. Veronique had been a firm believer in St. Augustine's view: lying was morally wrong. Over the years, Angelene realized some lies were necessary and morally just, like the Christians who hid Jews from the Nazis. There was nothing malicious in this lie. It was to protect Brendon.

"Was it Posy Partridge, the keeper from the girl's team? She's always hanging around the pitch asking for advice," Simone said.

Sofia plucked at the bow on her blouse. "You're still upset they chose me to plan the gala, aren't you?"

"No offence, Vic, but Sofia has a knack for putting on a bash," Simone said.

Victoria bit into a tart. "You weren't in town?"

"I was, but not at the pitch. I went to St. George Church and a bookstore." Angelene set down her plate and kept her eyes on Victoria. "Excuse me."

She wobbled to her feet and rambled out of the library. Sofia's sigh followed her. Little earthquakes erupted inside her. Angelene climbed the stairs, glanced over her shoulder, and tiptoed down the hall. She snuck into the eucalyptus and citrus-scented room and floated to the dresser. Nestled within the pages of a football magazine was some photos. She pulled them out and flipped through pictures of Charlotte and Maggie, Troy with his sunshine smile. She stopped at a picture of Brendon and ran her finger over his tousled hair and grin. Opening her clutch, she slid the photo in the pocket and tucked the rest back into the magazine. Angelene turned from the dresser and spied a Borussia Dortmund shirt hanging from the side of the laundry basket.

'Please forgive me.'

Angelene folded the jersey into a square and placed it deep within the giant rectangular purse. Walter had brought it home from London, raving it was the latest fashion. She had found it cumbersome and awkward. It was perfect now. She took one more glance around Brendon's bedroom and met the black bead eyes of a bear.

"You must be Monsieur Paddington. It's nice to meet you."

She squeezed her purse under her arm and hurried down the hall. Guilt sawed relentlessly at her gut. Lies, stealing.

'I'll punish myself: thirty-nine lashes.'

"You weren't hiding in the bathroom again, were you?" Sofia said.

Angelene gripped the banister, her cheeks burning.

"I walked right past it to that green and white room. The view of the forest is beautiful."

"I can't say I like it," Sofia said, straightening the bow on her blouse. "Ignore Victoria."

Sweat gathered in Angelene's armpits. She held her purse tighter.

"I have no reason to be with Brendon."

"Come have dessert."

Angelene summoned confidence, it ignored her. She dissolved onto the sofa.

Sofia ladled trifle into a bowl and passed it to Angelene. "I thought you might have joined Walter in Paris?"

"Not this time."

"Aren't you homesick?" Victoria said.

"Not really."

"You don't want to shop? Hermes, Vuitton," Simone said.

Angelene shifted among the cushions and picked through the berries and custard. Home, she still didn't know where she belonged or what it meant.

"Going back will open old wounds."

Victoria sucked the jam off her finger and wiped it on a napkin. "You've set Walter free in the City of Love?"

"He's working."

Sofia dunked a sugar cube in her tea and raised an eyebrow. "Walter is not a womanizer."

Angelene glanced up from her bowl, there was something unnerving about the way Victoria was staring at her. It could be guilt, paranoia. She was sure Victoria was taking inventory of her.

"I'm going to Brussels. David has a lovely weekend planned for us."

"David needs to give my hubs Taj a few pointers," Simone said.

"That Partridge girl is tall, built like an athlete. You never see her out of her Taunton Blues kit," Victoria said. She stuffed a cookie into her mouth and hooked her purse over her arm. "You ready, Simone?"

"I was hoping to say hello to Brendon."

Sofia set down her teacup and stood. "Thank you both for coming. I'll see you out."

Angelene flopped against the sofa. Her breath rushed from her lungs to her lips. She would have to stop the private meetings. It was part of a pattern: secret trysts, hiding, lying. She slid the clunky purse beneath her arm and walked to the foyer.

"I should head home, too."

It was hard to tell whether Sofia believed Victoria.

"Don't let Victoria scare you off."

"My head is full."

"I understand. I'm in need of a long soak," Sofia said. She opened the door and peered at the grey sky. "Shall I drive you? It looks like rain."

'It would be appropriate for God to cry.'

"I'll walk. It will help clear my head." She clamped her purse under her arm and shivered. "Something cold went through me."

"It's the ghosts," Sofia said. "David's mother sits at the piano. Richard roams from room to room. I still can't get rid of him."

"Are there any others?"

Sofia glanced at a photo of Brendon. Her voice was tearful. "One." She cleared her throat and forced a polite grin. "It's starting to rain. Are you sure I can't drive you?"

"If I don't see you, have a wonderful time with David."

The wind nipped at Angelene's legs and pushed her along the lane. She removed her shoes and held them in her hand. Rain seeped through the canopy of branches and soaked her clothes.

'You're disappointed in me.'

Mud oozed between her toes.

'Who will I have when Brendon leaves?'

Headlights shone through the blinding rain. She recognized the glistening black paint.

'You're always here when I need.'

The car made a U-turn and idled beside her.

"What the bloody hell are you doing? Get in."

Angelene rushed around the car and slid onto the leather seat. She wiped her arm across her face and twisted her drenched hair into a braid. "Walking home."

"Put this over you." Brendon reached into the rear seat, grabbed his blazer, and draped it over her lap.

"I survived the Untea party. I had a cheese and pickle sandwich."

"Did Mom call it that?" He parked under the willow tree and cut the engine. "Sometimes she themes her tea parties."

"Tweedle dee and tweedle dum were there."

"I'm going to grab my backpack. I want to change out of my uniform."

Angelene ran up the walkway and unlocked the door. She dropped her shoes and tossed his blazer onto the bricks in the front room. Angelene tore away her muddied stockings and scrambled up the stairs. She hurried down the hall, peeled away her blouse, shed her skirt, and kicked it into the bedroom. She laid her purse on the bed and wiggled into a pair of lounge pants and a sweatshirt. It had been a trying afternoon. A cup of tea might help the lingering jitters. Wine would be better.

Angelene stood at the top of the stairs. She could see Brendon's shadow on the wall. The strange flutter attacked her belly. She pushed it away and touched the spot on her neck where her cross used to lie.

"Are you decent?"

"I'm putting my jeans on."

"I'll bring you tea. May I have a glass of wine?"

"No, you may not. The house is a bloody mess."

"I was in a hurry."

Angelene rambled down the stairs and stopped at the kitchen island. An apple core had browned beside a wedge of brie, dishes sat in the sink, stale cigarette smoke hung in the air. She flapped her hands and sighed softly. Moving to the stove, she set the kettle on the burner, then reached for the canister of tea bags and turned to face Brendon. The little quiver lit up her insides—guilt for stealing, shame for lying to Sofia, something else. She didn't know.

"I'd rather have wine."

"You spent the afternoon with Mrs. McGregor. You'll drink the entire bottle."

"She's a horrible woman."

"I made a fire," Brendon said. He opened the fridge, grabbed milk, and poured it in his mug. "Did you smoke an entire pack? The house stinks."

"Walter made me spiky red."

"What is it this time?"

They walked to the front room, the scent of cedar masked the cigarette smoke and incense. Angelene stretched along the sofa and tucked her feet under his thighs.

"I didn't want to go for tea. He said I must. I said I was wearing a navy dress. He said to wear a black skirt. I said I would wear a white blouse. He said wear black."

"You should have told him to fuck off."

The conversation with Walter littered her brain, guilt strangled her, and a new feeling appeared. It was murky green.

"Victoria told Sofia she saw me at the pitch." Angelene blinked at the red spots flashing in her eyes. "Simone said it was Posy Partridge. Who's she?"

"The keeper for the Taunton Blues," Brendon said. He pulled her feet from beneath his legs and laid them across his lap. "What did Mom say?"

"She dismissed Victoria," Angelene said. "I practiced what to say, read a book on etiquette, I got to your house, and nothing came out. I couldn't speak until Victoria said you weren't smart."

Brendon grinned and sipped his tea. "Gobby cow. What did you say?"

"I defended you, like you do me."

"What did Mom think of that?"

"I couldn't tell. She wanted to have a nice party."

Angelene dug under a mess of illustrations, found a half-smoked butt, and placed it in her mouth. "Simone wanted to say hello to you. She wants you to date her daughter."

Spots flashed and flickered within her gaze.

"Eshana jumps from one footy player to the next. She's dated a striker from Chelsea, a midfielder from Liverpool, and a defender from Tottenham. She's working her way through the Premier League."

"It'll be the Bundesliga next, a goalkeeper."

"She isn't my type. She's more bloody fake than Mrs. Batra."

The spots spread, painting the room red. Her insides were on fire. God was angry with her. She stole. She lied. Normal had been suffocating.

"I scrub Walter's floors, do his laundry, hang his clothes in straight fucking lines and blocks of colour." The teacup flew across the room and shattered against the wall. "I never should have married him. I should have taken him as a lover and been his slut in Paris." She grabbed a mug from the coffee table and hurled it at the fireplace, bits of blue porcelain sprinkled over the bricks.

"Are you done? Would you like to take a swing at me?"

"You should have seen the smug look on Victoria's face. She was happy you might have done something wrong."

"She thinks Will and I should share time in net."

Angelene flicked ash from her shirt and dropped the cigarette into a glass of water. "I want to tear everything up, including myself."

"We really would have a mess, wouldn't we?" Brendon said. He wound his arm around her. She shot him a warning look. "I'm not going to kiss you. The house is messy enough without you throwing more bloody stuff around."

Angelene snuggled into his chest and clutched his hoodie. "I thought if I put on the right clothes, it would be okay. I don't belong here. I should have stayed in Paris."

"I wouldn't be able to give you this." He handed her an ink illustration of a cornflower, the words 'ihre Kornblum' above the bouquet. "I drew it in Latin and asked Rachel the German way to spell it."

"That's so sweet." Angelene placed the drawing against her breast and yawned. "I'm tired." She gave him a little squeeze and curled into the corner of the sofa.

Brendon glanced at the mess: broken glass, overflowing ashtray, piles of burnt incense. "I think I met another one of your devils."

"They were all raging inside me today."

Brendon plucked a blanket stuffed between the cushions and laid it over her. "I'll stay until you fall asleep."

"Roman used to sit with me until I drifted off. I had terrible nightmares as a child. One night, I dreamt a man snuck into my bedroom and stole my most precious thing. Roman held me and hummed Edelweiss."

"I'll stay, but I'm not singing."

"Je t'aime parce que tout l'univers a conspiré à me faire arriver jusqu'à toi."

"I really need to pay attention in French."

"It's a quote from *The Alchemist* by Paulo Coelho. 'I love you because the whole universe conspired to make me get to you.' The universe had a plan to bring Walter to Parc Floral and me to Taunton."

"Walter is a persistent guy. He wouldn't have left Paris without you."

"I think there's a bigger plan."

Sleep swept her down a rabbit hole.

Down, down she fell, tumbling into a field of cornflowers. She jumped to her feet and brushed off her knees, greeted by a rabbit, limestone Victor Hugo and a boy with incredible light.

Where am I? This is a curious place.

She wandered through the cornflowers and stopped at the edge of a forest.

Will you come with me?

Mammina doesn't let me play in the woods.

I need your light.

The path snaked through gnarled limbs and tangled roots. She stumbled into the clearing alone. Tweedle dee, in her too-tight dress, sat across from Tweedle dum, who sipped tea from a gargantuan cup. The rabbit rested in the middle of the table, munching on cookies shaped like carrots. At the other end, the queen wore a robe of black and a crown of thorns. Dark, sullen music seeped from the burls.

Who invited her?

She doesn't belong here.

I'll have tea and leave. I must follow his light.

Would you say hello for me? He's a pretty thing. I could devour him.

Please don't, you'll steal his light.

What do you say, queen? You're the guardian of his light.

Off with her head!

Angelene jerked, clutched her neck, and gazed around the room. She was safe at home, but things were different. The floor was clean. Pencils were in the jar. Illustrations tucked into her sketchbook. The drawing of the cornflower leaned against a candleholder. Angelene stood, held out her arms, and steadied herself. She walked to the kitchen. The sink gleamed. The scraps of food had disappeared.

She carried herself up the stairs. The macabre music from her dream played in her ears. Lumbering to the bedroom, she walked into the bathroom, and lit candles lining the window ledge. She put the plug in the drain, turned on the taps, and tipped in patchouli-scented bubble bath. The hot water scorched her skin. Her mother swore a soak was as good as a baptism. It was a chance to wash oneself clean. She could hear her mother's voice, *'scrub, Angelene, scrub.'* She closed her eyes. The memory burned bright.

I missed you, Roman. You were gone a long time.

I was in London. I brought you a copy of Through the Looking Glass. Alice reminds me of you.

Because of my blonde hair?

Something you said before I left. 'When I woke, I was Angelene Hummel but as the day went on, I lost myself a few times.' The same thing happened to Alice.

Angelene plunged under the water, twisted her hair around her hands, and pulled. A scream forced its way out. Electricity surged through her veins. *Stay, run, hide, fight.* She burst through the bubbles and panted.

"Changing, always changing. From Mademoiselle Hummel to the lady of healthy things to Mrs. Secretary of Defence. All in a matter of a day."

Angelene dragged herself from the tub and scrubbed her body dry. She walked to the bed and nestled under the blankets. Her eyelids grew heavy. She blinked, trying to banish sleep. She didn't want to go back to the queen and her thorny crown. The strange dream world was just as odd as the real world. She didn't fit. Happy thoughts and cheerful things, sunshine and songbirds. She needed spring.

Your eyes are the deepest blue, like spilled ink.

I thought you were sleeping.

I had a nightmare.

I'll tell you a story, snuggle next to me. Once upon a time, there was a girl named Petite Oiseau. She lived in a nest of yellow ribbons high in an oak tree. One day, a boy looked up and saw the girl. She was the prettiest girl he had ever laid eyes on. He called to her to come down and walk through the fields of lavender with him. Her voice sang out, 'I have no wings to fly.' Each day, the boy wandered through the streets collecting feathers, and each day before he went home, he visited the nest and placed a feather in the nub until she had the most beautiful wings any bird had ever seen. They soared together through the sky. You will fly, Angelene.

19 'Sheeps'and love bites

B rendon

The decision to hold the world's greatest party stood.

Brendon wrapped his hand around a list tucked in his pocket. The plan was fail proof.

"I'll miss you," Sofia said.

"You're going to walk around Bruges and Ghent, eat chocolate, waffles. You won't have a minute to miss me."

"Remember what I said."

"No friends over."

"Amelia will pop in Sunday morning to check on you."

"She doesn't need to do that. I'm not doing anything but watching the Dortmund match."

The part lie slipped from between his pristine white teeth. It was his plan on Saturday.

"You can stop worrying. All I'm doing tonight is watching my last match. I recorded it on my phone."

"That's it? Football?"

"You'll miss your flight if you don't get on the road."

It was getting harder to look into her eyes. Sofia's gaze had turned from suspicious to a worried, 'I-may-never-see-you-again.' It kicked him square in the stomach. He grabbed her train case and followed her to the Maserati.

"Don't you think you over-packed?"

"I picked out all your father's favourites."

Brendon raced back to the foyer and wheeled out the remaining suitcases. Sofia held his cheeks in her hands and gave him her best 'do-as-you're-told' look.

"Stay away from Angelene."

"Shouldn't I check in, make sure she's okay?"

"Watch your football. Ti amo, sweetheart."

He embraced her and completed the performance with the most incredible hug. He had done it, survived her 'I-hate-good-byes-I-love-you-too-much-to-leave' look. Padre Diavolo flipped the excitement switch. It was time to get to work.

Brendon raced into the house and up the stairs to change. He had a hundred things to do: empty the great room, lock the liquor cabinet, roll up the handwoven rugs, lock the door to the laundry room so no one discovered the wine cellar, lock the pool, set out tin cans in the garden for cigarette butts. Guilt invaded the 'yes, Mammina, I promise, Mammina, I would never do that, Dad' space in his brain; Padre Diavolo could wrestle with that.

Brendon quickly changed and raced down the stairs. He grabbed his great-grandmother's Cantagalli plate and a Limoges vase. The Marti et Cie clock had to go, and the apple-shaped tea caddy his mother said was a rare find. He carried them into the den and placed them on the desk. The doorbell snapped him out of his daze. He opened the door. Vivid gold spread across the moors.

"I wanted to thank you for cleaning my mess. I'm good at making all sorts of messes."

Brendon glanced at his feet and shrugged. "You were tired and upset. I didn't think you would want to deal with that when you woke up."

"It was sweet and, as usual, other people manage my chaos." Angelene gazed around the foyer. "Did I interrupt you?"

"I was putting Mom's antiques away."

"Is she redecorating?"

"I'm having a party."

A look of disapproval passed over her face. "You mustn't."

"I've told all my friends."

She reached for his wrists and gripped them. "Don't answer the door. Sofia's beautiful things."

"I've been smart this time. I made a list of everything I need to put away. I'll make sure everyone stays in the great room. You can help me."

"If Sofia knows I was a co-conspirator, she'll never forgive me."

Brendon laughed. "Do you remember sneaking out and getting pissed? I'll grab the keys."

He ducked into the den, opened the desk drawer, and fumbled around scrapbooks for the key ring.

"I suppose Père diable has been whispering to you."

"The prick's been pestering me all week." Brendon rattled the keys and grinned. "The skeleton key is for the laundry room; the pool key has a P on it. Once you've done that, meet me in the great room."

"I won't be blamed if you get caught."

"You were never here."

Brendon sauntered into the great room and took an inventory of all the furniture and antiques. There wasn't one thing in the room that didn't mean something to his mother. Pushing back the coffee table, Brendon rolled up the rug and shoved it towards the doorway. He walked to the mantel and swept his arm across it. The photos fell like oversized dominoes.

"I locked both doors."

"Can you lock the liquor cabinet? Dad has an expensive bottle of scotch in there. It's the little key."

He laid the bundle of frames on the sofa and his heart clunked. Brendon chased the feeling away. She was his friend, nothing more.

"What about the Klimt painting?"

"I better take it down."

"I'll carry it. Be careful not to touch the canvas. The oil and perspiration from your fingers will leave residue and ruin it."

They strolled to the corner of the room, stood side by side, and stared at the painting. Brendon reached above the credenza and carefully grabbed the frame. "I don't know why Dad doesn't like this painting. The blonde looks randy."

"Stop staring at the girl."

"Are you sure you can carry it? It's as big as you?"

"Give it here," Angelene said. "Is there a key to the den? No one should go in there."

"There's a key for every room in the house."

He gathered an armful of collectibles and followed, impressed at how gentle she was with the painting.

"Sofia has a Cipriani sculpture?"

"It belonged to her great-grandmother."

Angelene carefully leaned the painting against the wall. "It's beautiful."

"I'm going to grab my pictures."

"You didn't keep them on the mantel?"

"Have my friends take the piss."

They walked back to the great room. Brendon scanned for more treasures. "I'll grab the clock. It's one of the few German things Mammina loves. Can you get the lamp?"

Angelene unplugged it and wound the cord around her hand. "What does she have against Germany?"

"It stole me."

"The chairs by the fireplace were a present for David. They're upholstered in fabric from the Mastrioni family mill."

"I'll move them to the wall, drape a sheet over them and pray no one uses them as a trampoline."

"I'll pray, too."

Brendon teetered the chair on its legs and hobbled it across the floor. He sat on the armrest and felt his pulse grow. Angelene picked up an item and examined it. She took a moment with each, lightly touching the curve of a bowl or studying the details before she moved to the next.

"One last thing to do." Brendon pulled a remote from his pocket and pointed it at the armoire. "You can't have a party without music." A vibrant tempo travelled around the room. "Still got the keys?"

Angelene raised her wrist and jingled it. He slid the remote into the armoire and closed the doors. He had done it, followed through on a promise, and protected the illustrious Rosewood Manor.

"Have you eaten?"

"I was working on a painting and lost track of time."

Brendon touched her elbow and guided her into the kitchen. Beer, alcopops, and crisps littered the counter. He reminded himself to put the alcohol in the garden and crisps on the coffee table. If Amelia's alphabetized pantry was out of order, he'd never hear the end of it.

"How many cigarettes have you had?"

Angelene dropped onto a stool and held up two fingers.

A note card addressed to her 'little man' leaned against the pepper mill, a smiley face ended the instructions. He slipped his hand into a strawberry print oven mitt, warm air scented with lemon and dill permeated the air.

"Would you like butter for the veg? I use olive oil spread. Amelia says she could polish the floors with it."

"You don't need to feed me. I can go home and make something."

"Do you want milk or water?"

"Water, please, you eat."

"You'll start painting and forget, or smoke instead."

He turned on the tap and filled a glass. Brendon grabbed the jug of milk and plunked it on the island. He set out a plate and arranged half the fish, rice, and broccoli.

"I planned to make harira, it's a Moroccan soup. Roman loved it, he'd make it for mother and me."

"Just planned?"

"For three days now. I had Malcolm take me to Tesco for the ingredients."

Brendon piled fish and rice on his fork and frowned. "Don't tell me you haven't eaten for three days?"

"I've had some yogurt, some brie, an apple or two. Not a meal but, I've eaten."

"Bloody hell, eat up then and take a bag of crisps with you."

"Are you talking about sheeps?"

"A sheep like baa? Crisps, they're crunchy, made from potatoes."

Angelene smiled. "In France, we don't snack on them. We eat them with a meal."

"Mom would die. I put them on a sandwich once, and she nearly had a heart attack. Take the salt and malt. They're my favourite."

They ate in silence. She took tiny bites, savouring each mouthful before the next. The moment sank deep into Brendon's bones. She looked beautiful, fragile like crystal. Drop her, she'd break.

"What colour are you right now?"

Angelene stared up at the ceiling. A few seconds passed before she spoke. "Pink, green, red, murky, muddied. Éperdument amoureux, madly in love."

"With me?"

Angelene glanced at him. Her grin was slight. "The idea of love."

Brendon touched her fingers. A little spark drew him to her, like they had been friends in an earlier existence, kindred spirits, like he had been madly in love with her before. Angelene pulled her hand away and flicked her fingers as if ridding herself of the connection.

"What can I help with now?"

Brendon took their plates, rinsed them, and set them in the sink. "You can help with the beer and sheeps." He stacked a pack of Fosters on top of a box of Becks and nodded towards the snacks. "Throw some on top. Don't forget the salt and malt."

"I'll eat them with my soup."

Angelene tossed bags onto the boxes and filled her arms with the rest. They walked to the great room and she dropped the armful of snacks. The music changed to a slower beat. An instrumental version of a movie theme song Brendon couldn't put his finger on. All he could remember was being stuck in the cinema, listening to Maggie cry for three hours.

"Dance with me."

Angelene shrunk away and twisted the cuffs of her sweater. "Non, I haven't danced with Walter. It isn't right."

"I won't kiss you. I promise."

"God won't be happy."

"If we were at a party, Dad would expect me to. I'll be a perfect gentleman." He held out his hand. "I won't step on your toes. I was Mom's date for the gala three years ago. She taught me the proper way to dance."

They swayed in silence. Her palm was moist in his. Brendon clung to the moment, knowing it would be just that—a moment. He wished he could stretch it out, make it last. It was three and a half minutes of utter bliss.

The CD shuffled. A poppy beat boomed from the hidden speakers.

"Was that so bad?"

"I'll ask God to forgive me."

"God doesn't have to forgive anything. I've danced with Charlie, Kate, even Mrs. Batra. She giggled worse than Maggie. Just enjoy it for what it was, a dance with a friend."

"I should go."

"I didn't mean to make you uncomfortable."

He followed her to the foyer. She cradled the bag of crisps in her arms.

"I enjoyed listening to your heartbeat. It was prettier than that song." Angelene opened the door and wagged her finger. "Don't listen to Padre Diavolo. He'll convince you to do all sorts of dreadful things."

"Like sneak off in the night and get pissed. Tu me manques."

"Faire de beaux rêves, mon ami."

Brendon closed the door; the 'in love' feeling swarmed him. He wanted to hold her, chill on the sofa, watch football and eat 'sheeps.' Padre Diavolo had to flip on the excitement switch fast. The idea of a party with friends, friends of friends, and strangers had lost its appeal.

The door burst open. Troy smiled and clapped Brendon on the back. "This is going to be brilliant."

"There are more beer and cider in the kitchen. It needs to go on the loggia."

"I saw Mrs. Pratt."

"Did you say hi to her?"

"She was halfway down the hill. I didn't want to make eye contact."

They sauntered to the kitchen. Brendon leaned against the kitchen island and stared at his feet.

"What are you going on about?"

Troy tore open a box, grabbed a lager, and chugged it. "Her eyes are magical. Green, grey, sparkly, stormy." He scrunched the can and tossed it in the sink. "I had a dream I was humping her."

Dreams of making love to Angelene had haunted Brendon since the day he adjusted her strap and touched her skin. He wouldn't call it magical powers, just attraction.

"Charlie and I were doing it when it happened."

"I was snogging Maggie and imagined it was Angelene. Does that make you feel better?"

Troy snatched a bag of crisps and slammed his hands against it. A spray flew into the air and scattered across the floor. "Not really. A snog is one thing, but shagging, that's bleeding bad."

Brendon placed the opened beer case on another and lifted the stack. "Promise to hump in one room. You did it in three last time. Amelia was pissed off she had to wash all those sheets."

Troy grappled with three cases of cider; his face brightened. "I love waking up with Charlie. Morning humps are brilliant. You're both sleepy, like a beautiful dream."

"What about morning breath?"

"You really know how to ruin things," Troy said. He walked into the great room and out to the loggia. "Spoon, wanker."

"Humping in the morning is ace. I'll remember that."

Troy's eyes lit up at the wall of alcohol. "Where did all this come from?"

"I picked some up after school. Todd Watson bought the rest."

They set down the cases and walked back inside.

"That swot?"

"He was bloody desperate for an invitation. I met him at Tesco. He filled the boot of my car."

"I guess when your best friend is a Bunsen burner, you'll do anything." Troy gazed around the room. "You cleared everything by yourself?"

"I had a plan and stuck to it."

The doorbell chimed. Relief washed over Brendon. The longer he had to talk about his plan, the harder it would be to keep his accomplice a secret.

"That'll be Charlie."

"How do you know it isn't guys from the team?"

"She doesn't like to be late."

Brendon opened the door and stumbled over his feet. Charlotte bounced into the foyer and into Troy's arms.

"I brought those frilly knickers you like."

Brendon's eyebrows raised. "You brought frilly knickers?"

Maggie swung her overnight bag at him then poked her finger in his stomach.

"Which room do babes and I get?"

"The one at the end of the hall, past Mom and Dad's."

"That's the blue and white room. I've always wanted to sleep in that bed, posh pillars and a canopy. It's fit for a queen."

"It's perfect for you, luv."

"Don't be jumping all over it. It's from the tutor period."

"Cheers, mate." Troy took Charlotte's hand, and they walked away.

"It's pronounced Tudor, with a d, wanker. We *are* studying Henry VIII," Maggie said. She shuffled from foot to foot, clamped her teeth into her bottom lip, and chewed. After a few nibbles, she spoke. "I still can't believe you're doing this."

"Please don't ruin my night by being mom-like."

"I'm putting my stuff in your room."

"You're staying over?"

Headlights pulled Brendon's gaze from Maggie.

"The queen slag and her troupe of tarts are coming. There's no way I'm leaving you alone with her."

Brendon didn't know what to say. For the first time in his life, he was happy to see William.

"Looks like the party can start now. I've arrived." William smiled a smug smile. "This is going to be ace."

"The beer is on the loggia. Go to the great room."

"Is that what you toffs call a sitting room?"

"Just go, bloody wanker."

"Did I interrupt something? You seem a little tense," William said.

Maggie nibbled her thumbnail. Her eyes flickered to Brendon. "I'm spending the night. Tell your tarts to stay away from him."

"Maybe tonight will be the night." William laughed, shaped his hand into a circle and poked his finger into it.

"Please go. You're giving me a bloody headache."

William snickered and slapped Brendon's chest. "Rachel's always up for it."

Maggie hiccupped, swayed, and stuck her tongue out at William. "Gosh, I hate that dolt."

"Have you been drinking already?"

"Charlie and I split a bottle of champagne. I lied to my mom and said I was staying at Charlie's house. I feel awful about lying, so don't be a wanker and make me feel worse."

A group of First players barged through the door, followed by some girls Brendon recognized from Latin. A succession of Taunton College students and the Taunton Blues, led by Posy Partridge, greeted him with enthusiastic hellos. Brendon took Maggie's bag and set it at the bottom of the stairs. He trailed the mob and scanned the room. No one was jumping on the sofas. The smokers were in the garden. Small groups had congregated in corners. Maggie's friends from drama stood in a cluster by the fireplace, full of animation and gestures.

"Get this into you, mate. You've got that gloomy look on your face all the girls find dishy."

Brendon cracked open the beer. "One, Mags. You're worse than me when it comes to alcohol."

Maggie twisted off the top of a beer and squished under his arm. She slung her arm around his waist to say, 'he's mine.' "People like that slag think I'm boring. I'm going to prove them all wrong."

Rachel waved and called over the music. "Du bist die Liebe meines Lebens."

"Cheeky cow!" Maggie slurped her drink and scrunched her nose. "I think she just said you are the love of her life."

"I wouldn't know. She can't tutor me anymore. Tutor with a T."

"Who's being cheeky now?" Maggie said. She guzzled the beer, set the bottle on the floor, and reached into her sweater pocket for a cider. "Why is she coming over here?"

"Don't you be looking at the queen slag, babes. I'm not in the mood to give you a pinch tonight," Charlotte said.

Troy stared at the coffered ceiling. It was hard not to notice Rachel. Her jeans looked as if she had poured them on. An oversized V-neck hung off one shoulder, exposing a galaxy of freckles. Her hair was wild and untamed. Femme fatale was on the pull.

"Your home is brilliant. Will said you have an indoor pool and a ballroom. Who has a ballroom?"

"The house is old."

His teammates snickered at his red cheeks. Maggie scowled into her drink. Padre Diavolo wanted to introduce himself to Rachel.

"Can you give me a tour?"

"Go back to your friends," Maggie said. She laced her fingers through Brendon's and made a point of flashing her ring. "Go on, your perfume is making me nauseas."

Rachel twirled a strand of hair around her finger. "I'm going for a ciggie. You want to come, knuddelbär? We can talk about the lineup for tomorrow's Dortmund match."

"He isn't going anywhere with you."

"Relax, Thornton, I'm not chatting up your man. Auf wiedersehen, knuddelbär."

"Why do you have to be like that?"

"She's a slapper, trying to tell me she wasn't chatting you up. Rubbish!"

Maggie gulped the cider and pulled another from her pocket. She belched, teetered, and nodded towards the loggia. "It looks like she's giving the cigarette a BJ."

"What do you know about giving a BJ?"

Troy tried to keep his face neutral. "The party is banging."

Brendon forced a grin and kept watch on the crowd. So far, so good.

"Let's get you some crisps. You need to soak up that alcohol," Charlotte said.

"That's a bloody smashing idea."

"I'm not leaving your side. You'll be staring at the tart's fat arse. Troy another." Maggie burped and snapped her fingers. "An alcopop this time."

"Let's go, Magpie." Charlotte kissed Troy's cheek and tugged Maggie away from Brendon. "Babes, give Brendon a pinch if he stares at the tart."

Brendon balled his hands, sparks fluttered. The party had grown. Conversations merged. Laughter spilled over the music. Everyone was enjoying themselves, everyone but him.

"I need some air."

"You got the sparks, mate?"

"I need to take a few breaths before I say something I'll regret."

"Don't be too long. You need to take care of your girl."

Brendon nudged through the crowd and walked onto the loggia. A tepid, earth and pine scented wind rushed by. Overhead, the sky was inky blue, sprinkled with stars. Padre Diavolo had flicked off the excitement switch.

'*I'm as blue as the sky.*'

He smiled to himself and swept an empty can off the concrete bench. Angelene was rubbing off on him.

"Hiya, knuddelbär." Rachel sat beside him. Her knee rested against his.

"You have thirteen freckles on your shoulder." Brendon traced from freckle to freckle. They came together to create a star.

"Does Thornton practice giving the evils in the mirror?"

"It's the alcohol. Maggie doesn't get mad, she cries."

"You look fit tonight, knuddelbär, a little sad, still dishy."

"You've had too many fizzy pops."

"I've had one, and it's the truth." She traced her finger over his tattoo. "What's the matter?"

Brendon stared at the farmhouse and shrugged. "I thought I was up for a party. I guess I'm not."

"Babysitting Margaret mustn't be fun."

"All it takes is two, and she's pissed. I think she's up to four now. That doesn't include the champagne she drank with Charlie."

"I'll stay after everyone leaves and help you clean up."

"Maggie's staying over. She'll throw a fit if you hang around."

Rachel got to the end of his tattoo. She continued along his vein; tiny shivers travelled up his spine. It was Angelene's thing to do—follow the veins in his hands and arm. She said it carried his light.

Brendon glanced into the great room. Gemma Fowler wore the same irked expression as Maggie.

"Pull Tilly off Will. Gemma doesn't look impressed."

He laid her hand in her lap and tapped a German flag painted on her thumb.

"It's the other way around. Will's been chatting her up all night."

Brendon turned and grinned. Her eyes were wistful amber.

"Do you want to stay and help?"

"Anything for you, knuddelbär." She rose and touched his cheek. "You make me tingly. Ich liebe dich."

Brendon returned to the great room. Crisp bags sprouted from the sofa cushions. Battered tins cluttered the floor. He scooped up a handful and walked to the fireplace, where he had stashed a pile of garbage bags.

Brendon snapped one open, dropped the cans in and slumped onto the chair. Small crowds of people stood around the room. There were no holes in the walls or scratches in the parquet. Everything was okay, everything except Maggie. He stared up at the ceiling and stretched his arms, it was time to be a wonderful boyfriend.

"How many alcopops did you drink?"

Maggie clamped her hand over her mouth, her eyes widening. "I'm going to barf."

Brendon's gaze left the creature stirring in Maggie's belly to the loggia. Rachel was picking up cigarette butts. She had kept her word.

"You better get to the loo before you chunder all over Mom's floor."

"Why is the ginger tart still here?"

"Lots of people are."

Brendon wound an arm around her and guided her up the stairs. Her stomach pitched and heaved against his palm.

"Hurry, Mags."

"I'm trying, but my legs feel like they're filled with jelly."

"Don't honk on Mom's runner. It came from her Nonna's home in San Siro."

"Will you shut it. I'm focusing on walking."

Brendon pushed open his bedroom door and released his grip. She staggered to the bathroom. A rainbow of colours and undigested crisps spilled into the sink. Brendon jerked his collar over his nose and sank onto the toilet seat. The smell of fruity vodka and what he thought was roasted chicken crisps seeped through the fabric.

"Oh my gosh." Maggie bounced off the rim of the sink, stumbled over the threshold plate, and knocked her head on the edge of the door. "Why is your floor slanted?"

"It's you, not the bloody floor. Get into bed."

She tugged at her puke-splotched sweater and fell onto the mattress. "Can you help?"

"Unzip it."

He grasped the pull, found a vomit-free spot, and yanked her limp arms from the sleeves. "I finally get you out of your clothes and you're pissed."

"Your bed smells like barf."

Brendon switched on the lamp, walked to his laundry basket, and dug out a T-shirt. "Wear this."

"It's dirty."

"Sleep in your clothes then."

He tossed the T-shirt at her. She swayed back and forth, her eyelids blinking slowly.

"I can't find the armholes."

Brendon sighed, left his spot, and helped her with her shirt. Maggie tumbled over knocking her head against the headboard.

"My jeans."

Brendon stared at her zipper. Padre Diavolo came out of hiding and snickered. '*Look at your girl, pathetic, can't handle other birds, can't handle her liquor.*'

He undid her jeans and slid them over her hips. "Sit up so I can get my shirt over your head."

She flung herself up, hiccuped, and held up her arms. "Turn off your lamp and lie with me."

"You might need the loo again."

Maggie shoved the blankets aside and crawled under. "Lie beside me."

Brendon flopped onto the bed., the mattress bounced. She groaned and clutched her stomach. The scent of vomit and vanilla wafted from her skin.

"Do you want to... you know."

"You're bloody pissed."

"I'm up for it."

"Go to sleep."

She squished herself next to him, whispery moans warming his skin. He could hear the door open and close. Troy was doing an excellent job of saying goodnight to his guests.

Brendon shimmied off the bed, draped the blankets over her, and headed downstairs to the great room. His stomach did a funny little tumble. Rachel hadn't left.

"How's Maggie?" Troy said, smiling behind a sandwich piled high with an assortment of meat and cheese.

"She's passed out."

"Are you leaving?" Charlotte said. She stole a corner of cheese sticking out from the bread and placed it on her tongue. "We've tidied everything up."

"I want my tour," Rachel said.

"We're going to bed, right, mate?"

Charlotte raised her eyebrows and shot Brendon a glassy stare. "You should be with Magpie. She's never been this bladdered before."

"I promised Rachel I'd show her the pool and ballroom, then she's leaving. Right, you're leaving?"

"If you want me to, then I will, knuddelbär. I wouldn't want to get you in trouble with your friends."

Troy squished the last bite into his mouth and pointed an accusatory finger. "No dancing in the ballroom." He took Charlotte's hand and helped her up. "And no swimming."

Brendon held up his hands and gave his best, 'I promise' grin.

"I was talking to Rachel."

"Behave." Charlotte leaned into Brendon and planted a kiss on his cheek. "Especially you, Miss Jones. Don't try to work your tart charm on my friend. He's taken."

Guilt sizzled his lungs and burned his stomach. Rachel was beside him, ready to pounce. Maggie was upstairs, passed out. The song he and Angelene danced to filled the room.

"Show me the ballroom, knuddelbär."

He shook the memory from his head, tried to make sense of his emotions: do the right thing, follow his heart, keep loving the girl he shouldn't love, or listen to his ignored body part.

"I've only seen a ballroom in movies."

"Don't get too excited. It's an empty room with a piano in it."

Rachel hooked her arm through his.

"Really?"

"A gentleman would escort a lady to the ballroom."

They strolled arm in arm. He went over the list of what went where, which photo adorned what table until they reached the darkened room. He pushed a switch. The chandeliers lit the expansive space. The smile on her face was dreamy and filled with wonder.

Rachel walked over to the piano and ran her fingers across the cover. "Do you play?"

"Dad does, well, did. He hasn't played in years. I'll show you the pool."

"He never taught you?"

"He tried. I would sit for a minute, then kick the football around. The ballroom makes an impressive pitch."

They wandered down the hall to a set of French doors. Rachel pressed herself against the glass and squealed dramatically. "Is that a fireplace? By a pool, bleeding brilliant. You're so lucky."

"I guess."

Rachel stared at him like he had two heads. "Have you looked around you?"

"They're just things. Things don't make you lucky or happy. Mammina loves me, that's all that matters."

"How could she not, knuddelbär, you're adorable. And your daddy, does he love you too?"

They strolled back to the great room, heat crept over Brendon's cheeks. "I think he'd love me more if I were going to uni."

Rachel sank onto the sofa and tugged him with her. "You've never liked school, have you?"

"I'm a bloody terrible student."

"That must upset our Lord Chancellor."

"He's proud I made the pros, only because it's part of the code: pursue and conquer. I know he wishes I were more like…"

Brendon could feel eyes burning into him. He heard scampering feet and rustling curtains. His pulse quickened as a draught passed over him.

"Like who?"

Brendon rubbed the chill from his arms and grinned. "My dad, who else."

"You know everything there is to know about football, and you're learning German."

Rachel edged closer; he squeezed himself deeper into the cushions.

"Where did Tilly run off to? Didn't you come together?"

"She left with William."

"Poor Gemma."

"William fancies Tilly. Gemma is like Magg…" She stopped herself and licked her lips. "Tilly is having a hard time pulling her number one."

She pressed her breasts against him. Padre Diavolo was back, begging him to touch her.

"I might have sick on me. Maggie vomed."

Rachel brushed her lips over his neck, stretched her legs over his, straddling his lap.

"What are you doing? Maggie is upstairs." He sank further into the sofa, cushions separating, the frame stuck in his back. "Troy or Charlie could come down."

Rachel licked and sucked along his collarbone. "Do you think those two are going to stop humping to check on you?"

Padre Diavolo stirred up the tingles. Her fluttery kisses reached his ear. "Fancy a snog, knuddelbär?"

"Not a good idea."

"I'll give you a kiss, and if you don't like it, I'll stop."

She traced the outline of his lips, the kiss was hard, then soft.

"Kiss me back, knuddelbär."

Warmth diffused from her lips and slowly spread through his body. With it came insecurity. He didn't know what to do: push her off, run his fingers over her back? He could use her, get his first time over with. It was obvious she wanted it, and once he had given her his virginity, she'd cross him off the list and move on to number two. Should I or shouldn't I, danced in his head.

Padre Diavolo gave his approval.

Brendon shoved his hand up her shirt and cupped her breast. Troy said more than a handful was too much. He disagreed.

Rachel wound her legs around his waist. He fell on top of her. She fumbled with his belt, tugged at his jeans and boxers. Padre Diavolo instructed him to undo her zipper. It took some tugging to pull her jeans over her hips. Her knickers were lace. She was a natural redhead.

"Brendon, where are you?"

He placed his forehead against Rachel's and cursed. She nudged his jeans further over his hips.

"Ignore her."

"I'm going to barf again," Maggie called.

Madre Innocente jabbed her staff of guilt into his gut. Her army of remorse charged through him. Brendon mumbled a string of curse words and pulled up his jeans and boxers.

"Doesn't your devil want to play? What did you call him? Father Satan?"

"I played with him before, and he got me into trouble."

"Brendon, hurry!"

Rachel grabbed her jeans and wiggled into them. "Just my luck, knuddelbär. I'll see myself out."

"I'm sorry."

"No, you're not, you're relieved. See you soon."

He rushed to the foyer. Maggie clung to the wooden railing, teetering precariously on the top step. He hurried up the stairs and unclamped her hand from the banister.

"Is that Rachel? Why is she still here?"

"She forgot her purse."

Maggie coughed and gagged. "Gosh, I didn't think there was any sick left."

He lugged her down the hall and steered her into the bathroom. The sugary smell of artificial fruit hung in the air. He shoved her towards the toilet. She tumbled into the bowl and fell to her knees. A splash of pink and orange vomit filled it. Madre Innocente scolded him for not holding her hair back. Maggie moaned and rested her head on the toilet seat. He took her hand and pulled her limp body from the floor.

"Are you going to sleep with me?"

Brendon helped her onto the bed and yanked the blankets over her. "I'll be right next door. It reeks in here."

"I love you." Maggie licked and smacked her lips; the words dripped from her mouth. "From the moment Charlie introduced us, maybe before that. Maybe it was in maths. I stared at you an awful lot."

He stifled a yawn and glanced out the window. All the lights in the farmhouse were out. He wished Angelene sweet dreams and started to leave the bedroom.

"You never said it back."

"I, uh, love you."

Brendon waited until her eyes closed, asked Madre Innocente to look after her, and shuffled to the bedroom next to his. He dove onto his stomach. Exhaustion bulldozed over him. His mind on fire. He had to put the day to bed and forget about the almost hump, drunk Maggie, and the silly feeling of love.

Sofia

Furious gusts blew through the trees. Cold and snow rushed over the moors, brittle and icy. Drifts of snow suffocated the roses. A menacing whirl of white surrounded Rosewood Manor.

Where's Brendon? Where is my son?

He was in the forest.

I told him to stay out. He'll get swallowed up by the storm.

He followed her.

Run, quick.

Protect yourself from the storm.

I must find my son.

Brendon!

"Brendon."

Sofia woke, eyes wide. She laid her hand on her racing heart and her other on David's arm. It was a dream. Sofia took a deep breath and hoped that's all it was.

Angelene

Angelene puffed on a cigarette. His lamp light was on, but he was not in his bed. She felt it. Goldilocks had tripped into it.

"I had my first dance tonight. God, please don't be angry with me. I used to dance on Roman's feet until mother forbade it."

She took a long drag and crushed the cigarette on a plate. "Brendon danced, and then I was too. I was dancing. I felt his heart and the music. I felt bliss for the first time."

Angelene pushed on her heated cheeks. Her breath hitched, and she crawled under the blankets.

"I know, God, it should be shame I'm feeling."

20 Ghosts

Brendon

Goldfinch chirped. The sun played peek-a-boo behind the clouds. Brendon rolled his head across the pillow and scratched at his rumpled hair. He yawned, walked to his bedroom, and peeked around the doorframe. Maggie stared over the blankets. The heady stench of vomit and sweaty vanilla hung like a toxic cloud over his bed. Brendon opened the window. A leaf pirouetted in the breeze, landing on the bench where he had sat with Rachel. A wave of nausea engulfed him. He had almost had sex.

Maggie inched her way up the headboard and flinched. "My head hurts. My throat feels like sandpaper. All I can taste is sick."

Brendon slipped into the bathroom. Reminders of Maggie's evening floated in the toilet bowl. Jerking his shirt over his nose, he swung open the cabinet, and grabbed a bottle of pills. He filled a glass with water and marched back to Maggie.

"Take some pills. I need to clean my bathroom and have a shower."

Maggie groaned and folded her arms over her chest. "Can't you sit for a minute? I feel awful."

"Give me ten minutes. I slept in my clothes. I can't get the smell of barf out of my nose."

Madre Innocente was up early. He had fallen asleep with the guilts and woke with them.

"Can I have a kiss?"

"Are you bloody mad?"

"Did we... we didn't. Remember when Davina got bladdered and did it with the twins, Jude and Jaden?"

"I may be a wanker, but I wouldn't take advantage of you when you're pissed. Bloody hell."

A door closed, footsteps and a voice as bright as the birds approached. There was only one person Brendon knew who sang Nicki Minaj's *Right by My Side* after she had a cuddle with her babes.

"There's my sweet little muffin. Have you got a poorly tumkins?" Charlotte fanned the air as she stepped into the bedroom. "You ready? Daddy needs his car."

Maggie held her stomach and burped. "I'm afraid to get out of bed. The room is spinning."

Charlotte laughed at the state of Maggie. Hair sticking up, cheeks a pale shade of green. She tugged Brendon's arm and chuckled harder as a series of burps and groans filled the air. "Bend down."

He stooped in front of her. Charlotte flung her arms around his neck and squeezed. "Thanks for letting babes and I stay over. It was a brilliant evening."

"I'm glad you had a nice time."

"You'll let Charlie give you a hug, but you won't come near me." Maggie licked her lips. The words sounded sticky. "You're a terrible boyfriend."

"She smells like coconut."

"Go shower. I'll get Magpie up."

Brendon shut out Charlotte's mothering and flushed the fruity remnants away. He yanked off his T-shirt, a purply red mark shaped like Australia adorned his collarbone. There was the proof he was a shitty boyfriend. He had been busy concentrating on not prematurely exploding, he couldn't remember when it might have happened.

Brendon stripped out of his clothes and stepped into the shower. Memories flipped through his mind like a stack of photographs. He had to clear his head and focus. There was an entire house to put back together. He washed his hair, ran a washcloth over his body, rinsed and turned off the taps. Brendon dried himself, wound the towel around his waist, and reached for a bottle of cleaner. He aimed it at the sink, squirted the lemony bleach into the basin. The toilet was next. Brendon gave it a good dousing, snapped a rag, and scrubbed the scent of vomit away. He washed his hands, brushed his teeth, and slowly opened the door. Charlotte was fluffing Maggie's hair. He ducked into the walk-in and shrugged on a T-shirt, the evidence hidden.

"Doesn't Magpie look better?" Charlotte said.

"You're the colour of mushy peas, Mags."

"You're a wanker. Don't let me get drunk again."

"Here, muffin, have some gum."

"I told you to stop." Brendon strolled to the dresser and pulled open a drawer. "Close your eyes, I'm putting on my boxers."

Maggie placed the gum in her mouth, gagged, and chewed. "Brendon, Charlotte is right here."

"It's not like she hasn't seen a bare arse before."

Charlotte tilted her head from side to side and tapped her lip. "You're fit, not as dishy as babes."

"I'm going to drop my towel," Brendon warned.

"Go to the loo. Charlie will sneak a peek."

"You cheeky cow. I had my look."

"Close your eyes."

"Just do it, Magpie. I need to stop by the bakery. Netflix, my sweet little crumpet, and doughnuts. What a beautiful Saturday it's going to be."

Maggie peered through her fingers as she spoke. "Haven't you seen enough of him?"

"Never."

Brendon slid on his boxers and tossed the towel into the hamper. He finished dressing, then walked to the walk-in to grab a hoodie, another layer to hide the evidence.

"Thanks again, luv. I didn't make the bed. The sheets are mussed."

"I planned on changing them. I can't have one of mom's guests rolling around in crumpet's spunk."

Maggie stared up at him. Her blue blossom eyes were bloodshot. "Can I have a kiss now? I chewed some gum."

Brendon pecked her forehead. "That's the best you're going to get. I'll walk you to the door."

They left the bedroom; pale light stretched across the foyer, bounced off the chandelier and cast tiny prisms on the stairs. Charlotte yelled an enthusiastic, "See you, babes."

Brendon mouthed, 'I'll call you,' and waved. He strolled to the kitchen and dug in the pantry for coffee. His thoughts pulled him in all directions, from setting up the house to breaking the Gentlemen's Code. Brendon spooned coffee into the basket and clicked on the machine; it hissed and gurgled. Part of him wanted to ring Angelene and see if she would help. The other part, the rational part, said to put some space between them. The feeling of love was getting out of control, and it didn't feel warm and fuzzy like Troy said.

"Morning, mate." Troy plopped onto a stool and sniffed the air. "What's that smell?"

"Bleach. Maggie honked all over the loo."

"I was having a brilliant hump while you were cleaning up barf."

"Do you have to rub it in? I finally get Maggie in my bed, and she's pissed."

Troy chuckled and reached for an apple. "Did Rachel stay long?"

Brendon turned to the cupboard, grabbed two mugs, and poured coffee. He wanted to tell Troy about Rachel's lacy knickers and that her 'more than a handful of breasts' were lovely, but he kept the tingly secrets to himself. Troy was like David Cook, the poster boy for monogamy.

"I showed her the ballroom and pool, then she left."

Troy bit into the apple and screwed up his face. "You sure? Your cheeks are a pretty shade of pink."

"Tilly left with Will," Brendon said, handing Troy a mug.

Change the subject to something scandalous. Give him the gossip before it was the hot topic at school.

"Rubbish, mate."

"It's true. Gemma left crying," he said, yanking open the fridge, grabbing the jug of milk and cream.

Troy crunched around the apple and tossed the core into the sink. "Rachel stayed longer, didn't she? We've been friends for thirteen years. I know you."

"I kept my hands to myself."

"What did you do? Snog? Your first BJ?"

A hot flush stained Brendon's cheeks. "Do you want brekky? I can fry you up all that greasy stuff you like."

"Don't change the subject."

"It was her. I swear."

Troy tore a banana from the stalk, snapped the stem, and peeled it. "You didn't hump her, did you?"

"Maggie woke up before anything bad happened."

Troy gobbled the banana in three bites and laid the peel on the kitchen island. "I knew it. Did you touch her jubblies?"

Brendon rubbed the back of his neck. He'd give Troy the watered-down version, save himself a lecture.

"Rachel climbed onto my lap and kissed me."

"She kissed you?"

"She's bloody relentless. I asked her to stop, but she was grinding her fanny against me and did this thing with her tongue. It was one hell of a snog."

Troy flung the peel towards the sink then tore into an orange. "Dry humping gets you every time."

"Are you going to tell Charlie?" Brendon sipped his coffee. It was bitter and hot, like the guilt searing his insides. "I feel bad enough. I ignored Maggie all night. Can you imagine what she would be like knowing Rachel and I snogged?"

"Did she taste like cigarettes?"

"She must have chewed some gum. Her mouth was minty."

"You need to stay away from Rachel," Troy said. He popped an orange segment in his mouth and gave Brendon a scolding look. "She'll get you into heaps of trouble."

"I've been told."

Troy swiped the orange rinds into his hand and walked to the sink. He hooked his foot under the cupboard door, jerked it open, and deposited the peels into the compost bin.

"I won't tell Charlie if you promise to stay away Rachel."

"I'll avoid her like the plague," Brendon said. "Do you have chores to do?"

"I promised Callum I would wrestle with him if he collected the eggs. What do you need?"

The tension drained from Brendon's body. The PG-13 version—accepted.

"I've got to put the house back together before the Dortmund match."

"I'll help. It was an ace party, mate."

They left the kitchen and headed toward the den. Brendon pulled the keys from his pocket and unlocked the door. "It's organized by room.

The things on the desk belong in the great room. The junk on the coffee table, in the foyer."

"I'm afraid to touch this stuff."

"Just be gentle."

"Doesn't everything have to be lined up at specific angles?"

"All I need you to do is move them from here to their homes. I'll do the arranging."

Troy exhaled long and slow. "You're lucky I like you."

"I'll give us ninety minutes to get it done, the length of a match. After that, I'll make you something to eat."

"Is there any pizza dough in the freezer?"

"Amelia made some the other day. I'll take it out. You ready?"

"The first half just started. You best get that dough out of the freezer."

It would be a miracle if they cleared everything from the den in ninety minutes. Brendon imagined himself on the pitch. The referee blew the whistle. The first half had begun.

Brendon waved goodbye to Troy and walked across the lawn. He wandered to the forest's edge and contemplated the trees that stretched and spiked through the grey-blue sky. From within the shadows, the brambles rustled and birds chirped. The gnarled hornbeam branches didn't look frightening in the afternoon sun. Sofia had been adamant about him staying clear of the forest—it was off-limits. He'd be defying her again. Deciding he had done enough rule-breaking, Brendon turned and flinched.

"Jesus Christ."

"Jesus isn't here. He's having tea with friends," Angelene said. "I was going to explore the forest for some inspiration. Will you come with me?"

Brendon gazed nervously at the dense canopy. "I can't. I've got to be a good boy for the rest of the weekend."

"I don't know the property."

"Mom and Dad made up a bunch of stories to keep me out. I'd probably lose you in there."

The forest hummed with life. Leaves shushed, branches clacked, the trunks moaned. A whisper of light broke through the wavering treetops, lighting the path. It was a forest, not a raging beast.

"I did sneak in when I was ten."

"Now the truth comes out."

"It was Uncle Walt. We started building a fort. Mom was pissed off when she found out. I promised I would never step foot in the woods again."

"Walter's a troublemaker. Shall we?"

"Who's the troublemaker now?"

They stepped onto an uneven path dotted with mossy rocks, patches of foxglove, and toadstools. The green and brown foliage grew thicker. The air was damp, scented with the tang of pine needles, earth, and bark. Light disappeared.

"You see that over there," Brendon said, pointing to a burl in an oak tree. "Below the bump and behind the mushrooms."

"I see it."

"It's a faery door."

Angelene looked up at him and smiled. "Who told you that?"

"Walt did."

"Faeries are naughty. Roman told me you must be kind to the faeries, or they'll play tricks on you. What did Walter say?"

"They're beautiful and randy."

The air became cooler. Twigs snapped and crunched under their feet. Brendon stopped at the tangled roots of a hornbeam. A tingly sensation prickled up his legs and spine. The trees whispered, *go back*, a shadow floated over the roots, something watched him, waited. Brendon suppressed a shiver. The shadow disappeared into the knotted roots, and the air cleared.

"Doesn't look like much, does it?"

Rot had warped the boards nailed between four alder trees. The makeshift plywood roof had bowed under the weight of broken branches and damp detritus.

"You never tried to finish it?"

"I've never seen Mom so mad."

"Spiky red?"

Brendon ducked under the crumbling shell, brushed twigs and curled leaves to the ground. "Spiky red doesn't describe it."

"It would have been a fun place to play." Angelene picked up a stem of pine needles and swept it across her palm.

"Walt and I had so many adventures planned. It was the dressing room at Signal Iduna, our pirate ship."

"Would you like to pretend we're at the stadium now?"

Padre Diavolo screamed, *'Kiss her.'*

"I'll be in the real one soon enough."

"How was your party?"

"Maggie got pissed. She spent most of the night barfing." He hesitated and rubbed the back of his neck. "Rachel was there."

A brisk wind stirred up the leaves. Angelene snuggled into his arm. "I told you to stay away from her."

"Who said I went near her?"

"Your words are sludgy green."

"I kissed her."

"We've kissed."

Brendon chuckled and dug the toe of his trainer into the dirt. "I wouldn't call that a kiss." He breathed in her lavender-scented hair and shooed away the 'in love' feeling. "If Maggie hadn't woken up, I would have humped Rachel on Mom's bloody posh sofa."

"You protected your light."

"There's evidence."

He pulled his arm out of his hoodie and hiked up his T-shirt. Angelene poked at the purple splotch.

"Mon Dieu. Did she put her mouth there?"

"She would have put it anywhere if I let her."

"Put your shirt down. Zut alors! You've kissed me, which you claim wasn't a kiss. You've kissed Taunton's Salome."

He wiggled into his hoodie and swiped a pinecone from the ground. Brendon peeled back the sections and flicked them into the air. "Who is Salome?"

Angelene drew his arm around her and rested her head against his chest. "Read the Gospels of Matthew and Mark for the full story, but she was responsible for the execution of John the Baptist. She danced before Herod, and he promised her whatever she wanted. She asked for John's head on a platter. That girl who put that disgusting mark on you will do the same. It will be your light."

Brendon rested his chin on the crown of her head and laughed. "I have no intention of kissing Rachel again. I do, however, think about kissing you all the time."

"Please don't start talking about that. I don't like it."

"You give me the feels. I know it's wrong, but I like the feeling."

"The boy with liquid blue eyes... no, I won't let it happen again."

Brendon whipped the pinecone. He held her hand and kissed the top of her head. "I've kissed Charlie like that, so don't get pissed off. It's just a friendly kiss, mon ami." He snapped a plant growing among a patch of ferns and handed it to her. "It isn't a cornflower, but it's something."

"It's nightshade, the devil's berries."

"Someone must have slipped me some last night. I feel like shit for snogging Rachel."

"That's a silly word, snogging. It sounds as bad as kissing."

"Kissing is the greatest thing on earth, other than football."

"It'll take a lot of convincing for me to believe a kiss is anything but exchanging spit."

"You won't let me kiss you, so you'll never know."

Kissing her will lead you to a place you should not go. Wanting it is just as dangerous.

The whispering words passed along the branches and rustled the leaves. Brendon glanced around the forest and shivered. She trembled against him.

"I wish I had been like you and Maggie."

"Maggie might be okay with it. My goolies are aching."

"What you have is precious," Angelene said, her voice weak. "Mine was stolen. Don't take it from Maggie and don't fall victim to Taunton's Salome."

"I'm sorry that happened to you."

"Roman told mother to protect me."

Brendon rested his chin on her head and held her tighter. "Roman sounds like a good man."

"He used to send me postcards from all the places he travelled. Mother got jealous and threw them away. She told Roman the postcards never came. He knew she was lying. He would sneak them into the flat and I would hide them in the jewellery box he gave me."

"How could she be jealous? You were just a child."

"She loved Roman. She would deny it, but I knew. She was afraid of the love she felt for him and chased him away."

Angelene's soul was his again. A few more bricks dismantled from her wall.

"What happened? Did he stop showing up?"

"Roman came to visit after a business trip. He brought me the prettiest yellow dress for Easter Mass. Mother was angry with him, worse than spiky red. She was a mixture of green, crimson, and electric black sparks."

Brendon's heart knocked about. He remembered a painting of a little girl in a yellow dress, a horrible monster clawing after her.

"He gave Veronique peonies and put them beside her bed. The flowers were cheap compared to my dress. She screamed." Angelene snuggled deeper into his chest. "I never heard her scream like that. She must have bottled it up for years. I was so frightened, I ran to my room and sat on the windowsill with my fingers in my ears. That's when I saw Roman walk away. It was my turn to scream."

Brendon pressed his lips against her hair. He'd never turn his lamp off, always say 'see you soon' and help find all her missing pieces.

"Mother cut up my dress. There were shreds of yellow fabric and peony petals everywhere. We saw more of Paulo and Gustav."

"That was a long time ago. You're in Taunton now, no one can hurt you anymore."

"It doesn't matter where I am. The scars live in my heart and mind. I have years of evidence on my body."

He turned over her hand, pushed his thumb between the bracelets, and traced his thumb over the scar. "Why did you do that?"

Angelene jerked her hand free, fixed and adjusted the beads. "I don't talk about it. God wept and forgave me."

"What if I want to hear?"

"I haven't talked about it with Walter. He's embarrassed."

She tucked herself deeper into the shelter of his arm.

"You can trust me. I won't judge you." He brought her trembling hand to his lips. "I haven't yet."

"I was sixteen. Douchette asked me to make him raclette. All I could think about was the time Roman made it for me and we sat in the window eating it. The pot of potatoes boiled over; the cheese burnt." Her chest rose in shallow breaths. "Douchette hit me for spoiling his supper. He split my lip open, then bent me over his bed, shoved my face in the sheets. I can still smell the repulsive, sweaty odour. The noise, the terrible grunting."

"Bloody hell, he fucking raped..."

"I told no one. I ran to my flat, straight to the bath, and tried to scrub him away, but I couldn't. The stench lingered; the sounds remained. I asked God for help. All he did was cry." Her hand was clammy in his. Her heart thumped against his ribs. "It rained all night and into the next day. I stayed in the tub, scrubbing and scrubbing until I was raw. I hoped slicing into my skin would release the scream bottled inside me."

"Somebody must have been looking out for you."

"I thought it was Roman wrapping my wrists and crying, little bird, what have you done."

"Who found you?"

"Douchette," she whimpered. "Brendon, I feel like I'm drowning. I can't breathe."

"What can I do? Do you need to walk?"

"My sweet boy, always trying to help."

Brendon yanked on his cuff and blotted the tears on her cheeks.

Angelene sniffed and looked up from his chest. "You aren't disgusted by my scars?"

"We all have some."

"You'd say anything to make me smile."

"Look." Brendon pulled down the waistband of his jeans and pointed. "There's my scar."

She traced her finger along the jagged line on his hipbone, his belly quivered.

"How did it happen?"

"An attacker was trying to catch the rebound and slammed his foot into what he thought was the ball." He let go of his waistband and grinned. "I made the save."

"Who knew football could be so dangerous."

"A scar is a reminder we've healed. You should be proud you survived."

Angelene stretched her arms and yawned. "I'm tired. I need sleep."

She shone differently now. The burden of horrible memories sank her shoulders. Her light pulsed behind her scars, begging to break free.

"Try to think about happy things, like your friend the rabbit and football."

"I'll read the Hunchback. Spend some time with Quasimodo."

"Give me a bell if you want to talk. All I'm doing is changing sheets. Mine reek like barf. Troy and Charlie, let's just say, she was getting a piece of Troy's light all night and this morning."

Brendon released a long, pent-up breath. Exhaustion wrapped around him, squeezing tight.

The crowd cheered and threw yellow ribbons onto the pitch. The roar of the fans had his heart knocking violently.

Knock, knock.

Brendon gazed sleepily around the room. The furious knocking rose from the foyer. His eyes jerked open. It wasn't a dream or his heart. Every horror movie he had watched flashed through his mind. It was after midnight, windy. He was alone. The knocking grew louder and more frantic. Hesitantly, he climbed out of bed. This was what every character did in the movies, searched the house and ended up butchered. He gripped the banister; the knocking persisted. He made it to the foyer and stared at the door. There was no peephole to see who was on the other side, no identifying rhythm. He was positive a six-foot seven machete wielding madman lurked beyond the door.

"Who is it?" he said, masking the quiver in his voice.

"Please open the door."

A whoosh escaped from his lungs. "Bloody hell, you scared me." He grabbed Angelene's wrist and dragged her inside.

"Have the ghosts followed me?"

Brendon scratched his hair, dazed. Rosewood Manor had its own host of ghosts. Had she brought more with her?

"I thought about happy things, about you, then you faded away. No goodbye, no see you soon, you just vanished." She paced, rubbing her arms. "I thought about Roman, then I saw him walk away. I have a horrible ache in my belly. All the ghosts were in my room tonight."

"Did you call Walter?"

"He accused me of being drunk." She swayed. Her accent was thicker.

"You have been drinking."

"What did you expect me to do? I hoped one would help me sleep, and when it didn't, I had another."

His eyes shifted to a series of red welts on her arm. "Would you like to stay here?"

"I can't be alone. It isn't safe."

He took hold of her hand and escorted her up the stairs. "Which room? Springtime in Ireland? The Art déco masterpiece?"

"I want to stay with you."

His brain stuttered. He tried to decipher her words. Stay with him? In his bed, or have him nearby?

"You can hold Paddington. He's good at keeping ghosts away."

"I need you. I feel God in your fingertips."

"Only until you fall asleep."

He went to the walk-in, tore a Nike T-shirt from a stack and handed it to her.

"I've got to wee."

This was the worst ideas he had ever had. It wasn't like he was going to make love to her, just sit beside her until she fell asleep. He wouldn't lie under the blankets or hold her. He flushed the toilet, washed his hands, and froze in the doorway. She didn't look like a woman. She looked like a terrified little girl. He slid onto the bed, pulled blankets over her, and pushed Padre Diavolo from his mind.

"Tell me something wonderful."

"My Nonna's spaghetti, football."

"Was Borussia Dortmund always your favourite team?"

"The black and yellows forever."

A breathy laugh tickled his side. "Do you like Emma the bee?"

"You know Dortmund's mascot. What's Bayern's?"

"Berni the bear."

"And Man U? Troy will be disappointed if you don't know."

"Fred the Red after the club's nickname, the Red Devils. PSG is a lynx."

"Bloody hell, that's impressive."

"I've had a lot of time to read about things." She yawned and curled into a tight ball.

Brendon leaned his head against the pillow, losing himself in the rhythm of her breathing. Happiness engulfed him, his breathing slowed, and his eyelids grew heavy.

Angelene

Angelene danced in a field of buttercups and cornflower.

21 Twisted

Brendon

Brendon woke with the anxious thudding of his heart. He had drifted off to visions of being in net surrounded by 80,000 Dortmund fans. Angelene had been one of them, in a yellow dress, and now she was here, in his bed. Brendon turned to his side, stared at a photo of Maggie, and flipped the frame over.

"Are you awake?"

Angelene threaded her arm around his waist, her breasts squished into his back, his belly tightened. He turned his attention to the gentle splats of rain dribbling down the window and concentrated on what he was going to work on at the pitch. Her body was warm, inviting. Troy's bragging about morning sex infiltrated his thoughts.

"I shouldn't be here. You shouldn't be here. Bloody hell, Angelene."

She withdrew her arm, pushed the pillows against the headboard, and rested against them. "I haven't slept that peacefully in a long time. You have a gift, like Roman."

Brendon rolled over and grinned. It was a stupid thing to do, fall asleep with her. If it meant she had a night of peace, then the dumb decision was worth it.

"I wish things could have been better for you."

"It's only a few chapters." She slid across the bed and shivered as her feet hit the floor. "I haven't finished my story yet."

"Would you like coffee?"

Angelene lifted the T-shirt and dragged it over her head. "I don't know when Walter will be home. I've left a mess again."

Brendon picked up the pillow and held it to his nose. It smelled of lavender and patchouli.

"Can you invest in a bloody bra?"

"I don't like them. All I do is pull at it." She dressed, walked around the bed, held his cheeks in her hands. Little flutters floated in his belly. "You stay away from Salome, no more of that nasty kissing."

"I don't need another love bite."

"It's ugly. She bruised you." Angelene scratched at his stubble and placed the tiniest kiss on his nose. "Thank you for keeping the ghosts away."

"We're here for each other."

He'd help her write the next chapter in her story and title it, 'The night we chased the ghosts away.'

The rain had stopped. A slice of sunlight broke through the trees, making them shine like glass, the bark crystalline. Brendon scraped his fingers through his hair. A melodic hum of *Arthur's* theme seeped into the kitchen. Amelia was as particular as his mother. She knew every inch of the house, what went where, and the angles Sofia preferred. He spooned up the last bite of yogurt and berries and hoped it would meet her approval.

"Good morning," Amelia crooned. She set down the grocery bags and dug through the drawer for an apron.

"Checking in on me?"

Brendon stood, rinsed his bowl, and placed it in the dishwasher. He chugged back a glass of milk and shoved a half-eaten piece of toast into his mouth.

"I'm freshening up the house and making one of your great Nonna's recipes."

"You drove all the way out here to make sauce and open windows?"

"It's Janina's bolognese. It must simmer. You'll be responsible after I leave."

"I'm going to the pitch, then Maggie's."

"When you get back."

Brendon kissed her cheek and grinned. "You can look through the entire house. You won't find a thing."

"Who says I'm looking for anything?"

Brendon left the kitchen and bounded up the stairs. Despite the broken sleep, he had a surprising amount of energy. He side-shuffled down the hall, preparing himself for a morning at the pitch. He stepped into the walk-in and ran his fingers over a row of Bundesliga shirts.

"Ame!"

"What are you hollering about?"

She stomped into the room, cradling a stack of clean towels.

"My practice jersey. I can't find it."

"Your First shirt is right there."

"Not that one."

He moved from the closet to a mountain of clothes piled on the chair and tossed handfuls to the floor.

"Which one? You have half the Bundesliga in there."

"The only one that matters. Dortmund."

"It wasn't in the basket when I did the laundry."

He bent down and peered under the bed. No dust bunnies, no magazines, or lost socks.

"If you would put your clothes away," Amelia scolded.

Brendon pushed himself up, marched to the laundry basket, dumped it, and kicked through the pile. He yanked on a dresser drawer, rooted through socks and boxers. The second drawer, nothing but never-worn pyjamas.

"You have a cupboard full of jerseys to choose from."

Brendon grabbed his ball cap and yanked it over his mussed hair. "It's signed by the keeper. Every time I wear it, we win."

"Don't be superstitious. You've only lost one match so far, and you said it was because no one's head was in the game, including yours."

"You don't understand."

"I hope you aren't expecting me to clean up this mess."

"Why would I?"

"Don't be cheeky." Amelia stacked towels on the vanity. She came out of the bathroom and stopped. "I should be putting the blue sheets on, not taking them off. I have a system."

Brendon swiped his keys off the dresser and glanced nervously from the mess of clothes to his bed.

"Who has a system for changing sheets?"

"I do. It makes things easier."

"Maybe you put the blue sheets on by mistake."

"I never deviate from my system."

Brendon cursed, pounded down the stairs, and slammed out the door. Sparks darted around his body. He revved the engine and flew down the driveway. What could he say? His room was hot. He felt feverish. That would send Sofia into a tailspin, worrying he was sick.

Brendon blew through a red light, grumbled under his breath, and screeched into the car park.

"We've been waiting almost an hour," Troy said. He bopped the ball with his head and caught it. "I left Charlie with Callum. Little bugger made her eggy bread with Mom's strawberry jam."

"I couldn't find my Dortmund shirt."

"We win when you practice in it."

"Let's hope Nike can bring us luck."

Brendon tromped to the net. Of course, Amelia would have a process for changing sheets. She had a system for everything: grocery shopping, dusting, cleaning the bathrooms. He cursed Amelia and her routine.

"We don't need a shirt for luck, Mr. Wonderful."

"Fuck off, Will."

"I came here to have some fun, not listen to you two," Troy said. He dashed in front of William, stole the ball and fired it towards the net. Brendon reached and snagged it.

"Did you have fun on Friday night?" William said. He aimed. Brendon jumped, caught it, and tossed it onto the pitch. It came soaring back at him. He dropped to his knees and snatched it.

"I heard Rachel stayed after everyone left."

"He gave Rachel a tour," Troy said, slamming his foot against the ball.

Brendon tipped the ball over the crossbar. Sparks whirred and inflamed his limbs.

"That's not what I heard."

Brendon picked up the ball and whipped it at William.

"You didn't think Rachel would keep her gob shut, did you? She told Tilly, who told me."

Troy batted the ball between his feet. "Can we just play? It was a mistake. He regrets it."

William thrust out his lower lip and puckered his brow. "Poor Brendon. Did Maggie ruin it for you?"

"You need to keep your bloody trap shut. We snogged. That was it."

Brendon lifted his ball cap and ran his T-shirt over his forehead. The entire weekend had been an onslaught of poor decisions.

William snickered. "The poofter almost got down to it."

"You're any better? Running off with Tilly."

Brendon whipped his gloves to the ground. Sparks fluttered and burned.

"How did it feel to touch some jubblies?" William said.

"Put your gloves back on, mate. Will, you try to get the ball past me."

William smirked. "What was her fanny like?"

"You should know, you fucked her."

"I tried. I couldn't get hard. She's had a lot of knobs in her beaver."

"I left Charlie to listen to this." Troy picked up Brendon's gloves and handed them to him. "Keep breathing. I can see the sparks."

"Is that a love bite? You dirty wanker."

Brendon charged across the pitch and seized William. "You need to keep your fucking mouth shut. If Maggie finds out about this, you're bloody dead."

"Let him go, mate. He isn't worth it."

"Always bloody Switzerland."

"Someone has to be. Let go of him. We need to practice."

"You wouldn't know where to put your knob," William teased.

Brendon twisted William's collar and dragged him to the ground. William kicked, the studs on his cleats battered Brendon's knees. Everything went fuzzy and black. He tightened his grip. William coughed and sputtered.

"If anything gets around school or Taunton. I'll see you're never in net."

"Get off me," William said, tossing handfuls of grass at Brendon.

The trees, grass and bleachers came back into focus. Sparks whizzed through his body like a firestorm.

"Have a drink." Troy knocked a bottle of water against his chest. "Cool off."

"Do that again and my fist will be in that dishy face of yours," William said.

Brendon tossed the bottle aside and glared. "Try me."

"You two poofters enjoy the rest of the morning."

Brendon swiped the bottle from his feet and chugged it. He was doing everything he promised his father he wouldn't do—let his anger control him. Another promise broken.

"I didn't get a chance to defend because of you two dolts," Troy said.

"Get out front. I'll try to get one past you."

"I hope Will keeps his mouth shut. Maggie will be gutted if she finds out," Troy said.

Brendon dribbled the ball and ran towards the net. "He will."

"You think?"

"He was shaking in his football boots."

Troy poked his foot between Brendon's feet and grinned. "Too easy. I can see why you're a keeper."

Troy raced down the pitch. Brendon ran, fuelled by the sparks, and dove just in time to stop the ball from going into the net.

Brendon finished his sandwich and tossed the wrapper into the bag. He plastered on his best dimpled grin, strolled up the weed-infested walkway, meeting Maggie at the door.

"You look better than the last time I saw you, not so green."

He hastily brushed his lips over Maggie's cheek and kicked off his shoes.

"You look awful."

Brendon glanced at the smears of dirt on his elbows and knees. "I just came from the pitch. What did Rosie say when you got home?"

Clothes hung over the railing, books and toys trailed along the staircase and spilled into the foyer.

"I got in so much trouble."

He followed her to the front room, flopped on the sofa, and stretched his legs across the coffee table. Jack's footsteps thundered overhead.

"I told her Charlie, and I drank champagne," Maggie said. She leaned in, sniffed his neck, and scrunched her nose. "You smell sweaty."

Brendon dug between the cushions, grabbed the remote and flicked through the stations until he found the football scores. He smelled his armpit. "Bloody hell, I can go if it's bothering you."

"You used to go home and shower."

Footsteps pounded down the stairs. Jack raced into the room, fired a block at Brendon, and thumped away.

"Bloody hell, how do you tolerate him?"

Maggie shrugged. "I kind of have to. He's my brother. Do you want a cuppa?"

Brendon dropped his head against the cushion. *Thump, thump, thump*, echoed through the house. He couldn't focus on the highlights or Maggie. His brain was shuffling through kissing Rachel, Angelene and her knowledge of football mascots, waking beside her, Amelia's system for changing sheets. Sparks were simmering in his belly. With every crash and bang, another lit.

"How do you stand the noise?"

"I'm used to it," Maggie said. She wound the cord of her sweater around her finger and stared into her lap. "What do you want to do?"

"Watch the bloody highlights in peace."

"Can't we talk? Tell me about practice."

Brendon clicked off the television. The house was unbelievably silent.

"It was the usual."

"Did anything happen?"

Brendon reached between the cushions and extracted a bright blue block. He examined the ridges, the little nubs, and plasticine wedged into the holes. This could be a set-up; bribe him with tea, stare at him with eyes that said she honestly cared about football.

"You sent your spies out, didn't you?"

"Are we in a *Game of Thrones* episode? I'm trying to make conversation."

Jack thumped into the room and shoved his finger up his nose. "Make me lunch."

"Looks like you're about to have it."

Maggie gave him a 'you're-being-a-baby' look and turned to Jack. "I told you an hour ago to get out of your jimjams and I would make you something."

"Batman and I had important stuff to do." Jack wiped his finger on his pyjamas. He licked at chocolate something staining his upper lip, dug into the other crusted nostril, and pulled out a green glob. "What are you looking at?"

"A bloody disgusting brat."

"I'm looking at a big dolt."

Brendon held up a pillow as a series of colourful blocks flew towards him.

"Will the two of you stop," Maggie said. "I'll slap some peanut butter on bread, then belt up."

Jack grabbed a handful of blocks and aimed. "I'm going to tell you wouldn't make me anything to eat cause you were too busy snogging."

"Will you make him a sarnie before he takes my eye out."

Maggie groaned and stomped from the room. "I feel like I'm babysitting two."

"I hate you." Jack dropped the blocks, tugged two cushions from the sofa, and stacked them into a tower. "You smell gross. Give me the remote."

"You do my fucking head in."

"You swore. My mom never let you come over again."

"Good, I won't have to listen to you bang around the bloody house."

Bubbly laughter gurgled in Jack's throat. He lay on top of his tower of cushions and snorted. "Maggie barfed yesterday. It was her favourite colours, pink and green. Mom said she better not have gotten soused with you."

"Fuck off."

"Brendon," Maggie said. She dropped the plate on the coffee table and slammed her hands on her hips. "Leave Jack alone. Come with me."

Brendon kicked through the pile of blocks and followed her into the foyer. "Where are we going?"

"To my bedroom."

He booted a path through the toys and stopped at the bottom of the stairs. He didn't know how much longer he could keep up the charade. His lunch was about to come up. His muscles ached. All the memories of the weekend swelled around him. He was drowning in his bad decisions.

"You're breaking your mom's number one rule. No Brendon in your bedroom."

He made his way upstairs and stood in the doorway. Everything was pink, frilly, and smelled cloyingly sweet. Stacks of things were everywhere, piled on the vanity, in corners, on the floor. Stuffed animals and textbooks cluttered the bed. It was as chaotic as the rest of the house.

"Jack could use this against me."

"Horrible Henry is on. He'll be glued to the telly for an hour."

"No wonder he's such a brat."

"I have three tubes of Sherbert Dip to bribe him with." Maggie twiddled the ear of a stuffed bear and dropped onto the bed. "He broke a Hummel figurine last week. We tried to mend it as best we could. I can threaten him with that."

Brendon lifted his ball cap and swiped his hand over his sweating brow. If he sat beside her, she could accidentally tug his T-shirt and expose the continent-sized love bite. He had no excuse for snogging Rachel or falling victim to the 'in love' feeling. He backed away and bumped into the pouf. He wasn't proud of his behaviour. Maggie's blue blossom eyes made him feel worse.

"Are you going to shave that stuff off your face?"

"Don't start nagging about the stubble. I get enough aggro from Mammina."

Stunned by the tone of his voice, Brendon forced himself to remember all the things that made his heart flutter two years ago after his first date with Maggie. All he felt was empty. A chorus of clapping and 'Brendon smells gross' exploded through the house, followed by a chair scraping across the floor. Maggie jumped from the bed and ripped open the vanity drawer. Brendon's eyebrows raised. The entire drawer was full of sweets. Jack chanted faster, *thump, clang, bang.*

"Will you do something about him."

Maggie swiped a handful of sweets and kicked the drawer shut. "Gosh, you're miserable."

Brendon's breath was heavy in his chest. He stepped over a tower of books, stared out the window. Dismal grey swaddled the weatherworn bricks and gardens. Swallows perched along the telephone wires. Every memory of Rachel and Angelene resurfaced, painful and sharp. The girl he wanted was married. The other he used to satisfy all his unsatisfied parts. His bad decisions hit him hard.

"Jack should be quiet now. He's eating ice cream. I gave him the sweets."

"I'm going to go."

"You just got here."

Brendon frowned at the display of photos lined up on the vanity. It was hard to look at himself.

"Is it Jack? He'll settle down now. I put on a Batman movie."

"It isn't your brother."

Sparks, heat, longing rattled his insides.

"Is it because I got bladdered?"

"I don't care you were pissed." He shifted from foot to foot and sighed. "I want to go home."

"Did Rachel really forget her purse?"

"Bloody hell, why are you always going on about Rachel and Mrs. Pratt.?"

Maggie crossed her arms and dug her teeth into her bottom lip. "I haven't said a word about Mrs. Pratt."

Brendon punted the pouf into the vanity. He couldn't count his breaths. The sparks were furious.

"I can't fucking breathe."

Maggie's lips quivered. He grabbed her arm and pulled her into his chest. She was springtime. Angelene was winter. Rachel was blazing, like the summer sun.

"I'll call you later."

"Do you promise? You said you would ring yesterday. You didn't."

"I'll bloody call."

Madre Innocente skewered him with her staff. Every part of him hurt.

"I need help with the history assignment."

Maggie ripped a tissue from a squished box and dabbed her nose. "At least I'm good for something."

"Don't be like that." Brendon fished his keys out of his pocket and nodded towards her vanity. "Why do you have so many pictures of me?"

"I like looking at you."

Brendon kissed her and waited for the flutter. He kissed her again, gentler, slower. Nothing. He took hold of her hand and led her from the bedroom, waiting for the tingles or swell of his heart. Nothing happened.

"Bye, wanker."

Jack charged past. A handful of blocks fell like colourful bullets at Brendon's feet.

"Unfuckingbelievable."

A 'you-deserve-to-be-tortured-by-my-brother,' smirk quirked Maggie's lips.

"History. Don't forget. I promised your father I would help you."

Brendon clacked his heels and shot his arm out in a salute. "Heil Thornton."

"Don't joke about that," Maggie said, opening the door. "I expect you to do your part of the assignment."

He kissed her. Nothing. Was he falling out of like, had two years been long enough? Had too much happened over the weekend, and he wasn't thinking clearly?

Brendon collected the clothes scattered on the floor. He shoved handfuls of boxers into the drawer, threw his dirty laundry back in the basket, and froze. Amelia had changed his sheets. Angelene's perfume lingered, crept off her skin, seeped onto flesh or fabric, clinging, screaming 'Remember me, I'm always here.' Amelia broke into a full-blown performance if she felt moved by a song. A show tune might have distracted her. The mess might have annoyed her, and she pulled the sheets away without bringing them close to her face. Brendon held his cross and raised his eyes to heaven.

"Please God... bloody hell, who am I fooling?"

Brendon grabbed his history textbook and notebook and walked down the stairs. There was nothing he could do except hope his tantrum annoyed Amelia and she didn't notice the smell. It was time for act two, appeasing Maggie. He set his phone to speaker, clicking on the television.

"You're watching the highlights."

"No hello?"

"Do you have your book open?"

"Page 235."

"Turn off the telly. The assignment is on page 325. Tell me one of the key events of Henry VIII's life."

"He was fat and humped a lot of women. Bloody brilliant save. That's another clean sheet for Dortmund."

"Brendon."

"In 1531, he declared himself head of the English Church."

"Sweetheart, we're home."

"My parents are home. I'll call you back."

Sofia and David waltzed into the great room like they had just stepped off the set of a steamy romance. Sofia's lips were set in a dreamy, lovestruck grin. Cupid had pummelled David with his arrows.

She floated to the sofa and wound her arms around his neck. "I missed you."

"You're bloody strangling me."

"Doing your homework?" David said. He gazed from the open textbook to the television. "With the telly on and talking on the phone." Disapproval overtook the lovestruck look.

Sofia rubbed David's shoulder and grinned. "I have wonderful news. Your Nonna is coming to visit."

"Don't you mean coming to give her approval? You better warn Walt."

Sofia's gaze swept over the room. The mantel had been set up correctly. Cuckoo clock in the middle, his smiling mug on either side. The armchairs positioned at the perfect angle in front of the fireplace to keep his father warm when he read. The Klimt hung.

"Everything good, Mammina?"

"I can't look at you when you're grumpy. You get this look in your eye, and it frightens me."

Brendon leaned across the sofa and planted a kiss on her cheek. "I can't wait to see Nonna. Instead of one woman nagging, I'll have two."

"No more football until you finish your studies." David clicked off the television and placed the remote in the armoire. "I hope you talked to your mother. Angelene is shy. Nicola is bold."

"Mom says it like it is. Women could learn from her."

"Tell her to be gentle," David said. His brow furrowed at the doodles on the paper. "Was Maggie helping you with your homework?"

"Someone has to."

"This is just like the last time and the time before that. You say you're going to apply yourself and all you focus on is football."

"We had a lovely weekend. I can smell the Mastrioni Magico bolognese simmering. I'll see he does it in the morning."

"He can do it now." David's brow creased as he flipped through the notebook. There were more drawings than notes. "What have you been doing all weekend? Wasting time at the pitch? Lying in front of the television?"

"Who cares how many wives Henry VIII had."

"You don't like French, Latin. You hated your maths class. Need I go on?"

"Do you know how embarrassing it was, yanking me from the U19 squad? All my friends got to hang out after training. I had to study."

Sparks sizzled like little sticks of dynamite, crackling and exploding.

"Imagine an educated football player. When you're too old to play and not everyone's hero, you'll have something to fall back on."

"I'm not bloody smart like you."

"Why don't I go make tea," Sofia said.

"You'd best get it done or…"

"Or what? You going to keep me from going to Dortmund, make me redo sixth form until I get the grades you'll be happy with."

"I'll be happy to see you go."

Sofia gasped. "Dio santo! What a thing to say."

"Aren't you tired of fighting with him? It's been a struggle since year one."

Brendon gripped his textbook. Every ounce of him thrummed with fire. Curse words danced on his tongue, ready to spit like bullets.

"I'll be in the den. The assignment will be bloody finished."

Brendon stormed from the great room, followed by Sofia's sigh and David's annoyed growl. He slammed his elbow on the light switch and tossed his books onto the desk. Flopping into the chair, Brendon imagined the sparks flying out of his fingers and toes. He took himself back to Friday, the soft curve of Rachel's belly, the swell of her breasts. He remembered Angelene curled into a tight ball, her breath warm against his ribs, her heartbeat in sync with his. Brendon jerked open the drawer and dug under file folders. He gripped a frame and stared at the picture.

"You fucking prick. Why'd you have to be so smart."

He whipped the photo back in the drawer and slammed it shut. A quote from *The Tempest* popped into his head. It was the only Shakespeare play he liked, 'Hell is empty, and all the devils are here.' They lived in Rosewood Manor.

Troy

Troy petted Lucy's feathers. The chicken clucked and settled onto his lap. He didn't know how long he had been sitting in the coop. The sun was setting, painting the horizon in shades of soft pink and gold. It had been hard not giving Brendon a punch for snogging Rachel, even harder keeping the secret from Charlotte. He felt like he was going to burst with all the stuff hidden inside him. It wasn't like he had done anything as bad as snogging another girl. The thoughts of Angelene were harmless. They just caught him off guard. Sure, he had snuck a peek now and then, but his thoughts always came back to Charlotte. Angelene had a way of lingering in his head. She gets stuck. He wasn't sure how. He thought Angelene had lovely eyes, but that was it. She was everything he didn't find attractive. He preferred brunettes, hated smokers, too skinny, too fragile. Yet something drew him to her. He was almost positive whatever those things were had a hold on his best mate.

Troy ran his hand over Lucy's feathers and stared across the pasture. Clouds gathered around the trees that separated Spence Farm from Walter Pratt's back garden. Their shadows grazed the barn and the person approaching him. His heart lurched, and he cursed, something he rarely did. Charlotte liked that about him. He was Switzerland, and he refused to drop an F-bomb.

"Bleeding heck, Lucy, it's Mrs. Pratt."

He focused his attention on the barn and the light inside. His dad was in the milking parlour with Brian sanitizing the equipment. Troy liked dealing with the chickens. He never enjoyed cleaning the udders before placing the milking machine on. He didn't enjoy farm life, but it was where he lived, and he had to do his part whether he liked it or not.

"Bonjour."

"Hey, Mrs. Pratt. Out walking again?"

Troy rolled his eyes at the stupid comment. He was tongue-tied and didn't know why. She stood at the gate, swathed in Walter's Royal Navy hoodie. The wind, which was picking up, had pulled strands of hair from her ponytail. She looked as chaotic as her eyes.

"Walter drove into town to get us a takeaway. We're having curry tonight."

"It looks like it might storm. You should probably head back."

"Do you believe in ghosts?"

It was a strange question to ask him, but something Troy expected to come from Angelene.

"One time I was at Rosewood Manor. Brendon and I were watching a footy match. Mrs. Cook was out. Amelia had gone home. I felt something cold rush over my skin, and I could smell biscuits and damp earth. I could have sworn someone was sitting next to me. The feeling lasted a few seconds, then it disappeared. It could have been a ghost. It might have been my imagination."

Angelene opened the gate and plunked onto a bale of hay. "There have been ghosts in Walter's house all weekend."

Troy set Lucy down. The chicken clucked around his feet, pecked at the ground, never moving too far from him.

"Charlotte says there's a ghost in my house. She said something was staring at her while she was having a shower. I told her it was probably Callum. He has a huge crush on her."

The tiniest smile lifted Angelene's lips. "I can see why he would. Charlotte is a beautiful girl. I envy her. The power that beauty can bring."

A little tug yanked Troy's heart. She was doing it again, whatever *it* was. How could she not see how pretty she was? Some boys in his geography class had commented on Walter Pratt's wife. They saw whatever Brendon did. Maybe he saw it too and was afraid to admit anyone other than Charlotte made his heart swoon. Troy plucked a feather from a patch of clover and passed it to Angelene.

"For your collection. Mom said you want feathers."

Angelene took the feather and placed it in her hoodie pouch. "I'm in love with your farm, the cows, and chickens. Look at that one. It hasn't left your feet."

"That's Lucy. I raised her." Troy petted the chicken. It clucked and cooed. "Don't get too close to her. She's very protective of me. Charlie gets a peck on the ankle whenever we're in here together and she gives me a cuddle."

Troy flicked at the pull on his sweatshirt. His gaze moved from Lucy to the light on in the barn to his house. He could see his mom in the sitting room crocheting. Callum curled up beside her reading.

"I'm making you nervous." Angelene tugged at a stem of traveller's joy and ran her finger over the feathery fronds. "Walter said I was giving off weird energy."

Troy zipped his sweatshirt up to his chin and turned to look at her. He couldn't read her face. He felt bad for her. Another quality Charlotte admired about him. His compassion and empathy for others. She would be okay if he held Angelene's hand for a moment.

Troy scooted across the hay bale and hooked his pinky around hers. Angelene glanced from their entwined fingers to his face. Her eyes were the saddest green.

"You *do* make me nervous, Mrs. Pratt. Only because I can't stop thinking about you after we talk."

"Charlotte knows you love her."

"I tell Charlie everything. I can't seem to bring myself to tell her about you or the things that come into my head when I think about you." Troy wound his pinky tighter around hers. "Can I tell you something? I promised I wouldn't say anything. It's eating me up, keeping it inside."

"I understand what that feels like. I'm not one to share the mess in my head."

"Brendon snogged another girl, and not just any girl, the randiest girl in Taunton. Rachel Jones. He has a love bite on his collarbone."

He let out a long sigh and thought he saw something flicker in Angelene's eyes: jealousy, sadness? It was hard to determine which had rattled her.

"Not a nice thing to do to Maggie."

"She'd be gutted if she found out and I knew." Troy unhooked his pinky and stretched out his legs. Lucy strutted and pecked around his ankles. "Something is up with my mate. He hasn't been the same since coming home from Dortmund."

"He needs to stay away from that girl. She'll steal his light."

Troy didn't know whether Angelene meant Rachel or herself.

A ping rose from Angelene's pocket. She laid the traveller's joy over her lap and pulled out her phone. "Walter wants to know if I want mustaki or morba."

"Get the morba. It's a favourite of mine."

Angelene tapped in the reply and slid her phone into her pocket. "I should go. I didn't mean to trouble you."

Troy watched her walk away. He summoned Charlotte into his head and opened the door to the coop.

"Lucy, time to go in."

Lucy led the flock into the coop. Troy followed behind and scooted some stray feathers from the roosting bar. He tidied the nesting boxes and topped up the bedding with chopped straw. He gave Lucy a final pet for a job well done and closed the door. The wind whipped up sand and hay. Troy rubbed the chill from his arms. Angelene was with him. In the wind, her touch, she was there.

"Hey, numpty, Charlie is on the phone." Callum leaned out the door, the phone in his hand. "She tried your cell."

Troy sprinted across the lawn and grabbed the phone from Callum.

"Am I glad you called... you have no idea how much I missed you... can I stop by after dinner? I need to see you."

Angelene

A heavy ache lingered in Angelene's chest. She had slipped into her old pattern, seduced by the light. It could have been Brendon's devil playing tricks on her. She knew Padre Diavolo well, and he was dangerous to Brendon's light. Angelene tucked the feather into a book and stared beyond the trees. The memory was vivid.

Mademoiselle Hummel, what are you doing in here?

I'm looking for Professor Piedmont. I need to talk to him.

Pierre won't be in for a while.

Has something happened?

Pierre mentioned you had stolen the light. He kept repeating it. Please stay away.

Angelene shuddered. The walls creaked. A howl swept over the blackened moors.

Where have you been, little bird?

I was washing Monsieur Douchette's feet. Mother wanted quiet.

My coat is on the chair, little bird. There is a gift in every pocket. I need to speak to your mother. Veronique, what are you doing sending that precious girl to him? You must protect her.

I'm late with rent. He said he would wait if she anointed his feet like Mary Magdalene did Jesus. It's an act of kindness.

That man is not Jesus. You can't trust him around her. I will pay your rent if it means Angelene is safe.

She stared at the glow in Brendon's window and dug her fingers into her forearm.

I have a gift for you, petite oiseau. Mother and I visited the lavender fields in Valensole. You should have seen it, purple as far as the eye could see. Your hair will smell as beautiful as the fields.

What did your mother say?

I told her it was for a girl at school.

That was a lie.

Not entirely. You're a girl, my girl. This will help you find your light.

"Dinner is ready."

The sound of Walter's voice jolted her from her memories.

Walter cupped her chin and stared into her eyes. "Lost in thought."

"I'm thinking happy thoughts to keep the ghosts away."

She rubbed at the indentations and jumped from the nightstand. Walter smiled his crinkly smile and sat on the bed. He took hold of her wrist and gently tugged her beside him.

"There are no ghosts in the house, just memories."

"There was knocking on the walls, taps from the attic."

"Old houses make noises."

Angelene hung her head and fiddled with her bangles. "You thought I was drunk."

"Weren't you?"

"I was tipsy. I couldn't sleep. The sounds were coming from every corner."

Walter wound his arm around her and kissed her forehead. "I know you were scared. I should have listened and consoled you."

"I'm trying not to run to alcohol. It's a terrible habit. I have so many to get rid of. Please be patient."

"I have something for you."

An image of her curled beside Brendon slashed through her mind, striking her, electrifying the ache in her chest. "I don't deserve presents."

Walter reached into his pocket and held up a chain, at the end, a simple cross. There were no diamonds, no flash, just a plain thread of gold.

Angelene touched her mouth. Tears blurred her eyes.

"I know how important the church is to you."

She gazed from the cross to his soft blue eyes and flung her arms around his neck. "I had to pawn mine. It was my favourite gift from Roman."

"Louboutin and Chanel don't seem to impress you. I thought this might make you happy," Walter said. "You're always touching your neck, searching for the necklace."

Angelene lifted her hair; Walter clasped the chain. She glanced down at the shimmering cross.

"I feel like a piece of me has returned."

"I'll keep trying until we find all the pieces, little bird."

Angelene clasped her hand around the cross. A sting, icy and sharp, pierced her heart. *'Please God, keep me away from his light. Something strange happens when I'm around Brendon. I don't understand it. It frightens me.'*

22 La DouleurExquise

Brendon

According to Edward Weiss, Taunton's most trusted doctor, there were four stages to anger: annoyed, frustrated, infuriated, and hostile. By age seven, Brendon had learned at when he needed to put out the fire. At various times over the weekend, he had been at one stage or another. The conversation between Sofia and Amelia had him intrigued, sweating, and on the verge of blowing.

"Does Maggie still wear that sweet perfume?"

"She smells like a bakery. Every time she visits, I get a craving for a faery cake."

Brendon stiffened and pressed his back against the wall.

"Margaret hasn't started smoking, has she?"

"She's a saint. What's with all the questions?"

"I was gathering the sheets on Sunday to get a head start on my Monday list. I have a system. A certain colour each week."

"And."

"They were the wrong colour."

Brendon cursed. Amelia Potter was the only person he knew who found joy in being excessively regimented.

"All this fidgeting because of the wrong colour sheets."

Brendon loosened his tie, skipped frustration, and slid into infuriated.

"I know that smell. My sister thought it masked the pot she smoked, patchouli oil."

Sparks flashed in Brendon's vision, and he stormed into the kitchen. Sofia looked at him with curious eyes.

"Did Maggie spend the night?"

"I said patchouli, not vanilla."

"What the bloody hell are you accusing me of, Ame?"

He shoved bread into the toaster, undid a button, and jerked his collar open.

Sofia set down her mug a little too hard and stared at Brendon. "I asked you a question. Turn around and look at me."

'*Get a fucking grip.*'

"It was Charlie."

"Go on."

"There was a party in the forest, close to the rugby club. I'm not allowed in the forest, any forest, so I stayed home. I wouldn't want to break the rules."

Heat crawled up his chest and stained his cheeks. He breathed, released the breath, surprised he wasn't spewing fire.

"Charlotte doesn't smoke," Amelia said, flapping her apron ties.

Brendon slammed his fists against the island. "Stay out of this. You've already said enough."

"Brendon David, control that temper."

"This is fucking daft. Charlie got drunk. Troy had a few and didn't think he should be driving. We carried Charlie to my bed and let her sleep while we watched the telly."

The toaster popped. Brendon ripped the toast from the slots and whacked a layer of jam across it.

"It's an odd perfume choice, don't you think?"

He wrapped it in a paper towel and stared at Sofia. "Charlie is always changing her perfume. I can't fucking believe you're asking me these bloody questions."

"Stop swearing."

"I fucking won't. I'm mad."

Sofia glanced at Amelia, then back to Brendon. "Why didn't you tell us Sunday night?"

"Dad wouldn't shut up about my homework. I've been angry since then. I'm almost at the hostile stage. I might lose all my fucking strikes today."

"You know the rules. No one in the house."

"Next time I'll let your little meatball drive bladdered. Sound good?"

"You're impossible this morning."

"You better hope the sparks go out before I get to school. Bloody unbelievable."

Amelia twisted her apron straps around her hand and lowered her chin. "I'm sorry, Brendon. I didn't mean to make you mad. I just thought Sofia should know."

"Your loyalty is bloody commendable. I need to go before I'm late and Ms. Hudson makes me sit in the hallway."

"I suppose I shouldn't ask for a kiss," Sofia said.

"You've got to be bloody kidding."

Brendon stormed from the kitchen, snatched his backpack off the floor, and prayed the sparks fizzled out before he got to school.

The sparks stuck with Brendon all morning and continued to simmer in his belly. He had sent Angelene two texts and no reply. The buzzy noise in the garam masala-scented dining hall dove into his ears. He checked his phone. Still no reply. They had spoken briefly before he fell asleep. She couldn't say enough about Walter. He had bought her a necklace—a cross. He was a saviour, and even though she hadn't said she loved Walter; Brendon could hear a strong 'like' in her voice.

"If my mom asks, Charlie got pissed and slept it off in my bed."

"Why would Charlie sleep at yours when I live five minutes away?"

"You were bladdered too."

Troy laughed into his soda. "Did she find out about the party?"

Brendon swallowed a mouthful of salad and shook his head. "Amelia changed my sheets. They smelled like perfume."

"So why did you say it was Charlie? Do you fancy my girl?"

"I couldn't say it was Maggie. Mrs. Thornton would never let her stay over, and if Mom visited the salon and said something, it would create a bigger mess. Mrs. Donovan and Mom have never liked each another. It was the safer bet."

"Where did this party happen?"

"In the forest, beside the rugby pitch."

Troy gobbled some tikka masala. His eyes twinkled playfully. "The forest? That's a daft place for a party."

"If I said it was at yours or one of the guys from the team, she'd find out. Mom knows bloody everybody."

Brendon pressed on the ache in his stomach.

"You got the collywobbles?"

He dropped his fork into the salad. A splatter of thyme-smelling dressing dotted the tablecloth. He stared at his cell, still no text.

"My stomach is in knots."

"It's pre-match jitters."

"Can you watch my stuff? I've got to go to the loo."

"You going to honk?"

"I'm going for a wee, bloody hell."

Brendon clutched his phone, lumbered past the tables, and burst through the doors. He glanced up and down the hall and tucked himself beside a trophy case. He needed her voice. He had one class to get through before the match. Dragons in the belly were one thing. Sparks could get him a yellow card or worse, a red. Brendon tapped his foot and cursed each ring.

"Are you ignoring me... I don't care about bloody Walter or the beautiful gift he gave you, Amelia told mom my sheets smelled like patchouli... you're fucking right it's bad... I can't, I have to go to history, I was late everyday last week... Calm bloody down, I told mom it was Charlie... I can't come right now, I've been a prick all morning, Dawson's waiting for me to fuck up... I said no, I'll come after the match... I don't care if you need me now, where the fuck have you been? I've been texting all morning."

Brendon burst through the door, his pulse crackling with the rhythm of the sparks. Whispers of bets buzzed around him. 50p he would toss a chair; two pounds he would scream the F-word. He weaved around the tables, kicked a chair out of his way, and plunked down at the table. Choking back a bite of chicken, he swallowed it with a gulp of water. Anger stirred within him. He had been there for her, kept the monsters away, listened when she told him Walter had given her a cross. He had been there when Walter hadn't. He was there to help rewrite her story.

"What's the matter?"

"Nothing." His voice was cold and sharp.

"Don't be an arse. I'm just asking."

Brendon impaled a pile of lettuce and shoved it into his mouth. "Mom called when I was in the loo and started in about Charlie sleeping in my bed."

"You shouldn't feel guilty about something that didn't happen."

"You think someone will tell Maggie about Rachel?"

Troy shoved his plate away and grinned. "Feeling guilty? Just tell Maggie, she'll cry, you arse-lick. She'll forgive you. She loves you."

Brendon poked his fork into a piece of chicken and pushed it through a puddle of dressing. Angelene made him believe he was important by inviting him into her world. He was stuck in her messy life, drowning.

"You have two choices. Come clean or break up with Maggie and hump the tart."

"She promised to come to Dortmund. She promised we'd walk in Westfalenpark."

"Are you talking about Rachel? She'd say anything to knock you off her list. Now finish that veg, you need fuel for the match."

"She's never had a boyfriend or danced with a boy before."

The weekend and all its tender moments swarmed Brendon's brain. Angelene wanted him, not Walter.

"What do you care about Rachel? You fancy her?"

"I thought I did."

Brendon texted an apology and stared at the screen. No reply.

"Let's walk before you explode."

Students snickered and whispered. Someone rejoiced in their winnings. The bet: Troy would save the day. Brendon wiggled his tie and unbuttoned the top button. He needed her, and she was too busy. She needed him, but the time wasn't right. His thoughts were messy, like her.

Scattered wisps of clouds scudded across a vivid blue sky. It was the kind of day that begged for footy matches and walks in the park. Groups of students gathered under the beech trees, sat on the steps of Evans Hall. A couple had parked under the famous willow tree. Some students loitered around the privet hedges to see what Brendon Cook would do. Explode, curse, run away.

"Are you practicing your breaths?" Troy said.

"I've been trying to breathe since the weekend."

"Let the explosion happen. We could go to the car park; you can let it all out."

"Niall Jacobson and Emily Howard are humping in his Honda. No thanks."

"It isn't good to keep it in either. It'll fester, mate, and you'll bring it to the pitch."

A string of curse words spewed from his mouth. Brendon jerked his shirt tails loose and rubbed them over his sweating chest.

"That was impressive. A dick fuck prick, bloody doing as you're told c-word. I promised Charlie I would never say that word. You feel better?"

Brendon glanced at his phone. Still no reply.

"You want to do sprints? A few quick ones to burn the sparks away."

"I'm sweaty enough."

"I'm trying, mate. Breathe down the hall and think about being between the sticks."

"Breathe, got it."

"Promise me and think happy things."

All his happy thoughts had been stolen by the girl who hated the title of wife and now suddenly loved it.

"I'll think about a brilliant save the Dortmund keeper made."

"No jubblies?"

"That only reminds me of the daft thing I did."

"What's more than a handful feel like?"

"I thought they would be squishy like a marshmallow. They were firmer than I thought."

"You're becoming a man." Troy slapped his shoulder and turned to leave. "Tuck your shirt in."

Brendon burst through the door. The musty smell emanating from the heat vents choked him. He glanced at his phone. One message. Brendon hastily tucked in his shirt, looked around, and growled. Maggie wanted to know where he was.

"Just in time, take your seat," Mr. Clark said in a tone that was both surprised and irritated.

Sparks buzzed through his limbs. He kept his lamp on so she'd know she was safe. He had done everything for her, and now she ignored him.

Maggie reached across the aisle and touched his arm. He jerked it away and dropped his forehead against his palm.

'She put me through hell. On purpose. Sucked me into her poor-me bullshit. You're married. I know this. Maybe I'm the idiot.'

"Your final assignment is on what you feel was Henry's greatest accomplishment. No papers on how he could pull a woman. It's been done. That student failed."

Brendon tapped his pen on the desk. The sparks were out of control. He had held Angelene's hand, listened to her sad stories, stuck up for her when Walter hadn't.

"Asleep, Mr. Cook?"

Whispers of 'here we go' and 'ten quid Cook's going to blow' filled Brendon's ears.

"Do you know what we're discussing?"

"Henry VIII."

"You have no hero status in my class. Answer the question on the board."

Brendon gripped a handful of hair. "Have you heard about the stages of anger? I'm about to reach the fourth one. Please let me bloody breathe."

"Answer the question." Mr. Clark poked a stubby finger against Brendon's text and barked, "You aren't on the correct page."

The stench of coffee breath assaulted Brendon's nose. Salad tossed about his stomach. He begged Madre Innocente to come out of hiding, shower him with calm and good judgement. Padre Diavolo cackled, *'Stick your pen in his eye.'*

"Every teacher at Taunton College knows what your punishment will be if your grades slip. One call is all it would take."

Brendon dropped his pen, clutched the corners of the desk. The room clouded. "Are you threatening me?"

The veins in Mr. Clark's neck throbbed. Silence swept through the classroom. "Answer question one. We spent Friday discussing it."

"If you weren't so bloody boring, I might have paid attention."

"Pardon me?"

Brendon lifted the desk and clunked it against the floor. "If you weren't so fucking boring, I might have listened."

"Get out!"

"Turn to page 355, Brendon, the answer is there," Maggie pleaded.

"Out, Mr. Cook." Spit showered Brendon's sleeve. "All my years of teaching, I have never met an idiot quite like you."

Brendon rose and knocked the chair to the floor.

"Pick that up."

"Fuck off."

"Mr. Dawson will be notified about your behaviour."

"Tell him. I don't care."

Brendon stormed past Mr. Clark, swung the door open, it banged against the wall, and rattled the map above the blackboard. He marched to his car, whipped his backpack in the rear seat, and crumpled behind the steering wheel. The game of being there for one another weighed heavily on him.

"Guten Tag."

"Shouldn't you be in class?"

"I told my teacher I had unbearable cramps and needed to go home."

"I have some paracetamol in my rucky."

Rachel laughed. "I told a porkie, knuddelbär. It's an easy excuse when I want to skive off school."

"Would you like to sit?"

Rachel skipped around the BMW, jerked open the door, and slid onto the seat. "Why are you sitting in the car park?"

"I got kicked out of history."

"Oh, knuddelbär, that's so dishy."

"I've never seen Mr. Clark so mad."

Brendon stared at his palm and traced along his lifeline. Angelene saw strength. He didn't feel strong. Padre Diavolo and his orchestra of sparks had beaten him down.

"I need to relax so I can play my best today."

"You want to come to mine?"

"I've got to find Dawson and apologize. You have no idea what could happen if I don't make this right."

Rachel leaned across the console and wrapped her hands around his arm. "I'll make you a cuppa. You can watch some highlights."

"The bus leaves at 3:30. I have to change into my suit, or Liam will fine me 5 quid."

"You can change at mine." Rachel shook out a cigarette, lit it, it bobbed up and down as she spoke. "You're really tense. Not good when you have a footy game to play."

Padre Diavolo stopped lighting the sparks and snickered. '*Fuck school. Fuck your father and his expectations. Fuck little bird, let her break her own patterns.*'

Brendon started the engine. The collage of Victorian buildings faded in the distance.

"Want a drag, knuddelbär."

"No, thanks."

"You're such a good boy."

Cursing, lying to his mother, kissing Uncle Walt's wife, fantasizing about Rachel. There wasn't an ounce of decent behaviour left.

Rachel flicked the cigarette out the window. She pulled out a piece of gum and tossed it in her mouth. "Would you rather have a proper drink? Mom's friend visited from Berlin, there's lager in the fridge. Turn left, second house."

Brendon turned onto a cul-de-sac lined with brown, rectangular boxes. The street was quiet. It was a newer subdivision with cookie-cutter houses, beautifully landscaped gardens—quiet and leafy.

Each house faced the tree-adorned street with the same white-framed windows and brick-edged gardens. The only difference between Rachel's home and the others was the pots of cyclamen and pansies blooming outside the front door.

"Tea or beer?"

Brendon parked the car and wrestled with the jitters in his belly. One drink before the match wouldn't hurt. He'd add it to the list of stupid things he had done today.

"Beer. One."

"Coming right up. Follow me."

'*Will power, Brendon. Ignore Padre Diavolo.*'

He rubbed his brow, sighed, and stepped into the floral-scented foyer. The white-tiled floors shone. The wood gleamed. Brendon's gaze drifted across the various shades of white from the entry to the sitting room. The only speck of colour was the rattan settee, the walnut coffee table, and the blue floral pillows. Everything from the armoire to the fireplace looked as if covered in snow. The house breathed silently around him.

"Shall we go to my room, knuddelbär?"

"Can't we sit in there and watch telly?"

"I have a telly in my room."

His nerves were tattered, jumping in every direction. Sparks zipped and fizzled.

"You're not doing anything wrong."

"Everything about this is wrong."

He followed her up the stairs. Matte white continued down the hall, into the bedrooms and bathroom.

"My bedroom, knuddelbär."

Brendon poked his head into the white, golden brown and smoky-blue room. He had expected a temptresses' lair with red walls, black satin sheets and handcuffs dangling from the bedpost. He got a neatly made bed in virginal white.

"It's warm in here."

He took off his blazer and laid it on an aquamarine fan-back chair.

"Sit. I'll grab the drinks."

Brendon smiled stiffly and plunked on the edge of the bed. He glanced at a photo of Rachel and Tilly, all smiles, dressed to impress. A piece of paper stuck out from beneath the frame. She had listed the prices of tickets to a Dortmund match and decorated the words in hearts. It would cost sixty-five pounds to fly to Dortmund.

I would fly home and take a train. We would walk hand in hand in Westfalenpark.

Brendon rolled his knuckles over his forehead, forcing her voice from his mind. She wouldn't sneak away from Walter to hold his hand. Walter was a prince now.

"One Helles for my knuddelbär."

Brendon took the glass and ran it over his inflamed cheeks.

"Here's to a win." Rachel raised her glass and clinked it against his. "Prost." She took a long sip then set her mug down. Hopping onto the bed, she sat behind him, and kneaded his shoulders.

"Does it feel good?"

The glass slipped in his sweating palm. She pressed her breasts into his neck and undid his tie. He could picture Angelene pacing, praying, clutching her cross, pleading for forgiveness. He should be with her discussing the patchouli-scented sheets.

"I should go. I'm in enough trouble."

He cursed Padre Diavolo for changing the angry sparks to tingly ones and sending a wave of heat to his groin. Rachel had undone his tie and the buttons on his shirt. Brendon chugged the beer and set the glass next to hers. His shirt floated to the floor.

Rachel climbed off the bed, faced him, and jerked her tie loose.

"I shouldn't be here."

Angelene's pretty words cluttered his brain. He pictured Maggie chewing her fingernails. Sparks of both kinds fluttered.

"Go on, knuddelbär, take my shirt off."

She guided his hand, her breasts sprung from their cage of cotton. Brendon touched the heart charm dangling from her belly button. He peeled away her shirt, his fingers tickled down her spine and stopped at the zipper.

"Undo it."

Yes, no, bombarded his head. Padre Diavolo switched on the pleasure sensors. He unhitched the clasp and tugged at the tiny pull. Rachel stood before him in a turquoise lace bra and panties.

"Your turn now."

Protect your light. She's no good. She'll serve your head on a platter.

Rachel climbed onto the bed and patted the space beside her. "Hurry, I'm cold."

"Cold? It's about a hundred degrees in here."

He slid his trousers off; her bra landed at his feet. Brendon counted twelve freckles between her collarbone and sternum. He crawled under the blankets, his face and body heated. Rachel's minty ale tasting mouth clamped on his. She had him trapped with her arms, legs, and lips.

"You can touch me," Rachel said.

Brendon glanced from her breasts to the turquoise triangle, both places looked inviting.

"Haven't you touched a fanny before?"

He placed his lips on hers and tucked his fingers under the elastic band. To hell with Angelene and Maggie, his devil wanted to play.

"Go slower, knuddelbär, like this."

She laid her hand over his and guided his fingers in slow circles. She gasped against his mouth and reached into his boxers. All the gossip that had floated around the dressing room was true. She knew how to please a boy, and she was pleasing him. Pleasant twitches surged through his body. He fought the sensation, struggling to hold on.

"Bloody hell, I'm sorry."

She grinned and kissed his nose. "Don't apologize, knuddelbär, it was bound to happen."

She reached over him. His lips parted as her nipple grazed his mouth. She wiped his belly, dropped the bundle in the bin, and nibbled his chin.

"I love the stubble."

"Mom hates it. Maggie complains it scratches."

"Don't use that name in my bedroom."

"Who is she? Voldemort."

Her fingers skated over his ribs and abdomen. He laughed. "Will you bloody stop."

"You're smiling. Your eyes were dark before. They're twinkling now." Rachel kissed his shoulder and the space below his ear. "I have a brilliant idea. Let's get starkers."

She lifted her bottom and wiggled out of her panties. Brendon fumbled with his boxers. He didn't want to be a gentleman or the 'I always do as I'm told' boy. He didn't want anything but this moment.

He opened his mouth, danced his tongue over hers, and slid his fingers between her thighs. A tip Troy had shared crept into his mind. Start with one finger, then two, and crook them like he was tickling the inside of her belly. Rachel moaned. He sank his fingers deeper, and she gripped his forearm.

"Am I hurting you?"

"Keep doing what you're doing, knuddelbär."

Brendon had no idea what he had done, but by the look on Rachel's face, Troy's trick had worked.

"Do you have a condom?"

"In the nightstand," Rachel said, through delighted gasps.

Brendon yanked open a drawer, pushed aside papers and books until he found a strip of foil packets. He stared at the square, his body quivered, and not in a 'I'm about to lose my virginity' way.

"Are you going to put it on?"

"I'm working up the nerve."

"You're so cute, knuddelbär, allow me."

He lay on top of her, his breath rapid. He couldn't remember whether Troy said to go slow or fast. All he knew was the feeling was amazing. Her breath was warm on his neck. It surprised him how tightly she held him.

"I'm afraid you'll think this is a mistake, knuddelbär."

He silenced her with a kiss. It was a mistake. A horrible, fantastic mistake.

Brendon savoured the incredible warmth between them, sighing heavily in her ear. Padre Diavolo applauded, and Madre Innocente struck his belly with her staff. He stared at his clothes heaped on the floor. A cold realization slapped him back to reality. He had screwed up again.

"That was brilliant."

"Can I use the loo? I need to change into my suit. The bus will be leaving soon."

"Ignore my mom's beauty products. She's worried about getting old." Rachel gathered the blankets around her. The dreamy smile faded from her lips. "Can you pass me my ciggies?"

Brendon tossed the package onto the bed.

"You feel like an arse, don't you?"

He gathered his school kit. His heart dropped to the pit of his stomach, crushing the sweet memories.

"You'll keep this a secret?"

"I'll take it to my grave."

"I mean it, Rachel. No one can know about this. Maybe place a star beside my name instead of crossing it off."

He clutched his clothes; his mind wandered. Did he kiss her? Should he thank her for an enjoyable time?

"I can't be late for the bus. Liam fines us."

"I get it, you're taken." Rachel blew out a mouthful of smoke and rested her head against the pillows. "Can I ask you something?"

He was getting impatient. The room felt hotter. He needed to run and fast before he fell back into her bed.

"Where did you learn to do that? For a boy who's never touched a fanny, bleeding heck, knuddelbär, that was a brilliant tingle."

"Troy. If I could ever get my hand down Maggie's knickers, I needed to know what to do."

"Know any other tricks?"

"I'm going to miss the bus. My bloody suit is in the car."

Rachel dropped her cigarette into the glass and pointed to a kimono. "Pass me my dressing gown."

Brendon lowered his gaze and handed her a cherry blossom print robe.

"Go to the loo. She who shall not be named will never find out."

Her body disappeared under the silky fabric. She ran her hand over his bottom.

"Bloody hell, don't you ever quit."

"You have a brilliant bum, knuddelbär."

Brendon touched his cross. *'Thanks for fighting off Padre Diavolo. You're never here when people need you.'* He walked down the hall and snapped on the bathroom light. A floral scent clung to the seashell-print shower curtain and Roman blinds. Different sized wicker baskets stuffed full of serums and lotions sat on the countertop. Brendon dropped his school uniform to the floor, turned on the tap, pumped some fruity-smelling soap onto his hands and washed Rachel's scent away.

"You decent?"

"You've already seen me naked."

Rachel opened the door and held up the garment bag. She wore a smile Brendon didn't expect. She was supposed to be a 'I got what I want, now leave' girl, not grinning at him like she was love struck.

"Is that an Armani suit?"

"Mom thinks Italians make the best clothes."

"Impressive. I'm making a cuppa. You want one?"

"I've got to get a move on... should we kiss goodbye?"

"It's never goodbye, knuddelbär and no, you don't have to."

Brendon hung the garment bag from the towel rack and slumped against the counter. Madre Innocente wrapped him in an itchy cloak of regret. A heavy breath emptied from his lungs. He couldn't change what he had done, just shove it aside with all the other bad decisions and try to forget it happened.

Brendon unzipped the bag, trousers, shirt, tie; he looked the part of a respectable footy player. He took one last look in the mirror, grinned an 'you're-a-bloody-dolt' grin and shoved his school kit in the bag. He walked down the stairs. The kettle whistled. Brendon opened the door. Heavy clouds washed the sky in grey.

"I'm leaving."

"Bist bald, knuddelbär. Viel gluck, mein Freund."

Brendon sprinted to his car. He had ten minutes to get to the pitch. His head was full of regret, his stomach in knots. He needed someone. He needed Angelene. Brendon kept his eyes on the road and tapped his phone.

"Pick up, please pick up."

The phone rang and rang. Brendon parked the car and tried again. Sparks flickered. It went unanswered. He inhaled, long and slow, plastered a grin on his face and tried to stir up the dragons. Brendon stared from one teammate to another; their faces were sullen.

"Why does everyone look so bloody miserable?"

Troy kicked a stone and looked at him with an 'as-if-you-don't-know' smirk.

The bus shook. Liam slammed down the stairs. His clipboard flew towards Brendon's head. "You spoiled eejit."

"What the bloody hell have I done?"

Liam charged towards him, finger pointed, nostrils flared. Brendon batted Liam's finger away and took a step back. He had seen Liam angry, but not where his face was crimson and the veins in his neck were ready to burst.

"Why are you acting like a bloody nutter?"

"You're benched. The headmaster called your mamm. What were you thinking bunking off school?"

"Let me call my mom."

"You think your charm will work on her? There's no reasoning with that woman."

Brendon glanced at William. "We'll lose."

"You should have thought about that before you made a holy show of yourself."

"Mr. I'm so tough, I should have been a rugby player." Brendon cracked his knuckles and stepped closer. Sparks exploded like grenades. "You're going to listen to my mother?"

"Do you know how much influence she has? Do you have any bleeding idea how much money she's dumped into the team?"

"You knew about the daft rule, didn't you?"

"Your father and I had a pint, and he mentioned it. He said you made a right bag of things in Dortmund. I'm not going to argue with our Lord Chancellor."

"My parents have you by the goolies."

Liam grabbed Brendon's lapels and shoved him into the bus. "You show up here in your posh suit, stinking of ale and perfume, expecting to play when your mamm warned you. I want fifty quid."

"For what?"

"For missing the team meeting." His Irish lilt got thicker as he spoke. "For drinking before the match. For disrespecting your coach and breaking the rules. Do you want me to go on?"

"You have no idea what my day has been like. Sparks all day."

"You should have practiced your breaths. Now get your bleeding arse on the bus and keep your gob shut. You better be in top form, McGregor."

Brendon brushed off his suit jacket and ripped his backpack from the ground. He stomped aboard the bus, jammed his knapsack on the overhead rack, and dropped onto the seat. Sparks burned and swirled.

"Talk to me, mate?"

"Liam said to keep my mouth shut."

Brendon scrolled through the music on his phone; the sparks dimmed, he could finally breathe.

"Your mom could have you benched for the entire season. You should have found Dawson and begged for mercy."

"She's teaching me a lesson, avoiding aggro from my dad. She'll feel bad. She always does."

"Where did you go?"

"For a drive."

Troy leaned in and sniffed his neck. "With who?"

Brendon flicked Troy's nose and gazed at his phone. She hadn't returned his call or sent a text.

"Myself, that's who."

Troy's face twisted. "You reek of Rachel's perfume and spunk. You also have a daft look on your face, like you did something bad."

Brendon turned away from Troy. How does someone smell like sex? He had washed his hands, rinsed his mouth with mouthwash he found stuffed in a basket of potions and lotions. He leaned his head against the seat and stared at the steel rack.

"Charlie said Rachel complained about girly cramps and left psych. You better not have spent the afternoon humping."

"I wasn't humping Rachel."

"I swear if you hurt Maggie."

"I haven't done anything. You always have sex on the brain."

"Why would you pick this day to tell Mr. Clark where to go? Weston is two points behind, now Will's in net. Bollocks."

Brendon couldn't agree more. The entire day had been bollocks.

Sofia

Sofia walked into Johnstone, Harrnsworth, and Miller law offices. She smiled warmly and nodded towards Kate's office. The secretary pulled down her glasses and returned the smile.

"Go in, Mrs. Cook."

Kate's corner office was bright and welcoming. An arched window overlooked the garden, filling it with natural light. Kate's desk, an ornate, gargantuan structure, sat squarely in the middle of an area rug. A notebook, Toby mug filled with her pens and pencils, three framed photos, one of Sofia and Kate sipping espresso on a piazza, Brendon signing the contract with Dortmund and her and Walter at last year's gala, decorated the expansive desk. The built-in bookcases housed a variety of law books and journals. Two floral barrel chairs. It was more home than office.

"Sorry I didn't call." Sofia set a cup of cappuccino on the desk and dropped into a chair. "I hope you aren't busy."

Kate glanced up from her notebook. "I'm trying to figure out how I can help a client keep her home and children. You're just the break I need."

"She's a mother. Wouldn't it make sense she gets the home to raise her children?"

"Not when you're having an affair."

"I need your help."

Kate removed the plastic lid and blew on the milky foam. "It's just like you to get right to it."

"Do you still have that friend? The private investigator?"

Kate's brow wrinkled. "Hugh? I wouldn't call him a friend, more of a colleague."

"If I ask you to do something, promise not to tell David."

Kate took a small sip and shook her head. "I know what this is about, and the answer is no."

"Money isn't an issue."

"I thought you were over worrying about Angelene?"

The cup crinkled in Sofia's hand. "How do you know it isn't about Lukas or a new groundskeeper?"

"No one knows roses like Peter, and you already asked about Lukas," Kate said, her smile wavered. "There's only one person causing you to worry. She's five feet tall and blonde."

"I need to know about her family." Sofia squeezed the cup tighter. She shoved her pinky between her bangles and flicked. A few beats passed before she spoke. "The professor she worked with."

"Why? Angelene doesn't like to talk about her past. You should respect that."

"Do it for Walter."

Kate wheeled back the studded Edwardian chair. She walked around the desk, perched on the corner, and folded her silk-clad arms over her chest. "What else is troubling you? You're fiddling with your bracelets."

When Sofia became a mother, she took on the challenge like she did everything: headstrong and confident. Over the years, she found motherhood changed her; she worried, she got scared. She loved fiercely, found it hard to let go.

"It's Brendon."

The smile returned to Kate's face. Not mockingly, more like an 'I-hear-you-but-worrying-has-made-you-crazy' grin. "Angelene is not out to harm Brendon."

"The picture she drew from memory, at the restaurant in Burnham, she kept glancing at him over her cocktail. All five of them."

"He's an attractive kid, and not just his handsome face. He's worth a fortune."

"Angelene looks at him differently."

Kate rose, unclenched Sofia's fingers from the cup, and tossed it into the garbage bin. "We need to leave her alone."

"Amelia thought she smelled Angelene's perfume on Brendon's sheets. He said it was Charlotte. When Amelia gets a hunch, it's usually right. Her stomach was in knots the day I had to run into the forest."

"Why would Brendon have Angelene in his bed? Is Amelia suggesting they're having an affair?"

Fear settled into Sofia's chest. As far back as she could remember, women had always flirted with Brendon. This was more than flirting. There was a longing in Angelene's eyes, like she wanted to crawl inside him, cling to his heart and lungs.

"Simone made that ridiculous comment; she'd love to get Brendon between the sheets."

"She was on her fifth margarita." Kate left her perch and sat beside Sofia. "Have you spoken to Dr. Weiss, walked in the forest like he suggested? It might put an end to all the fear you carry around."

"David and I are dealing with it. We have been for years."

"When Brendon went to Dortmund in August, you redecorated a bedroom. When he was there last spring, you dug out all his baby pictures and started scrapbooking," Kate said. "What do you do when he leaves the house?"

"Hold my breath," Sofia said softly.

"Once he's home, you release it."

"You're not a mother. You don't know what it's like to have a child."

"You're right, I don't. But I know how it feels to love someone so much, you feel your heart break every time they walk away."

A Royal Dalton vase caught Sofia's eye. A hollow, achy feeling stuck between her ribs. "I still have the pieces of the Royal Dalton figurine Brendon broke. I remember the look on his face when he handed me the five pounds he got for his birthday. He made me a pasta necklace, painted each noodle red to match my lipstick. The string snapped, but I kept every damn macaroni."

"This bedsheet nonsense has you worried."

Sofia shivered and clutched Kate's hand. "Have you ever looked into Angelene's eyes?"

"They're sad and green."

"Some background information, please."

A whispery wind rustled the leaves and pushed the clouds through a sooty sky. Goldfinches chirped and fluffed their yellow feathers in a concrete birdbath.

'Maybe Angelene envies Brendon's wings. She's looking to repair hers and only wants to steal a feather or two.'

Kate reached for her cappuccino, took a sip, and crossed her legs. "Why do I have a sense there's more?"

"I feel terrible. I promised David."

"What did you do?"

"Mr. Dawson called. Brendon told his teacher to fuck off."

"Is that all?"

"Isn't that enough?" Sofia said. "He was supposed to see Julian. He left. This is not the first time either. He's been buying Boots out of paracetamol."

"I'm surprised he goes at all."

"David is so upset."

Sofia tapped her fingernails against her purse. She had never been a punisher. She reacted, then softened.

"I called Liam and had him benched."

Kate finished her cappuccino and tossed the cup into the garbage. "Way to hit below the belt."

"David and I told him if he didn't take his studies seriously, no football." Sofia watched the birds fly into the trees. She flicked her bracelets, *click, click, click.* "I'm sure it's to see her. They always find one another."

"Who?"

"Angelene." Sofia looked at Kate, doubt in her eyes. "The mysterious intruder, Walter's party. The damn sheets."

"Brendon was probably at the pitch or driving around trying to cool off."

"The whole time I was talking to David, I could hear Walter laughing."

Kate placed her hand over Sofia's. Her tone was gentle and understanding. "Walter thinks you're overprotective."

"Walter can go to hell," Sofia snapped. "If he hadn't called Lukas, I wouldn't be losing my son."

"Someone would have discovered Brendon."

Sofia had never forgotten the championship game. A group of scouts had swarmed Brendon. He knew all the moves. He could read the play as if stepping into the minds of the other players. His confidence was outstanding and all at the age of seven. She had protected him from their sales pitch. They were there to steal her son. Angelene was no different from those men.

"I wouldn't ask if I didn't think it was important. Ask Hugh."

"I'll take you for curry. That place on High Street is getting brilliant reviews," Kate said. "We'll have a G&T, sort through your worries, then you can decide if you want me to ring Hugh."

Sofia pulled her wrap tighter around her shoulders. "Did I make the right decision? The only thing Brendon looks forward to is football."

"If it saves you arguing with David, then yes. Brendon will get over it like he always does with a few curse words and some brooding."

Sofia wasn't so sure.

Angelene

Night came with chaotic splatters of rain, charcoal smudged skies, and frantic winds. Angelene enjoyed a night when God was furiously screaming at the world, not tonight. He was angry with her. She was tired. Tired of pacing, tired of waiting for God's forgiveness. She started the day yellow, said goodbye to the chocolate brown walls and hello to a hallway the colour of a chick's feathers. When Brendon called about the scented sheets, the yellow drained away and she was sickly grey. Cigarettes had not helped the tearing of her insides. Wine helped for a minute, then the tornado of emotions would reappear. She needed Brendon. He did not come.

A knock echoed through the house. Angelene plucked a bent cigarette from within a mound of ashes and squeezed her eyes closed.

'I knew you would come. I don't need you now.'

She broke the cigarette in two and tugged at her braid. "Go away."

The knock grew louder—spirited, forceful. Angelene walked to the foyer and stared at the door. She brought her cross to her lips and kissed it.

"I want you to go away."

"Open the door. I need to talk to you."

"God is furious with me. Can't you tell by the rain and wind?"

"You promised to be there for me. Open the fucking door."

Brendon burst into the foyer. She stumbled from the force and pinched the cross between her fingers. His energy was static and electric.

"Go sit by the fire. I'll bring you a towel." She crushed her cross into her palm and marched to the laundry room. "You weren't there for me either."

Angelene whipped the towel at him and plunked onto the ottoman. "All day I paced trying to think of something I could tell Sofia. You should have come."

"I had one class and then I had to catch the bus for the match. I couldn't drop everything and run to you, not today. It looks like you've been dealing with the problem."

She followed his gaze to a bottle of wine and ashtray full of butts. "What was I to do?"

"Call Walter. He bought you the necklace. He's bloody wonderful now. You could have invented a story and made him feel sorry for you. You're good at that."

"Padre Diavolo is extraordinarily powerful right now. Your eyes are so dark."

"The little fucker has been pestering me all day."

Brendon's black mood seeped into Angelene's skin. It tasted like soot. His thoughts jumped from his mind and stabbed into hers.

"Did you win?"

"Lost. 4-0."

"You let in four goals?"

"I couldn't play." His words slammed against her, black and sludgy.

"Are you hurt?"

Brendon ran the towel over his neck and balled it in his hands. "I told my history teacher to fuck off. The headmaster called Mammina, and he told her about the other classes I bunked off."

"You shouldn't have listened to Padre Diavolo."

"It wasn't bloody Satan, it was me. I've skived off school to help you. I've needed you all bloody day."

Staticky black surrounded him. Slashes of red, like fiery lightning bolts, lit up his abdomen and groin. "What have you done to your light?"

Brendon shifted on the bricks, clenched and unclenched the towel. "I went to Rachel's house."

Angelene shook out a cigarette, lit it, and inhaled sharply. The tornado of emotions raged. This was not her boy in magnificent brown. It was his clothes, his citrusy smell and beautiful face, but it was not him.

"I had sex with Rachel."

Angelene choked on a mouthful of smoke. "You broke up with Maggie?"

"I cheated on her."

"I warned you to stay away. I told you to protect your light."

"If you had picked up the phone. If you had understood, I needed to go to class. If you were just there."

Angelene smashed the cigarette into an ashy plate. Swampy green and hot red invaded her sickly grey.

"Don't blame me. I needed you and you fucked that disgusting girl. You're dirty."

"I was pissed off, and she was there. Rachel was fucking there, not you," Brendon said, whipping the towel. "All that shit you said. Bloody hell, we kissed. You can say we were drunk, and it meant nothing. It meant something to me."

Angelene pressed her hands over her ears and squeezed her eyes shut. "Stop, please stop."

"You slept in my bed, held my hand; you don't hold Walter's." His voice was brittle and cold. It swept over her skin like a winter wind.

"No more, please. I can't listen to you."

"You used me."

"Ask God for forgiveness. Stay away from that girl and your light will be bright again."

"I have nothing to say to God. Mom has been asking him the same question for nineteen years and he still hasn't answered her. What makes me special?"

Angelene pushed herself off the ottoman and paced. Her gut twisted; the pieces of the pattern that had fallen away came together.

"I thought we could be friends. I've tried before; it ended horribly. I will not let it happen again."

"Stop fucking pacing. We're here for each other now." He rose and stepped in her path. "We can forget about the day and start over."

"I don't like you."

"Because I had sex? Everybody fucking humps. I'm still the same person."

His words were sludgy brown with shades of weepy blue.

"It's for the best we end this. I promised God I would be a better wife. Walter has been very patient. I'm starting to love..." The words broke off. She wasn't sure she loved Walter yet, but it seemed the right thing to say. A wife loves her husband. It was normal. Normal kind of fit.

"Give Walter time and he'll be that cocky prick ordering you around. He'll complain about the yellow walls, and you'll paint them blue or white to appease him. Who'll be there to say it's okay? Not me."

He barged past and slammed the door. Angelene dashed to the foyer, flung the locks in place, and ran up the stairs. She fell to the bedroom floor, yanked out the jewellery box, and spilled the contents. Grabbing a news article, she ran her finger over Brendon's face. She lay the article in the box and held up the Dortmund jersey.

"I can't be your friend. La douleur exquise, you want my affection, I can't give it."

She laid the jersey over her lap then looked at a sketch of the Pont des Arts. Her heart split.

"We held hands along the footbridge. You were going to build me a castle on the Ile de la Cite so I could have cake with Marie Antoinette's ghost."

She set the drawing inside and picked up a postcard of the Black Forest. Angelene flipped it over; she read the words, longed for them, breathed them into her wrenched lungs, 'tu me manques, little bird.' Angelene pressed her lips against it then put it back. The tornado inside her grew to a hurricane, blowing and smashing into her lungs and heart. She clamped her hands against her temples; voices screamed at her, biting into her flesh. She was no good, a cancer, infected by the devil.

Angelene scrambled to the bathroom and whipped open the medicine chest. She shoved aside bottles of aspirin, aftershave, and vitamins. She whacked the door closed, bolted from the bedroom, and raced down the stairs. The voices mocked violently. She thumped to a stop. The paring knife she had used to slice an apple sang to her from the cutting board. Angelene clutched it and sank to the floor. She folded down the waistband of her jeans and gazed at the blue vein pulsing through her tissue paper skin. She was slow, steady, her breath blew out as hard as the wind.

Roman, hurry, it's coming.

What is it, little bird?

A monster.

There are no monsters. I checked before you went to bed.

Mother said Satan takes little girls away when they're bad. She said she saw the devil in me.

You're wearing the cross I gave you. You said your prayers. God is protecting you.

Every time I close my eyes, I see him. He's a fat little man with stinking breath and hooves for feet.

Have we chased winter away with Ursli today?

Maman said you were all hers.

Snuggle next to me. We need to help Ursli find his cowbell.

What if I dream about the wicked man and you aren't here?

I'll always be with you, little bird.

Angelene stretched her shirt and dabbed at the bubbles of blood. "What do I do when I need someone? Who will help me when life gets tangled and I trip?"

She grabbed the edge of the kitchen island and dragged herself off the floor. An ache settled into her forehead. Exhaustion dripped like honey, slow and oozy, following her like a sticky puddle to her bedroom. She stopped at the foot of the bed and held her fingers to her mouth.

"Your lamp is on."

The pattern of run, hide, clutch, smother, wound around her. She pressed her palm against the tickle in her belly. Brendon had succumbed to fevered red. The loss swelled and choked her. La douleur exquise.

23 L'appelDu Vide

Brendon

What are you doing?

Playing footy, Granddad.

Call me Richard. I can't stand that you call me that. Don't you see the antiques? Can't you see the money I've invested in the foyer, and you play football. Your damn mother traipsed into my home and thought she could change everything. Then you came along after your father told her to wait. I wish you would go. To Milan, London. I don't care.

Daddy said this is Grandmother's house.

Your father was a spoiled little brat, just like you. Take your football outside.

Mommy has planted roses. I'll get into trouble if I go near them.

Go. Get out of my sight. Play in the bloody forest.

But I'm not allowed.

Go.

A book fell from Brendon's hand and landed on the floor with a thud. He opened his eyes and gazed around the room. He was in his bedroom. Richard wasn't towering over him, screaming. He was alone. A replay of the Dortmund, Leverkusen match was on the television. His homework spread out on his bed. The sparks crackled around his body, and if he were to attach a colour to his words, it would be blue. He had always liked the colour. He hated it now. All his poor decisions assaulted him, coated in shades of blue. He had kissed Walter's wife. He cheated on

Maggie with the girl no boy fancied. He bunked off school, and for what? A woman he couldn't have, a whim, hope. He was no better than his grandfather Richard. A cheat, a liar, a cruel, untrusting man.

Questions swarmed Brendon's head. What had happened between him and Angelene? Had it been doomed from the start? Had it meant anything to her? Was it too much—the patterns she talked about, the boy with liquid blue eyes, God's forgiveness—and she had to end it? Was she a nutter like Victoria McGregor had spewed around Taunton? Was she in love with Walter?

From between the folds of blankets; his phone buzzed. Brendon dug under the duvet. His heart clunked to a stop. He stared at Maggie's phone number, thought of her blue blossom eyes, shy smile, and the sweet sound of her laughter. Springtime Maggie. She was the better choice than wintry Angelene and sultry Rachel. Maggie had been his first girlfriend. David and Sofia loved her. Brendon had revelled in his parent's approval and the attention Maggie gave him. Margaret Grace Thornton, with all her knowledge and innocence, had been the one. He didn't know whether it was Richard's infidelity gene or the game Angelene played that twisted his want for her. It could be Padre Diavolo who lusted after Rachel's curves.

Confusion stormed Brendon's brain. His phone rang again.

"Hey, Mags."

"I've called twice now. Are you alright?"

Brendon pushed himself off the bed and walked to the window. The rain had stopped. Wind whipped through the trees. Lights were on at the farmhouse. Walter would have arrived home. Did she have a meal prepared for him? Had she greeted him with a kiss?

"My head's all over the place. Sorry."

Silence.

He could picture Maggie on her bed surrounded by her stuffed animals, gnawing on her lip, that incredible brain of hers on fire with worry and fear. He had heard the bets at school. Brendon Cook had gone off Margaret Thornton.

"Where did you go after Mr. Clark yelled at you?"

"I told you. I drove around."

"Rachel left school. Gemma bet five pounds you were with her."

"Gemma's still pissed off. Will left my party with Tilly."

"I bumped into Rachel at Tesco, and she stared into her enormous boobs. She usually smirks or whispers knuddelbär. She couldn't look at me."

Brendon could come clean. He could use Troy's tactic: beg, buy her a gift, grovel some more until she forgave him. Had he followed the Gentlemen's Code, none of this would have happened. It was the code that made him run to Angelene: help a woman in distress, shield them, protect them.

"I should have let Walter do that."

"What are you talking about?"

'Think, Brendon. Maggie's smart. She puts things together.'

"I'm in my head. I should have asked Walter to speak to my dad before he dragged my arse home from Dortmund."

"I doubt anyone could have said a thing to change your dad's mind. All you had to do was work on your A-levels. You'd still be in Dortmund if you had done what your dad asked. School isn't that hard, Brendon."

Sparks whirred. He tried to shoot them out of his fingertips. They lingered. Brendon returned back to his bed and sat. He guzzled water that sat beside his bed and hoped it would douse the annoying flickers. It didn't help.

"You were chuffed I was coming home." Sparks sizzled around his words.

"Don't snap at me. Of course, I was happy, but not in a snide way. I love you. Do you know how hard it was to let you go?"

"You placed a bet I'd be home after term started. You told Charlie I wouldn't last because I'm an angry dolt. You said I'm more Richard than David Cook. You didn't even know Richard the prick."

"The entire town knows who Richard Cook was. He has quite the legacy. He was a cheating, lying dolt... Brendon, did you do something?" He could hear the hitch in her voice.

"I haven't done a bloody thing."

"I'm going to go. I need to call Charlie."

"She's with her little crumpet. Mrs. Spence is teaching her how to crochet."

"Something doesn't feel right."

"You've got yourself all worked up for bloody nothing. I drove around, end of."

"Goodbye, Brendon. Call me back when you feel like chatting."

Brendon cursed and tossed his phone onto the bed. A shadow darkened his bedroom floor. The hair stood up on his arm. He met the eyes of Richard: condemnation, hate.

"I want to talk to you about school."

"You lectured me over dinner, Dad. Mom made sure Liam benched me. I won't do it again."

David walked into the room, grabbed the chair, and plunked it beside the bed. "How much faith do you think I put in your word?"

"None."

"All we ask is that you finish your A-levels. Is that so hard?"

"When you're me, yes. I've never been good at school."

"You've never applied yourself." David looped his arms through his suspenders and wiggled his tie loose. "The day Lukas showed up with the sporting director from Dortmund and offered you the contract, what did you say?"

Brendon remembered the exact time, when, where. He had finished playing a match, made some amazing saves. He didn't know Lukas and the sporting director were in the stands watching. It was at 8:15 pm, the dressing room, Thursday, September 6. He had just turned sixteen in August. Brendon Cook was the youngest keeper ever signed to the Bundesliga. His mother tried to fight it. She swore at Lukas, a lengthy string of Italian. Brendon knew it came from a place of deep love and fear of losing her son. David was proud he had followed the code, but signing the contract came with a condition—complete his A-levels. Dortmund could have him when he graduated. Brendon, having been over the moon happy, vowed he would do whatever daddy wanted to get himself to Dortmund. He tried. When Taunton First put him on loan with the U19 squad, he promised to continue his studies in Dortmund. He couldn't keep his head in the game and concentrate on maths and science. Promise broken. The second time he flew to Dortmund, it was on the condition he studied. History and English took him away from what he loved. The sparks led him to a place he regretted. Promise broken.

"That I would finish my A-levels."

Brendon dragged his fingers through his hair. The light in Angelene's bedroom turned on.

"I screwed up."

David stood and picked his textbook off the floor. "I won't tell you again. School first, then football. You've only got until July, and then you're free from here and me."

"Why do you always say that?"

David handed him the book and walked to the doorway. "Because you've been angry with me since we flew home. I do this because I love you and I want the best for you."

Brendon grabbed his pen and flipped open his notebook. "I won't bunk off school."

There was a moment of silence before David spoke. "I don't like to see your mother upset."

There were two things Brendon wished he inherited from his father—a love for academia and now—monogamy. If there was ever a love story that needed to be told, it was of Sofia Mastrioni, the heiress of a textile mill, and David Cook, the gifted lawyer turned politician.

"I'll have my Latin done tonight and history before the match tomorrow."

"Your mom wants to play chess. She has beat me the last three times. Will you join us later?"

Brendon grinned, glanced at the farmhouse, and nodded. "As soon as I'm done."

"We can watch the highlights after she beats me again. Beatrice keeps getting after me to watch more games."

"Your secretary is a brilliant footy supporter."

"She makes it seem like I'm the only person in England who doesn't watch football."

Brendon watched his dad walk away. He promised again. Promises after promises broken. He could do it. He could focus on school, what was nine months? He could ignore Rachel, change seats in Latin, and be the best boyfriend Maggie had ever had. No more Angelene. No more secret meetings or running to her for comfort and understanding. He would forgive his dad, after all, it was his fault. School, footy, Maggie.

Brendon leaned his head back on the pillows and stared at the coffered ceiling.

Blue.

He was blue.

Bleeding blue.

Troy

The scabiosa, or pincushions as his mother called them, swayed in the breeze. They covered the ditch out front of Spence farm in a sea of purply-blue. They were the same colour as the sky and how Troy felt—bruised on the inside. He plucked a handful; something made him turn and glance at Walter's home. Shadows fell around the house. One was as dark as night and had eyes that glowed red. Another stretched across the lawn and up to Rosewood Manor like a sinister, twisted thread, stretched taut. One danced around the chimney. Another howled like the wind. The hair on the back of his neck prickled. One shadow was icy cold and as blinding as a snowstorm.

Seven shadows.

Seven devils.

Seven ghosts.

Troy covered his eyes, the flowers drooped and brushed against his neck and when he opened them; the shadows were gone.

"Babes, I'm done crocheting with your mom. Come see the blanket I've started. Red and yellow for Man U." Charlotte touched his arm, and he jumped. "Babes, are you okay?"

He glanced once more at the farmhouse. There was nothing but trees, smoke billowing from the chimney, Walter's Aston Martin.

"I feel blue, like a heavy feeling, and I don't know why."

Charlotte wrapped her arm around his waist. "Ahh, babes, you can't feel sad. I popped us popcorn. The movie is set to play. Daddy said I could stay the night, randy old bloke, told me he wanted some alone time with his girl. Come inside."

Troy held up the bouquet and gazed at Charlotte like it was the last time he would see her. He breathed in her flowery sweet perfume, counted the lighter flecks of blue in her eyes, the bow in her upper lip, and the two tiny freckles that dotted her nose. He pressed his lips against hers and savoured the taste of cherry lip balm.

"I love you." Troy handed her the flowers and held her cheeks in his hands. "You know you're my girl?"

"Always and forever. When I told you I was going to be Mrs. Donovan-Spence, I meant it." Charlotte paused and stared into his eyes. Ocean blue met cobalt blue. "Did Daniel Winsor tell you Alfie Holden gave me a Double Decker candy bar? I gave it back, babes. I told him I only accepted sweets from you."

Troy grinned and took her hand. He glanced once more toward Walter's home. The atmosphere turned sour and bloated. He tugged Charlotte towards his house to rid himself of the sticky feeling. He could hear his brothers wrestling in the sitting room, Harrison Spence cheering on his sons. He saw his mother laughing and felt the warmth of Charlotte's hand. The world turned bright again.

"Brendon told Alfie to back off, or he'd punch him."

Charlotte smiled, stood on her tiptoes, and kissed his cheek. "Good. Leave the fighting to him. You stay Switzerland."

"What movie did you pick?"

"A horror movie so we can cuddle. I'll turn your blue around. You'll be back to your brilliant, twinkly self in no time."

Troy glanced at the farmhouse. A shiver, icy blue, travelled up his spine, and something whispered to him, *'A storm is coming, run.'*

Maggie

She ran.

The storm was fierce. Leaves shivered. The trees swayed. Sludgy rain battered the houses.

The world was black and white.

Turn around, look at the monster.

I can't. I'm frightened.

You must, you hold the key.

I don't understand.

It came here uninvited. It cursed the town, draining it of colour and light.

Things are going to happen. I see it. It's beyond the trees.

Run. Face it.

Wind whipped her hair. Rain thrashed against her skin like stinging nettles. Gnarled branches reached for her.

She ran deeper into the forest.

It's a clue. It's leading me somewhere.

Yes, girl, run. Just past the trees,

She couldn't breathe. Her heart sputtered and stopped. The world was bleeding blue.

Maggie sat up with a start, pin straight, her shoulders pressed against the wooden kitchen chair. She blinked and rubbed her eyes with the heels of her hands. It took her a moment to realize where she was. She heard Jack bouncing on the sofa. He and Batman had saved Gotham City. Her father talked about his day. He had worked on a classic MG. Rosie had highlighted Simone Batra's hair.

All was right in the Thornton household.

Maggie glanced around the kitchen table. She was preparing an extra lesson for the student she tutored. Shakespeare's words jumped from the page and stormed her heart.

'By the pricking of my thumbs, something wicked this way comes.'

Sofia

'Why am I so afraid of you? Because you took something from me. You'll take again.'

The trees creaked and whispered. The path was narrow and twisted, tangled with brambles. Skeletal trees like ghosts clattered. Sofia rubbed the chill from her arms, gazed at Rosewood Manor, followed the ivy until she reached Brendon's bedroom window. His light was on. She turned. So was Angelene's.

It was as if there was a direct path from his room to hers. A thread.

'Is Hell so overcrowded Satan's bouncers are tossing people out?'

Sofia wiped the thought from her mind. She was being silly. A worried mother. She turned and gasped. David held out a red rose, amused by the startled look on her face.

"We really need to take Dr. Weiss's advice and go for a walk in the forest."

Sofia fell against his chest, listened to the beat of his heart, inhaled the scent of his skin.

"I should have planted blue roses. Everything feels so blue."

David kissed the crown of her head and lifted her chin. "It wouldn't be Rosewood Manor without red roses. Just like you wouldn't be Sofia Cook without your red lipstick and silver bangles."

"Why do I feel like this?"

Sofia took his hand and glanced at the farmhouse. Dizziness struck her like someone was gripping her neck and cutting off her breath.

"Maybe we should skip chess and talk instead. You're shaking."

"I need a distraction."

"You did the right thing, Sofia. Brendon won't hate us for long. In fact, I got a smile out of him. He'll join us after he's finished his homework. He must learn to keep a promise."

"It's more than having him benched. I feel it, David, it sits in the pit of my stomach, gnaws and gnaws like a warning."

David opened the kitchen door and kissed Sofia's forehead. "A lot has happened in the past few weeks. You said goodbye to Brendon, and we had to bring him home. Walter got married and brought Angelene into our lives. Our life is a little messy right now, but we always handle messy very well. We're Sofia and David Cook."

"What would I do without you?"

David touched the wrinkle on her brow. "That's something you'll never have to worry about." He poured her a glass of wine and held it out to her.

'His hands,' she thought.

What those hands had achieved: law school, MP, Secretary of State for Justice, Lord Chancellor. She loved the power in them, prominent veins that carried his strength to his fingers. Fingers that touched her, caressed her, let her know the world was okay.

"Tell me I'm being irrational and it's mom guilt."

"You're being silly."

Sofia stared into his hazel eyes. They were more green than brown. She saw her entire world.

"Promise me everything is going to be okay."

"Your mother is coming. It'll get interesting. I warned Walter."

Sofia grinned. "Nicola Mastrioni is on the way. No one messes with her family. She'll see to it."

Walter

Walter held up a little glass bird. The light above the kitchen island shone through the blue glass. It was the perfect gift for his little bird. Blue seemed fitting for his wintry bride.

Walter put the bird in his pocket, shut off the kitchen light, and climbed the stairs. He smiled at the scent of lemony disinfectant. Angelene was proud of herself. She had cleaned the entire house, put the laundry away, smoked outside, and had dinner prepared for him. Chicken paillard and ratatouille Angelene. Her secret, every good chef needs a secret ingredient, a splash of balsamic vinegar. She told him over dinner, normal fit okay, not so squishy. Husband felt rather good, too.

Walter knocked on the bathroom door. Candlelight flickered across the wall. Patchouli-scented bubbles wafted in the warm air.

"Am I disturbing you?"

Angelene held out her hand. He took hold of her wet fingers and dropped onto the toilet.

"I have something for you." He watched her shoulders stiffen and he chuckled. "I didn't buy you a new purse or dress. I saw this and thought of you."

Walter pulled the little glass bird from his pocket. He could have sworn there were tears in her eyes.

"It's beautiful."

"I want you to be happy. For us to be happy." He set the glass bird on the windowsill, grabbed the loofah, and moved it over her shoulders. "You are a beautiful woman, Ang. Do you believe me?"

She drew her legs to her chest and cradled them, didn't tense under his touch. Walter watched the water run down her spine. He ached to press his lips against her skin, feel her underneath him, but he wouldn't push. Things had been pleasant. Normal was okay.

"I want to see what you see. It's hard."

"Soon, little bird."

Walter dunked the loofah into the water and ran it over her neck. "What have we learned about one another this week?"

"You love Cumberland sausages because they're peppery. Your favourite Agatha Christie novel is *And Then There Were None*. You've seen every episode of *Doctor Who*. Now me."

"Your favourite books are *A Bell for Ursli*, the Hunchback, and *Tale of Two Cities*. You love Toblerone, which reminds me, I need to buy the bigger size next time. You devoured it in seconds." Walter hung the loofah from the tap and kissed the nape of her neck. "You love the chickens and cows at Spence Farm. How's that?"

"Pretty good for this week." Angelene lay back against the tub. Her smile was wistful. "Will you read *A Bell for Ursli* to me?"

"If it means we can chase your winter away, little bird, then yes."

Angelene

Angelene touched Walter's hand. Golden fingertips. She could feel them hum within hers.

'If anyone can make me beautiful. It's Walter Pratt.'

"Can you make me a tea?"

"I'll be right back." Walter kissed her forehead and stood. "I picked up some roly-poly. We'll have that when you're out of the tub."

She wanted to say, I love you. The swelling of her heart made her think it was love she was feeling. Something about the little tug frightened her. Love made people crazy. Her mother said so.

Angelene closed her eyes. The warm water lapped over her skin. The memory exploded in her mind like fireworks: bright, crackly light.

I'm sad, Roman. Everyone I love goes away.

You're sad about Francois. Don't think of him as gone. He is with God. He is always with you, little bird. In your heart and your memories.

But who will I have to protect me at school when the kids are mean? Where can I run to when Maman is grumpy? I feel so unlucky. Maman is never nice. I lost my best friend. I don't see you enough. My words are bleeding blue, Roman.

"Your tea. Black, just how you like it."

Angelene opened her eyes and stared at Walter. He handed her the cup and sat on the floor beside her.

"Are you alright? You're white as a ghost."

"Your words are blue."

"That's better than black, or what did you call them the other day, spiky red?"

Angelene wasn't sure his blue words were positive or if her blue mood was bleeding into him.

'Think yellow. His blue and your yellow make green. You'll be lucky green, Angelene Hummel now Pratt.'

"Are you familiar with Jean-Paul Sartre?"

"He was a philosopher," Walter said.

"L'appel du vide. The call of the void. It's that unsettling feeling, that unnerving, shaky sensation of not being able to trust your own instincts." Angelene took a small sip and listened to the bubbles crackle. "Have you ever been waiting for a train and thought, what if I jumped?"

"I've worried I won't have a speech prepared in time." Walter touched her arm and glanced at the little glass bluebird on the windowsill. "No more sad thoughts. We'll keep trying until normal fits perfectly."

"Will I ever be what you want? Can I be Mrs. Secretary of State for Defence? What if someone digs up my past and it's splashed all over the news and people look at you differently? Why did you choose me?"

'Why didn't I run?'

"People already look at me. I'm Walter Pratt. A successful forty-eight-year-old man who married a twenty-five-year-old." Walter dipped his fingers in the water. It was cool to his touch. He stood and pulled a towel from the stack folded on the vanity. "Come, little bird. You're turning into a prune."

Angelene pulled the drain. Bubbles slid down her body. She knew Walter was looking at her breasts. He tried to hide his desire. This part of normal was harder than keeping a tidy house and cooking dinner. Angelene reached for the towel, stepped out of the tub, and wound it around her body.

"Why me?"

"Because I saw something in you. I need you to see it, too."

She could see the disappointment on Walter's face, see it in the blue words that fell from his mouth. He wanted to make love. She couldn't bring herself to do it. How could she turn herself into that woman? When would that part of normal fit?

"Get dressed and meet me downstairs. I'll read you your book."

Angelene looked at the man with golden fingertips. His presence filled the room, pressing against her. An aura of successful black and the hottest red surrounded him. Women adored him. Men envied him. He had chosen her, of all the women in Paris, he had selected her.

Anastasia from Russia, lips, legs, dazzling under the spotlight. Kate Miller, smart, independent, quiet beauty. Branagh from Cork. Paulina from Prague. Elzbieta from Warsaw. Madeline from Toronto. Sofia's cousin Luciana from Parma. Angelene Hummel from the gutters of Paris.

"Would you like some roly-poly?"

Walter's voice tore her from her thoughts. From Clichy-sous-Bois. From the beige concrete beast she grew up in. From Francois, yellow ribbons, Roman Krieger.

"Please."

Walter held her cheek in his hand. She could feel his energy pulse against it. "Ursli awaits, little bird."

Angelene smiled. She patted herself dry and tossed the towel into the laundry basket. Pyjama bottoms, too big. Walter's Royal Navy hoodie, like a blanket.

Angelene perched on the nightstand and stared into the amber glow shining in Brendon's window.

L'appel du vide.

'I've never been able to trust myself. My instincts have led me to all sorts of places. They led me to you, my boy in brown, and now I'm bleeding blue. What will ever become of us?'

Acknowledgements

I want to express my deepest gratitude to the people who stood beside me through every draft, doubt, and late-night breakthrough. To my family, whose patience and encouragement carried me farther than they know. To my friends, who reminded me to breathe when the words refused to come. And to the readers—thank you for giving this story a home beyond my imagination. Your time and trust mean more than I can ever say.

About the author

Jennifer has always believed in the power of stories to heal, challenge, and transform. Growing up with a notebook never far from reach, she learned early that writing was both refuge and revelation. When not crafting characters or building worlds, Jennifer can be found with a cup of coffee in hand, wandering through bookstores, or collecting moments that later find their way onto the page.

Playlist

Music plays a huge part in my writing. Songs often inspire a character, a plot, or help create a scene. A huge thank you to the following artists that rode along on Brendon and Angelene's journey.

Sol Seppy Enter One

Daughter Smother

Sia Breathe Me

Agnes Obel Familiar

PJ Harvey Angelene

Tom Walker Leave a Light On

Apparat Goodbye

Ursine Vulpine Without You

Cloves Don't Forget About Me